Praise for

THE WORLD AT HOME

"Moyer brings wartime San Francisco to life in a coming-of-age story packed with romance, temptation, and a flash of mystery. . . . Irene shines as a young woman finding her voice and spirit during one of the most complex, adrenaline-fueled moments in American history."

—Meghan K. Winchell, author of *Good Girls, Good Food, Good Fun: The Story of USO Hostesses during World War II*

"Moyer has written a richly detailed love letter to the city—its fog, its views, and its potential for romance and loss—with beautifully drawn characters that grabbed my heart. The world seen through Irene Cleary's eyes is one I won't soon forget."

—Kirsten Mickelwait, author of *The Ghost Marriage* and *The Ashtrays Are Full and the Glasses Are Empty*

Praise for

A GOLDEN LIFE

Named a Best Indie Book of 2024 by Kirkus Reviews

". . . a delightful escape into the golden age of film, with compelling characters that make the novel simultaneously enthralling and contemplative . . . irresistible . . . will enchant until the final page."

—*Library Journal*

"The author captures 1930s California with meticulous detail and has masterfully created characters with depth and authenticity. . . . A delightful human drama about accepting the past and forging a future in 1930s Tinseltown."

—*Kirkus Reviews* (starred review)

"In the expert hands of Ginny Kubitz Moyer, *A Golden Life* is a dazzling story set in Hollywood's dream factory. . . . a fabulous read!"

—Adriana Trigiani, author of *The Good Left Undone*

"Ginny Kubitz Moyer writes with quiet authority and strong prose, creating a novel that is hard to put down and characters that remain long after the book is read."

—Laura Spence-Ash, author of *Beyond That, the Sea*

Praise for

THE SEEING GARDEN

2023 Foreword Indie Book Awards Silver Winner in Historical Adult Fiction

"This well-written and captivating novel about social manners and stifling expectations imposed on women shines a light on a piece of California history that has been overlooked. A delight for the senses with Moyer's artistic descriptions of gardens and mansions, *The Seeing Garden* is a page-turner of a story that is sure to inspire today's women who seek creativity and love."

—Ann Weisgarber, author of *The Glovemaker*

"This luscious literary romance has whiffs of a marriage between D. H. Lawrence and Rosamunde Pilcher. *The Seeing Garden* is a finely drawn portrait of a woman torn between two diametrically opposed worlds. The unforgettable setting is the icing on the cake in this truly captivating novel."

—Laurel Davis Huber, author of *The Velveteen Daughter*

"[Catherine's] struggles to fashion a compromise among her confused feelings and her aunt and uncle's pressing desires are beautifully evoked among the slow revelations of Moyer's well-crafted novel of society and American cultural shifts."

—*The Historical Novels Review*

"The prose and dialogue flow naturally, with the author spinning phrases that beautifully capture the passion of youth and love. . . . a moving story with strong female characters and twists that will satisfy readers who enjoy well-researched history alongside their romantic narratives."

—*Kirkus Reviews*

THE WORLD
AT HOME

THE WORLD AT HOME

GINNY KUBITZ MOYER

SHE WRITES PRESS

Published in 2025 by
She Writes Press, an imprint of The Stable Book Group

32 Court Street, Suite 2109
Brooklyn, NY 11201
https://shewritespress.com
Library of Congress Control Number: 2025908967
ISBN: 979-8-89636-018-6
eISBN: 979-8-89636-019-3

Interior Designer: Stacey Aaronson

Printed in the United States

For Scott,

who showed me the magic in the city

ONE

1944

I met Max and Cynthia Burke on the kind of day that makes you never want to leave San Francisco. If you know this city, you can picture the sort of day I mean. Walking up the steep street toward their apartment building, I felt that lift of spirits you get when the sky is blue and clear and the windows reflect the sun like little bursts of crystal, a day where the city seems to be showing off, flaunting the beauty of the bay and the hills beyond. Even in wartime, with gray battleships brooding in the water, it's a lovely place.

Admittedly, I don't have much to compare it to. I grew up here and have hardly ever left the city, to be honest. But there's always something new to admire, and on that September day the object of my admiration was Nob Hill, home to more luxury apartments per square block than anywhere else in the city. The Mark Hopkins Hotel, with its rooftop bar the Top of the Mark, was the only place in that expensive neighborhood I'd ever actually been inside.

Going up the street I quickened my pace, which wasn't easy; this hilly city makes you work. I was wearing heels and my latest creation, a dove-gray suit with deep red trim around the edges, consisting of a peplum jacket and skirt with a kick pleat. I'd saved hard to buy the hat, a red one with an upturned brim that seemed to be saluting the sky. I had one pair of good nylons left, and I carefully skirted the edges of a small hedge, for to snag them would be a tragedy.

It was my best outfit, and I needed to wear my best, for I was about to meet with Mrs. Cynthia Burke (formerly Miss Cynthia McNeil) about a dress she wanted altered. She had phoned my shop the day before, surprising me in the middle of a fitting. "I'm trying to find a seamstress who will be able to come tomorrow," she said. "I'm quite eager to start on remaking this dress."

She had actually called for Anna Orlova, who used to own the shop. When I told her that Anna had passed away in December—an awkward thing to say over the phone—she said with earnest sympathy, "Oh, I'm so sorry. It was my hairdresser who gave me this number. Miss Orlova made a dress for her once. But you're a seamstress as well? Perhaps you would be free."

I explained that I'd been an apprentice to Anna and the shop was now mine, and that I'd be delighted to come the next day at any time that was convenient. So we settled on three o'clock, and I said a poised goodbye as if I were used to making dresses for the socialites of Nob Hill, managing to contain my wild excitement at the astonishing opportunity that had just appeared on my doorstep.

On the sidewalk opposite the imposing Fairmont Hotel I paused, taking a moment to catch my breath. Just beyond the hotel was the Burkes' apartment building. It was L-shaped, with ornate entrance pillars and a paved forecourt, its doorway flanked with manicured trees growing in fancy planter boxes. I had seen it once before, coming back from the Top of the Mark in April, but had never dreamed I'd ever be invited inside.

My confidence began to waver, so I paused and opened my compact. The red precision of my lipstick gave me a quick shot of courage.

Beneath the hat my light brown hair, dressed in Victory rolls, looked as neat and glossy as the hair of a woman in a magazine.

"You walk like you're someone," said a soldier I danced with my first week at the USO. I tucked that comment away in my memory and bring it out anytime I need a little confidence. My posture has always been excellent (I have the nuns to thank for that), and when you grow up as I have, without the benefit of family, you learn to compensate for it in how you carry yourself.

Overall, I'm fairly pleased with my looks. I don't have a pinup's figure, but standing up straight makes up for that. My light brown hair is thick, and I'm good at styling it. I've got hazel eyes that taper a little at the corners, and I like my mouth and teeth. The one thing I've always disliked, and it's a big thing, are my freckles. They're not like my friend Trixie Dubuque's freckles, cute cinnamon-colored ones which lie sprinkled across her nose as if someone tapped them out of a sifter. My freckles are more the rule than the exception, one leading into another, as if someone has laid a whole sheet of them over my skin; even the fronts of my arms and legs are covered. I've found that when I meet people for the first time, there's often a beat of surprise in their eyes, as if they need a moment to absorb what they see. My friend Louise likes to say that people (by which she means men) talk to her chest instead of her face. For me, they talk to my freckles and always have.

I patted a little powder on my nose, appraising myself with a critical eye. A twenty-year-old woman with her own business doesn't want to look any younger than she is, which was why I'd chosen my most sophisticated hat. Tilting the mirror, I took a moment to admire its crimson elegance.

My watch said it was five minutes to three, so I put away the compact, snapped shut my pocketbook, and happened to look up right into the eyes of a sailor who was stepping onto the sidewalk in front of me. He had golden blond hair and brown eyes, a combination so startlingly familiar that for a moment my heart seemed to stop. I froze there on the sidewalk, staring at him. Then he nodded and said, "Good morning, Miss," and he and his companion continued on, their voices floating behind them as they walked in the direction of the bay.

It was good that a woman pushing a baby carriage came up behind me and asked, "Pardon me, are you crossing?" for I had to smile, say yes, and collect myself enough to start walking. And I was caught up again in the currents of San Francisco in wartime, a busy city that does not stop, that hardly lets you think.

The Burkes' apartment building had a doorman wearing a double-breasted coat and a peaked cap. He tipped it to me as I entered and gave me a welcoming smile, which I needed, for in the courtyard I'd just passed what looked like a Rolls Royce gleaming in the sun.

The lobby was a glorious blend of mirrors and marble and floral arrangements on pillars. As I pressed the button for the elevator, trying not to look obviously impressed by my surroundings, I couldn't help but marvel at the surprising twists of fate. It didn't seem possible that I, Irene Mary Cleary, was about to meet Cynthia McNeil Burke.

In some ways, I felt I already knew her. For years I'd seen her photos in the newspaper: Cynthia McNeil at the fashion show, at the opening night of the Opera. She was often with her father, Harrison McNeil, who owned a shipping company, or with her mother Eleanor, who was a slightly less slim double of her daughter. There was a younger sister and an older brother, but it was Cynthia who had always fired my imagination. I'd been aware of her ever since she was eighteen and had a lavish coming-out party, which had been given its own full-page article in the *San Francisco Chronicle*. Trixie and I, both thirteen years old, had lain on the floor with our faces inches away from the newspaper, admiring Cynthia's white dress with a diagonal line of rosettes on the bodice.

The elevator was taking its time, apparently going nearly to the top floor before coming back down. Watching each number light up in turn, I thought about Cynthia's most recent appearances in the newspaper. The last six months had certainly been a whirlwind for her, beginning in March, when she had been a bridesmaid in the wedding of Fred Gibson and Betty Sweeney. The wedding was a big event by wartime standards, for the Gibsons, like the McNeils, were old city money. Photos had been taken on the steps of St. Luke's Episcopal Church, and the *Chronicle* had included a huge picture of Cynthia alone, smiling at the camera from underneath her cloud of blonde hair, in a gorgeous floor-length dress with what looked like darker piping on the bodice. "In sea green chiffon, Cynthia McNeil almost upstages the bride," said the caption.

"Gosh," I remember Trixie saying as she studied the photograph. "That's a terrible thing to say. They've managed to insult both women at once." I'd been so enraptured by Cynthia's dress I hadn't even noticed.

The bride, Betty, was not a native of San Francisco. She was from Florida, the daughter of an admiral who had come west due to the war, and the photos showed her to be pretty in a sweet, cute way, like the fresh-faced girl in the movies whose unconscious charm defeats the more glamorous femme fatale. In the photos, Fred Gibson, a surgeon at Letterman Army Hospital, held her arm and looked down at her proudly.

It was disappointing that Cynthia's own wedding had been a civil one, in another city. A month after the Gibson wedding, she'd gone to Chicago, where she'd met and married Max Burke. He was the owner of a string of successful nightclubs, described by the paper as "watering holes for the local elite." The *Chronicle* had run a photo of the two of them on the steps of Chicago City Hall: Cynthia in an elegant suit, holding a massive bouquet; Max Burke, a tall man with a solid build, holding her elbow. "Cupid Strikes in the Windy City!" the paper had exclaimed.

They were a stunning couple, her blonde elegance paired with his dark good looks. *It's proof that beautiful people seem to find each other*, I mused as the elevator pinged and the doors slowly opened. Wealthy people did, too, of course. It was a world I didn't know, one where you had a family solidly behind you, where you had a home on Nob Hill and a country estate on the Peninsula—a world where your money would open every door.

Was I envious? Not exactly, for the world the Burkes inhabited was one I'd never presumed I could enter. It had always seemed too far away for envy. I knew I would never have Cynthia's cool refined beauty or a penthouse apartment. I'd never have my photos in the society pages.

There was a time you thought you'd have a family, though, said a tiny voice inside as I entered the elevator, but as soon as my thoughts drifted into that familiar and dangerous groove I shied away from it, like you do when your tongue hits a sensitive place on your tooth. I didn't want to think about it anymore, although the memory of Johnny drifted back to me often, like an unwelcome phantom. I pushed the button and stood waiting, making myself stand even taller than usual.

Focus on the present, I told myself as the doors closed, *and on the future*. After all, I'd never have imagined my life would ever intersect with the Burkes, and yet I was about to enter their apartment, to walk quite literally into their world. Maybe the boundaries in San Francisco were more porous than they'd seemed. *Today could change my life*, I thought with a thrill as the elevator moved me noiselessly upward.

Cynthia Burke herself opened the apartment door. I'd have recognized her anywhere: the hair styled in immaculate blonde waves, the perfectly arched eyebrows above wide-set eyes. But it was her complexion, more than anything, that filled me with awe. It was the sort you see in advertisements in women's magazines, rose-petal skin without a single blemish.

It was a mark of her exquisite manners that she did not visibly react to my freckles. She smiled warmly and said, "Miss Cleary? I'm Cynthia Burke. It's lovely to meet you. Please, come in."

The paneled foyer led into a living room with a huge window overlooking the city and the bay. I'd never been in an apartment with such a view, and I suspect few people have. Curtains in a light blue print framed the window, with walls the color of oyster shells and carpet a touch darker. There was a beautiful formal portrait of Cynthia over the fireplace, a crystal vase on the mantel, and an arrangement of lilies, looking like porcelain, on the polished coffee table. Everything was delicate and feminine.

Cynthia indicated a place on the divan and offered me tea. She sat down in a small gilt chair opposite, smart in her gray skirt and light blue cashmere sweater. I couldn't help noticing her ring; it was a single diamond, almost cartoonishly large, like the kind mined by the dwarves in *Snow White*.

"I'm so glad you could come today," she said as we drank the tea, which appeared so quickly it must have been prepared and waiting. "I've an event coming up, and nothing in the stores appealed to me. I know it's not patriotic to complain, but good material is so hard to come by now."

I nodded my sympathy, putting my cup down carefully in the saucer. It was white china with a silver filigree, subtle and elegant.

"So I thought of remaking this dress I wore once, five years ago. I've always loved it. And the fabric is better than anything I'll find now, I think."

"I'd be happy to take a look at it, Mrs. Burke."

"Here it is," she said, going over to a standing screen by the fireplace and unhooking a hanger from its edge. She held the dress up, and I caught my breath.

The fabric was exquisite, dark rose satin, the rich kind that looks like cool water rippling in a brook. It was a long evening dress with a high scoop neck and a fitted bodice, tight through the hips then flaring out gradually from there to the ground. The sleeves were long and full, falling gracefully to a band at the wrist. It was a design of five or six years before, pretty but no longer stylish, and I was immediately thinking about how to transform it. Cynthia watched me silently, waiting for my assessment.

"What if," I said, "you cut down the neckline?"

"I was thinking that. Perhaps a square neck?"

"No, that would look too severe. I'd do a V-neck, I think. What sort of jewelry were you thinking of wearing with it?"

"Just the diamonds," she said. I could not imagine myself or anyone I knew saying "just the diamonds" so casually. "A pendant on a silver chain, with a matching bracelet and earrings."

"Definitely a V-neck," I said, getting up. I took off my right glove to finger the dress material, turning it over and assessing the seams. "You could replace the sleeves with very thin straps, I think. I could use the sleeve material on the bodice, shirring it slightly? Just to give it some texture."

We talked a while longer, and I got more and more excited by the possibilities; you would almost think the dress was mine. I told her I could draw up a sketch of my ideas, and she agreed with heartening enthusiasm.

"It's a lovely dress," I said as she hooked the hanger back over the screen and we both sat down again. "Was it worn for a particular event?"

"A sixteenth birthday party at the country club, for a friend of mine. Actually, I was friends with her older brother. But we know the family well."

"I hope you will enjoy wearing it just as much a second time."

She flashed me a look, an odd one as she picked up her cup; I don't know quite how else to describe it. Then she smiled again. "I'm sure I will. I look forward to seeing your designs."

There was a sudden noise from the foyer, the sound of a door opening and closing. Cynthia's face changed, this time to an unmistakable look of irritation. Into the doorway came Max Burke, instantly recognizable from the photo I'd seen, smoothing back his hair as if he'd just taken off a hat.

He went right to his wife, bending to kiss her cheek. "Hello, Cynthia," he said, but she did not turn to make it easier for him.

"You're back early."

"Less traffic than I thought." He saw me then, straightened, smiled. "Oh, I didn't know you had a friend over." He strode toward me with an outstretched hand. "We haven't met yet, have we. Max Burke."

I was too seized with awkwardness to take his hand at first. Cynthia said coolly, "This is Miss Cleary. She's here to help me with a dress."

"Oh. Well, nice to meet you," he said, still holding out his hand. I took it, feeling naked without my gloves. His hand was warm, which made me realize just how cold my own must have felt. It was a relief when he let go.

It was hard not to stare, for I had never met anyone like Max. He was just as handsome as his photo: tall with broad shoulders; dark, almost-black hair, thick and well-groomed; alert brown eyes; a high forehead; and a mouth that turned up slightly at the corners, which gave the impression that he was thinking of something amusing or at least pleasant. I was surprised to see that he had a heavy five o'clock shadow, giving him an almost piratical look. But what I felt most of all was his masculinity, which made an immediate impression, like walking into a cloud of cologne. The impact was only heightened by the decor of the room; his broad frame and stubble seemed out of place in such an elegant setting. I was so momentarily overwhelmed by my thoughts and so determined to keep them hidden that I didn't even notice his reaction to my freckles.

Cynthia had stood up and crossed to the mantel, opening a silver box. "Would you care for a cigarette, Miss Cleary?"

"Thank you, no." I was relieved that my voice sounded normal. Max moved swiftly towards her, reaching into his breast pocket for a lighter, but she had lit a cigarette for herself before he could do it for her. She moved back to her chair, and he remained standing by the mantel, hands in his pockets, looking after her.

"So you're a dress designer?" he said abruptly, turning toward me.

"Yes, Mr. Burke." I didn't normally call myself that—"seamstress" was the word I was used to—and for a moment I felt like an imposter.

"It's a new dress?" he said to his wife.

"No. I'm remaking another one."

"Which one?"

She raised her eyebrows toward the rose satin. "That one."

He glanced at it and turned quickly back to her. I was surprised to see a look of alarm come into his eyes. "The one from the dance?"

She said nothing, just lifted the cigarette to her lips.

"I'll buy you any dress you like, Cynthia," he said. "You don't need to remake that one."

"Of course I don't *need* to," she said, and I was shocked by the tone of her voice; it was close to contempt. "But I've always loved that dress." She smiled warmly at me, such a contrast to the tone she'd used with her husband. "So you'll let me know when you have the design, Miss Cleary?"

"Yes, Mrs. Burke. I'll call as soon as it's ready."

"Excellent. Thank you very much."

"My pleasure."

"Let me see you out." She got up, straightening her skirt gracefully. Max remained standing by the mantel, eyes following her as she passed him into the foyer. I picked up my pocketbook and stood irresolutely for a moment, surprised by currents between them that I could not understand, uncertain how to say goodbye to him in a way that seemed both friendly and professional.

Then he looked at me. With his wife gone it was the obvious place for his attention to turn, but I felt flustered all the same. As before, I had an overwhelming sense of his physical presence: the breadth of shoulder, the five o'clock shadow, the brown eyes. He said nothing, so I summoned all my poise.

"It was nice to meet you, Mr. Burke," I said.

"You too, Miss Cleary." I was surprised he'd remembered my name. His gaze moved to my shoes then up to my hat, as if assessing my ensemble, my skill as a designer. There was a businessman's approval in it, which bolstered my confidence, but when his eyes met mine again I felt discomfited, my fragile poise deserting me.

"Goodbye then," I said awkwardly and quickly left the room.

TWO

When I got home over an hour later, my feet were throbbing. I'd taken the streetcar over to Van Ness, but when the next one came it was jammed full of servicemen, and I wanted to walk anyhow, to process the experience and let the idea of the dress crystallize. By the time I had returned to my place at the corner of Steiner and Sacramento, I could picture the dress as if it were hanging right in front of me.

I've always been good at making something out of nothing, or almost nothing. Back at the orphanage I loved to spin stories out of my imagination, stories inspired by hours reading *The Blue Fairy Book*. The other kids at Mount St. Joseph would sit rapt as I invented tales of princesses, trolls, and fairies. I liked to make the main characters orphans, for obvious reasons, and my stories ended with the good and clever living happily ever after. In a way, my fairy tales were no different from the saint stories the nuns told us, stories of people who were virtuous and faithful. "They got their reward in the end," Sister Rosemary would always say. She was a short woman with a bright, eager face, beloved by all the kids at the orphanage. The dramatic white cornette worn by the Daughters of Charity hid her hair and made her seem ageless, like a perpetual child.

"But didn't they die?" I remember asking.

"Many of them did," Sister said. "Some in terribly painful ways.

But their reward was a life in heaven, where there is light and beauty and music, all the time."

Light and beauty and music. How I had loved that description, as if heaven were a magical kingdom like in the fairy stories.

And how I had loved imagining myself as the heroine, the girl who lived happily ever after.

The key was sticking in the lock again, and if you didn't apply just the right amount of pressure, it wouldn't turn. With grim determination I leaned on it, and finally it engaged. The shop door swung open as I made a mental note to call a locksmith.

In spite of my shop's quirks, it's always been a great setup, just one block away from the bustling businesses on Fillmore Street. My building is on the corner with windows on two sides, giving me terrific natural light for my sewing. Downstairs is one big room, with a tiny storeroom behind and a flight of stairs leading up to a small apartment.

When Anna died and left me the business, I began pouring my extra time and any extra funds I could find into transforming the shop. In Anna's day it was functional and clean but nothing special; I've dressed it up with light green paint on the walls and violet-blue curtains around the three-way mirror and the storeroom entrance. There's a big folding screen hiding a dressing area, a screen which I painted the same violet as the curtains, with a design of gold and green scrolls. There's always a vase of iris on the counter by the door, and I added a framed picture of Paris and other tasteful knickknacks for a little cosmopolitan flair. For, while Anna was content to mend and work from patterns, I've got bigger ideas and dreams. "You have original ideas," she said to me once, "and I am teaching you the skills you need. With both, there is no telling where you can go."

Including, it seemed, to the heights of Nob Hill. The memory of where I'd just been made me grin, and I ran upstairs to the apartment, where I took off my hat and shoes, carefully unrolled my nylons and put them aside, and called Trixie at her dorm at San Francisco State College. I had to wait while the girl who answered the hall phone went in search of her, and I massaged my bare feet and stared out the window, thinking of satin and diamonds.

"Irene," said Trixie at last. "How did it go?"

"Wonderful. It was a rose-colored evening dress she wants me to remake. She loved my ideas."

"I'm not surprised," said Trixie. I could picture her on the other end, dark hair falling around her thin and serious face, her mouth curved in a grin. "What's she like?"

"Just like the photos. Her complexion, Trixie! I felt like such a hayseed."

"Is she nice?"

"Very nice. Strange with her husband, though."

"Oh, he was there? Strange how?"

I replayed the odd interactions in my mind. "Kind of short, like she was annoyed with him or something."

"What's he like? He looks so handsome in the papers."

"He is." The word seemed inadequate to express the force of his presence, but for some reason I didn't want to try to explain it. I didn't have the chance anyhow, for Trixie had put her hand on the receiver and was talking to someone else.

"I've got to go," she said a moment later. "Doris needs the phone. Some of the girls and I are going to the movies tonight. Want to come?"

"If only I could. I'm behind on Mrs. Geller's suit. I was going to work on it today, but then Cynthia Burke called. I'll be burning the midnight oil to get it done."

"Those rich people," said Trixie good-naturedly. "Making us peasants do their every bidding."

I laughed. "Goodbye, peasant. Have fun tonight."

Trixie and I have known each other since we were eight years old. It's thanks to her that I learned something about how a real family works, for she—unlike practically every other kid at the orphanage—actually had one.

She came to Mount St. Joseph in March of 1932, with her younger brothers. Her mother had tuberculosis and had been sent to a sanatorium on the Peninsula, and Mr. Dubuque, unable to be both father and mother to three kids, had no choice but to take them to the sisters until she returned. I was in the hall when they arrived, and I can still see the scene vividly: Mr. Dubuque, looking stricken; five-year-old John, attaching himself to his father's leg and refusing to let go; and eighteen-month-old David with his toy bear, already being cuddled by Sister Rosemary. And I remember Trixie frowning, as I later learned she always did whenever she felt strong emotion.

"Irene," said Sister Margaret, the head of the orphanage, after Mr. Dubuque had left, "why don't you show Trixie the chapel? I'll take the younger children for some milk."

So Trixie and I went to the empty chapel, with its stained glass and huge statue of Mary standing with her arms outstretched. Trixie surveyed her with the intense interest I would come to know as one of her key characteristics. "She's pretty," she said.

I was pleased that she thought so, too. "It's Mary. Jesus's mother."

"I know." Trixie looked up the statue's blue robes. "My mother has a bed jacket this color."

We were both silent, thinking of mothers: one known and loved; mine unknown, but no less real in my imaginings.

"She's got tuberculosis," said Trixie. "I might not be able to see her for a whole year." The quiver in her voice made me want to console her.

"Well," I said, "I like it here. The sisters are kind. I've lived here my whole life."

"You never had parents?"

"No. My mother died first, then my father."

"So who brought you here?"

"My father. I was a week old."

"How do you know?"

"Sister Rosemary told me." She hadn't really. All she'd said about my past was that my parents had loved me very much but couldn't keep me, that they had loved each other, and that I'd been brought to the orphanage when I was a week old. In the absence of more detail, I'd filled in the gaps myself. "My parents would have kept me if they could. But my mother died when I was just a few days old." I had told the story to myself so often it seemed true.

"Why didn't your father keep you?"

"For the same reason your father can't keep you, I guess. He had to work. And then he died and couldn't get me."

Trixie looked back at the statue of Mary. She reached out a hand and touched the bare foot stepping on the serpent. Even as a child, I recognized the gesture for what it was: assurance of something solid in a world that had changed completely.

"You can pray to Mary," I told her, proud to have remembered what the sisters would have said. "You can ask her to pray for your mother."

"Will it work?"

"It always does," I said, just as Sister Rosemary would have done.

Mr. Dubuque came every Saturday to see his children, taking them to the park or the beach or the zoo (he'd made the mistake of taking them home the first weekend, Trixie said, and John had refused to leave and had to be carried back out to the car). Trixie and I became such fast friends that one day she asked if I could come along too. He applied for permission to Sister Margaret, and—much to my joy—it was granted.

It was all so new: riding in a car, being with a man instead of sisters, going to the park and then to get ice cream sodas. I was so well-behaved for fear that I might not be asked back that at first Mr. Dubuque thought I was mute. He talked about his wife so much that his adoration for her was evident even to a child. *That must be how my father felt about my mother*, I thought.

"I got a letter from Mama today," he said. "They are letting her sit up and knit. She has nice roommates. The food is good, she says."

"Does she miss us?" asked John.

"Just as much as we miss her," said Mr. Dubuque.

I had been certain the prayers would work, so it was no surprise when, twelve months later, Mrs. Dubuque came to get her children. I studied her avidly, fascinated to meet a real, live mother. She was a pale, pretty woman with blonde curls and big eyes underneath a cloche hat, and she fell on her children and kissed them with abandon.

"My sweethearts," she said, burying her face in their hair. "My babies." Even Sister Margaret had tears in her eyes.

When Trixie introduced me, Mrs. Dubuque gave me a kiss on the cheek, which delighted me. "You've been such a good friend to Trixie. I hope you'll come and visit us often. If Sister says you may, of course." I glanced hopefully at Sister, and she smiled and gave me a nod.

So that's how I entered a house, a real home, for the first time. The Dubuques lived in a chocolate-colored stucco house just below Golden Gate Park, and it was there I saw what it was like to have a father who whistled as he came home from work and a mother who ironed while listening to the kitchen radio. When I graduated from high school and the orphanage and was living in the boardinghouse on Gough Street, I had a standing invitation to the Dubuques' house for Sunday dinner. I helped them trim their Christmas trees, decorate Easter eggs, and celebrate birthdays. It was a wrench when, just after Anna's death, they moved to Minnesota to be near Mrs. Dubuque's parents. The closest thing I'd had to a family home was gone, packed away in boxes.

Before they left Mrs. Dubuque gave me the violet-blue living room curtains, a white fluted vase, and a framed print of Paris I'd always loved. "They'll be perfect for the new shop you want to create," she told me. It was typical of her; somehow she always knew what a young girl needed. *Just as my own mother would have known*, I mused, *if she'd lived*.

The clock struck five thirty, pulling me out of my reverie. The sky was still blue, but the shadows meant that time was passing. It was time to make a cup of tea and get to work piecing that suit for Mrs. Geller.

The dented tea tin on the kitchen shelf was almost empty, and the old mug into which I poured the water had a chipped handle. It was hard to imagine a more dramatic contrast with the fine china I'd used earlier in the day. Watching the steam rise, I wondered what the Burkes were doing. I imagined them getting dressed to go out to a show or a fancy nightclub, or maybe having a quiet dinner for two in their picture-perfect apartment. *I've actually been there*, I marveled, feeling the thrill of the privileged insider. It was astonishing to think that I had actually sat on their sofa, that I knew exactly what color their carpeting was.

Then I thought of Cynthia ignoring her handsome new husband, brushing past him as if he did not even exist. I remembered his eyes following her, then landing on me. And I realized there was a lot about the Burkes—quite a lot, in fact—that I didn't know at all.

THREE

After a weekend hunched over the sewing machine, it was a relief to hand the suit off to Mrs. Geller. She was delighted with it, in part because I charged her less than Anna would have done. Instead of a gray-haired Russian woman with years of experience, the regular customers have had to adjust to a twenty-year-old freckled girl altering their clothes, and I knew right away that some of them would need a little incentive to keep from taking their business elsewhere.

My work speaks for itself, though, and the customers' satisfied faces make me hopeful about keeping the business afloat. When it comes to sewing I'm a perfectionist, a fact that Anna noticed the very first time I made a buttonhole for her. Her faith in me had given me faith in myself, which was good when I had a project like Cynthia Burke's dress ahead of me. I was eager to start on my sketches and I'd have done so the moment Mrs. Geller and her suit walked out the door, but I was scheduled to volunteer at the USO on O'Farrell Street, so it had to wait.

Trixie came by and we rode downtown in the streetcar. It was packed and before long two soldiers were standing above us, holding the straps. We were chatting about this and that, and it was clear the guys were listening to us while trying not to make it obvious that they were.

Since the start of the war, this city has been bursting with men, servicemen either stationed somewhere around the bay or passing through on their way to the Pacific. Some of them are bold, initiating conversation on the street and aggressively turning on the charm. Some are gentlemen, polite and well-mannered, while others are wide-eyed and overwhelmed by the big city. The two fellows on the streetcar definitely fit into the last category. They didn't seem to know each other well, either; I guessed they were probably just two of a pack of servicemen on leave who had splintered up for the night.

When we got off the streetcar and made our way towards the USO, it was clear the soldiers were headed in the same direction. Trixie finally turned to them and smiled. "Are you going to the USO, by any chance?"

The guys lit up like Christmas trees. "We are," said one. "You are too? I'm glad." He was blond, thin, with a wide smile. The other guy was stockier, with deep-set dark eyes and a cleft in his chin. They couldn't have been more than nineteen or twenty.

We chatted on our way there. They were Earl from Georgia and Dave from Illinois. It was their first time in San Francisco and their first USO. "Just looking for a place to have fun," said Earl. "With nice girls and maybe dance a little too. Some of the guys went—well, they went other places." He looked embarrassed. "But I figure you can't go wrong at the USO."

"This is a good one," I said, as we climbed the steps upstairs. "There's ping-pong and dancing. There are places to write letters home. And if you need any mending the senior hostesses can do it for you."

"That's what I need," said Dave. "A little bit of home. But with pretty girls like you."

Apparently he did have some boldness in him after all. I smiled in my best USO manner and said, "You'll find lots of them here."

It had been Trixie's idea to volunteer as junior hostesses for the USO. She'd stopped by the shop one afternoon in early February with cannoli from my favorite Italian bakery. I'd had the shop for almost two months and was exhausted. "You need to get out," she said as we sat at the table. "You're working too much. And you wanted to help the war effort, right? If you volunteer at the USO you get to do both."

It was tempting. "What would we do there?"

"Whatever they need. Mostly be a friendly face for guys away from home. They have dancing and ping-pong tables, and sometimes they show movies. You can pour coffee and serve doughnuts if you don't want to dance. It'll do you good, and it'll do me good because I don't want to apply alone. And it'll do the country good."

"But you need references, don't you?"

"One of the senior hostesses there knows my mother. Mama will write you a letter, don't worry."

So a week later we applied to the USO at O'Farrell Street, near Union Square. Mrs. Latham was the head senior hostess, a woman in her mid-forties, with gray-blonde hair worn in a neat twist. "I have a son in the Pacific," she said to us, "so this work is personal for me."

I was glad I was wearing my light blue dress with the round collar and tie at the neck. I'd opted to look pretty and girlish rather than sophisticated: a good choice, I realized, as Mrs. Latham explained the purpose of the USO.

"This is a home away from home for the boys. They're far away from all that's familiar. And this city"—she indicated San Francisco with a tilt of her head—"has many diversions that are less than healthy for young men. The USO is a wholesome alternative. That's why we don't let just any girl volunteer." She gave us each a keen glance, perhaps wondering if a smarting conscience would reveal itself in our demeanor, before continuing. "Our application process may seem rigorous, but it helps us ensure that our junior hostesses have impeccable conduct and morals. You understand how important that is."

"Of course," I said, just as Trixie said, "Yes, Mrs. Latham."

Mrs. Latham picked up the paper I'd brought in, studied it a moment, then looked at me. I was alarmed to hear her tone shift, as if aware she had to speak with delicacy. "Irene, we don't usually take girls without families to vouch for them. It's nothing personal, just a need to make sure we can best serve the interests of the young men in our care."

I remember I kept smiling bravely as I felt my stomach swoop in that old familiar way. It was like being in high school again, hearing girls talk about their families, knowing that my family was a group of sisters and an assortment of orphans. I sat up straighter, fighting back the lump in my throat.

"However," Mrs. Latham continued, "Mrs. Dubuque is certainly effusive in her praise of your character." She read the letter silently as I waited. "The family has known you since you were a child, is that right?"

"Yes, ma'am."

"It sounds like you've spent a great deal of time with them over the years."

"Yes, I have." I glanced at Trixie, who gave me a hopeful smile.

Mrs. Latham nodded and put the letter down. "In that case," she said, "I am happy to accept you."

The relief was audible in my voice. "Oh, thank you, Mrs. Latham."

She smiled at me, more gently than she had so far. "It's not your fault that you don't have a family," she said. "You've made the best of your circumstances, which is all one can ask." She stood up and extended her hand. "Welcome to the USO, Irene."

My first night as a hostess, a week later, had been a revelation. Simply put, it was more concentrated male attention than I'd ever known before. I'd gone out with boys here and there, and I'd had a semi-serious romance with my senior prom date, Henry Llewellyn, the summer before he joined up. But at the USO, with four men to every girl, it was an entirely different experience.

"Dance with every man who asks you," Mrs. Cohen, another senior hostess, told the new volunteers. "This is about them, not about you. Imagine how crushed they would be if you turned them down." And in fact the men had lined up, quite literally, along the dance floor waiting their turn. It was really something.

I might have quailed at the thought of making small talk with so many strangers, but it was remarkably easy. The guys were usually around my age and touchingly grateful for female company. That first night, there was a red-haired sailor who made me laugh so hard I got a stitch in my side, and a soldier with a crooked smile who told me I was a great dancer. I remember the very shy fellow who was achingly nervous until he started talking about his dog back home. He loved that dog so much I got tears in my eyes. "It's not like Buddy can write to me, like my family can. I hope he knows I didn't want to leave him." He'd thanked me with real gratitude when the dance ended, and I remember watching him disappear into the crowd and feeling glad I'd given him a respite from his paralyzing shyness.

"Take a break from dancing, Irene," Mrs. Latham had told me that first night. "You'll wear yourself out." But I didn't, because taking a break meant disappointing the men who were waiting. If they could go off to war and maybe die, I decided, then I could dance a little more. That was my philosophy, every time I went there to volunteer. There wasn't an evening I didn't come home with aching feet.

But it wasn't entirely patriotism and sacrifice. The truth is that I got something from the USO, something I'd never had before. To those servicemen who came and went, I was just Irene, a normal American girl. Sure, some of them asked about my life, but in the space of a dance or a ping-pong game there wasn't time to get into the details. Besides, we had been trained that we were there to entertain the men, not to talk about ourselves, so I could easily avoid owning up to my orphan status. Just as the men could hide their individual pasts behind a uniform, I could hide mine behind a USO name tag and a welcoming smile.

Until one day, that April day, when I didn't hide it. And everything changed, in ways that were too painful to remember.

Dave and Earl were delighted to be there. I could tell there was something about the USO—friendly and wholesome, with mature female chaperones like a dance at a school gymnasium—that reminded them of home. They asked us each to dance, but I'd been assigned to help with coffee, so I promised to look for them later.

Mrs. Cohen, petite and businesslike, greeted me as I slid behind the table. "I'm glad you're here tonight. It looks like a big crowd."

"I'm happy to help, Mrs. Cohen."

She put the coffee on, and I got out napkins. "Peggy was supposed to do this tonight, but she phoned in sick. Even when she's here, she gets talking and forgets to check the coffee. Sweet girl, but a little flighty."

At a pause in the music Trixie stopped by my counter. "How's the dancing?" I asked.

"Great. Do you want to switch? I can take over the coffee."

"I'm all right."

"Are you sure?" She dropped her voice so the airman with her could not hear. "You haven't done the coffee duty since . . ."

"I'm fine. Really." My tone must have convinced her for she smiled and went back to the dance floor.

I turned to the coffee, pretending to check its progress. If I looked out at the crowd it was too easy to picture a certain sailor, blond and with a slow, beautiful smile, watching me from across the room.

"How is the sewing these days, Irene?" asked Mrs. Cohen. "Is it keeping you busy?"

"Very busy, yes." I was glad to be pulled away from my thoughts. "I'm remaking a satin evening dress for—a new customer." I didn't want to mention her name; it seemed like bragging.

"Good," she said briskly. "I'm sure you'll do it well. You're a good worker."

It always made me glow inside, any acknowledgment of my competence or skill. As I thanked her and looked out at the dance floor, I thought again of the dress in Cynthia Burke's apartment. I imagined it transformed, the height of style and grace, moving through an evening crowd like a rose-colored dream.

FOUR

"Oh, this is perfect," said Cynthia, "just perfect." Her eyes were shining as she studied my design. "Exactly what I hoped it would be. That little twist of fabric around the waist—that's a lovely addition."

"I'm so glad, Mrs. Burke." And I was, both glad and relieved. I'd been confident about my sketch at home but walking back into that luxurious apartment, I'd momentarily doubted my right to be there.

"What's the next step?"

"I'll take some measurements, and then I can begin to work. I can take them now, if you're free."

She checked her watch. "Perfect. I've the Red Cross, but not until one."

We passed through her bedroom, where a uniformed maid was dusting the picture frames. The walls were blush pink and the carpet so soft I could feel my heels sink into it. The spacious dressing room next door had a row of white built-in wardrobes and a huge floor-length three-way mirror, like the one in my shop. She stood before it in her slip and I measured her, making notations in my book. Her underclothes were beautifully made, nothing like the ones I got from Sears and J. C. Penney.

As I moved deftly about her with my tape measure, I thought of my own bedroom, with its uncomfortable narrow bed, its small window, and the mismatched bureau and nightstand I had inherited from Anna. It was hard to imagine sleeping in a room as luxurious as Cynthia's and having an equally beautiful space dedicated simply to getting dressed. I wished the wardrobe doors were open, so I could catch a glimpse of the glories inside.

Just as I was making the last notation, the door on the other side of the room opened. Max Burke was standing there in a dark gray suit, looking handsome and surprised.

"Max," said Cynthia, reaching for a silk dressing gown.

"Sorry, I didn't know you were here," he said to his wife. "Don't you have the Red Cross?"

"Not until one," she said, drawing the ends of the gown together. "Do you need something?"

He glanced at me, nodded briefly in acknowledgment, then turned back to his wife. "Those train tickets for Los Angeles. The twenty-fourth? Is that all right?"

"I told you, Max, I don't know. Just make your plans without me."

"There's no point in getting them if you can't come, Cynthia."

"Then don't get them." It was there again, the same tone as before, one of exasperated contempt. "I can't tell you any more than that."

I stood there, uncertain as to whether I should leave, pretending to make notations in my book. The air felt close and warm.

Max put his hands in his pockets and turned to me. "Miss Cleary," he said abruptly. "A tailor. Do you know any good ones?"

"A tailor?"

"I need tuxedo pants hemmed by next Wednesday. The fellow who made them can't finish the job. His son, the war—" he tilted his head to the side, a family's grief summed up in one gesture. "Anyhow, I thought you might know one."

"I don't, I'm afraid. There was an excellent tailor in my neighborhood, Mr. Yamagami, but he—well, he's—"

"Unavailable," he finished briefly. "You don't know anyone else?"

"I'm sorry, no. Perhaps you could ask one of your friends?"

The last word seemed to hang in the air, as words sometimes do, and I felt myself blush. It sounded so juvenile, as if I had suggested that he speak to his pals or his buddies. And then I was not just embarrassed but annoyed: annoyed with him, and at the fact that his questioning had made me feel like a schoolgirl.

Then I saw the hard, cold glance that his wife darted at him, a glance that seemed to say, "What friends?" It surprised and unnerved me; so, too, did the way he bent down and picked up the pencil that I didn't even know had fallen out of my notebook. I took it and murmured my thanks.

"You could do the pants, couldn't you, Miss Cleary?" Cynthia stood with crossed arms, the wide sleeves of her silk dressing gown making her look like a medieval queen.

"Yes," I said slowly. "I could."

"You do men's tailoring?" Max asked.

"I can, yes."

"You can. But you don't like to?"

Truth to be told, I hated working with men's clothes. I also hated that he'd sensed my reluctance and exposed it. "I'd be happy to help you out, Mr. Burke," I said in my most professional tones.

He studied me silently. I could feel my color rise.

"For goodness' sake, Max, just have her do the pants," said Cynthia. "You can start them now, can't you, Miss Cleary?"

"Yes, Mrs. Burke. I'd be happy to."

"Why don't you go wait in the living room, then." She turned to her husband. "Max, put on the pants and meet her out there. I've got to get ready anyhow."

"I'll make an appointment for tomorrow," he said to his wife. "It doesn't have to be done today."

"She's here now."

"But I've hardly seen you all day, Cynthia," he said, his voice low.

"Yes, you've been busy, haven't you," she said. She turned to me and indicated the door. "My husband will join you in the living room."

I've always disliked hemming men's trousers. Anna did, too. "Some men like it too much, having a woman at their feet," she muttered once as the door closed behind a particularly demanding male customer.

I knelt on the floor and started on the right trouser leg. Max's shoes were expensive, highly polished, black as onyx. There was a whiff of rich leather when I got close.

Sometimes I'm painfully aware of the intimacy of my profession. What other job brings you so close to someone else's body, to the person they are underneath the outline created by the clothes they wear? Though I could not see Max's calves, I had the impression of solid muscle. I cleared my throat and put in the first pin.

Far above me he spoke. "You didn't expect to do this today, did you."

"It's all right, Mr. Burke. I'm happy to do it."

"I can tell."

It was clear from his tone that he'd seen through my fib. I worked on in silence, concentrating grimly on my pinning.

"You seem awfully young to have your own business," he said.

"I'm not as young as I look."

"I figured. You look about seventeen."

I could feel myself coloring under my freckles. "There will come a day," Mrs. Dubuque had once said, "when you will be thrilled to have people think you're younger than you are." But it was not that day, and when I spoke my voice was sharp in spite of myself.

"I'm twenty," I said. "If you really want to know." Then I could have bit my tongue; why on earth had I said the last six words? They made me sound more like a schoolgirl than ever.

He said nothing in response. The silence in the apartment was extraordinary. Perhaps it was the plush carpet, the heavy drapes. Maybe the wealthy had better windows, blocking out the foghorns and traffic sounds below.

"Step apart, a little, please," I said, and he did.

I wished I could stop my cheeks from burning. I thought of serious things: military fortifications around the bay, the newspaper announcing local casualties, the electric bill I needed to pay.

"How long have you been in business?" he asked.

"For myself, about nine months. I worked as an apprentice to a woman who left me the business when she died. I've—I'm changing it a bit."

"In what way?"

"I'm hoping to do more than just the basics."

"You want to design dresses, you mean. Not hem pants."

"Something like that."

"I saw the design you made." He indicated the sketch, still on the end table where Cynthia had left it. "It looks like a totally different dress. It's impressive."

I was surprised. I thanked him.

"Do your parents help with the business?"

"I'm an orphan."

"Since when?"

"Since always."

I added another pin before he spoke again. "That suit you're wearing. You made it yourself?"

"I started with a pattern, but I changed it somewhat."

"It was your idea, putting those colors together? The light green with that brownish trim?"

"It was, yes."

I saw him nod above me. It felt like a compliment.

Reaching for a pin, it occurred to me that he was not in the war. I wondered why. He was young enough to enlist, probably thirty; what kept him out? Maybe he had some hidden disease, like hemophilia or something.

As I straightened the hem, accidentally brushing his ankle, I thought of all the diseases I could name. *Smallpox. Measles.* I concentrated as hard as if it were a quiz show and I would be eliminated if I were to stop. *Pneumonia. Mumps. Influenza. Whooping cough.*

At last I was done and sat back, surveying the two hems for evenness. It wasn't a bad job, especially given how flustered I'd been for most of it.

"All done," I said, trying to get up gracefully, which was difficult in my straight skirt. He reached down and caught my hand, helping me up. "It shouldn't take me long to do these, Mr. Burke," I said, backing away and tugging my skirt into place. "When do you need them?"

"Tuesday, if possible. Tell me where to find your shop, and I'll pick them up."

"It's no trouble for me to come here."

"And it's no trouble for me to go there. I'm always driving about the city." Reaching into his jacket breast pocket, he took out a small leather pad and pencil. "Write your address down. If you write your phone number, too, I'll call before I come."

When I handed it back he glanced at the pad as if making sure he could read my writing before returning it to his pocket. "Have a seat. I'll be right back."

His presence was so vivid that it felt like a different room once he had left. Instead of sitting down, I went to the window, studying the view in a way I had been unable to do before. It was absolutely stunning: the buildings sloping down the hill, the blue stretch of the bay with Alcatraz in the center and the hills of Marin County beyond, the streets where you could see tiny cars glinting in the sun like the heads of pins. Up here you could feel like a queen surveying her realm, as if all this belonged to you. I mused on how strange it was that you never got this same feeling of possession at ground level. When you were close enough to a thing to touch it, you should feel more ownership, but you didn't; it was only at a height that the city really seemed to belong to you, when it was so small it seemed you could tuck it into your handbag. It was like the feeling I'd had at the Top of the Mark, once before, looking out at almost the same view.

"Miss Cleary."

I started and turned. Max Burke handed me two parcels, neatly wrapped in brown paper. "My pants, my wife's dress. She says to call her when you need her to come in for the fitting."

"Thank you."

"And don't forget this." He picked up the sketch and held it out to me. It took me a moment to shift the parcels around, and as he waited he looked at my drawing. His expression was almost somber. I remembered that it was the dress he hadn't wanted his wife to remake.

As I took it from him, my fingers brushed his. I felt my color rise and slowly put the sketch in my pocketbook to avoid looking up into his eyes until the last possible minute. When I did he was studying me, a faint line between his brows, as if trying to figure something out.

Then he smiled. Brief as it was, I could tell it was not the kind of smile men give to dazzle or charm. I was astonished to see admiration in it, and respect.

"Thank you for your help, Miss Cleary," he said. "You'll hear from me soon."

FIVE

My love of clothes began the Christmas I was nine. Every year the trustees' wives would come to the orphanage to distribute gifts, a thrilling event that began with the parade of big cars rolling up to the curb. From the dormitory windows we'd watch the chauffeurs walk briskly around the vehicles, opening the doors for women in fur stoles and hats.

That year, when I was called up for my turn, a gray-haired trustee handed me a package that was thin and flat, clearly a book. I was too well-behaved to show my disappointment; everyone knew that the large boxes were usually the better gifts, like dolls or china tea sets.

But when I actually opened the gift everything else vanished, for it was a book of paper dolls. I'd never had anything like it before. It was a family: Mother, with marcelled hair and profuse eyelashes; Father, a pipe forever stuck in his mouth; dark-haired Jimmy, blonde Jane, and Baby, a child of indeterminate gender with a large amber curl on his or her forehead.

"How nice," said one of the trustee's wives, pausing by my chair. "Just think of the fun you'll have dressing those children for adventures."

"Yes, ma'am," I said politely, though it wasn't the children I was fascinated by, but the mother. After living with women who wore the same black robes day in and day out, I couldn't get enough of Mother's printed outfits. House dresses in green and red with white cuffs and collars, her hands holding a feather duster or a pie; a long flowing nightgown and robe of pale peach; navy slacks with wide legs and a striped boyish sweater, a kerchief tied around her neck; a white tennis dress; a pretty suit of bottle-green, with a fur stole and a hat with a wide flat bow on the brim ("For playing bridge and shopping!"); and, best of all, an evening gown in dark violet, a diamond brooch at the neckline, the sleeves short and ruffled ("For glamorous nights out with Father!").

Trixie and I cut the dolls out the next day, starting with Mother and her wardrobe. Father came next, so that Mother would have someone to take her dancing, then Jane, and finally Baby. (Jimmy, truth be told, was never liberated from his pages. We had no interest in little boys or their clothes.)

We played with the dolls so much that the paper tabs grew soft and limp. Mother's neck weakened and had to be reinforced by Sister Margaret with cellophane tape. I was relieved at the success of this operation, for to lose her would have felt like losing far more than a toy. I couldn't have articulated it at the time, but Mother and her wardrobe were teaching me that there was a connection between clothes and life experiences. With the right wardrobe, it seemed a woman could do anything.

Then one day I wondered what the evening dress would look like with long sleeves. The idea was so captivating that I sketched it on white paper with my crayons. I liked the look of it, so I sketched it again, this time in red, putting a huge silk poppy in place of the diamond brooch. I was learning another lesson: One creative idea can open the door to many more. I filled sheets of paper with my drawings.

"You've certainly gotten a lot of enjoyment out of those paper dolls," said Sister Margaret as she watched me sketch. They were paper dolls to her, but to me they were the door to a world of colorful possibility, a world that I knew even back then was exactly where I belonged.

One of the brightest things in my adult wardrobe was my bathing suit: a halter one that bared the midriff, with a little skirt underneath. It had a splashy print of multicolored flowers against a white background, and I loved it, even though any bathing suit meant that my freckles were on full display.

"Cute suit," said Louise as I came back from the changing rooms. We were at Ocean Beach on one of those gorgeously warm September days in the city. "Did you make that?"

"I found it on sale at Macy's."

"Lucky you," she said, adjusting her own polka-dotted one-piece. "Wish I could wear a halter. It would just call even more attention to my chest." She grinned as if she were complaining, but I knew she wasn't.

Louise is a friend of mine from Notre Dame des Victoires, a Catholic high school for girls not far from Union Square and way across town from the orphanage. I ended up there on a special scholarship from Mrs. Detweiler, one of the trustees, who saw promise in me and made the arrangements. It meant a ridiculously long ride there by bus and streetcar, but since it was where Trixie was going, I didn't mind at all. It was allied with the French parish of the same name, and we all had to learn French if we didn't already know it. Luckily, I was a quick study, and Mrs. Dubuque helped tutor me on weekends.

The beach was packed, unsurprisingly; San Franciscans put up with so much wind and fog that no one can resist the lure of a hot day. And there were servicemen, too, in small groups or alone with a girl.

"Poor things," said Louise, indicating a group of sailors nearby. "It must be hot in those uniforms." She flopped down on her stomach, propped up on her elbows, blonde hair around her shoulders. "Should I call them over? They look lonely."

"I thought we were here to talk about me," said Trixie, taking a swig from her bottle of Coke. "And my problems." Her boyfriend Dennis, stationed somewhere in Europe, had been writing letters that seemed far less romantic of late. "Like the fact that I suspect Dennis has met some elegant French girl who's totally turned his head."

"Or some lucky WAC," I said, thinking of the Women's Army Corps in their sharp uniforms and all the places they could go.

"So make him jealous," said Louise. "Start talking about some other boy."

"I can't," said Trixie. "I don't care about any other boy."

"You volunteer at the USO. You meet tons of them."

"That's different. We're not supposed to go out with the boys we meet there." Trixie glanced at me apologetically, as if realizing what she'd just said. I smiled to let her know I was all right.

"Look," said Louise, "I know how to remedy this sit-u-a-tion." She sat up, tossing back her hair. The four sailors standing a few yards away were staring at her. She waved, and as if they had been waiting for her cue, they immediately started over.

"Lou*ise*," said Trixie under her breath, but the damage was done.

It's typical Louise, this kind of thing. She's pretty and has a boldness that I don't have, and Trixie doesn't, either. I think it comes from years of independence; her father is a businessman who divides his time between San Francisco and New York and her mother typically goes with him, leaving Louise at home with the housekeeper, an older woman named Hetty. "We leave each other alone," said Louise in high school, the first time I met her. "She makes me dinner, I eat it, then I study and listen to the radio. I might as well be on my own. Like you, I guess," she added cheerfully. The thing she didn't realize, though—never actually had, in all the time I'd known her—was that her independence and mine were totally different. Even when they were miles away, she had a family and always would.

The sailors, we learned, were on shore leave. Two were the gentleman type, one was wide-eyed, and one was bold. He gravitated toward Louise and within minutes was next to her on the blanket, lying on his side and leaning on one elbow like a pose in a magazine. Trixie and I put on our best USO welcoming faces and chatted for a bit with the others, but our hearts weren't in it. Mine wasn't, at least. Maybe it would have been better if they'd been in army uniforms instead of navy ones. It was just too familiar.

"I'm going down to the water," I said finally. "It's so hot today." I smiled apologetically and raced away to the water's edge, where the ocean—always so cold—made me seize inside. I was ankle-deep and a wave crashed into shore then rushed back out, giving me that old disorienting feeling, as if I were the one moving instead of the water. The sand beneath me seemed to give way, but I didn't fall. I stood up straight, locking my legs and digging my toes in the sand for a foothold, and rode out the wave.

That night in bed, more tired than usual after the sun, I thought about my parents. I often did that when I was drifting off to sleep, a habit which started at the orphanage. I would listen to the breathing and bed springs of the children in the other cots and stare at the moonlight spilling onto the dormitory floor. Like a movie in my mind, I would see the moment that my father brought me to the orphanage:

. . . It was a dark night, with clouds covering the moon. The man in the patched coat moved slowly toward the front entrance of Mount St. Joseph, holding a basket lined with blankets. Inside it the baby slept, and he was glad, for if he had to look into the hazel eyes that were just like her dead mother's, he would never be able to do what he had to do.

He had planned to put down the basket, press a kiss on her forehead, and leave, knowing that soon the sun would rise, and a sister would open the heavy door and find the sleeping baby. But just as he was bending over his daughter's head, the door opened. A short sister with a childlike face was standing there, her eyes full of kindness. He pulled off his old hat, gripping it hard.

"My wife is dead," he said. "And I'm too poor and too ill to care for our daughter. Please keep her until I can come back."

"Of course," said the sister. Her eyes, normally so merry, were grave with compassion. "Come in. Let us give you some breakfast."

"No," the man said, fighting back tears. "I have to leave. I love her too much and I loved her mother too much. I have to go while I still can." And before Sister Rosemary could do anything, he bent to kiss the baby and then turned and ran, coat flapping, into the dawn. . . .

I'd pictured the scene so often that it had settled into my bones. Stories you hear over and over become a part of you, and stories you tell yourself are no different. It was only after I had left the orphanage and moved into the boardinghouse, eighteen years old and with a new distance from the home I'd always known, that I realized how little Sister Rosemary had actually told me about my arrival. The man with the patched coat, the basket . . . those details had come from my own imagining, not from her. It had been a jolt to realize that, but it was a comfort to recall what Sister had in fact told me, so many times over the years: "Your parents loved each other, Irene." The words had become almost like the Hail Mary, like a prayer you know by heart. "They loved you too. They would have kept you if they could."

I snuggled down into the sheets. Whichever other parts of the story I had grown out of believing, I still had that.

SIX

I finished Mr. Burke's pants the next morning. He'd said he needed them for an event on Wednesday, but I was in the shop all day Tuesday, minus a quick run to the corner grocery for milk, and he never called to pick them up. Around four thirty, I gave up wondering and turned my attention to the christening dress I was making out of a white evening gown ("I've got no need for the gown anymore," said the mother wryly, her baby squalling in her arms, "with my husband overseas and this little fellow changing my figure."). It was the sort of sewing challenge I enjoyed.

The radio was on, as it usually is; when you've lived all your life with lots of other people it's strange to be on your own, and the background noise is comforting. I lay the gown out on the table, paused a moment, then took my shears and cut into it, which is such a brave action because it's an irrevocable one. "Measure twice, cut once," Anna used to say, and I think of that every time I take my scissors in hand. Oddly, though, I've always loved making that first cut. You have to have total confidence in what you're doing. Maybe it's that little bit of risk that gives it a certain thrill.

Behind me a drama of some kind was on the radio. A woman was saying, with a sob in her throat, "You couldn't wait for me, Frank," and he said, "No, I couldn't. I had to live my life." "But I loved you," she said, "and I was only in Albuquerque because my aunt was dying.

She took so long to die. And all the time I thought only of you." *Poor old aunt*, I thought with a grin as my scissors sliced through the fabric. These radio dramas were ridiculous, but at least they were voices in a quiet shop. "You loved me?" said Frank, his voice husky with feeling. "Then why did you marry Jerome?" "Why did you marry Imogene?" asked the woman. "Because I was lonely," he said. "But what will we do now, Eloise? What will we do?"

It went on and on as the light changed, the afternoon shifting to evening. When the program ended, I neatly folded the pieces on the cutting board and switched off the radio. Still no call from Max Burke; I wondered if I should call his apartment the next day. I went to the front door and flipped the sign to CLOSED.

On a hook behind me Cynthia's dress was hanging in a green garment bag, ready for me to begin work. As I stretched out the crick in my neck I stared at the bag, picturing the rose satin inside, hanging in rippling folds.

It was quiet in the shop, the only sounds the muffled noise of traffic outside. A few pedestrians passed by with the purposeful walk people have in the evening, when they're on their way home to family and dinner. Fog was creeping in from the west, and though the shades were open, the angled sunlight meant that no one on the sidewalk would be able to see inside. No one could see me. I was totally alone.

Almost before I knew it, I was unzipping the garment bag and whisking the dress into the screened changing area.

My cardigan, blouse, and skirt were soon off, and standing in my bra and half-slip I carefully lifted the dress over my head. It shimmered over me like pink water. Slowly, deliberately, I put my arms into the sleeves, my heart pounding. The dress was too long; it pooled at my feet, and without closing the keyhole fastening, it did not lie on my chest as it should. But the material against my skin was cool, soft, luxurious. I'd never worn anything like it before.

There was a mirror in the dressing cubicle but a better, three-paneled one was just outside, and after a glance at the street I boldly went and stood before it, lifting my skirt clear of my feet. The color was surprisingly flattering, and I couldn't stop staring. Although I was going to cut away the long blousy sleeves, I liked how they felt and how they covered my freckly arms, every inch of me transformed by the fairy godmother that was the dress. I lifted my hair, imagining it pinned high, and turned my body sightly to admire the drape of the skirt over my backside. This was a dress to wear to a ball, to some place with potted palms and high French windows and an orchestra playing. With a dress like this even an outsider could be accepted, could be welcomed on a cloud of champagne and moonlight and music—

It was almost violent, the sudden rapping on the glass. It made me jump. I turned quickly from the mirror, instinctively holding my arms over my chest. Max Burke was peering in at the glassed front door. I couldn't tell if he could see me.

I darted back behind the screen and took off the dress, which was hard to do because I was trembling. *Stupid, stupid Irene*, I said in my head. I forced myself to slow down, for in my haste it would be easy to damage the dress. By some miracle I managed to get it safely back on the hanger.

He knocked again as I was putting on my blouse, with its three small buttons high in back. Normally I could do them myself if I craned in just the right way, but it took time and I was too flustered, so in the end I left them undone and put the cardigan on. It would hopefully cover them up and the gap would not be visible.

Walk like you're somebody, I told myself as I emerged from the cubicle. Max was still just outside the shop, half-angled toward the street, taking a cigarette box out of his breast pocket.

I opened the door and he turned, putting the cigarettes away. "Miss Cleary. I wasn't sure you were here."

"I'm sorry," I said, my cheeks burning. "I was just—" and I gestured vaguely toward the back, as if to indicate something nonspecific but benign: in the ladies' room, unable to hear your knock.

He took off his hat as he came in. "I was in the neighborhood, thought I'd call in to see if the pants were ready. I called at lunch, but you weren't here."

"Yes, of course." That fifteen minutes when I'd been to the corner grocery: *What impeccable timing*, I thought grimly. My heart was still pounding as I picked up the folded pants. He was looking about the shop, taking in every detail. His gaze rested on the quartet of small gold-rimmed glass plates I'd found in Anna's apartment and had mounted on the wall between the windows, an addition Trixie had said was particularly inspired.

"Would you like to try on the pants?" The moment I said it I remembered his wife's dress, hanging in the changing cubicle, probably askew on its hanger. I opened my mouth to speak, then shut it, for there was nothing I could say.

He looked at me, apparently noting my discomfiture. "No. I don't need to."

"Let me wrap them up," I said. I found some brown paper and turned to the counter to fold the pants. It helped to have something to do, though I was still conscious of him standing several feet behind me.

"It's getting foggy out there, isn't it," I said.

"Just starting to."

"Too bad," I said, creasing the paper around the fabric. "It's been so sunny lately."

"Your top button is undone," he said suddenly. "On your blouse."

"Oh." I gave a little laugh. "Yes, it's quite hard to get to."

"Here," he said, and before I could do anything I felt his fingers on the nape of my neck. I just stood there in shock, frozen. His movements were brisk but still careful, as if he feared pulling my hair.

"Thank you," I said when he had finished. My back and neck were rigid, like those of a statue.

"Oh," he said in some surprise, "they're all undone."

"I know," I said, breaking away in case he reached for my neck again. I turned to face him, the counter biting into the small of my back.

I was glad I could hold the parcel in front of me. As if sensing my discomfort, he immediately took a few steps back.

"I was surprised when you knocked," I said. "I didn't have time to do them up." It was a stupid thing to say. If he hadn't seen me in his wife's dress, I'd just given him a reason to wonder why I was undressed at five in the evening.

"It's a crazy place for buttons," he said. "They look impossible to do."

He was absolutely right, but the awkwardness of the moment made me defensive. "I'm used to doing things for myself."

"Yes," he said, putting his hands in his pockets. He studied me. "I can tell you are."

It was said thoughtfully, almost neutrally, but there was a hint of admiration in his tone that did not escape me. His eyes left mine, once again surveying the shop.

"I know a thing or two about that," he said finally, taking the packet from my hands. He pulled a five-dollar bill from his billfold and put it down on the counter. "Thank you for the alterations."

"That's too much, Mr. Burke. It's only two dollars."

He was putting on his hat. "Keep the change."

"But it's too much," I said, pride making me speak even though I needed every cent he was offering.

"Two dollars for the trousers and three because I burst in on you after closing time. It's only fair." He lifted an eyebrow, as if daring me to argue. "Good evening, Miss Cleary."

When the door closed behind him, I watched him go to his car, a huge silver Cadillac parked directly in front of the shop. Two young boys on the sidewalk turned to admire it as he drove away.

After closing the shades, I took off my cardigan and went upstairs to my apartment. I undid the button he had done and then did them all up again, from the bottom to the top.

SEVEN

"Irene, do you think there are different kinds of rich people?"

"Sorry?" I'd been drifting, staring out the window of the diner, and Trixie's voice brought me back. We were having lunch on Fillmore, the day after Max came to the shop.

"Do you think there are different kinds of rich people?"

"I don't know. Why do you ask?"

"I'm reading *The Great Gatsby*. It's full of rich people, and the richest one—Gatsby—is kind of an outsider. It's interesting." Trixie's face, under her brown bangs, was absorbed; she's always loved thinking about big questions like that. "In the book there's a difference between the people who have always had money and the people who have made it themselves. The newcomers aren't accepted. I'm wondering if it's really like that."

"When I get to know some rich people, I'll ask them," I said flippantly.

"You know the Burkes," teased Trixie.

"Not as equals." I hadn't told Trixie about the visit of Max Burke to the shop the day before; I wasn't sure why. Maybe I didn't want to admit that I'd tried on his wife's dress as if I were slipping into her skin, a place I had no right to be. I flipped the metal lid of the cream pitcher up and down.

"I guess Louise's parents are kind of rich. But I've never spent much time with them, they're always somewhere else." Trixie's voice changed. "Irene," she said, "I'm a little worried about her."

"Why?"

"I think she went out with that sailor the other day. You know, after we all left the beach." Her expression was troubled. "I think she goes out with a lot of them."

I knew what she was referring to. No one wanted to be known as a Victory Girl, a V-Girl, someone who slept with servicemen just for kicks. They were also called sea gulls, the girls who you saw slipping out of hotels early in the morning. But I couldn't believe it of Louise. "She's probably just going out for drinks. Dancing."

"Maybe. But I wish she'd volunteer with us at the USO. She could meet plenty of guys that way without . . . well, without taking risks."

Except, of course, for the risk I'd taken. Even the USO wasn't safe, in some ways. It wasn't sex you had to fear there, but something more innocent and dangerous. It was seeing a guy across a dance floor and believing that you were in a fairy tale, where there was actually such a thing as happily ever after.

Moments after I returned to the shop, the phone rang. "It's Mrs. Fred Gibson," said the girlish voice. "I hear you are remaking a dress for Mrs. Burke? I was wondering if you'd be available to make me a new suit."

I threw back my head and grinned ecstatically at the ceiling before composing myself. "I'd be happy to, Mrs. Gibson," I said in my most graciously professional tone.

So at four o'clock the following afternoon I was walking into another luxury flat, this one only a few blocks from the Burkes' home. Betty Gibson, just as in her wedding photographs, had glossy brown hair and a Deanna Durbin–type prettiness. She was probably my age, but she seemed so much older, with a ring on her finger and a beautifully appointed home. A huge photograph of the wedding party sat on the mantel, the same one that had been in the newspaper. There was Cynthia in her chiffon dress, almost—I remembered the caption—upstaging the bride.

I took Betty's measurements in the bedroom, which had a big three-way mirror. "My mother-in-law gave me this fabric," she said, "and I thought it would be lovely as a daytime suit." It was silk in a deep buttercup yellow. "She's such a doll."

We'd barely started when there was a knock on the door. "Betty? It's me, Dolores."

"Come in," said Betty. The door opened to admit a woman in her late twenties, angular and elegant, with jet-black hair and a pine-green suit and hat. The two women air-kissed.

"Gladys said you were getting fitted. I figured you wouldn't mind some company." The woman glanced at me. "New seamstress?"

"Yes. This is Irene Cleary."

"Dolores Kittredge," said the woman. "Nice to meet you." I murmured my greeting, and she sank into a boudoir chair, drawing off her gloves, a massive ruby glinting on her left hand. She fingered the fabric. "Pretty color. That sort of thing isn't easy to find these days."

"Fred's mother gave it to me. She was going to make something with it but never did."

"Anne Gibson is a peach," said Dolores. "You're lucky. My mother-in-law is an absolute witch and always has been."

"She can't be that bad."

"Can't she?" Dolores opened her pocketbook and lit a cigarette.

"Hold your arms out, please, Mrs. Gibson," I said. In the mirror behind us, Dolores pensively exhaled a ribbon of smoke.

"You saw Cynthia Burke at Vanessi's the other evening, didn't you?" she said after a moment.

"I did. She looked lovely."

"Her figure's better than ever." Dolores studied the end of her cigarette before asking casually, "Did she look happy to you?"

I was instantly intrigued but hid it by focusing on the tape measure. Betty was less suave; she involuntarily turned her head toward Dolores and her body went with it, then she apologized to me and resumed her pose. "Why do you ask?"

"Just curious. She didn't look happy, did she?"

"Thank you, Mrs. Gibson," I said, and she took her arms down.

"I think he's a nice man," said Betty staunchly. "A little . . . rough around the edges, maybe."

"It's more than the edges," said Dolores. "You saw him, ordering that champagne for the whole table even though it was the Shaws' party, not his. Cynthia looked like she was going to die. And the way he was so friendly with the waiter?"

"That was a little bit awkward."

"More than awkward. It was showing off. He doesn't know where to stop."

I looked down at my notebook, writing the measurements, remembering Max's fingers on the base of my neck.

"Give him time," said Betty. "Maybe Chicago is different. He just doesn't know how we do things here."

"Listen to you," said Dolores with an indulgent smile. "You've been in this city, what, a year?"

"It takes some people longer to adapt, maybe," said Betty. "And there are worse things than not knowing how to act at a dinner party."

"I suppose so." Dolores took a long drag on the cigarette. "Of course," she said in a different tone, "I suspect he does know how to act in the bedroom."

"Dolores Kittredge."

"Come on, Betty. Don't tell me the thought hasn't entered your head."

There was silence. Glancing up from measuring Betty's wrist, I saw in the mirror that her face had turned crimson.

"The man oozes sexual appeal," said Dolores. "It's the Italian in him, or whatever it is. And he can certainly wear a tuxedo. He was sitting next to Gordon the other night, and my God, it was like Don Juan next to Elmer Fudd. And it wasn't Elmer Fudd I wanted to go home with."

"Dolores Kittredge. Say five Hail Marys."

"Oh, please." Dorothy stubbed out her cigarette. "If they're honest, every woman there was thinking the same thing." She glanced meaningfully at her friend, but Betty, by now in command of her feelings, met her gaze in the mirror with pert defiance. "Fine. Not you, Miss Newlywed. But everyone else."

"Then she should be a very happy wife," said Betty definitively.

"You would think," said Dolores. "But if she were really enjoying that side of things I think she'd be nicer to him."

I looked down at my notebook, reviewing my notations. There was silence that seemed oddly pregnant; I glanced up to see Betty opening her eyes meaningfully, telegraphing a message to her friend in the mirror. Dolores leaned forward, her long legs folded together like scissors.

"Of course," she said in a louder tone, as if to indicate she was speaking to a new audience, "Miss—sorry, what was your name?"

"Cleary. Irene Cleary."

"We always talk like this when we get together." Dolores gave a pointed smile. "Two friends chatting. Not the kind of thing that needs to leave the room."

"Of course." I gave a brief professional smile, then turned back to my notebook. "I wasn't listening anyhow." It was easier to lie when I was looking down at the pad.

After leaving the Gibsons' apartment I walked slowly east, not in a rush to get home, pausing to look down the undulating streets to the bay beyond. Sea gulls wheeled above me, and across the street an army officer and a blonde woman were kissing as if they weren't out in public in broad daylight. A child ran past me, another boy behind him, their excited cries increasing as gravity took over. It wasn't the view you got from the Burkes' apartment, but it was still beautiful. The water in the bay was bright sunlit blue, like a picture from a postcard. You could almost forget that there were nets below the surface, placed to catch enemy submarines.

Life in the city had changed instantly, that terrifying day in December of '41. It was my last year before leaving the orphanage, and I can still hear Estelle Delgado, whom I shared a room with, crying hysterically when Sister announced the news about Pearl Harbor. The entire orphanage prayed a rosary, and when I went to school even my teachers, who normally seemed unmoved by anything outside Latin or mathematics, were shaken and distracted.

There were blackouts and metal drives. For months everyone was afraid of a Japanese attack over the water. Walking toward the streetcar stop from school, Trixie and I would see huge lines of young men snaking around the block at the army recruitment office. Our Catholic school uniforms made us conspicuous; occasionally one of the guys would call out, "Pray for us, girls," said sometimes as a joke, and sometimes with great seriousness. I always did.

But I think the neighborhood that changed the most was one not far from Anna's shop. A few blocks down Fillmore was a community of Japanese shops and businesses, including a tailor shop owned by Mr. Yamagami. Before the war started I'd occasionally go to his shop on errands for Anna, usually to outsource a particularly difficult piece of men's work. I always enjoyed going there. Mr. Yamagami was a widower, courteous and kind, with a son who played baseball—there was a photo of him in uniform behind the counter—and a daughter, Helen, who was studying history in college. When I saw her, she was often engrossed in a book. I remember one time she was reading a novel by Steinbeck, and she told me with pride that he was from Monterey County, where her father had grown up and where they still had aunts and cousins. "My uncle has strawberry farms there, outside town. They grow chrysanthemums in their yard, and you should see all the different colors they come in. The prettiest flowers you've ever seen. Even roses can't compare."

Then there was the December day when the American flag suddenly went up in their shop window, along with a neatly hand-lettered sign saying AMERICAN BORN. Months later, the government posted notices all around the neighborhood: INSTRUCTIONS TO ALL PERSONS OF JAPANESE ANCESTRY. I passed one as I came to the shop to pick up a man's coat Mr. Yamagami was finishing for Anna. There was no one behind the counter, so I rang the bell, and when Mr. Yamagami came out there was a change in his manner, a sober abstraction mixed with something like shame. As I took the package, he added several spools of thread, saying, "Please, Miss Cleary, I hope you will accept these." I'd wanted to protest but something in his eyes stopped me; he knew, as I did, that Anna would get far more customers now. I thanked him, and as I turned away, I could hear what sounded like Helen sobbing in the back room. On the step outside the shop I paused, putting the thread in my bag. I was even more shaken when a middle-aged woman walking by gave both me and the shop a look of white-hot hatred.

As an orphan, it's always been easy to feel like an outsider. But as I walked back to Anna's shop, I realized that the Yamagamis—and every Japanese person in the whole country, probably—knew that feeling in a way I never would.

I stopped at a flower seller the next day and bought a small bouquet of orange chrysanthemums. When I got to the Yamagamis' shop, the front door was locked and the shades were down, though I thought I saw movement inside. "They're going," said the red-haired woman sweeping the step of the bakery next door. "They're all going." I knew which "they" she meant.

In the end I set the flowers by the front door, propping them up against the frame. The woman stopped sweeping and looked at me curiously. I nodded and left, heading up Fillmore Street.

When I reached the corner, I looked back. I could still see the flowers, a tiny orange speck against the gray front door.

EIGHT

After a few days of focused work on Cynthia Burke's dress, it was time for her to try it on. It was a nerve-racking experience. Even though I had faith in my skills, so much of the original dress had been cut away that it would be impossible to start over.

Thankfully, she loved it. Her expression changed when she saw herself in the shop mirror, with the rapt look every seamstress wants to see. "Oh, this is beautiful," she said. "Even prettier than I'd hoped for. It's a totally new dress. But the things I liked about it before are still there, too."

"I'm so glad, Mrs. Burke," I said, exhaling fully for the first time that day. "If there's nothing you'd like to change, I can have it done for you on Monday."

It was a polite way of saying she could take it off, but she didn't seem to be in any rush. She kept looking at her reflection and smiling. No wonder: I knew how it felt to have that satin against your skin, to feel transformed by the power of a dress.

At last she did take it off, emerging from the changing room in her powder blue suit with the silver fur stole. "Thank you for letting me come today," she said. "I was so eager to see the progress on the dress. You're so wonderful to fit me in last minute."

Her kindness made me glow. "I'm so glad, Mrs. Burke. I've enjoyed working on it." *Even to the point of trying it on*, I thought guiltily.

The little bell rang as the shop door opened. It was Mrs. O'Leary, the widow who lived one block over. She was a longtime customer and friend of Anna's who still loved to drop in to chat, even when she had no work for me to do. At the sight of Cynthia Burke in her impeccable outfit she stopped short, glancing at me in surprise.

"I'm sorry," she said, shifting her shopping bag to the other hand. "I can come back later if you're busy."

"No, please," said Cynthia. "Miss Cleary was nice enough to take me last minute. I apologize if I've taken your appointment." She turned to me, putting on her gloves. "Just call when you're ready with the dress, and I'll come by and get it."

"I'd be happy to bring it to your home, Mrs. Burke."

"Thank you," said Cynthia, "but the dress . . . is a bit of a surprise. It's better for me to come here." She smiled again, nodded at Mrs. O'Leary, then left.

"My goodness," said Mrs. O'Leary, shrugging off her old brown overcoat. "Such beautiful clothes. She's like a movie star, isn't she? And so polite, too."

I nodded, but my mind was replaying what I'd just heard. A surprise, Cynthia had said. But Max knew I was remaking the dress and had seen the sketch. Who was the surprise for?

That night I couldn't sleep. I tossed about, finally reaching for the light switch and turning it on. Just after midnight, said the clock. I turned off the light and lay staring out the window at the boring view of bits of roofs and the back ends of neighboring buildings and the small irregular patch of sky.

The bed was a narrow one I'd inherited from Anna, with an iron frame and an increasingly saggy spot right under my hip. I'd crawled under the bed at one point and sure enough, there was a busted spring. Cloth I could fix but metal springs were beyond my capacity, so I did my best to ignore it, but that night I couldn't. The saggy part felt lower than usual, and I felt low right along with it. Why, I wasn't sure.

I started thinking of all the beds I'd ever slept in. There was the cot in the orphanage, one of sixteen girls in a big echoing room. Then there was the twin bed with the green metal headboard when I was in high school and Sister Margaret let me move into a smaller room with Estelle Delgado. After leaving the orphanage two years ago, there was the maple bed at the ladies' boardinghouse on Gough, a converted Victorian where I lived with a bunch of girls who were working as typists or secretaries. The landlady, Mrs. Maloney, was friendly unless you missed curfew, at which point you were looking for a new place to live. "If you're tempted to test her, don't," warned one of the typists. "You'll never find another bed in this town." She was right; ever since the war started, the city has been packed with servicemen and shipyard workers and even wives of soldiers who follow their husbands across the country until they get here and can follow them no further.

But coming from the orphanage, I didn't mind the curfew. I didn't mind the fact that the partitions dividing the once-huge rooms were flimsy, or that my room was right next to the bathroom. I was working full-time for Anna, and my head was full of ideas. At night I'd lie in bed, hearing the girls as they returned from dates (there was always a rush for the bathroom just after curfew, and the pipes were so noisy there was no point in trying to sleep until it was over), and I'd dream of clothes. I'd imagine ones I could design from scratch and remember those I'd seen in magazines and shops. Sometimes I'd stay up late changing my own store-bought clothes, adding trim to a sleeve or changing the buttons or altering the neckline to make it more flattering. Anna would advise me on the technical aspects of these changes, but the ideas were all mine. She'd look at my handiwork and smile approvingly. "You have come so far since you started here," she said once. "Nothing can stop you now."

I reached for my robe and bunched it, creating a barrier to keep me from sliding onto the sagging spot. Anna had never known it, but something almost did stop my work. Just before she died, I came close to joining the WACS. I had gotten the idea from Estelle, my former roommate, whom I ran into one day in her new uniform. She practically shone with purpose. "Think of enlisting, Irene," she said. "I feel like I'm part of the war. Like I'm actually doing something."

We were all doing something—rationing, saving newspaper—but I knew what she meant. And for a while, the idea kept rattling around in my mind. I'd lie in bed, and the clothes I envisioned were a smart new uniform and hat. I was restless and wanting to travel, maybe because the war was making me see how big the world really is and how small a part of it I actually knew. It was a revelation to think that in a few months, I could be lying down to sleep in another country altogether. *Why not?* I asked myself. *What can stop me? Who needs family or money when you have a willingness to serve your country?*

I got as far as a visit to the recruitment office and the making of an appointment. While I was there, Anna collapsed while helping a customer. When I heard the news and called the hospital, they wouldn't let me come. "She can't hear you anyhow," said the nurse, telling me to check back the next day.

But early the next morning the phone rang. The doctor told me to come to the hospital to pick up Anna's things. "There is no other family we can notify?" he asked.

"No," I said, my tears wetting the phone cord I was winding around my hand. "She had no family."

It struck me then—for the first time ever, surprisingly—that Anna and I had been very much alike.

She left me the shop and the apartment. I was astonished to discover it. "I can't help thinking that Miss Orlova suspected this," said the lawyer, a thin, balding man with a tidy office on Fillmore. "She called me just two weeks before she died to amend her will."

"Who was she going to leave it to before me?"

"She was going to leave the shop and apartment to the San Francisco Ballet. I gather she did some work for them, at times?"

"She helped sew costumes, yes." I thought of the white tutus for the swans in *Swan Lake*, hanging along the back of the shop like fluffy clouds. "She was from Russia and she loved the ballet." One time I saw her pause in her sewing, listening to Tchaikovsky on the radio and looking rapt and far away, as if she were not just hearing but seeing something beautiful. For a moment she was not merely a middle-aged seamstress but a woman full of dreams. It occurred to me that I could have asked her what the music meant to her, but I hadn't. We spoke mainly about sewing, rarely about ourselves.

"She told me," said the lawyer, "that the ballet would be all right without her, but she was not certain that you would be. She did not mean that as an insult, Miss Cleary. She described you as competent and gifted, but she was aware that your lack of family was a challenge that you would always have to face. This was her way of giving you a safety net. A business, a base of customers. A place to live too."

A place to live. For I would be moving, of course, out of my congenial boardinghouse and into the flat above the shop, the flat that still held Anna's things: the small brown sofa, the drop-leaf table with its lace tablecloth, the icon of a sober-faced Christ above the low cabinet in the living room. They would be my responsibility now.

It wasn't that I was ungrateful. I was astonished and touched by her legacy. But as I thanked the lawyer and got up, it was clear that my dream of the WACS was over. At the age of almost twenty, my future would not involve traveling the world. It would be rooted, firmly and deeply, in the city I had always known. Any new worlds I wanted to discover, I realized, would have to be here.

NINE

It was the first Friday in October, one of those glorious fall days in the city that make you willing to forgive the foggy overcast of summer. Buttery evening sunlight drenched the shop, and the vase of iris glowed like something in a painting. Benny Goodman was on the radio for the five o'clock hour, and I whistled along as I swept up snippets of thread and then pulled down the shades. I had plans to meet Louise and Trixie at the movies at seven, and after finishing Cynthia's dress I was ready to celebrate. It hung in its garment bag in sophisticated splendor; I'd give her a call the next day to let her know it was available.

Just as I was about to go upstairs and find something for dinner, there was a knock at the door. My heart sank. The shop was closed, but a woman who wants alterations is a tenacious creature, and I can't afford to turn customers away. I assumed my most welcoming smile and opened the door. Max Burke was standing outside.

"Sorry," he said. "I took a chance you'd be here. I should have called."

"It's all right," I said, backing up to let him in. I was flustered by his presence, his maleness, the slightly astringent smell of his after-shave. By the memory, too, of the last time he'd come by the shop when he'd reached for my undone buttons. "How can I help you?"

I was afraid he would ask to take home his wife's gown, the one she had wanted to pick up herself. Instead, he put his hat on the coat rack. "Do you have a minute?"

I nodded and indicated a chair by the door, but he pulled it out for me, then went to get the nearby club chair for himself. He sat down, hands clasped together, leaning forward and facing me, while I sat with my back perfectly straight.

"I'm curious about you," he said without preamble. "I'll tell you why in a moment. You've had this shop how long?"

"Almost a year."

"How much of it did you decorate?" A wave of the hand indicated the curtains, the screen, the print of Paris, the gold-rimmed plates.

"Nearly all of it." I looked down at his clasped hands, with dark hair visible at the base of his wrists. "The curtains were given to me, and the colors—those were my ideas. I painted the screen to match."

"The walls? Were they this color when you came?"

"No, I chose it. A friend helped me paint."

"He did a good job."

"It was a girlfriend, actually," I said, then wondered why I had bothered to correct him.

"It's a bold choice, that purple-blue with the green. And the gold bits here and there. I've never seen that combination before."

"It's all there, in an iris flower." I lifted my chin in the direction of the vase. "You just have to look."

"Sure, but who bothers to look? No, some people are visionaries, and I think you're one."

I almost scoffed at the word, but he was looking at me with those dark brown eyes, steadily and seriously. I remembered that he was a successful businessman who probably knew a thing or two. "Thank you," I finally said.

"I don't know anything about design, but I do know something about business," he said. "I know what makes a person want to come through the front door, whether it's a restaurant or a seamstress's shop. You've got an eye for what works. I saw it the first day we met, that suit you wore, and in the design for my wife's dress, too. Everything." Once again, he waved his hand to indicate the shop. "You have style, Miss Cleary, and I have a proposition to make."

I had absolutely no idea what was coming next. It seemed an age before he spoke again.

"I'm opening a nightclub," he said. "A crazy thing to do in wartime, they say, but soldiers have to drink somewhere. Last week I found out that the fellow who was going to design it has fractured his leg, will be out for months. So I'd like your help in decorating it."

"*My* help?"

"Yes."

"But I'm not a decorator."

"Says who?"

"Says me. I mean, I."

"I say you are. Do you really want to argue?"

"Yes."

His eyebrow lifted, as did the corners of his mouth; I could tell he was enjoying the argument, and it stirred something in me, too, some bit of life.

"I make clothes," I said. "I don't know anything about decorating a nightclub."

"Have you ever been to a nightclub?" he asked.

"Of course." I was glad I could answer in the affirmative. "I've been to the Rose Room."

"Did you like the decor?"

"I suppose so. I didn't really notice."

"Which means one of two things. Either you were so focused on your date that you didn't notice anything else, or the decor of the place was totally unmemorable." He leaned forward. "Here's the thing, Miss

Cleary. The Rose Room could be any bar in any city in the country. I'm thinking of opening a place that is pure San Francisco, a nightclub that captures the feel of this city. The color, the atmosphere, all of it. Completely San Francisco."

"You'd better find a fog machine then," I said, and he laughed. I realized it was the first time I'd ever heard him do so.

"That would be original but bad for the upholstery." He took out a cigarette and offered me one. I shook my head and got up to get him the ashtray. "Look," he said when I sat down again, "I've been in this city for two months, and already I can see it's not like anywhere else on Earth. And with the war, with so many people coming here, it's being discovered. Soldiers, sailors, shipyard workers. They're discovering it, and they'll go back home and miss it terribly."

"But the people who live here are already in San Francisco. They don't need a bar to remind them."

"But this will be the first of many. If it does well here, I'll take it on the road. We'll have one in Chicago, New York. Even in Los Angeles, maybe." He spread his hands out as if indicating a marquee. "The Spirit of San Francisco."

"That's a terrible name for a nightclub," I said involuntarily. I was instantly embarrassed by my bluntness, but to my surprise, he grinned.

"I know it is," he said.

Apparently it was a test, and I'd passed. He sat there, holding his cigarette, smiling at me from behind the spiral of smoke. It was crazy, but my spirits were rising like a balloon.

"You'll give me ideas on design, color, fabric. You wouldn't have to draft or do anything like that, of course; I'll be working with an architect. We'll be meeting over the next two months or so. I'll pay you three hundred dollars up front for a consultation fee."

The three hundred dollars staggered me. I opened my mouth,

closed it again. "I've got customers," I finally said. "I have work to do here."

"You can still do it. I'm not asking you to close up shop. We can meet evenings, weekends."

The life of a businessman was unfamiliar to me, but this schedule went against everything I'd ever heard about how newlyweds spent their time. With the words of Dolores Kittredge echoing in my ear, I said tentatively, "Won't you be busy, evenings and weekends?"

"No," he said. He ground out his cigarette, then turned back to me. His eyes were alert, appraising. "What do you think? Do we have a deal?"

Three hundred dollars. It was unbelievable, like something you'd get from a fairy godmother in a story. Or not a godmother but a godfather, dark and surprising, able with some sleight of hand to produce a gift you'd never have imagined.

"It's a deal, Mr. Burke," I said.

He smiled and reached out his hand and I shook it.

"Good," he said. "Excellent. And if we're working together, forget the "Mr." Just call me Max."

"Max," I said tentatively, as if I hadn't already said his name a hundred times in my mind.

I was almost too late for the movie. "We'd practically given up on you," said Louise, pressing a ticket into my palm and steering me into the foyer of the theater.

"Sorry," I said. "I'll explain later." And for the next two hours, while everyone around me laughed at *Arsenic and Old Lace*, I sat lost in thoughts of my own.

We walked around Union Square afterwards to see the shop windows, and as we did I told the girls all about Max's visit.

"I can't believe it," said Trixie. "Three hundred dollars? For decorating his nightclub?"

"Yes." I put up my coat collar. "I was as shocked as you are."

Trixie's narrow face was serious. "That's a lot of money."

"Are you saying I'm not worth it?" I teased her.

"No, you are. You're the most stylish person I know, and I guess other people can see that too."

"Of course they can," said Louise. "Max Burke knows a good thing when he sees it. I think it's amazing, like something in a movie. And my God, he's handsome."

"You've seen him?"

"Only the photos, but that's enough. Cynthia Burke is a lucky woman."

Trixie still looked grave. It bothered me, somehow. I indicated the shop window in front of us, displaying a mannequin in a red wool dress and a tartan cape. A felt hat with a single large feather stuck straight up, like a radio antenna. "Look at this outfit," I said. "What would you wear it to?"

Louise laughed. "A highland fling? Or coming through the rye, maybe."

Trixie didn't answer, just looked at it thoughtfully. I squeezed her arm. "Look, let's go get a malted. My treat. Okay?"

She turned to me and smiled apologetically. "Sorry. I don't mean to be doubtful. I think it's great, Irene, and you deserve it. It's just surprising. Different. Not something we're used to, I guess."

I knew what she meant. This wasn't dancing with the soldiers at the USO. This was a totally different world, a world of business, of older men who were blunt and had money to spare. The blare of a foghorn echoed in my thoughts as we walked to the drugstore. My deal with Max was like leaving a known harbor and sailing out to sea, where anything could happen.

TEN

The next day I saw the violin player. He's often on the steps of the Presbyterian church on the corner of Jackson and Fillmore, a few blocks from my place. I first noticed him the week I met Johnny, and the two are somehow linked for me. Sometimes I hurry by when I see him; I don't want to remember.

He's old, probably about seventy, and he always wears the same brown tweed suit and mustard-colored vest and dark green tie. His hair lies in a white fringe around his head, longish and needing a trim. Trixie thinks he looks European, like a refugee from Vienna or Warsaw or somewhere.

He stands there and plays, with cars and streetcars and bicycles moving by, and you can actually see people stop on the sidewalk to listen like they do to Orpheus in the story. He doesn't seem to notice that he has an audience, never even looking up at the people pausing before him, and somehow I like that; it's as if he's so absorbed in the tunes he is drawing out of his violin that nothing else matters. Anna always liked classical music and often had it on the radio, so at times I've been able to recognize the pieces he plays.

This time it was *Song to the Moon*, and I stopped to listen. He didn't look at me, of course, just kept on playing, his face rapt and intent, the arm holding the bow revealing a frayed shirt cuff. The real world didn't exist for him; he was on a busy street but he was somewhere else entirely. And in spite of the shabby clothes and battered case at his feet, I could tell he was happy.

Some songs reach deep into your soul, moving to the hidden corners like water, running past all the barriers you've built inside. I just stood there listening, holding my bag of groceries, and I could not turn away until he was done. It hurt, the memories that were coming to the surface, but I could not stop them.

I met Johnny last April, at the USO. I was on coffee duty with Mrs. Cohen when I saw him across the floor, in a knot of other sailors over by the windows. He drew my eye right away, with his golden hair, his stature, the way his strong chin and full mouth made him look both manly and gentle. As I waited for the coffee to brew I kept glancing over. It wasn't just his looks that caught my attention, it was also his manner. He wasn't the brash, joking type who makes himself the center of attention, nor was he the restless type to scan the room, alert to the movements of every junior hostess. There was a stillness about him as he stood with his hands in his pockets, an ease that captivated me. *What was that French phrase they taught us in school?* I mused as I arranged the cups. *Bien dans sa peau*—he was at home in his own skin.

Then I glanced up from the cups, and my heart skipped a beat, for he was looking right at me. He smiled. I smiled back.

"Irene," said Mrs. Cohen behind me, "the coffee is ready."

"Yes, Mrs. Cohen," I said, picking up the new pot and forcing my attention to the line of servicemen gathering for coffee. I poured and greeted the fellows brightly and tried not to glance over at the blond sailor, but after a few minutes I couldn't help myself and had to look. He was gone.

Tamping down my disappointment, I poured for a red-haired

airman and a burly sailor. I laughed when one fellow said, "You ladies serve this joe so much more neatly than they do in the mess hall." And then I was out of coffee.

"I'm sorry," I said, looking into the pot. "I'll have to brew more."

"It's all right," said the next man in line. I raised my eyes, and it was the blond sailor. He smiled. "I'll wait."

He was even more handsome up close. His eyes were brown, and he had the kind of strong cheekbones that Louise would squeal over. But what was even more astonishing was the way he was looking at me. For I knew, with absolute, perfect certainty, that the man standing before me was every bit as attracted to me as I was to him.

That had never happened to me before. Usually you meet a fellow and even if you both like each other, you can never quite tell what he's thinking, or maybe you're conscious that one of you is a little more interested than the other. But I knew from this sailor's eyes, from his smile, that he and I were feeling exactly the same thing, at exactly the same intensity, and I could sense that for him, as for me, it was unlike anything he'd ever felt.

"When you're done with the coffee," he said, "would you like to dance?"

I glanced at Mrs. Cohen, who was watching us with the hint of a knowing smile.

"Go ahead, Irene," she said, taking the empty pot from my hands. "I'll take care of this."

It's funny . . . earlier that evening, I'd been sitting on the streetcar on the way to the USO, trying to figure out how many men I'd danced with in my short time there. My estimate was two hundred. It's a staggering number, but it happens when there are five men for every girl. After a while, it's kind of hard to remember individual guys.

But when Johnny put his arms around me, it was like he was the first. That sounds corny, but it's the truth. We just kept smiling at each other.

"I'm Johnny," he finally said. "Johnny Pendleton."

"Irene Cleary."

"Irene. That's a nice name." A couple bumped into us, and Johnny apologized, which I found charming.

"This is my first time in San Francisco," he said. "I'm in town this weekend, on shore leave."

"I'm glad you came to the USO. There are a lot of other things you can do in this city."

"I'm glad too. Really glad." The smile he gave me made the subtext clear. I grinned back at him, not even hiding how delighted his words made me. There was no need to be coy or hold my cards close, not with him.

"Is there any chance . . ." He paused. "I don't know if it's okay, Irene, but is there any chance you'd be free to take me around tomorrow? Show me the city?"

It was against the rules for junior hostesses to meet up with guys we'd met at the USO, but for the first time in my life I didn't care about breaking a rule.

"I'd love to," I said.

"That's swell," he said. He beamed at me. I moved closer as the music played. It was "Heart and Soul" sung by Bea Wain, which I'd always loved and suddenly loved even more.

"You know, Irene," Johnny said, "I really like your freckles."

I wasn't expecting that. "Thank you. I'll have to give them some respect now."

"You don't like them?"

"I never have. They make me feel like a leper, sort of. No one ever has them in the movies or magazines."

He was silent for a moment. With another guy it would have been an uncomfortable pause, but I knew he was absorbing what I'd said.

"I'm not a girl," he said at last, "so I can't say how I would feel, in your shoes. But if almost no one else has freckles like yours—well, maybe that's a reason to be proud of them."

That almost made me want to cry. I think he could tell, because he squeezed my hand.

The song was winding to a close, and the guys waiting around the dance floor began to surge in that restless way they do when a bunch of girls are about to be free for partners. "I guess it wouldn't be sporting to dance with you twice in a row," he said with regret.

"No. But when this is over, I'll look for you outside. By the front door."

"I'll be there. See you then, Irene." He smiled at me, and I watched him walk off into the crowd.

As I put on my coat an hour later, I was guiltily glad that Trixie wasn't there. She'd probably say sensible things ("You might lose your place here") that would make me doubt my decision. Louise, on the other hand, would surely approve. "You only live once," I could hear her saying blithely.

But when Johnny turned to me on the sidewalk, his face breaking into delight at the sight of me, I didn't think about Trixie or Louise or anyone else. "Where shall we go?" he asked. "You lead the way."

"Let's walk around Union Square."

I felt proud showing off my city to someone who didn't know it. On one side of the square the grand St. Francis Hotel loomed impressively in the moonlight. We walked along past the benches and dark flowerbeds, talking as easily as if we'd known each other all our lives.

He was twenty and from New York City. It was his first time out West. "What do you think of San Francisco?" I asked.

"I love it," he said with enthusiasm. "I've always wanted to come out here. I wanted to go to college at Stanford, but Dad wouldn't let me."

"Why not?"

"Tradition. All the men in my family go to Princeton." He paused and looked up at the column in the center of the park, the full-breasted woman holding a trident and a laurel wreath. "Who's the gal?"

"Honestly? I have no idea. Some tour guide I am."

"Don't feel bad. If you came to New York, I probably couldn't answer half your questions."

"I've always wanted to go to New York. What's it like?"

He thought about the question seriously, as if wanting to make sure he gave the right answer. "I guess it's hard to be objective about the place you're from. But it's a fine city, really. Always something going on. And when you want some peace you can escape to the park. We're right across the street."

"What's your family like?"

"We're a pretty close bunch. Dad's a lawyer, Mom is on a million different charities and boards: the opera, the Red Cross, you name it. I've got an older brother who's married and two sisters in high school. And then Hildegarde, the youngest, who's eight. We call her Hildy." He smiled. "I miss her most of all."

I loved imagining him as the beloved older brother. "It must be hard, being away from them."

"They write often," he said. "Even Hildy. My mom writes twice a week, without fail. When I read her letters I can just imagine her, sitting at her desk in the library. Like she always does when she writes letters."

"You live near the library?"

"No," he said. "I mean the library at home. In our house."

"Oh, of course," I said. But I felt my stomach swoop at the image of an elegant woman sitting in a book-lined room, in a home passed down through generations of Princeton men.

"Are you cold?"

"No, I'm fine." The way he was looking at me, I wished I'd said yes. I indicated a bench that a couple had just vacated. "Shall we?"

"So tell me about your family," he said as we sat down. We angled toward each other, his knee almost touching mine.

"I don't have a family," I said. "I'm an orphan."

His face changed: a look of interest and compassion. "I'm sorry."

"It's fine. I've never had one. I was given to the orphanage when I was just a week old. You can't miss what you never had, right?"

I meant it to be a rhetorical question. To my surprise, he pondered it seriously.

"I don't know," he said after a moment. "I think maybe you can. Can't you?"

He was right, and I knew it. I'd always known it, actually. His gaze held mine in the moonlight, and I realized I could say things that I had never told anyone else, things that I'd hardly admitted to myself. Even more astonishingly, I found that I *wanted* to say them, wanted to acknowledge them out loud.

"It is hard, sometimes," I said slowly. "My best friend has a family, and they've been wonderful to me. But when you're with them you see what it's like to have a home, to do things like Christmas and birthdays. Even little things, like having dinner together every night." I looked down at our knees, still only inches apart. "It was a good orphanage, and I was happy there. But it's not the same thing. You're one of many people, not one of a few who really matter to someone. Who matter deeply. And that's—well, it can feel very lonely sometimes."

In the silence that followed, I felt a sudden flash of doubt at my candor. I'd only just met Johnny, and I was spontaneously revealing the most vulnerable parts of myself. But he didn't seem ill at ease, nor was he looking uncomfortably about the square for some way to change the subject. He was regarding me with a steady gaze, encouraging me to say more.

"You mentioned earlier," I added, "that it was a family tradition to go to Princeton. I can see how that would be a burden at times. But I wish I'd had a chance to try having that burden."

"I can see that," he said quietly. A foghorn sounded off in the distance, as if signaling its agreement. "My parents are so much a part of my life that it would be hard not knowing them. Not knowing anything about them."

"I do know one thing about my parents," I said, smoothing my skirt over my knees. "I know that they loved each other very much. It's not much to know, but it . . . it helps."

I was going to say more, but I was stopped by the way he was looking at me: with a smile that was not just happiness, not just desire, but something like wonder at the fact of my very presence. It's hard to explain the effect that look had on me. It thrilled me to my toes, and it made me feel totally safe, both at the same time.

For a moment we just sat there, smiling at each other in the moonlight. Then he reached up. Gently and sweetly, he tucked a strand of hair behind my ear. Even as it was happening, I knew I would never forget what he said next.

"Well, however it happened, Irene Cleary," he said in a low voice, looking almost shyly into my eyes, "I'm glad you're here."

ELEVEN

The first thing Max wanted me to do was see the building where the nightclub would be. "Meet me at my office downtown," he said on the phone. "We'll go there together." I arrived at five fifteen on a Monday, walking into the tall building on Montgomery Street just as scores of businessmen and typists were streaming out.

His secretary surprised me. Shc was a severe middle-aged woman named, somewhat incongruously, Mrs. Bliss, with spectacles on a chain and sensible shoes. Somehow Max had seemed the kind of man to have a young secretary with a ruffled blouse and pretty legs. Mrs. Bliss showed me into his office, and I waited as Max got his suit and hat and handed me a check.

"Your commission. I said I'd pay up front."

I took a moment to admire the check. How odd that a tiny piece of speckled paper could represent so much richness. I thanked him and put it in my pocketbook, and when I looked up Max was surveying my outfit, a china blue jersey dress to which I'd added a braided white and blue belt, along with the same red hat I'd worn the first day I went to the Burkes' apartment. Under his scrutiny I used to feel flustered, but now I felt empowered, all the more so when he said, "I like it. Patriotic without going overboard."

On the way out we said goodbye to Mrs. Bliss, who was covering her typewriter for the night. "She seems efficient," I said as we waited for the elevator.

"Mrs. Bliss? She's a professional. Been in this city forever, knows everyone worth knowing."

"Your wife knows a lot of people, too, I'm sure."

"Not in the business world," he said shortly. It was clear that he didn't want to talk about Cynthia. She'd been by the shop earlier that day to pick up the dress, and her delight at the finished product had been evident not only in her praise but in the sizable tip she'd given me. I wondered if she knew I was working with her husband on his nightclub. I'd almost said something at the shop, but it was an awkward subject to bring up out of nowhere, so in the end I hadn't.

The nightclub was on Geary, just two blocks from Union Square, a place built probably shortly after the earthquake. It had a large foyer with two imposing columns leading onto a high-ceiled room with a marble-topped bar running along one side. There were two rooms to the left, a smaller one in which faded red booths spoke of years of whispered conversations over cocktails and a big one where a covered grand piano sat on a small platform.

"What do you think?" Max asked.

"I love it." There was something unique about the place, obvious even to someone like me, who had been almost nowhere. "You can really feel the past here, can't you," I said as we made our way back to the first room. "If that's what you want people to feel, I mean."

"I don't have a problem with the past, Irene." He leaned back against the marble bar, an attitude which made his chest seem even broader than usual. "Especially if it's not mine." He cocked his head to the right, indicating where he wanted me. "Come here. Take a look at the ceiling."

I joined him, leaning back on my elbows just as he did. Tipping my head, I studied the ceiling, which was tiled in squares of various colors. "That's beautiful."

"Should I keep it?"

"Absolutely. Those are all the colors of the city, aren't they? Blue like the bay. Orange like the bridge, and green, like the park. With a little white, for the fog. It's all right there."

He sprang up and began to pace around the room, arms crossed, smiling at the ceiling as if liking what I'd said. I watched him. It was exciting to be there, to be swept up in his vision, and I was about to ask him a question about his plans for the flooring when he suddenly glanced at his watch. "Six o'clock. Okay if I put you in a taxi? I've got another appointment."

"Of course." The dismissal was abrupt, almost rude; I thought of Dolores Kittredge saying he was rough around more than the edges. But if he was going to pay for a taxi, a rare luxury for me, I wasn't going to complain.

I felt so different sitting in the back seat of the cab, being carried through busy streets like the Queen of Sheba or something. The city seemed different too. As we paused at an intersection, my attention was caught by the flower cart on the corner. I'd seen it a million times, but this time the roses and dahlias and chrysanthemums and iris seemed to glow in their buckets like scattered bits of a rainbow. I was in San Francisco, just as I'd always been, but somehow it felt like an entirely new world.

At noon the next day I was pausing for a cup of tea when the shop bell jingled. "Hello," said a voice. "Anyone here?"

I ducked out from the back room. It was Pauline Benson, the ballet dancer who lived a few blocks away. "Sorry, I was just having some tea. How are you? I haven't seen you in a long time."

"Irene, hi. Yes, it's been ages. Since Anna died, poor woman." From a bag under her arm she produced a bundle of lavender-colored chiffon. "I've a repair job for you. Kind of a tricky one, I'm afraid."

It was an evening gown with a long skirt and horizontal tear along the back hem. "Given the placement of the rip, it'll be hard to do," I said, "but I'll try. It might be visible from close up, though."

"That's fine. I need something to wear for an event next week and I don't have time or money to get something new." She stood straight and tall; I always think my posture is good until I see hers. Her dark ponytail was like a question mark curling behind her head.

"Something fun?"

"A date with a man who gives money to the ballet, so it's only wise to accept. But he's forty at least. I'm inventing a sick mother at home, just in case things get tricky."

"Hopefully it won't be too bad an evening. I can have the dress done on Tuesday, if that works."

"That's perfect, thank you. Oh, and that tear? Someone stepped on it four whole months ago. I shouldn't have put it off so long. Anyhow, I'm so glad you're here and can take it." She looked about the shop fondly. "I wasn't sure what would happen to this place, once Anna died. She was a nice woman. Reminded me of some of my ballet teachers, with her accent. And she was a perfectionist, too, in her way."

I thought of how Anna loved helping with the costumes. The whole shop and apartment would have belonged to the ballet, in fact, if not for me. I folded the dress carefully. "What are you doing now? Which ballet, I mean?"

"We're rehearsing *The Nutcracker*." She said the name as if aware it would be unfamiliar to me.

"I've never heard of it."

"No one has. It's never been performed in the United States

before, not the whole ballet. It's about a little girl at Christmas, who goes to a magical land of sweets. Kind of a fairy tale."

"A show for children?"

"No, for everyone. There's not much story, but the music is pretty. We're all just figuring it out as we go. Mr. C.—that's Mr. Christensen, Willam Christensen, the director—he had to write to the Library of Congress to get the whole score. I guess it's sort of exciting, doing something new." She gave a wry smile. "But we're scraping the bottom of the barrel, honestly. Most of the male members of the company are in the war, and there's almost no budget, either. We're all pitching in and doing things. Making our own costumes, even. But who isn't, in wartime?"

I thought of the rows of white tutus Anna had made for *Swan Lake*, how she'd worked on them as carefully as if they were for her most demanding customer. "I could help you with costumes."

Pauline's eyes widened in surprise. "Could you really? Honestly? We can't pay you, I'm afraid."

"I know. But I'd like to help out."

"Oh my goodness, you have no idea how fantastic this is. Thank you so much."

"When exactly would you need me?" I thought of Max. "I've got another project at the moment, and it'll probably keep me busy for the next few weeks."

"Not for a while yet. I'll be in touch." She grinned as she picked up her bag. "You're a champ, Irene. I'll guarantee you a good seat for the first performance."

"That's exciting. I'll see ballet history being made."

Pauline rolled her eyes playfully. "I'm not sure this ballet will make it into the history books, but we'll see. At least it'll help people forget the war for an evening."

TWELVE

Mrs. Lockwood, black-haired and imposing, studied me from underneath her elegant hat. She'd come to my shop with her sixteen-year-old daughter Nancy, with a pink taffeta formal they wanted remade for a school dance. "I got your name from my neighbor," said Mrs. Lockwood, her eyes narrowing as she took in my freckles. "I didn't expect you to be so young."

"Oh, Mother, really," said Nancy. "You don't have to be old to know what you're doing."

I smiled my most poised smile. "I promise you I am an experienced seamstress, Mrs. Lockwood."

"Well," she said, looking about the shop, her gaze resting on the vase of iris, "I'm willing to give it a try." As the appointment went on she seemed to soften, particularly as I kept up some friendly chatter with her daughter, who attended Convent School, the girls' school on the top of the hill. I toyed with telling them I'd gone to Notre-Dame des Victoires—it would have been a point in common, Catholic schools—but it was likely to invite questions about the year I graduated and who my family was, so I kept it to myself.

Just as I was pinning Nancy's neckline (she wanted it lowered three inches, her mother didn't, and I offered to show them what it would look like with an inch and a half), the phone rang. It was Max.

"I hope you don't have plans tomorrow evening," he said. "I'd like to take you to dinner and talk about the club."

"That would be fine," I said in a brisk tone, aware of the Lockwoods listening in. "What time would suit you?"

"You have a customer there?"

"I do, yes."

"Thought so. Let's say five. I'll pick you up. Where would you like to go?"

"I can't say right now," I said cautiously. "I'll have to let you know later."

"All right." I could picture his mouth curved up in a grin, enjoying the situation. "Two options. If you want to go to a French restaurant, say 'I estimate it'll be five dollars.' If you want to go to a place on the coast, say, 'My best guess is six dollars.'"

"My best guess is six dollars," I said. "If that's agreeable to you."

"It's absolutely agreeable. In that case, I'll pick you up at four thirty so we can get there before dark."

"That's fine. I'll see you then. Goodbye."

"Goodbye, Irene," he said, amusement in his voice.

"I'm sorry about that," I said, setting the phone back in its cradle. "Thank you for your patience."

"It's a busy time, I know," said Mrs. Lockwood. "Lots of girls needing formals for the first high school dance."

When Max arrived the next day, I was ready and waiting in my jersey dress with the sweetheart neckline. It was deep red, almost a perfect match for my lipstick. Thankfully my last good pair of nylons was still intact after a disconcerting brush with a rough fence. Although some women were handling wartime shortages by wearing leg makeup, I'd found it wasn't so easy for freckled girls to do.

"Nice dress," said Max. He helped me on with my coat. "Looks like autumn."

He closed the car door for me. It was only the fourth or fifth time I'd ever sat in the front seat of a car, and it was by far the nicest vehicle I'd ever been in, with gleaming chrome and pristine white upholstery.

"Hope you don't mind being out a bit late," he said as he started the engine. "You said you wanted to go to the coast, so I'm taking you south of the city."

"Where to?"

"Moss Beach. A great local place with ocean views."

In the close space of the car, I was more aware than usual of his physical presence. He smelled of a mix of tobacco and some musky kind of soap. I shifted slightly in my seat.

"Where is Mrs. Burke tonight?" I asked as we drove west.

"In Atherton, at her parents' place. She goes down there often."

"You don't go with her?"

"It's easier to work from the city."

My question seemed to linger as we drove past the Panhandle, the long rectangle of tree-lined land at the end of the park, then into the park itself. I yawned and tried to stifle it with my hand, but he noticed.

"Late night?"

"No, it's just that I didn't sleep well. I haven't for ages."

"Why not?"

"I have a terrible bed. One of the springs is broken, and it sags. I really need to do something about it."

"There's nothing fun about a broken bedspring." The comment, and the conviction with which it was said, surprised me; Max Burke was the last person I would expect to have had experience with that sort of thing. We were at the end of the park, right where it meets the ocean, and he turned the car to the south.

"Do you get out of the city much?" he asked.

"Almost never."

"You should. Expand your horizons."

I resented the implication that I was a provincial. "It's hard to do when you don't have a car."

We drove along the coast highway, with its dunes and beach and thunderous ocean waves. A few hardy souls were walking on the sand, in spite of the brisk wind.

"The zoo is just ahead," I said after a moment. "I've been there. I used to go as a kid."

"What was your favorite animal?"

"The tiger. I couldn't believe how big he was. And how powerful." It had made such an impression, the muscle rippling under the orange coat as he stalked about the pen. "One time we got to see them feeding him. I kept thinking how I'd never want to be in a room with him."

"So you liked something that scared you."

I'd never thought of it that way. "I suppose so."

It wasn't long before we'd left the city behind. The coast road grew more and more dramatic, until it finally became a narrow thread that hugged the high cliffs with a sheer drop to the ocean on the other side. It would have sent Trixie with her fear of heights into a panic, but I eagerly craned to look over the edge. The rough gray water below made me think of stories of pirates and shipwrecks. "This is quite a road," I said as he expertly followed a curve. "It must be something to drive a car here."

"Know what they call this stretch of road?"

"I've no idea."

"Take a guess."

"I can't possibly guess."

"Sure you can. Let's see how creative you are. If you can't come up with anything good, I'm taking back the three hundred dollars."

Though I didn't know him well, I could tell he wasn't serious. And something about the evening—the smash and churn of the waves on the rocks, the feeling of breaking free of my normal routine—made me rise to the challenge. "The Cliff Road," I said.

"You can do better than that."

"Water's Edge."

"Even worse. One more guess."

I looked at the cliffs rising in a straight line to our left, then at the water to my right, and a song title came into my head. "Between the Devil and the Deep Blue Sea."

I expected him to laugh, but his tone was almost grave. "Not bad. Very close, in fact."

"What's it really called?"

"Devil's Slide."

A little shiver crept over me. Maybe it was the shift in his tone, but I didn't like the name. It made me realize how easy it would be to slip over the edge and fall like a stone into the water below, with no way of climbing back up to solid ground.

After a time, the road moved inward and away from the water, becoming straighter and more sedate. There was the occasional farmhouse sitting in the middle of fields and cypress trees and gently rolling hills. Finally we took a right turn, driving through a tiny neighborhood of homes. They looked around fifty years old at least, with gables and broad porches and small plots of land. Victory gardens were evident in many yards, and one large house bore a gold star in the window. A woman with gray hair sat on the porch knitting, and a black Labrador at her feet lifted his head as the car drove by. I wondered who had died—her son, probably. It was a peaceful picture, the woman and the dog, but it was a home that had known sorrow. I watched her move the needles, her head with its coronet braids bent over her work, one way to keep grief at bay.

Max turned into a large gravel lot, where rows of cars caught the last of the sunlight. As we parked, I saw we were actually on a bluff, the ocean stretching out before us. The restaurant was a white stucco building with a red tile roof and curving windows facing out to sea and a sign proclaiming FRANK'S PLACE.

Inside was laughter, the buzz of conversation, the noise of glasses and silverware, and the sound of a piano playing in an adjoining room. The yellow-haired hostess smiled. "Good evening, Mr. Burke. How nice to see you again." Her eyes slid to me then neutrally away, as if she were used to men she knew arriving with women she didn't.

"How are you, Vera. I called yesterday for a table. This is Miss Cleary, who's helping me with my new nightclub."

"Welcome, Miss Cleary. Yes, we have your reservation, Mr. Burke. Please come this way." She led us past a large well-stocked bar and into a room beyond, one with large windows looking out on the bluff and the ocean. Max directed me to the seat with the better view.

At my request, he ordered for me. I couldn't focus on the menu, for I was too fascinated by the sea before me, the piano music in the other room, and the people dining around us, couples mostly, with one table of two well-dressed men craning to track the movements of a busty girl sitting coyly at the end of the bar.

When I looked back at Max, he was watching me and smiling. It felt like the smile of a man giving a young girl a treat, benevolent and amused, and I was suddenly aware of the gap in experience between the two of us. I've never liked feeling at a disadvantage, even though I've felt it for most of my life, but somehow with Max it was particularly insufferable.

"Do you and your wife come here often?" I asked bluntly.

The smile vanished and he reached for his water glass. "This isn't really her place."

"I see." Some desire to regain my dignity made me almost cruel. "You don't seem to have the same places, do you."

It was clumsily said, but my meaning was clear. Max had just opened his mouth to respond when the waiter came by with our drinks—he'd ordered me a glass of champagne and himself a sidecar—and he was silent until we were alone again. "Look," he said. "I know the whole city is fascinated by my marriage, but I didn't bring you here to talk about that. I'm not paying you three hundred dollars for that. All right?"

His voice was low and charged and for once he did not appear to be smiling. We looked at each other across the small table.

Then I smiled briskly and said, "Of course. This is business." I opened my pocketbook and took out a notepad and pencil. "Let's talk about your ideas. I'll take notes."

"For God's sake, put that away."

"Why?"

"Because you look like a secretary. This is a meal, not a board meeting." At my raised eyebrow he smiled wryly, as if conceding a point. "I'm sending you a mixed message. You're here for business but not for business. Well, it's my kind of business. I want to eat, drink, talk, enjoy the view. But you aren't Mrs. Bliss, and I don't want you to be. Understand?"

I didn't, not really, but I've always known how to nod along. So I slipped the notebook into my purse and took a sip of champagne. The bubbles rose to my nose; it was an exciting, novel feeling.

It was fun talking about the nightclub. Max had ideas that were big, broad; he needed someone to pin them down, to point out their virtues and flaws. It was like when a woman comes into my shop with a dress in mind, and I listen and acknowledge her vision before steering her toward what will fit her shape and budget.

Max wanted the nightclub to represent different parts of the city. The room with the piano could have hanging lanterns and other echoes of Chinatown, the other small room could represent Golden Gate Park, and the main room with the bar could be the bay. "How would I do that?" he asked. "I was thinking a section of the Golden Gate Bridge, cutting across a corner of the room. It could form a booth, maybe."

I grimaced.

"You don't like it," he said instantly.

"No. That would be too much."

"Too brash, you mean."

"Yes. You want to be subtle. This whole idea is original, but it could easily be overdone." I took a bite of my scallops, which were delicious; I was glad he'd ordered them. "If you want something that is going to last beyond the war, beyond the servicemen who will go anywhere, you need to tone it down."

"You're saying," he said, putting down his fork, "that there's a fine line between bad and good taste, and right now I'm on the wrong side of the line."

"Exactly."

He grinned. When he smiled like that, he looked almost boyish.

"It's hardly the first time." He drank the last of the cocktail. The waiter, passing by, asked if he wanted another, and Max surprised me by refusing. He glanced at me. "More champagne?"

I hesitated; it gave me a warm and rather melting feeling in my core, along with a confidence that was both exciting and disconcerting. "If you aren't having another, I won't either."

"I never have more than one." He waved the waiter away and then took out his cigarettes. I shook my head when he held out the box. I'm not much for smoking, though sometimes I will if I'm in an uncomfortable situation, like on an awkward date. I've found it can be a helpful distraction.

As he lit a cigarette for himself, I gazed about the room. An older couple, the woman looking like she had once been ravishingly beautiful, held hands across the table near us. A man sitting at a corner table seemed vaguely familiar, with his straight, slicked back hair and generous nose and expansive way of drawing his arm about the booth behind him. He caught me watching him and smiled with a nod, as if my interest were not unexpected. Normally I'd look away in embarrassment, but this time I smiled in response, which made him glance at Max and then back at me with new interest. The smile was still on my lips as I turned to Max.

He was studying me through the screen of smoke. "You like this place, I guess."

"I do. It's different."

I watched his hand holding the cigarette as he brought it to his lips. There was that dark hair again, in a sort of V at the base of his wrist. I found myself wondering if it was on his chest, too. That champagne; it was good I'd stopped at one glass.

"Are there places like this in Chicago?" I asked.

"Plenty. This used to be a speakeasy, you know."

"Did it really?" I glanced at my fellow diners and tried to imagine them dancing the Charleston and drinking contraband liquor.

"Apparently they used to smuggle alcohol onto the beach below. It's a good place for it."

"Just like Cornwall."

"Where?"

"Cornwall, in England. I read a book about it once. There are lots of coves that are good for smuggling. Lots of pirates too," I added. "You'd fit right in." I was suddenly aware I'd said something that would have been better kept to myself. "It's your hair and eyes mostly," I said, trying to cover my embarrassment. "Are you part Italian?"

"No."

"Spanish?"

He shook his head.

Curiosity kept me on the subject. "What are you?"

"Does it matter?"

"Yes. I think so."

"Why?"

"Well"—I wasn't sure how to explain—"it's part of who you are, isn't it?"

"So what are you?"

"Me? I don't know. I'm an orphan."

"Cleary isn't your real name?"

"No, the sisters gave it to me. I was dropped off at the orphanage when I was a week old." His expression changed, as if that revelation had confirmed something he'd suspected about me. He looked like he was about to ask me another question, but I spoke before he could. "So you won't tell me what you are. I guess you like being mysterious."

"I will tell you," he said, leaning forward across the table, "since you seem so set on knowing. My father was from Poland and so was my mother."

I'd never have guessed that. "Burke isn't a Polish name."

"My name was Maximilian Bukowski. I changed it when I was eighteen."

"Why?"

"Because it's nearly impossible to pronounce."

"Bukowski," I said experimentally. "I don't think it's hard to pronounce." Then a thought occurred to me. "Did you change it because it's Polish?" He looked down at his cigarette. "What's wrong with that?"

"In Chicago? Nothing. Outside of Chicago, Buffalo, or Detroit? Plenty. I wanted a name that went everywhere."

I pondered that. "Can you speak Polish?" I asked.

"I can, but I don't."

"What do your parents think? Of you changing your name?"

"They don't think. My mother was a drunk who was hit by a car when she stumbled into traffic one day. My father died a few months later of guilt."

I was shaken by the story and how casually he said it. I hid the feeling by being pedantic. "You can't die of guilt."

"But you can die by hanging yourself from a rafter in the garage." The horror was visible on my face before I could master it. He acknowledged it with a brief smile. "It's a shock to you, Irene, but it's old news to me. I don't cry about it, and I haven't since I was seventeen. I took the small amount of money I got from my father and invested it, opened a restaurant, then opened others. I started over. That's what matters." He reached for the ashtray, tapped some ash into it, then lifted the cigarette again to his lips. "So it's your turn now, Irene. What are you?" He studied me. "I'd guess Irish."

"You and everyone else. It's the freckles."

"But your eyes," he said thoughtfully. "I don't see Irish there. I see Polish, or Russian. It's the shape of them."

"How funny. You're the second person to say that."

"Who was the first?"

"Anna. The woman who trained me to sew. She was Russian."

Off in the larger room there was applause, and a moment later a female voice began to sing along to the piano. It was a song I didn't know, one that sounded like nicotine and loss. I studied Max. He was holding his cigarette but not smoking it, lost in thought. I was used to him being alert, quick, and responsive, not pensively gazing at some point in the center of the room as if seeing scenes no one else could.

"Max," I ventured tentatively, "what was it like living with your parents?" He looked at me in surprise. "It's just that I grew up in an orphanage. I never knew my mother and father."

"Sometimes that's a blessing."

"If you can't talk about it, it's all right."

"I can talk about it," he said. "I choose not to, usually. There's not much to tell after I was fourteen. That's when I left, was barely home."

"Where did you go?"

"Friends' houses, the street, the bus station. Home wasn't the kind of place you'd want to be, Irene. My mother would be falling down drunk by three in the afternoon, and when my father got home he would be so angry he'd beat her. When I was nine years old I tried to stop him and got a broken nose for doing so." He said it almost casually, while I absorbed the horror of it. "And then he'd hate himself for losing his temper. You can see why I left."

I studied him through the veil of smoke. "Do you think they ever loved each other?"

"That's an odd question. Does it matter?"

"I think so. To know that at the bottom of it all there was—there was something good."

He shrugged. "They must have loved each other once, or I wouldn't be here." He took another drag of the cigarette. "Though the act and the feeling can be two separate things, can't they."

I could feel myself blushing and was glad he wasn't looking at me. The woman's voice sang on, low and slow, some song about heartbreak and he done me wrong. "I'm sorry," I said.

"For what?"

"Asking you about the past. I can tell you don't like to remember it. It's none of my business."

He held the cigarette but didn't smoke it. A moment passed as he regarded me intently, thoughtfully.

"If you were someone else," he said at last, "I wouldn't have told you. I told you because I wanted to."

My skin began to prickle all over with something like a warning. *Don't say it*, my mind cautioned me. *Stop there, don't go any further.*

But instead I said, so low it was hardly audible, "Why did you want to?"

The singer's voice reached a crescendo and hung in the air for a moment, then applause filled the air. It seemed to roll around the restaurant, starting in the room with the piano, then the room where we sat, like a wave, and when it was at its peak Max leaned forward as if he didn't want anyone else to hear the answer.

"Because, Irene," he said, "you know how it feels to be on the outside."

THIRTEEN

I went to the USO the next evening. It wasn't my regular day, but I needed the distraction. After the evening with Max, I'd moved through my work in a sort of a strange haze, which I couldn't attribute to the champagne but rather to the surprising turns of our conversation.

It made sense: his past, the story of his parents, how he had remade himself into a successful man with a new name. What you saw in the paper, a handsome businessman in expensive suits, was only part of the story. What a change it must have been for him to marry into the McNeil family, the closest thing San Francisco has to aristocracy. Could that be the reason for his wife's barely hidden disgust with him? Could she really be such a—I hesitated to use the word, admiring her as I did—such a snob? And why had she married him in the first place, knowing his humble past? Unless she hadn't known his past before she married him.

"You know how it feels to be on the outside," he had said to me. I realized I was pinning the wrong pieces on the blouse I was making and had to start over. That's when I decided to go to the USO, to jolt myself out of my fog.

It was good to dance and socialize, and I played ping-pong, which was fun. Normally I would play to the best of my ability—and I'm actually pretty good—but you can always tell when a guy can't stand losing.

There was one rather intense airman who I could sense wouldn't take kindly to being beaten, so I intentionally missed a shot and gave him the game, and it was only then that he could relax and smile. Maybe I shouldn't have let him win, but I figured if he was fighting the Nazis then I could swallow my pride and give him a little victory.

I thought of Max. Was he the kind of man who needed to win at all costs? At times I thought yes, and other times I was sure the answer was no.

The next morning I was still in my red terry bathrobe, my hair tied up in a bandana, when I became aware of an altercation outside. Taking my tea to the window, I looked down. A furniture truck was blocking the sidewalk, and an elderly woman with a pug on a leash was giving the driver a piece of her mind. Two minutes later the shop door buzzed. It was Saturday and I wasn't open until ten, so I let it go, figuring it must be a mistake. It buzzed again and again, so I finally sighed, put on my slippers, and went downstairs.

I opened the door the barest crack and found two workmen standing outside. "Irene Cleary?" said the older one, reading off of a paper. "We have your bed."

"I didn't order a bed."

"There's one for this address."

"There must be some mistake." He turned the paper toward me, and sure enough there it was, my name. "But I didn't order a bed."

"Well, someone did." He looked at me with new interest. "Maybe it's a gift."

I backed away and in so doing I stepped on something. It was a white envelope, one that had clearly been fed through the mail slot in the front door. *Irene* was written in the same scrawling, bold hand that I recognized from Max's check.

Inside was a note, on monogrammed stationery:

I spent too many years sleeping on busted springs and I know how it feels. I hope this helps.

—M Burke

Color flooded my face. The two deliverymen were still waiting, watching me; the older one looked amused. I pulled the collar of my robe more tightly together and stood tall, like I was someone. "Bring it in," I said haughtily.

After they were gone, I stood in the doorway of the bedroom, still in my robe, staring at it. It was a double bed, with a rich dark wooden headboard and footboard, and he'd even sent along sheets and a cover—pale blue chenille, absolutely beautiful—to match. With my cup of lukewarm tea in hand, I leaned against the doorframe, taking it all in.

The bed was bigger than any I'd ever slept in, far bigger than the one the workmen had just carted away. It was as if my bed had grown in size, throwing off the proportions of everything else, dwarfing the room I knew so well; the effect was almost disorienting. I looked at it for a long while.

Then I got dressed, did my hair, and called Max at his office. I thought it was unlikely he'd be there on a Saturday, but he answered.

"Like it?" he asked.

"Yes. It was quite a surprise."

"I figured it would be. But you deserve a nice surprise, Irene. Besides, if you can't sleep well you won't work well, and I'm determined to get my three hundred dollars' worth. Speaking of which," he said, "let's go to Chinatown."

"Now?"

"Sure. We'll get ideas for the club. Or is the shop open today?"

It was supposed to be open until two. "No, not today," I said.

It was obvious that Max knew Chinatown far better than I did. Admittedly, that isn't saying much. Although it's only a few blocks from my high school, I'd never done much more than pause on Bush Street and gaze down Grant Avenue at the colorful temples and lampposts. You could find echoes of Chinatown elsewhere in the city, too; I'd often walked past Forbidden City on Sutter Street, the famous nightclub displaying posters of its all-Chinese entertainers, including young women in skimpy burlesque clothes. There were always servicemen standing in front of the posters, looking wide-eyed and thoughtful. But the heart of Chinatown itself was new to me, and I walked slowly, fascinated by a shop selling jade curios and a grocery store with a line of ducks in the window, strung up by their necks in a brown garland.

"You've never been here?" Max asked in his brusque way. "For a native you haven't seen much of the city, have you."

"You forget I spent most of my life in an orphanage," I said. "Which happens to be way down at the south end of town."

"What was it called? The orphanage?"

"Mount St. Joseph." I was going to say more, but he took my arm to pull me out of the way of a tiny old woman walking past us on the sidewalk.

"Here's where we're going," he said, indicating a doorway in a small alley.

It was a textile shop, run by an old man who seemed to have met Max before for he greeted him with an air of familiarity. Along the walls were bolts of fabric that took my breath away with their color and texture. How a place like this existed in wartime I couldn't begin to fathom.

"You had no idea this shop was here, did you," said Max. "For a decorator, that's criminal."

"Seamstress," I said absently, stroking a bolt of blue-green cloth that made me think of a pond in an emperor's garden. I looked around in delight, my mind spinning with ideas for dresses and suits.

We were there to think of the nightclub, though, and it didn't take me long to zero in on a bright red-orange silk. "This is perfect," I said. "It's the color of the Golden Gate. People will think of the bridge without even realizing that they are."

Max turned to the proprietor. "How much for all of the bolts?"

"But you don't know how much you need," I said. "Or what exactly we'll use it for."

"But we'll use it somewhere."

The man named a sum. I expected Max to pull out his wallet but, to my surprise, he made a counteroffer. They haggled back and forth amiably, which was something I had never witnessed before and something I am not sure I could have done. Max seemed to be enjoying himself, as did the man behind the counter.

Once we were outside, I remarked bluntly that it was puzzling to see a rich man resort to bargaining. You could say things like that to Max.

"How do you think I got rich?" he asked. "By knowing when to bargain. And he would have been disappointed if I hadn't. It was obvious."

It hadn't been obvious to me. He grinned at the bemused expression on my face, then indicated a nearby restaurant. "Hungry?"

It was a small place with Formica tables and a cracked tile floor, and we got the only available table. To my left I could hear a couple speaking Chinese as they ate with chopsticks. On Max's side was a table of sailors, young ones with loud voices, ordering five plates of chop suey. The waiter, scribbling on a pad, smiled resignedly.

"Chop suey's not Chinese," Max said to me. "But let them think it is. They can write home to Iowa or Vermont and say how they ate real Chinese food made by real Chinese people." He lit a cigarette. "'Join the Navy and see the world.'"

There was something in his tone that I hadn't heard there before. The waiter came by—"How are you, Alvin?" said Max, standing up to shake his hand—and I let Max order for us both.

Once the waiter was gone, I leaned across the table. "Max," I said in a low voice, "why aren't you in the war?"

It was a bold question. I half expected him to tell me to mind my own business, but he answered. "I tried to enlist. Turns out I have this thing with my heart. Every now and then it skips a little beat." He smiled without mirth. "Sounds like a Benny Goodman song. But the army didn't want me."

"Were you disappointed?"

"Yes." I waited for him to elaborate, but he didn't say anything else, just smoked his cigarette.

The tea, which was served in cups without handles, was green. To my surprise and to Max's obvious enjoyment, I loved it.

"You thought the only good tea was black tea," he said.

"Guilty as charged." I let the mellow, grassy flavor slide across my tongue. "I guess I'm learning a lot."

The last few words were drowned out by a sailor, whistling loudly as a young woman walked by on the street outside. "You don't see that in Little Rock!" said one of his companions, and the table dissolved into raucous laughter. I was beginning to wonder if there was something more than tea in their cups. It made me uncomfortable; I've never been at ease around rowdy groups of men. The waiter set down something doughy and starkly white, looking unlike anything I'd ever tasted.

"Pork buns," said Max. "Try one."

They were fragrant and rich with savory dark meat. After the first tentative bite I finished it quickly.

"I guess our shopping gave you an appetite," said Max as he lit his second cigarette.

"No wonder you like this place. Do you come here often?"

"Fu Manchu!" said one of the sailors at the next table, signaling for the waiter. "More tea, plee." Two of his friends sniggered as if it were a great joke. I could feel my blood pound in my veins. Max's eyelid flickered as if he were annoyed.

"I do," he said. "If locals eat here"—he tilted his head away from the sailors, toward the other tables—"you know it's good. I often come for lunch."

Just then a sailor stood up and put both fingers in his mouth and whistled in the direction of the sidewalk. It was a piercing whistle in such a small space and it made me flinch, as did the words he directed at the woman walking by outside. "Hey, China doll!" he yelled. "You can chop my suey anytime."

Out of the hush from the other diners, I was aware of the sound of a scraping chair. Max, putting down his cigarette, had risen to face the young man.

"All right, sailor," he said. "That's enough."

The sailor, surprised, stared at him. "Who the hell are you?"

"A man who's tired of seeing the customers wince every time you whistle. Come on, bud." Hands in pockets, he eyed him calmly. "Be a credit to the uniform."

The sailor wavered a bit, mouth open, taking in Max's fine suit and tie. I could tell he didn't know whether to back down or grow belligerent. He was young, with a huge pimple on the side of his chin, as if he were a high school boy playing at war.

"If you want to whistle at the girls, don't do it in a restaurant," Max said. "Go to the Forbidden City. That's what it's there for."

"I told you," said one of the sailors. "We should've gone there instead of that movie."

"You're the one who blew all that money on drinks," said the first sailor.

"Here." Max pulled out his wallet. "Go take in a show on me. Tell Charlie Low that Max sent you." Before the sailor could do anything, Max had pressed a twenty-dollar bill into his hand. "A contribution to the war effort." He sat down without waiting for thanks as the sailor, with a whoop of delight, displayed the bill to his friends.

Max looked at me calmly. "What were we talking about?"

I could barely hear him through the noise of the soldiers at the next table, pushing back their chairs, heading out with their new bounty. I was distracted, too, by the confrontation, by how calmly he had inserted himself into the fray. "Those sailors were drunk. They might have hit you or something."

"I know how to deal with drunks, Irene." He lifted the teapot. "More?" I nodded, and he poured the last of the tea into my cup.

"Have you been to the Forbidden City?" I asked him.

"A few times. And you?"

"No, of course not."

"Why 'of course'?"

I sipped my tea and thought of the posters, the dancers posing with their backsides tilted saucily in the air. "It's not a place most men would take a girl to, is it?"

"Depends on the man. And the girl. We could go tonight, if you're curious."

"No, thank you." I felt so prim saying it, like Sister Irene Mary, which Louise teasingly called me at times. "I wouldn't want to see our rowdy friends again," I added, an attempt to sound more worldly.

"Don't worry," he said. "If they're at the Forbidden City they wouldn't be looking at you anyhow. And that's no insult to you." He looked at my empty cup, then glanced at the bill and put down a five. "Shall we?"

I gathered my pocketbook and stood up. "You know," I said, voicing something that was gnawing at me, "giving them all that money—it's like rewarding them for bad behavior, isn't it? Now they'll just buy more drinks and get even more rowdy."

"So it would have been better to do nothing? Let them keep on bothering everyone?"

"Yes. I mean no. I don't know." He was standing near me, holding my coat, close enough for me to see a tiny scar at the side of his left eye. Somehow I had never noticed it before.

"Here's the thing, Irene," he said. "If I can pay to make things a little easier, for myself or other people, I do. This isn't the first time I've done it, and it won't be the last."

An image of the new bed darted into my mind. "So you pay to make beds appear and drunken sailors disappear," I said, making him grin as he helped me on with my coat. *Max the magician*, I thought.

On the way out of the restaurant, the waiter nodded. "See you next time, Mr. Burke," he said. "And Mrs. Burke," he said to me.

I was startled and glanced at Max, but he hadn't heard. I didn't know how to correct the mistake, so I just smiled and murmured goodbye.

FOURTEEN

Pauline's apartment, on Clay Street, was a whirlwind of disorder. "Watch your step," she said cheerfully as she led me down the narrow hallway past a bedroom and bathroom into the tiny living room. Clothing was hung to dry everywhere—brassieres, peach-pink dancing tights, black dance leotards, blouses—and a pile of pillows and blankets indicated that the divan did double duty as a bed. "My cousin Edith has been living with me," Pauline said, leading the way into the square kitchen at the back. "Her husband's overseas so she came out from Utah to work at the shipyards. And of course there's nowhere to rent in this town." She pulled out a chair at the table, which was covered with a flowered oilcloth. "You're so nice to drop off my dress."

"It's no bother. I needed a walk anyhow." I felt guilty, picturing my apartment above the store. It wasn't big by any means but compared to this tiny flat it was a palace. "I feel like I should be doing more to help. Renting out room in the store or something."

"You are doing something to help. The costumes for *The Nutcracker.* The company was thrilled to hear it, by the way." A kettle on the stove whistled, and she turned off the gas. "They were so fond of Anna."

Another thing I'd never known. "I guess I didn't know how much she did for you," I said as she poured the water into a teapot.

"Evenings and weekends, mostly. When her own work was done. Do you take sugar?"

"No."

"That's a relief. We don't have any more." She found a box of graham crackers, snapped one in two, and set it on a blue plate. "All I can offer to eat, unfortunately. I never seem to get a chance to shop." I showed her the dress I'd mended for her, and she was delighted. "Gosh, you're good. I'd have really hashed this up if I tried to do it myself."

There was the sound of a door closing, and a voice. "Hellllooo. You home?"

"We're here, Edith." There were footsteps in the hallway, then a petite young woman appeared in the doorway. She wore denim coveralls and had her hair tied up in a bandana. On the table she set down a metal lunchbox, like the kind a construction worker would have.

"Are you making tea? Tell me there's enough for me."

"Plenty. Edith, this is Irene Cleary. She's the seamstress who fixed my dress."

"Nice to meet you, Irene. Welcome to our messy home." Edith sank into a chair, unlacing her work boots. "Hope you don't mind me taking these off. My feet kill me by the end of the day."

It was fascinating, the contrast between her pixie-like appearance and the rugged outfit. "Where do you work?" I asked.

"At Kaiser shipyards, across the bay. I'm a welder."

"She makes iron melt," said Pauline. "My little cousin who used to love dolls now wields a blowtorch."

"It's the war," said Edith simply. "We're all doing things we never thought we'd do."

"Tell Irene about the brassiere," said Pauline as she poured the tea into three mismatched mugs.

"The what?"

Edith grinned. "They wanted the welders to wear these hard plastic brassieres. To protect ourselves. Some of us tried them on." She raised her eyebrows. "I'll leave it to your imagination."

I laughed. "You must have looked like department store mannequins."

"We sure felt like them. One of the girls wanted to keep it, just to wear as a joke next time she sees her husband again. I'd never do that to Bert. It would be too cruel after months apart." She grinned. "Like a weird chastity belt or something."

"Which reminds me," said Pauline with emphasis, "when he's here on leave I'm finding somewhere else to stay. Even if I have to sleep on the floor of Irene's shop. I'd rather not be around you two lovebirds."

"That suits me fine," said Edith. She sipped her tea with a reminiscent smile.

"How long have you been married?"

"Two years. We got married a month before he shipped out, so I came here. It's better than knocking around at home, doing nothing. And I always tell myself that the boat I'm building could be the one he ends up on." She stood up, stretching, and picked up her cup. "I'll leave you to discuss whatever you were discussing and drink this in a hot bath. Nice meeting you, Irene."

Pauline nodded at my cup as Edith disappeared down the hall. "How's the tea?"

"Great. Thanks."

"The one thing I can cook without burning it." She pushed the graham cracker plate toward me, and I took one. "You wanted to know more about the ballet. What can I tell you?"

"Everything, really. What's it about?"

"Well, let's see. It takes place on Christmas Eve. A girl named Clara gets a nutcracker for a gift, the wooden kind of nutcracker. Her godfather Drosselmeyer gives it to her."

"That's a strange gift for a girl."

"He's a strange guy. Kind of a magician. In the middle of the night he makes the Christmas tree grow bigger, and all the furniture gets big, and the Nutcracker comes to life and fights the Mouse King and kills him. Then he becomes a handsome prince."

"Let me guess—they live happily ever after," I said, unable to keep myself from rolling my eyes.

"Sort of, but not yet. They go to a snowy forest, then to the palace of the Sugarplum Fairy. There are all these dances from different places—Chinese tea, Spanish chocolate, Arabian coffee. And then Clara goes back home, and it turns out it was all a dream."

I crumbled the last bits of the graham cracker. "So it's not really a happy ending, then."

"I don't know. A dream can still make you happy, right?" Pauline twirled her ponytail around one finger. "The story's pretty silly, honestly, but the music is gorgeous. And I think Mr. C. is just figuring people want a little magic, a little fantasy. After so many years of war, you know?"

I could have explained how thoroughly I did know, but I didn't. I just nodded and took another sip of tea.

FIFTEEN

I'd become so focused on the male half of the Burke couple that it was a surprise when Cynthia phoned the shop the next day. "I have a favor to ask. I hope you'll say yes."

It was actually a favor for her younger sister Antonia, who was getting married at the McNeil estate on Saturday. "She's going to wear my mother's wedding dress. Would you be able to alter it for her? You'd have to come down to Atherton, I'm afraid, but we'll put you up for the night. Her fiancé is shipping out, so we had to move up the wedding."

They would pay fifty dollars, which at one time would have felt like a massive sum, but after Max's three hundred it wasn't the money that was the draw. It was the opportunity to see the McNeils' home, to walk into yet another new world, that appealed to me. "I'd be happy to help, Mrs. Burke."

The next day it was hard to stay calm. I boarded the morning train and sat primly in my gray suit and red hat, a small suitcase borrowed from Louise on the rack above me (my only suitcase was far too shabby to take), trying not to grin like a crazy person at the unexpected direction my week had taken.

I hadn't spoken to Max since getting Cynthia's call. The day we were in Chinatown he'd told me that he had some business in Southern California for a few days and wouldn't need me until at least the following week. Surely he'd be back in town for the wedding of his sister-in-law? I wasn't sure whether I wanted to see him at the McNeils' house or not.

The air seemed to grow softer as we got south of the city, the fog relaxing its hold and ceding to the mellow sunlight of autumn. I'd never taken the train so far down the Peninsula before. We stopped at various cities—Burlingame, San Mateo, Belmont—and I glimpsed downtown shopping districts, suburban homes, and a notable increase in the number of trees.

At Menlo Park's small Victorian-style station I paused awkwardly outside the main entrance, clutching my suitcase. Almost immediately a gray-haired man in a chauffeur's uniform appeared before me. "Miss Cleary? I'm Wilson, the McNeils' driver." I was surprised he could identify me so readily. Either I looked lost or Cynthia had told him to look for the girl with the freckles.

The car was long and black and gleaming, like a car in a movie. I sat in the back and looked about in wonder as we drove through quiet tree-lined streets. This was not San Francisco, where the houses stood shoulder to shoulder like people in a crowd. These houses were on huge lots, often set so far back that you could catch only a glimpse of them from the road. On some of the estates there were paddocks or swimming pools. Once we drove past a tennis court standing empty in the morning sunlight.

The McNeils' house was like a storybook cottage increased to mansion size, a huge three-story Tudor-style home with neat timbers on the facade and ivy cloaking the walls and mullion-style windows glinting in the sun. There were immaculate gardens all around it, and an American flag flew from its own pole on the edge of the front lawn.

The chauffeur opened the door for me, and I got out, then stood on the gravel drive, irresolutely clutching my purse. Should I ring the front doorbell? I watched as he took my suitcase out of the car, about to ask him what to do, when the door opened and a voice said, "Oh, you must be Miss Cleary! Thank you for coming."

I'd seen Mrs. McNeil in the newspapers, but it was still striking how much she looked like her daughter. Take away the fine wrinkles and subtract fifteen pounds, and she could have been Cynthia's twin. Even her outfit—a rose cashmere cardigan and a gray tweed skirt—was like one her daughter would wear. She shook my hand warmly then ushered me through an entrance hall and an impressive library, down a smaller hall, then into a huge glassed-in sun room—my goodness, I was in an actual conservatory—where a group of people, Cynthia among them, were sitting on wicker furniture and finishing breakfast.

Cynthia, greeting me with a big smile, made the introductions. There was her father, also recognizable from the photos, a handsome gray-haired man who stood up smartly and shook my hand in a strong grip; her younger sister Antonia, the bride, who wore denim slacks and a striped shirt and loafers; and her blond brother Harold and his pretty wife Judy, who was holding a baby and did not get up. There was also Great-Aunt Mabel, tiny and shrunken and asleep in a wheelchair, and her caregiver in a white nurse's uniform, who was introduced as Miss Hargreaves and who looked up from her knitting and nodded with a smile.

They offered me coffee, which I was too flustered to accept. "Silly me," said Mrs. McNeil. "You probably want to see the dress you're dealing with, don't you? Let's go on upstairs. Antonia? Come along."

"I don't know why you have to make this huge fuss, Mother," said Antonia, putting down her cup. "I was perfectly ready to get married in my blue suit." It was clear this was a conversation they'd had before.

"Girls should be married in white," said her father, unfolding the newspaper. "That's tradition."

"Cynthia wasn't," said Antonia. "Most girls aren't, in wartime."

"We can't let the war take everything from us," said her mother firmly. "Come. We don't have time to waste."

"Honestly," said Antonia, gesturing to the spacious back garden where gardeners were busily planting flowers in the borders. "All this fuss just for an hour and a few photographs in the paper."

"Give it a rest, Antonia," said her brother, reaching for the pitcher of orange juice. "You only get married once."

"Some people get married twice," said Antonia defiantly.

"Not in this family," said her father in a tone that finished the conversation.

The room where I would sleep and sew was like one in a magazine. The white furniture was obviously a matching set, and both the drapes and the bedspread had the same charming print of purple violets and tiny green leaves. A sewing machine had been placed under the window, which looked out on the front of the house. My suitcase, I noted, was already on a luggage stand at the foot of the bed.

The dress was ivory satin, with a high collar, long sleeves, lace insertions, and a sweeping skirt with a small train. I remarked on the beauty of the lace, and Mrs. McNeil smiled a little sadly. "I always thought Cynthia would wear this," she said. "We weren't expecting her to get married in Chicago."

"I'm sorry to disappoint you, Mother," said Cynthia, so lightly that it struck a false note. She was standing by the window looking out as if waiting for someone to come up the drive.

"I'm sorry too," said Antonia, kicking off her loafers. "I'm going to feel like a show pony in this."

But in fact she looked charming, and to my relief the fit wasn't too far off. I tucked and pinned, and as we stood in front of the mirror Antonia's mood seemed to soften. "Perhaps this won't be so bad," she said. "I just wish the neck weren't so high. I look like a giraffe."

I hesitated before offering to lower it—I didn't want to start an argument between mother and daughter—so it was a relief when Mrs. McNeil herself asked, "Would you be able to cut down the neckline, Miss Cleary?"

Another ten minutes, and we'd arranged it to our satisfaction. It was a good thing I was staying over; I couldn't imagine trying to finish the job in one day.

"Please let us know if you need anything," said Mrs. McNeil, checking her watch. "That's the house telephone. Mrs. Taylor will answer it. We'll send up lunch at one? And we hope you'll join us for drinks and dinner at six thirty. We're doing a buffet, a few neighbors will be by. Very casual."

"Oh," said Antonia, glancing outside. "There's one here already."

"Who?" Cynthia moved quickly back to the window.

"Fred Gibson. Alone. Where is his wife, again?"

"In Florida," said her mother. "Her sister had a baby, and Betty went back to help out."

I was sorry to hear it. It would have been nice to see a familiar face at dinner.

"I'll go down and meet him," said Cynthia, whisking out of the door as if not wanting the others to follow her.

SIXTEEN

At six thirty-five, I ventured downstairs. I'd made steady progress on the dress, fueled by the excellent lunch a uniformed maid had brought up on a tray, which made me feel like someone in a movie.

I went slowly, as much from nervousness as to admire the fresh floral arrangements and the beautiful wallpaper. On a side table in the downstairs hall was a framed photograph of Mr. McNeil with President Roosevelt, smiling like old friends, which perhaps they were. When a maid who was passing by saw me hesitating, she indicated the library. "They're having drinks in there, Miss Cleary."

"They" turned out to be all the adults I'd met in the conservatory, plus a few others: Antonia's blonde friend Letty and her husband Arthur, a robust male cousin named Jack, a middle-aged couple whose names I promptly forgot, Antonia's fiancé Bill, and Fred Gibson and his parents. "This is Miss Cleary, who is helping alter the wedding dress," said Mrs. McNeil, and Mrs. Gibson's eyes lit up. "Oh, how nice," she said warmly. "I think you're the one who made that beautiful yellow suit for my daughter-in-law?"

"I am," I said, grateful for both the compliment and the conversational opening. Mr. McNeil was at my elbow, smiling and pressing a drink into my hand. "It was such pretty fabric."

"I'm so glad she could use it," said Mrs. Gibson as I took a sip of the drink. I had no idea what kind of cocktail it was, but it was obvious I'd have to take it slow. "I thought the yellow would look charming on her."

"Betty's a dear girl," said Mrs. McNeil firmly. "What a shame she can't be here."

"She was sorry to miss it," said Mrs. Gibson. "But I'm glad she gets to spend time with her sister. I know they're very close."

"How's life in the hospital, Fred?" said Mr. McNeil.

At his question Fred Gibson, who had been standing aside and speaking to Cynthia, started and turned. "Sorry?"

"The hospital. Patching up our boys. How's it going?"

"Fine," said Fred shortly. "Fine."

"What's the most gruesome injury you've seen?" asked Antonia, curled up in an armchair.

"Antonia," said Cynthia sharply. "Please."

"I want to know. I'm going to train as a nurse when Bill is overseas, and I can take it. Shattered limbs, missing eyes, you name it."

"This is hardly appropriate talk," said her mother, with a glance at Bill, but he just shrugged and smiled down at his bride-to-be with affectionate amusement.

Fred looked more than uncomfortable; he looked, I noted with surprise, almost haunted. I also noticed how handsome he was, tall with a cleft in his chin, like a blond Bill Holden. "You don't want to know, Antonia," he said brusquely. "Excuse me." He put down his drink and walked out the French doors to the terrace.

Silence fell, broken only by the self-conscious tinkle of ice cubes. Mrs. Gibson's brow was furrowed with worry. "Please excuse him," she said. "He doesn't talk much about it. I think he's seen some rather awful things. They get the worst of the injuries from the Pacific, at his hospital."

"Of course," said Mr. McNeil. "Of course. Cynthia? Why don't you go out to him." Cynthia put down her glass and disappeared outside.

Mr. McNeil picked up the cocktail shaker. "Everyone else, please, drink up. Judy? A refill?"

As the party once again broke into little conversational groupings, I drifted over to the built-in bookshelves taking up the longest wall. Among the books were numerous framed photographs, both formal and informal. There was a striking one of a girl on a horse, jumping over a fence; whoever took the photo had timed it perfectly, capturing the horse's dynamism and grace.

"That's Cynthia," said Mr. McNeil, who had appeared at my side. "Sixteen years old. She had a good seat."

I had no idea what that meant but nodded as if I did. "Was it a competition?"

"It was. She came in second, a silly mistake on her part. Should have been first." He put his hands in his pockets, studying the photo. "We expect silly things from Antonia but not from Cynthia. It was disappointing."

It must have been, for him to be speaking of it to a stranger almost ten years later. Or maybe it wasn't the competition he was thinking of. I could think of nothing to say.

Then he turned to me briskly, indicating my almost-full glass. "Drink up, Miss Cleary. Enjoy yourself. We're glad you're here." He smiled, and I felt not like hired help but an actual guest. I wanted to ask about the photo with President Roosevelt, but then Cynthia and Fred returned from the terrace. Mr. McNeil excused himself and took Fred aside by the arm, probably apologizing for his younger daughter's bluntness.

"Where's Max?" asked the burly cousin, as if just realizing his absence.

"On business in Los Angeles," said Cynthia, picking up her cocktail glass. "He'll be here for the wedding."

"How's his nightclub coming along? Have you seen it?"

"No," said Cynthia. "He's working with some designer. I'll see it when it's finished."

Her tone was absolutely neutral, and it was clear she had no idea who the designer was. I felt my cheeks burn as if I had some shameful secret.

"Too bad he's not here," said the cousin, with a gleam in his eye. He smiled at the others, as if inviting them into a shared joke. "You can always count on Max to keep things interesting."

"Shall we eat?" asked Mrs. McNeil briskly. She lifted a hand toward the doorway. "The buffet is in the dining room."

What had been billed as a simple dinner was anything but. I wondered how they had managed to get so much food; it was as if rationing didn't exist. When he saw me choose a small piece of glazed ham, Mr. McNeil took a larger one and slid it on my plate with a wink.

After serving ourselves, we all settled into various chairs in the library. At first I'd thought a buffet would be less intimidating than being around a formal dining table, but it was hard to know where exactly to sit. It was a relief when Mrs. Gibson invited me to take a chair near the piano and then sat down next to me, asking me about sewing. She was a very kind woman. I remembered the conversation at Betty's and thought about what a nice mother-in-law she must be.

With the exception of Antonia's fiancé, it was clear that the guests had all known each other for years. "Do you live nearby?" I asked Mrs. Gibson.

"We have a place just down the road," said Mrs. Gibson. "My husband and I are in Atherton nearly all the time now. We gave the flat in the city to Fred and Betty when they got married."

"It's a lovely apartment," I said. "Such a nice view. But Atherton is pretty too."

"Fred and Betty come down here often, when he's off-duty at the hospital," said Mrs. Gibson. "We have a guesthouse, so they have privacy." She glanced at her son, who was eating with Cynthia and cousin Jack. "It's good for Fred to get a break from his work, I think."

Maids cleared our plates when we had finished, and Mrs. Gibson excused herself to go to the powder room. I glanced about the room, feeling the sense of well-being you get from a good meal and a comfortable home. It was how I used to feel at the Dubuques', but with an overlay of luxury. A log burned in the fireplace, making the large room feel cozy, and a cocker spaniel trotted up to me, sniffing my hands as if aware I'd just been eating. I love dogs and patted his silky head in delight.

Across the room Miss Hargreaves the nurse was helping Great-Aunt Mabel with her plate. I wondered how old she was; nearly a hundred, perhaps? Even in a wheelchair you could see the curve of her back, putting her head almost at the level of her shoulders. As I watched it occurred to me that in some ways, she was even more of an outsider at the party than I was. Various people had stopped by her wheelchair to say a polite hello, but other than Mrs. Gibson no one had paused for an actual conversation. I was just thinking of what I could say to her when Mrs. McNeil suddenly clapped her hands for attention.

"If you're all done," she said, "I'd like you to come outside. We need your help deciding where to have the ceremony." She glanced at her youngest daughter. "There's been a slight difference of opinion."

"The pool house courtyard," said Antonia. "Obviously."

"But the gingko tree is so pretty this time of year," offered Judy. "It would make a lovely background."

"The color won't show in the photos anyhow," said Antonia. "And what if the lawn is wet?"

"You see?" said Mrs. McNeil with mock, or possibly real, exasperation. "This is why we need other opinions. All wedding guests, come on out." With various degrees of enthusiasm, the partygoers got to their feet, stretched, put down their glasses.

I wasn't sure if I should join them; after all, I wasn't a wedding guest. Standing awkwardly by my chair I waited for someone to turn and include me, but Mrs. Gibson was no longer in the room and no one else seemed to remember that I was there. They all filed out without a backward glance, in chummy twos or threes, their overlapping conversations and laughter fading away as they moved down the terrace and into the darkness.

It was suddenly so quiet, with just the nurse, Aunt Mabel, and me left in the library. Even the spaniel had trotted outside with the guests. I stood alone by the piano, feeling my cheeks burn with embarrassment. Should I go upstairs, or did they expect me to wait until they returned?

Across the room Miss Hargreaves was patting Aunt Mabel's chin with a napkin. "There you are, Mrs. Sloan," she said. "All neat again." I wondered how long she had worked for the family. She gave me a brief smile, one employee acknowledging another, before turning back to her charge. "Shall we go upstairs?"

"No, I want to stay until they come back." It was the first time I'd heard the old woman speak.

"Well, just a little longer." Miss Hargreaves got up and came toward me with a certain urgency. "Would you mind if I left her with you for a minute?" she asked in a low voice. "I've a headache and need to take an aspirin."

"Of course."

"Thank you." She turned back to Aunt Mabel, who had nodded forward, her eyes closed. "She'll probably doze anyhow. I'll be right back." She left the room quickly.

Aunt Mabel did seem half-asleep, so after a moment I turned

back to the wall of bookcases. With the room empty I could examine them more closely than I'd done before. There was a snapshot of Mr. and Mrs. McNeil on the deck of an ocean liner and one of Antonia, much younger, on a pair of skis in the snow. I recognized cousin Jack, standing by a swimming pool with Harold and two other young men, their bodies bronze in the sun. There was a snapshot of the spaniel wearing what seemed to be a ribbon from a show, and one of the elder Gibsons and McNeils in evening clothes.

Then my eye was caught by a photo of Cynthia and Fred Gibson, both looking a few years younger. He was in a tuxedo and she was in a long formal gown, and they were standing side by side, looking not at the camera but at something in the distance. I took it off the shelf to study it more closely.

It's funny how sometimes people who are looking at the same thing seem even more connected than people who are looking at each other. There was a sameness to their posture and a similar expression on their faces as they watched whatever they were watching. It had been amusing, whatever it was, for they were both smiling. They looked so relaxed, so comfortable in each other's presence.

Then I almost dropped the photograph, for I recognized her dress. It was the rose satin dress with long sleeves that I had altered for her.

"That was a nice evening," said a voice behind me. I whirled about. Great-Aunt Mabel was awake.

I carefully put the photograph back on the shelf and sat down by her wheelchair. "I'm sorry. I thought you were asleep."

"People usually do," she said. "That was a lovely evening. Cynthia looked like a queen in that pink dress. Didn't she?"

"Very much," I said. "She is beautiful."

"It was a nice party, Marjorie Gibson's sixteenth birthday. You were there, of course. Remember the way it rained? So surprising for May."

And I realized with a shock that she thought I was one of their set, a family friend. I licked my lips, which were suddenly dry. "Yes," I said. What was the harm in playing along? "Yes, you don't expect rain past April."

"She's a good girl, Marjorie. Too bad she's all the way at Vassar and can't be here. She looked charming, in her blue. And Cynthia and Fred, dancing all night the way they did. Like Astaire and Rogers."

"Cynthia's a good dancer," I said recklessly. "She always has been." My heart was pounding. It was like I was someone else.

"Such a shame they didn't marry," said Aunt Mabel. "It was a surprise when Fred proposed to that Betty girl, wasn't it? Shows you what a silly quarrel can do."

"A big surprise." My heart seemed to be leaping out of my chest. I paused a moment, then plunged ahead. "I never knew what they quarreled about. Did you?"

"No. But Cynthia is stubborn, just like her father. Can't give in until it's too late. And now she's married to that other fellow. The dark one." She lifted a veined hand to her chin, as if indicating stubble. "Where is he tonight?"

"Los Angeles, I think."

"Marry in haste, repent at leisure," said Aunt Mabel. She closed her eyes, then opened them again and looked at me with a smile. "Tell me your name again, dear. I know you live in that big place with the palm tree, but I can't remember your name."

I was saved from answering by the arrival of Miss Hargreaves. "Thank you so much," she said to me, then she smiled at Aunt Mabel, raising her voice. "Have you had a nice chat? I thought you were asleep when I left."

"We were remembering Marjorie Gibson's birthday party," said Aunt Mabel. "We both had such a nice time there." She looked so frail and vulnerable, her head sunk low between her shoulders, and I felt suddenly sick about my deception.

"How nice," said Miss Hargreaves. She gave me a knowing look as if to say, *Thank you for humoring her.* I managed to smile back and then maids came in to clear the remaining glasses away.

In spite of the remarkably comfortable bed, sleep was elusive. It was the first night I'd ever slept outside of the city, and the silence was almost unnerving: no cars, no sirens, no foghorns, nothing but a sound I finally identified as the breeze stirring the ivy growing around my window.

It was impossible not to think about what Aunt Mabel had said. A lovers' quarrel that grew out of proportion, then the arrival in town of a sweet, pretty girl from Florida. A society wedding, then Cynthia's flight to Chicago where she—possibly nursing a broken heart and the consequences of her own stubbornness—found a husband of her own. Was it out of revenge, or what she thought was love?

I couldn't stop seeing the photo of young Cynthia and Fred side by side, with their shared backgrounds, shared memories, shared past. Anyone glancing at that picture would take them for a couple. Even now, when he had been driven outside by Antonia's blunt questions about his work, Cynthia was the one who had been sent out to comfort him.

I finally sat up and turned on the light. There was no point in wasting time when I could be finishing the dress. I put on my robe and slippers and set to work basting the underskirt.

And as I worked there in the pool of light in the quiet house, I realized something. The McNeils' library had photographs of cousins, friends, neighbors, even the dog—but nowhere, in that room or anywhere else, had I seen a picture of Max.

SEVENTEEN

"I was wrong," said Antonia, standing before the mirror. "I admit it." She pulled up her dark blonde hair in an updo, the better to admire the new boatneck I'd put on the dress. "I'm going to like wearing this."

"I'll refrain from saying 'I told you so,'" said Mrs. McNeil. She looked radiantly happy, standing with her hand at her heart, admiring her youngest child. "But it won't be easy."

"You can gloat, Mama," said Antonia, with an affectionate squeeze of her mother's free hand. "It's only fair."

"You look very pretty," said Cynthia, who was sitting on the edge of the bed and jiggling one foot up and down. "Bill will love you."

"More than he already does? Not possible." Antonia grinned at her own reflection. She did look so pretty and hopeful, lit by the autumn sunlight streaming into the bedroom. Even I, silently putting my pincushion away, couldn't help but feel moved.

Mrs. McNeil dabbed at the corner of her eye. "Well," she said. "I'd better pull myself together." She turned to me with gratitude. "You've been so helpful, Miss Cleary. And to come on such short notice. How can I ever thank you?"

"It's my pleasure, Mrs. McNeil. I'm glad it worked out so well."

"Can you stay for lunch? We'll be eating at one."

It was tempting, but I had work waiting for me back at the shop.

"That's very kind, but I'm afraid I have some projects that need finishing."

"Of course. We did rather pluck you away, didn't we?" She paused, her face alight as if an idea had just occurred to her. "Wait a moment. I'll be right back."

I was helping Antonia out of the dress when Mrs. McNeil returned and handed me an envelope. "Your fee, with a little extra," she said. "I also want you to have this." She passed me a folded packet of fabric.

I opened it, instantly made speechless by the luxurious feel of the cloth. It was a voluminous evening wrap of light blue silk, embroidered with a pattern of rust, orange, and gold chrysanthemums. Butterflies in the same colors danced among the foliage. It was the most beautiful fabric I'd ever seen.

"The cape," Cynthia said in surprise.

"It's some antique silk my husband brought back from China many years ago," said Mrs. McNeil. "I had it made into a cape which I've never worn. Not quite my style, as it happens. But there's enough fabric for you to make it into something new. A dress for yourself, perhaps. I'd like you to have it."

"Oh, I can't," I managed to say. It was one thing to accept a tip, quite another to take something like this. "I couldn't possibly."

"Yes, you can," said Mrs. McNeil firmly. "It's yours to keep. A token of my appreciation."

I stammered my thanks.

"Father may notice it's gone," cautioned Cynthia, her eyes on the fabric as it shimmered.

"He won't," said her mother wryly. "After thirty years of marriage, I know that much."

Cynthia drove me to the train station, at her own insistence. "Give Wilson the morning off," she told her mother. "He'll be run ragged this weekend. And I'll stop to pick up some nail polish to match my dress."

"All right, but don't be long," said her mother. "I want your advice on the flowers." The house was getting into wedding preparation mode already; workmen were unloading a marquee, and maids I hadn't seen the day before were busily polishing the staircase banisters. Mrs. McNeil thanked me again, and I shook hands with Mr. McNeil, who had come to the front door with his pipe. "Have a good trip back," he called to me as we drove away.

It felt oddly presumptuous getting into the front seat beside Cynthia, but the awkwardness quickly passed. We talked about fashion and the challenges of finding fabric in wartime, and before I knew it we were at the station. I expected her simply to pause the car as I got out and then continue on her way, but instead she parked off to the side of the small building and even walked me up to the entrance.

"Thank you so much for coming," Cynthia said. She made a slight grimace. "I hope it wasn't too much McNeil all at once. My family can be rather...overbearing."

The comment surprised me. "Not at all," I said with feeling. "They made me feel so welcome. I had a lovely time."

"I'm glad." She looked off in the distance. "I think I hear the train."

"I'd better run, then. Thank you for the ride."

Inside the station, I paused to belt my coat. I'd bought a round-trip ticket the day before and was just rooting in my pocketbook to find it, when I happened to glance outside through the small window to my right.

Fred Gibson was walking briskly toward Cynthia. There was no surprise on his face, or on hers, at having found each other there. He glanced about briefly, almost guiltily, and I saw her take his hand and pull him toward her, toward the building, where a corner of the wall hid them from view. Ten seconds later they reappeared, still holding hands, then quickly let them go as they walked to the car. She slipped into the passenger's seat, not even waiting for him to open the door for her, as if time were too precious to waste.

EIGHTEEN

Back home that night, I thought of Johnny. I was ironing and noticed that on the skirt of my favorite dress there was a grass stain on one of the white flowers, the sort of thing you would only see if you were really looking hard. And maybe it was the visit to the McNeils' and the sight of Cynthia and Fred stirring things up for me, but as I stood by the ironing board memories of Johnny came rushing at me, this time too strong for me to resist.

It was the dress I had worn six months earlier, that Saturday in April, the day after Johnny and I first met at the USO. It was mint green rayon, with a print of white calla lilies edged in coral, and there was a coral cardigan to match. The outfit had been far too light for the cool spring weather, but out of everything in my closet it best matched my jubilant mood. I was going to see Johnny again, spend the whole day with him; it was hardly the occasion for my navy blue wool.

We had planned to meet at the Stow Lake boathouse in Golden Gate Park, and when I arrived at nine thirty he was already there. At the sight of me his face lit up.

"Irene. You look beautiful."

He took my hands and kissed my cheek, and then we just stared at each other, smiling. On the way to the park, I'd had a moment's fear that maybe it was all in my mind, the connection I'd felt at the USO and in Union Square. But the minute I saw how he was looking at me, all doubt was gone.

We strolled to the edge of the lake, with its ducks and swans and the bridges connecting the shore to the small island in the center. A wooden boat moved swiftly past, with a soldier at the oars and a blonde girl smiling at him from underneath a blue hat. "Looks like fun," said Johnny. "Shall we?"

It was heaven, streaming through the water. He did the rowing, hardly breaking a sweat, as I sat back like an empress. I liked watching the dip and curve of his arms, and how the movement kept making him lean towards me, then back, then towards me. "You're really strong," I said.

"I row crew, at Princeton. I've always loved the water."

"Is that why you joined the navy, not the army?"

"You bet." He glanced behind him as another boat approached, this one full of high school girls, giggling as they tried to avoid hitting us. "My dad wanted me to join the army. I think he was surprised that I didn't."

"Why?"

"He thought the army was more prestigious. Dad's a great guy, but it was hard for him to understand that I didn't really care about that." He lifted the oars, holding them aloft a moment.

I'd have loved a photograph of him, sitting there in the boat in his navy uniform, so relaxed and happy. I told him so.

"Funny," he said, "I'd love one of you. Looking like a queen on a barge."

"A freckled queen."

"That's the best kind."

There's one problem with a boat; it's a little awkward for a kiss. I could see him thinking the same thing. We smiled at each other and then I looked beyond him and pointed. "We're almost at the bridge. My favorite spot."

"Let's check it out." He steered the boat easily underneath one of the arches. As we passed under I gazed up at the stone gliding above me.

"So tell me about the bridge," he said.

"I've always loved it. When I was a kid, I used to imagine it was the one from 'The Three Billy Goats Gruff.' I imagined the troll underneath, and the goats prancing over it."

He stopped rowing and we just drifted for a while, both of us looking at the bridge with its rocky stone sides arching over the green water like a brown rainbow.

"There wasn't much in my childhood that matched the fairy tales," I said. "But this always did." A gull wheeled over us and landed on the bridge, acknowledging us with a smart turn of its head.

"Have you been to that little island?"

"Once, with my friend Trixie and her family. It was so exciting. Then her little brother fell into the water, and we had to leave."

"You know what would be pretty," said Johnny, "is seeing this park in snowfall. But I guess it never snows in San Francisco."

"It actually did once, when I was eight. But I didn't get to play in it. I had influenza and was in the infirmary."

"For a kid, that's a tragedy."

"Oh, it was." I remembered it so well: the excited voices ringing through the echoing halls, me struggling to sit up in bed, the voice of Sister Germaine telling me I couldn't go outside. "I heard all about it from the other kids. There was only a little bit on the ground, but they made a tiny snowman and had a snowball fight. Apparently Sister Rosemary was a good shot." I hugged my knees. "I was always sorry I'd missed it. Even now, you hear people talk about the snow of 1932, and I don't have anything to share. That's a dream of mine, to see snow someday. To really see it."

"You'll love it when you do."

"It must be so pretty when it snows in New York."

"It is, although city snow isn't as nice as country snow. We go to

Vermont to ski, and that's where it's really beautiful, the woods in snow. You can't get cynical about it. Or I can't, at least. I'm like a kid every time."

"That's what I want to see. Snowy woods. Like on a Christmas card."

"You'll love it." He was silent, as if picturing it. "And it's so quiet when it snows, Irene. A quiet like nothing else. Like the rest of the world is—being reverent, for a moment. It's perfect peace."

The moment was shattered by the honk of a goose somewhere on the water. We both laughed.

"I guess that's my cue to row," he said, picking up the oars again. We smiled at each other across the boat. *I never want this day to end*, I thought, watching as he leaned toward me and back and toward me again, in a natural, effortless rhythm.

NINETEEN

Max called me the week after my Atherton visit. "Let's go scout ideas for the club," he said. "How about the park this time?"

When I got into his car, he opened the glove box and handed me a small flat package. "Something for you."

It was a large tablet of chocolate, wrapped in gold foil and a paper label of a Spanish señorita with a red rose in her hair. I lifted it eagerly to my nose, inhaling a whiff of dark, rich fragrance. "Where did you get this?"

"Like it?"

"I haven't had chocolate like this in a long time."

"Good. I bought it for Cynthia, but she doesn't like sweets. Didn't want it to go to waste."

I thought of how I'd seen Cynthia relishing a slice of iced cake the night I was at the McNeils'. Either she wasn't being truthful with him, or he wasn't being truthful with me. Either way, it was none of my business. I traced the chocolate, feeling the individual squares through the wrapping; it was all I could do to keep from snapping one free right then and there. I thanked him and put it in my pocketbook.

"So I hear you fixed Antonia's dress," he said as we drove away.

"I did, yes." After a moment I asked, "How was the wedding?"

"Fine. She looked great. You did a nice job."

"They seemed happy with it. Mr. and Mrs. McNeil, I mean."

He turned the car toward the park. I waited for him to say more, but he was silent. For some reason I couldn't stop picturing Cynthia getting furtively into the car with Fred Gibson. I didn't want to think of it.

"Do you like them?" I found myself asking him. "The McNeils?"

"Do you?"

"Yes, they were so nice. Welcoming. I thought it might be awkward, but they made me right feel at home."

We were at a stoplight, and he turned to look at me. I couldn't quite read his expression.

"I'm glad to hear it," he said, then the light changed, and he started up again. He didn't answer my question.

At the park we paused at the carousel, watching the children rotate slowly on their colored animals. Its carnival music filled the air, and mothers smiled and waved. Max surveyed the scene with keen interest.

"I want the room with booths to feel like the park," he said. "What about including this?"

"The carousel?"

"Sure. We could find a horse, repaint it. Or four, one for each corner of the room."

"No," I said with energy. "A carousel horse doesn't belong in a nightclub."

He looked down at me, clearly surprised at my tone. "That was a strong reaction."

"It doesn't." I tried to explain why. "It's—that's part of childhood. Sitting on a horse, going around in a circle and thinking you're going somewhere. It has nothing to do with a bar."

"You don't know much about bars, do you?"

"You think there's a place for"—I tried to find the words—"for childhood imagination? In a nightclub?"

"Absolutely. Why do you think people go to them?"

"To drink. To socialize."

"Sure, but underneath it all, they're looking for something. They're chasing something. It may be as much a fantasy as those kids on the horses, but it doesn't matter. It's what gets them in the door. The hope that something will happen in that club to change their life."

His tone was as charged as my own. For a moment we faced each other as the music began winding down behind us. Something in my expression made him raise an eyebrow.

"You don't believe me, do you," he said.

"Not at all."

He stood, hands in pockets, and studied me. "Then you're more of a cynic than I am, Irene," he said at last. "Who would have guessed?"

"I'm not," I said. "I mean, I never used to be." The music had stopped, and parents began surging forward to get their children. I turned and started walking away.

A moment later I felt Max's hand on my elbow. I pulled away from him, quickening my pace, and then he moved in front of me on the crowded path, so I had to stop.

"I don't know what it is," he said, his voice low, "but something here struck a nerve for you. I've said something that hurt you. I'm sorry."

"You haven't hurt me." With a supreme effort I managed to look him right in the eye. "I'm just surprised, that's all. But you probably know a lot more about people in bars than I do." I forced a smile. "So yes, we can do something with a carousel. If you want."

He kept standing there, a slight frown on his face. I remembered that time back at his apartment, when he asked about tailoring and had clearly seen through my lie.

Pulling my coat more tightly around me, I glanced beyond him into the depths of the park. "Let's see what else is here. The windmill, maybe? That's something you could work into the club."

We walked off in silence. A moment later there was music as the carousel started up again. I quickened my pace, so I wouldn't have to hear it and remember.

After our boat ride at Stow Lake, Johnny and I had wandered over to the carousel. We were holding hands, which felt at once absolutely exciting and perfectly easy. "This really reminds me of home," he said with nostalgia. "The Central Park carousel."

"Did you ride it often?"

"Every time I could. My nanny took us to the park every day. I could ride if I'd drunk all my milk and eaten all my lunch without complaining."

"And how often was that?"

"Every day she didn't give me peas," he said.

We stood hand in hand, watching the children go around, some of them patting the carved manes of their horses, others waving at mothers standing on the sidelines.

"Did you ride this, Irene? When you were a kid?"

"Not as much as the carousel at the zoo. I loved that one."

"Which animal did you like to ride?"

"The lion. I used to pretend it was a polar bear. In my favorite fairy tale, a girl rides a white bear east of the sun and west of the moon. I always wanted to do that."

The music was winding to a close, the carousel slowing. Next thing I knew Johnny was pulling me toward it with a grin.

"Come on, Irene," he said. "Let's see if we can find you a polar bear."

We didn't, but with Johnny there I didn't care. I chose a white horse with red markings and Johnny sat down on the brown stag next to it. I sat sidesaddle, not so much because it was ladylike as because I wanted to face him. He did the same, holding onto the pole with one hand.

The music started, and with a creak and shudder we were off. My horse went up and down but his stag was stationery. "You got one that doesn't move," I said, remembering childhood disappointments. "Want to switch?"

"No," he said. "I'm just enjoying the view."

He was so handsome in his uniform, his brown eyes bright with interest and fun. I glanced about me at the other riders just so I could have the pleasure of looking back and seeing him still smiling at me. As my horse moved I'd rise above him a foot, then glide slowly down, then up, then down. It was somehow comforting that he never moved, even though I did.

"I always liked it when the ride would end with me high in the air," I said. "So I'd have the thrill of jumping down." I shifted my grasp on the pole, which had that sharp metallic smell they always have. It wasn't comfortable sitting sidesaddle, but there was no way I wanted to stop looking at him.

"How's the horse?" he asked. "A good stand-in for the polar bear?"

"Perfect. I can imagine I'm gliding through a snowy landscape. Now that I know more about snow, thanks to you."

"I'm telling you, Irene. You'll love it when you see it. I hope I'm there when you do."

My heart soared. "I hope so too," I said.

The carousel music was winding down. Johnny watched me move up and down as my horse began to slow.

"So where will you end up this time?" he asked. "In the air or on the ground?"

"I'm happy either way. This is already the best carousel ride of my whole life."

With any other fellow I'd be embarrassed to show my heart like that. But Johnny just looked at me, his smile changing, deepening really, something new coming into his eyes.

The carousel hadn't even come to a full stop when he jumped off the stag. I was at just the right height that when he took my face in his hands, we were eye to eye, on exactly the same level. His hands smelled like metal, but his lips, when they finally touched mine, were warm and gentle and perfect.

TWENTY

Max didn't mention the carousel again, that day at the park. We walked around the windmill and looked at the bison and finished off at the Japanese Tea Garden—which had been renamed the Oriental Tea Garden—underneath the big pagoda. "Probably not the right time to have a Japanese feature in a nightclub," said Max, studying it. "Too bad. I like this."

He wanted us to go to Stow Lake, but I put him off, saying I was too tired. I didn't want anything else to remind me of Johnny.

It was obvious Max knew something was still bothering me. I could feel it in the way he looked at me, in the slight softening of his manner. At one point a group of teenage boys were clowning about on the path and one bumped right into me. Max immediately whisked me out of harm's way with a sharp, "Watch where you're going, kid." The boy apologized, lifting his hands, cowed by the authority in Max's tone.

But as we continued through the park, an idea for the club began to seed itself in my mind. I pondered it, glad to have something other than Johnny to occupy my thoughts. Max and I could represent the park through color, using various shades of green for the carpet and upholstery and maybe even the walls. Accents of white and mauve would be a nod to the spiky flower-like plants that grew everywhere along the borders. Instead of carousel horses, the wall would be covered with framed black-and-white photographs of various points of interest in the park.

When we got back to the car, I shared the idea with Max. He loved it. "Perfect. We can have a photograph of the windmill, one of the carousel, even one of the bison. Subtle and elegant. I like it."

"I'm glad," I said. "I need to do something to deserve those three hundred dollars. And the bed."

"That bed was a gift, Irene," he said. "Pure gift. Nothing else." We drove on for half a block in silence. "How is it, by the way? Comfortable?"

"Very."

"Good." He glanced sideways at me. "I hope you sleep well tonight. Looks like you need it."

After my sad little dinner of a cheese sandwich—thanks to Max's check I had the money to eat well, but I still found it hard to fit grocery shopping into my day—I put the teakettle on. As I waited for the water to boil I ate three squares of chocolate, careful not to tear the beautiful wrapper. It was achingly good, the perfect blend of sweet and bitter, and it was only with effort that I managed not to eat the whole bar. Wrapping it up carefully, I put it in a tin in the cupboard (I'd seen evidence of mice around and was taking no chances).

Once the tea was done, I took the steaming cup over to the carved chest in the corner, underneath the icon of the solemn Christ. There was a small gramophone on top, Anna's, which I'd rarely used; when your goal is just to have background noise, it's easier to keep the radio on than to stop and flip a record over. But this time I opened the cabinet and took out her stack of records, heavy in their cardboard sleeves.

They were classical ones: *Swan Lake*, and Chopin, and a ballet called *Coppélia*. A few were in Russian. But at last, I found the one I had been hoping for. Blowing dust lightly off the gramophone needle, I put the black disk on the turntable and watched as the arm slowly descended, making contact with a little scratch and pop.

Tea in hand, I curled up on the sofa. Pauline had said that maybe I'd recognize some of the songs from the movie *Fantasia*, and I did: there was the sprightly little dance that made me remember the mushrooms dancing in a circle, and the light, tinkly tones of—I checked the sleeve—the "Dance of the Sugar Plum Fairy."

The songs I'd never heard before were beautiful too. I was struck by a waltz which, true to its name, made me think of the flower sellers on the downtown corners. I'd never seen a ballet before, but I could imagine girls in dresses with skirts like petals, leaping and twirling on the tips of their shoes.

And there was a song that started off with light notes, like drops of water in a pool. It became more dramatic for a time, then turned into what was clearly a waltz, at one point with a chorus of female voices singing wordlessly like an angel choir. Putting down my mug, I closed my eyes and let the music wash over me. I was like the man playing the violin on Fillmore, his face rapt, transported by music to another place and time. I seemed to be in a forest, hushed and still, with girls whirling so lightly that their feet left no trace in the snow.

When I opened my eyes again I was crying. I turned to the window, which showed a slice of black city sky and the lights of the building opposite. There was no forest out there, of course, but for a moment I had almost believed there would be.

And then my thoughts left winter and went back to spring, to that Saturday in April. With tears still in my eyes, I let them go.

After Johnny and I left the carousel, we spent the rest of the day in and around the park. For lunch we had hotdogs near the bison field, and by the children's playground he bought cotton candy. We fed it to each other, laughing when it made the ends of our noses sticky.

We ended up near the Aquarium, under a palm tree, on the grass dotted with tiny fragile daisies. For two blissful hours we alternated between kissing and talking. We found that we both loved Christmas carols and comedies, preferred dogs to cats, and both hated oatmeal. I learned that he played the piano and he learned that I was afraid of mice. His middle name was Ronald—his father's name—and I told him mine was Mary. "Our nanny was named Mary," he said. "I adored her."

"All the kids at the orphanage were given that as a middle name. Girls, I mean."

"Irene Mary Cleary." I loved how he said my name. "It suits you."

"How?"

He thought before answering, in that way he had. "It's pretty and it's strong. And you're both those things."

"Sweet talker," I teased him, and we kissed for a long time.

His hands framed my head, and he traced my cheekbones with his fingers. When I was so close to him, I could see little things: the barest amber-colored freckle under his left eye, the way his eyes had a dash of green in the brown. The way he smiled at me, different from the way any other guy ever had.

"It's something isn't it?" he said. "That I happened to pick that USO, out of all the ones in the city. That you happened to be there that night, pouring coffee."

"It sure was lucky."

"Maybe it wasn't luck," he said slowly. "Maybe it was something else."

I was too overcome with feeling to answer. I pulled his head down to mine and we didn't speak for quite a while. Finally, two soldiers walking by whistled at us. "Having a good leave, sailor?" said one, and Johnny lifted his hand in a sheepish salute. But it broke the moment, and by one accord we pulled apart. My backside was damp with that feeling you get when you sit on a lawn that you'd thought was mostly dry. When I shivered, he put his arm around me and held me close.

"Do you want to get going?" he asked.

"Not just yet." I wanted to stay a little longer on our knoll, under the palm tree. It was holy ground now, as the lake was, and the carousel. And Union Square. *That's what love does*, I thought. *It makes the same old landscape into something magical and precious*. Then I felt a little jolt of awareness, a little thrill, that I had used the word love, even in my own thoughts. I moved closer to him, and his arm tightened around me.

"Irene," he said, "I know it's a cliché, the guy on shore leave finding a girl. But when I saw you across the room at the USO, it was like . . . well, it was like you knew me already, and you always had. I've dated other girls, but I've never felt that before. Do you know what I mean?"

I nodded.

He pulled away to look at me. "I really mean it. That song we danced to, 'Heart and Soul.' I don't just feel it in my heart, like I have with other girls. I feel it in my heart *and* in my soul. That's the new part, the soul."

There were tears in my eyes. I took his hand, kissed the knuckles, then I held it on my heart, his fingers splayed. "Heart and soul," I said. "Here's my heart."

"I can feel it beating." He took my other hand and pressed it to his chest.

"If only we could find the soul," I murmured. "Where do you think that is?"

Johnny grinned. "Sounds like a question for my philosophy professor." He bent down so our foreheads were touching. "But I'm kind of glad he's not here to ask."

"Maybe it's everywhere," I said, closing my eyes. "Maybe it's bigger than ourselves. That's why you can't touch it."

There was silence for a moment, then he pulled back so he could look at me. "Irene," he said, "that's exactly what I've been feeling. What I've been trying to say. This—you and me—it feels bigger than ourselves. Doesn't it?"

I nodded, too radiantly happy to speak. And as our lips met again, I realized that among the desire and joy and excitement, there was something else, too, something that I'd rarely ever felt before. It was a feeling of belonging, of the most pure and precious kind.

TWENTY-ONE

Between work at the shop and advising on the nightclub, the last week of October was a busy one. One cloudy day Max called me to come down to the club to meet Leonard Frank, the architect who was reworking the interiors, a gray-haired man with a pencil mustache and a supercilious attitude. Upon meeting me his glance flickered over my freckles with open disdain, and whenever I asked him questions, he addressed the answers to Max, who finally ground his cigarette calmly into an ashtray and said, "Fine, but I'm not the one who asked. Talk to Miss Cleary."

"There's not much for me to do here, anyhow," I whispered as we stood waiting for Leonard to finish his measuring. "I'm not even the one making the drapes. I might as well go back home."

"No, because we're going out to lunch when we're done," said Max. "And the 'we' does not include Leonard."

The restaurant Max suggested was in North Beach, a tiny eatery where you heard Italian more than English. I had chicken parmigiana and Chianti, making it my first time ever drinking wine with lunch. Max knew the proprietor, a man with a long white apron tucked in at his belt, who clapped him on the back fraternally the moment we came in. Max seemed to know everyone.

I said as much over the red-checked tablecloth. "It's what I do," he said. "I like getting to know a place and the people in it."

It was a cold fall day, but the restaurant was warm and cozy and smelled pleasantly of oregano. It looked out on Washington Square, with its green lawn and benches and the white sugar spires of St. Peter and Paul Church in the background. Pigeons wheeled about and people hurried by, bundled in their coats. I was glad to be inside, with hot coffee and biscotti for dessert and the low crackle of a radio playing Italian music.

"There was a place like this in Chicago," Max said suddenly. "Gave me my first job when I was ten."

"That's so young."

"I worked after school, evenings, weekends."

"What did you do?"

"Anything they needed. Swept the steps, washed dishes, ran errands. Emptied the mousetraps." At my grimace, he smiled. "It was better than being at home, Irene. And you learn a lot about a business at such a young age. You soak it all in." He drank the last of his coffee. "Luigi and his mother, Mrs. Patricelli. They were the owners. She used to mend my socks for me, when they got holes. When I opened my first nightclub I invited them as guests of honor."

"Did they come?"

"Yes. Briefly." He signaled to the waiter, who came with the check. "Thanks, Silvio." He glanced at it and reached into his coat for his wallet. As he did so, his black head bent, I studied him. I'd been with him enough over the past few weeks that his attractiveness, his masculinity, no longer had the power to render me awkward, as they had at our first meeting. He hadn't grown any less handsome, but now that I knew his story, his looks were no longer the most compelling thing about him.

He lifted his head to find me studying him. "What is it?"

"I'm just trying to imagine you as a little boy." I put my chin on my hand and leaned forward.

"Can you?"

In spite of the five o'clock shadow that he always seemed to have, in spite of the breadth of shoulder and strong jaw, there was something in his eyes if you looked hard enough. "Yes," I said at last. "I think I can."

He said nothing to that. There was no sound but the music crackling softly in the background. It took me a moment to realize we were staring at each other. I was the first one to look away.

It took me by surprise, the photo. I was in the streetcar going downtown, seated next to a man who was reading the newspaper, and I glanced at it idly, then did a double take. On the society page were photographs of a benefit for Letterman Hospital, and there it was: the rose evening dress in its remade splendor, with the V-neck and narrow straps. Cynthia looked radiant, her hair a golden cloud above her bare shoulders. She was standing next to Fred Gibson, with a young, pretty brunette girl on the other side. I craned my head to read the caption:

Mrs. Fred Gibson is still away in Florida, but her husband isn't lonely! Mrs. Max Burke shimmers in rose satin and diamonds and proud sister Miss Marjorie Gibson, just back from Vassar, wears blue silk with pearls.

There was no mention of Max, then I remembered that he hadn't been at the event. He'd taken me back home after lunch that day, telling me he would be spending the evening making phone calls. I wondered if he had seen the photograph, and what he thought of it.

Then the newspaper was folded abruptly, noisily, and the man behind it gave me the aggrieved look reserved for people who are reading over your shoulder. I smiled apologetically and turned to look out the window, staring unseeing at the buildings as they flashed by.

My earliest images of romance came from fairy tales. Romance meant a charming prince climbing up a hank of hair or cutting through thorns to win the princess. The fairy tales always ended at the wedding, of course; you never got to see what "happily ever after" actually looked like.

My image of marriage itself had to come from someplace else, and it came from the Dubuques. I don't think Mr. Dubuque ever forgot how close his wife had come to death. Even years after her recovery, he'd go out of his way to drop a kiss on her cheek or touch her shoulder. She was similarly affectionate, always calling him "sweetheart," and once when I was in high school and he came out wearing a new suit, she said to her children, "Isn't your father the handsomest man?" Trixie rolled her eyes at me, but I loved it. They were my image of what a married couple should be: loyal, loving, and unafraid to show it.

So the Burkes' marriage, with its obvious chasms and fractures, was puzzling. In the weeks following my return from Atherton, I couldn't stop thinking about it. When and how had things gone wrong? Max seemed guilty of nothing more than being Max: rough around the edges, outspoken, a man who had risen from unhappy circumstances to wealth and success. I'd never heard him say anything against Cynthia. But I'd seen her coldness with my own eyes, witnessed the disdain she apparently had no qualms about showing to others. With everyone else, myself included, she was warm and kind. With Max, she was almost derisive.

And there was Fred Gibson. She'd remade a dress from their past and worn it once again, apparently for him. I'd helped her do it, in fact. "It's a surprise," she'd said in my shop.

I thought of the newspaper photo as I stopped at the hardware store for mousetraps, a sadly necessary purchase. It was just a dress, right? Surely, she'd never actually break her marriage vows and have an affair with Fred, no matter how unhappy she was with her husband. And Fred, with a sweet young wife out of town? Certainly, he wouldn't, either.

But as I walked back from the store, I kept seeing the image of the two of them at the station. I kept seeing Fred's face, swiveling around with that guilty look, Cynthia pulling him out of sight for that brief moment. They didn't know I'd seen them. For my own peace of mind, I wished I hadn't.

TWENTY-TWO

It's strange to realize how much in my life has come from the charity of others. There were the sisters who raised me, who were literally called the Daughters of Charity. There were the Dubuques welcoming me into their life, and Anna leaving me the shop. And there was Mrs. Detweiler, a trustee at the orphanage, who was responsible for my high school education and for introducing me to Anna in the first place.

I happened to think of her because an errand took me past her old house on Franklin Street, on a brisk but sunny afternoon. It was an imposing Victorian, with gables and turrets and even a small side lawn. Pausing before it, I remembered how astonished I had always been that a woman could have such a huge house all to herself.

She was a widow, tiny and with steely-gray hair, who wore clothes that seemed from an entirely different era. She always came to the Christmas parties in a huge hat with a fake blackbird perched on the side. When Sister Margaret told me that Mrs. Detweiler was going to fund my studies at Notre Dame des Victoires, she had only to say, "She's the woman with the bird hat," and I knew exactly who she was. All the same, there was a wiry independence about Mrs. Detweiler that always kept her from appearing ridiculous.

Resting my hand lightly on the black arrow tips of the fence, I gazed up at the second-story windows. Mrs. Detweiler wasn't there, of course; my junior year of high school she had moved out of the city, and a few months later I'd heard from Sister that she had died. The house was evidently now a hotel, for a serviceman with a suitcase was coming out the front door, whistling.

Directly before me was the bay window of the parlor, where I'd gone for tea to discuss the scholarship. It was the only real house I'd ever been in other than Trixie's, and what a house it was: wood-paneled with ornate furniture and high ceilings and a portrait of the late Mr. Detweiler with his impressive mustache. There was a chow dog named Calvin, who was like a fluffy caramel-colored lion, and a canary in a cage. I remember sitting up straight on the stuffed armchair, fascinated by the silver tea service and the maid who wheeled it in.

Mrs. Detweiler fed the dog from her fingers and spoke frankly about the education I would receive at Notre Dame. I'd have to work on my French, of course, but my school reports indicated that I was someone who expected excellence from herself, and I deserved the best high school education I could have. I was proud that she'd chosen me. "I will do my very best, Mrs. Detweiler," I said, stoically sipping my oversweet tea (I wasn't used to having a sugar bowl at my disposal and regretted taking four cubes).

"Good," she said. "And if you show promise in any particular skills, we will encourage you to develop them. Every girl should know how to make a living, an honest one. Orphans in particular." She glanced at the street outside for a moment, her lined face growing severe. "Not every young woman is raised with the moral education you've had," she said as if to herself. "For all its beauty, this is a wicked city."

The word surprised me. "Wicked" belonged in fairy tales, describing stepmothers and jealous queens. It hardly seemed to fit San Francisco, with streetcars and traffic lights and policemen on every corner. "How is it wicked?" I asked.

She looked back at me, and I could tell she wasn't going to explain. "You needn't worry about that," she said, passing me a plate of cookies. "Just study hard, work hard, and remember all that the sisters have taught you. A good moral code is your best guide throughout life."

"Yes, Mrs. Detweiler," I said. I was still curious, but the cookies had apricot jam in their centers and were so delicious that I soon forgot.

But now, at the age of twenty in the fourth year of a world war, for some reason I found myself remembering.

"Irene," said Louise, clutching my arm. "Do you know what's behind the wall there?"

We were walking west on Pine Street, heading to the movies and then dinner. I looked at the building she was indicating, a large house with a gabled roof, rising up from behind a high stone wall.

"No idea."

"It's a brothel. Run by a woman named Sally Stanford."

"It is?"

"An airman I had drinks with told me about it. Lots of the guys go there, if they can afford it. It's sort of famous."

I stared up at the huge windows, but they were curtained and gave nothing away. "That can't be right. If everyone knows what it is, how is it not shut down?"

"He said it's because the city hall types go there too. They're regular customers."

"How would he know?"

She shrugged. "I guess if you know the right people, it's an open secret. Even the admirals go there, some of them."

I pulled my coat more closely around myself. It seemed incongruous that such activities could happen in the middle of a city, in a house sandwiched between normal-looking apartment buildings, a woman pushing a baby carriage past the front door. “I can’t believe it.”

“Well, I can.” She checked her watch. “Oooh, we’d better hurry. We’ll miss the movie.”

I cast a backward glance at the silent windows as we walked away. Louise was talking about how she’d heard that Errol Flynn was coming to town to sell war bonds, but for some reason I couldn’t get the house out of my head.

Even after the movie, when we were sitting in a booth at the nearby diner, it was still on my mind. “I don’t get it,” I said at last. “That house. How do those women do it?”

“Do what?”

“Be with men they don’t know. For money.”

Louise put down her glass. “It’s a job, I suppose.”

“That’s not a job. Not like mine.”

She shrugged. “I guess some women just like doing it. You know.”

“Actually, I don’t know, because I’ve never done it.” I said it with a laugh, but to my surprise she was looking at me with a strange intensity, with a sort of un-Louise-like question in her eyes. Then she leaned forward.

“Irene,” she said in a low voice, “I’ve done it.”

“You have?” She nodded. “With who? I mean, whom?”

She glanced to the side, then back at me. “If I tell you, will you promise not to tell Trixie?”

“I guess so.”

“I’ve done it with six different guys. Servicemen.”

I just stared at her. “Sorry,” I said after a moment. “Sorry. I’m just—I’m just surprised.”

“The first one was this dreamy marine,” she said, crossing her arms on the table and leaning forward. “Mike, from Tucson. We went dancing and started kissing and then took a cab back to my place. It wasn't great, the first time, but so much better since then. You learn a lot, actually, each time."

I watched her under the hard lights of the diner, this friend I'd known since I was fourteen. I thought of her parents' house, of her room with the pink ruffled bedcover and the lamp with the ceramic poodle at its base. The housekeeper Hetty, off in her own part of the flat, not hearing the late-night whispers and footsteps. "Did you—did you take them all to your house?"

"Most of them. Once I went to the guy's hotel. That was the airman I mentioned earlier. He had a suite at the Sir Francis Drake." She smiled reminiscently. "He was sharing it with two buddies of his and they were taking turns sleeping. Or not sleeping."

It was like the world had been tilted on its axis. I didn't know what to say.

"I've shocked you," she said. "I wasn't going to tell you. It just sort of came out."

"No," I said. "I mean yes, you've shocked me." I had a sudden memory of us together in Latin class, in our black school uniforms with the rounded white collars. "That sailor, the day at the beach. Was he one?"

"Jeff, from Mississippi. He had the cutest accent. Yes, he was the second one."

The waitress paused at our table, asking if we wanted anything else. "No, thank you," I said, and she tore the check from her pad and set it on the table.

"Why, Louise?" I asked when the waitress had left. "What do you get out of it?"

She grinned. "Believe me, when you've done, it, you won't have to ask. But it makes these guys so happy, Irene. You have no idea." She wrapped a straw paper around her finger. "For goodness' sakes, they're going off to war and they may not come back. Mike said he'd never done it before. I'm not sure I believe that, but if it was true—well, I could easily give him something to remember, couldn't I? And who wants to die a virgin?"

"But what if you have a baby?"

"They have prophylactics." It was a word I'd seen in print but never actually heard anyone say. "The army gives them out. And they're grateful, really grateful. I like to think I'm sending them overseas with good memories. My contribution to the war effort."

"You could sell war bonds. Or join the WAVES."

She laughed. "I'm too lazy to join, and I'd get bored selling war bonds."

"But what—what's your future? With them?"

"I don't want a future, just a good time. Look, you have the shop, and Trixie has college. I don't have either. I'm not complaining . . . I'd be a lousy college student. But this gives me a little thrill. Then when I'm a fat old married lady, I can look back on a time when I was young and exciting."

I was still trying to absorb it all. "Don't you care about them? I mean, don't you want to write to them or anything?"

"Not really. Oh, they always pretend they're going to write to me, but I don't believe them. Guys on shore leave will say anything to a girl."

For once I was glad Louise was too self-absorbed to think about how her words would affect me. She took out a compact and a lipstick and outlined her lips in red.

"But don't tell Trixie," she said, swirling the tube and snapping the top back on. "She wouldn't understand. And you know how she worries about things."

"All right."

"And I'm still the same Louise." She looked at me, her eyes sober for once. "That hasn't changed. I still like chocolate-covered cherries and Tyrone Power and all the other things I've always liked. I'm still me."

"I know."

"Just a little more experienced. A little wiser. That's all."

TWENTY-THREE

That night I couldn't fall asleep. I had finally grown used to the bed, to its comfortable mattress and the fact that it was big enough for me to spread my limbs like a jumping jack. It was luxurious, but at the same time it felt—I had to admit it—rather lonely.

I curled up on my side, bunching the cover under my chin. Louise's candid confession had startled me, going against everything I'd ever been taught about waiting until marriage. Sure, I'd always known that there were guys who would gladly spend a night with a girl they'd never see again, which meant there had to be girls who did the same, but there had always seemed to be an invisible gulf between them and me. I'd been accepted as a USO junior hostess because I was one of the good girls.

But I knew Louise. I knew that for all her charming self-absorption, for all her casual relationships, she was no scarlet woman. She was curious about things that we were all curious about. She'd acted on that curiosity, that's all.

Maybe it was a new world, one in which the old distinctions crumbled away. Virgin or V-girl; did it really matter anymore? Louise's parents would surely think it mattered, but they were off in New York. Whereas I had no parents, in New York or anywhere.

Turning on my stomach, I pressed my face into the pillow. If it didn't matter after all, if none of it mattered, then I had sure messed up. On that April day with Johnny, I'd made the biggest mistake of my twenty years of existence.

After the park, we had gone back to my place. Johnny looked about the shop, hands in pockets. "What do you think?" I asked, pulling down the shades.

"I love it. I'm trying to imagine you here at work. A tape measure around your neck, pins in your mouth."

"I use a pincushion on my wrist. Much safer."

"Smart gal," he said. He kept looking about, with that thoughtful, contented smile I loved. He noticed the print of Notre-Dame and moved closer to study it. "Nice picture. That's exactly how it looks."

"Oh, you've been there?"

"Right before the war. We sailed over as a family."

"Just Paris?"

"No. London, Venice, Rome. All the usual places."

I didn't know what all the usual places were; it was so far from my own experience. I watched the easy grace with which he stood studying the engraving, and my confidence in us began to falter. Without his uniform and my USO name tag, we would never even be in the same orbit. We'd never have met in any reality but the one created by war, a city and world turned upside down.

Then he turned back to me. It was astonishing how his smile always made my doubts vanish, like the sun drying a raindrop on cement.

"I'd love to go there with you," he said. He took both my hands, and we kissed. It was a different kiss inside the privacy of the shop, the world closed out by the drawn shades. My hands reached up along the muscles of his upper arms and his circled my waist, holding the place where my silhouette curved inward, with a warmth that thrilled me.

"Let's go up," I said finally. "I'll see what there is for dinner."

There wasn't much, but I grilled a pork chop for us to share. Johnny toasted bread and it was so cozy and companionable, having someone else there in my tiny kitchen. We kept laughing at the smallest things and pausing to kiss, and in the middle of it the bread burned, and we had to open a window and shoo the smell out into the darkening sky with a dishtowel. I found a can of green beans and added dill and vinegar, as Anna used to do when I was working late and we had dinner together. "This," said Johnny after taking a bite, "is the only way to eat green beans."

"You can thank Anna. I learned it from her."

"She must have been a wise woman," said Johnny. "Leaving you this shop. Knowing you could handle it even at such a young age."

"She was," I said slowly. "It sounds terrible to say it, but at times I didn't want it. Right before she died, I had hoped to join the WACS."

"Sometimes a gift can feel more like a burden."

"Exactly."

We were drinking from the bottle of cherry liqueur that a client had given Anna. It was delicious, and it relaxed me just as much as it made my senses hum. I could taste it on his lips when he leaned across the table to kiss me again. Our kisses were deeper this time. We laughed at how the corner of the table was in the way.

Before long we were on the divan, the sofa cushions kicked onto the floor. We were lying side by side and I couldn't get over the pleasure of feeling his body pressed against mine. But it was difficult staying on the narrow sofa; twice he had to pause in our kissing to catch me before I went over the edge. "Let's trade places," he said. "I keep thinking you're going to fall."

"Or," I said, surprising myself, "we could go into the bedroom."

His face was so close to mine it was almost hard to see him, but I could tell from his sudden stillness that he was absorbing what I'd said.

"Do you want to?" he asked in a low voice.

As we lay there, both of us barely breathing, I knew there were two answers to that question. Yes, I wanted to, because Johnny was Johnny, and the connection between us was unlike anything else. It would be so astonishingly easy to get up, take his hand, and lead him to my bedroom. There was no angel with a fiery sword to bar the way. I could do it if I wanted to, and that was an intoxicating thought.

But there was an image in my mind that held me back, an image put there by movies and magazines and morality class in high school and everything else. It was the image of a bride and groom, both of them radiant with joy. I'd always assumed my first time would follow a wedding, *my* wedding, that it would only come after pledging a lifetime of love. Even with the intensity of my feelings for Johnny, giving up that image was too quick a pivot for me.

He read my thoughts and smoothed my hair back gently. "I know."

"I want to, Johnny. But I always thought I'd get married first." I sat up so he could, too; it was too agonizingly tempting, lying with our bodies ranged against one another. I pulled the bodice of my dress in place, modestly moving my skirt over my legs. "But it's not easy."

He grinned wryly. "It sure isn't." Exhaling, he leaned his head against the back of the sofa. "I think you're right, though." He took my hand and for a time we were silent, but it was a comfortable silence. I traced his thumb with my index finger, wishing things were different, but at the same time glad that we could sit like that, still in harmony, feeling so at ease with each other.

Then he turned to face me, his eyes as serious as they'd been at the park. "You know, Irene," he said, "this isn't a now-or-never thing. It feels more like a postponement. Because I can see you being in my life for a long time." He paused, then went on in a rush. "I can see you being in my life forever. And maybe it's crazy, saying this to a girl I've just met, but you're not just any girl. And maybe the guy you end up marrying . . . well, maybe that guy might be . . . me."

He said the last word with a look on his face that I'll never forget, one that was hopeful and nervous and sweet. My face broke into a radiant smile, and then his expression changed, too, to a look of utter happiness. It took a moment to get my voice back.

"When the war's over, Jonathan Ronald Pendleton," I said, "let's pick up where we left off."

"It's a promise, Irene Mary Cleary," he said. He kissed me, not minding the salt of my tears.

When we got up a few minutes later to make tea, I was profoundly happy. My body still ached for his, but I knew we'd done the right thing. One rushed night in wartime couldn't compare to a languorous and confident one in the future, after a promise to have and to hold. My heart beat faster just imagining it.

And there was something else underneath my decision to wait, something I hardly acknowledged to myself. It was the belief that waiting was a sort of insurance that he would come back from the war. Finishing our unfinished business would be the reward for our self-control. Just like in the fairy tales, or in the lives of the saints, good things came to those who could wait.

I whistled "Heart and Soul" as I reached for the tea tin. Johnny started to sing along, and we were both so shockingly unmusical that we ended up convulsed in laughter. He wrapped me in his arms, and we kissed again, not letting up until the teakettle sang.

TWENTY-FOUR

Out of all the sisters at Mount St. Joseph, the two I loved the most were Sister Margaret and Sister Rosemary. They had known me the longest, having been at the orphanage even before I arrived. Like all the Daughters of Charity, they wore long black habits with rosaries hanging from their waists, and their headpieces were the distinctive, dramatic white cornettes that you could always spot from a distance.

We kids used to wonder how the sisters would look with hair, and we found out when I was five and the fire alarm sounded in the middle of the night. Women in nightgowns were suddenly in the dormitories shepherding us out, and it took us a moment to realize that they were the sisters. In the confusion of that evening we discovered that Sister Rosemary's hair was actually gray and that Sister Margaret's hair was red. I was surprised, thinking it should be the other way around.

Sister Rosemary was the one you went to for hugs. She was short and smiling, with teeth that overlapped in the front and round cheeks that gave her the look of a chipmunk. Even the crankiest babies seemed to calm down in her arms. In later years I wondered why she hadn't married and had children of her own, and when I asked her once she said, "You are all my children. Instead of a few, I get to have eighty. God is so good."

Sister Margaret was taller, more stern, with a prominent nose and angular face, but in her own way she was as loving as Sister Rosemary. You would not go to Sister Margaret for hugs, but somehow I felt more comfortable turning to her for other, sensitive things. She was the one I confided in when I was twelve and got my first period, for I knew she would not make a fuss but would quietly give me what I needed. Years before that, when I was eight years old, I'd gone to her when I was having nightmares of finding dead bodies hanging in the broom closet (inspired, no doubt, by the tale of Bluebeard in the *Blue Fairy Book*). She listened gravely and seriously; unlike Sister Rosemary, whose eyes were always darting and dancing about her, Sister Margaret gave you the sense of being fully and totally heard. That day she gave me something else, too: a little silver medal of the Virgin Mary, standing with her arms outstretched, rays of light coming from her palms. It was on a thin metal chain.

"This is called the Miraculous Medal," she said. "Over one hundred years ago, in Paris, the Blessed Mother appeared to Catherine Labouré, a sister in our order. This is just how she looked, when Sister Catherine saw her."

I caught my breath. "What did the Blessed Mother say?"

"She told Sister Catherine that she had important work to do. She said it would be difficult, but Sister Catherine would have the graces she needed to carry it through."

"What's she standing on?"

"She's standing on the globe. Let this be a reminder, Irene. No matter where you go in the world, or what you face, there are graces that will see you through."

She took it from my hands and fastened it around my neck. I tucked my chin down, gazing at it against the gingham front of my dress, feeling stronger already.

When Sister Rosemary saw my medal, she knew it instantly. "Oh yes," she said. "You will be protected. The medal promises to protect everyone who wears it."

"It will?" This was a part of the story that Sister Margaret had not shared. "So nothing can hurt me?"

"Nothing at all," said Sister Rosemary, picking up a ball and tossing it back to the children on the other side of the playground.

I looked down at the medal as it glinted in the afternoon sun. It was more than a promise of grace, then. It was a magical shield in a fairy tale, even more powerful than Sister Margaret had said. I wondered why she had left that part—the best part—out of the story.

The nightmares, for what it's worth, never came back.

The first week in November, Pauline invited me to a rehearsal for *The Nutcracker.* "You can meet everyone at once that way. Like buffalo gathering around a watering hole."

The ballet studio was on Van Ness, not far from the Opera House where the company performed. Crossing the street, I gazed up at the ornate gold dome of nearby City Hall as it glinted in the autumn sunlight. There were temporary army barracks in the nearby square; the white tents looked humble beside such imposing buildings.

Pauline had told me to enter the studio and go upstairs, where I found her in an anteroom lined with chairs and sofas. She was in practice tights and a black tunic, chatting with two other girls who were similarly attired. "Irene!" she said joyfully as I entered. "Welcome to the ballet."

She introduced me to other members of the company. When they heard I was "the new Anna," as Pauline put it, they were full of praise. "We can't tell you how much we appreciate your help," said a young woman named Lois. "We'll have to sew our own costumes, and most of us don't know what on earth we're doing."

"And it must be so hard to find the material in wartime," I said.

"Yes, talk to Russell. Where is he? There he is." A tall fellow about my age was pulled forward and he shifted the apple he was eating so he could shake my hand. "Russell Hartley. He's designing the costumes. This is Irene Cleary, the seamstress I told you about."

"I was so glad to hear about your offer," he said. He had light brown hair and glasses and a friendly smile.

"I'm happy to help. It must be hard, designing costumes with all the wartime restrictions."

"A nightmare. For one thing, you can't buy more than ten yards of fabric at a time. This show has 143 costumes." At my expression he grinned. "Exactly. I'll have to send the dancers out individually to buy their own fabric."

"Wait till you see his designs," said Pauline to me. "He's really good, even if he was born yesterday."

"What's it like," I asked him, "coming up with costumes for a ballet?"

"This one's like starting from scratch. None of us have ever seen the ballet. Mr. C."—he pointed to a fortyish man with a receding hair-line, standing and chatting to someone by the door to the studio—"Willam has been talking to some of the Russian expats who remember it from way back when. But mostly, I'm just using my imagination."

The studio door opened, and a group of dancers filed into the anteroom, pink-faced and bringing with them an aura of sweat and satisfaction. "Our turn," said Pauline, adjusting her ponytail. "Irene, you can come in and watch."

It was a rehearsal for "Waltz of the Snowflakes." There was a Snow Queen, performed by a woman named Jocelyn, and a man named Joaquin was the Snow Prince. Willam demonstrated the choreography, and it was fascinating to watch the dancers stop and start, to see how abruptly they went from the graceful attitudes of ballet to the intent focus of the pupil. I'd seen dancing in the movies before, but never in person, and I marveled at how the women seemed to soar as they twirled and leapt before me.

Their clothes fascinated me too. "What are your tights made of?" I asked when rehearsal was over.

"Normally nylon, but it's wartime, so wool or cotton. We knit them ourselves if we need to," said Pauline.

A blonde dancer took a pair from her bag and held them out to me. "These are cotton ones. They sag so terribly you have to yank them up all the time."

I fingered the tights, surprised to feel hard disks in the waistband. "What are these?"

"Pennies. We sew them in so we have something to grab onto when they sag."

"That must make it hard to dance."

"I'll say," she said. "Just one more reason to wish the war would end."

It was dark by the time Pauline and I walked to the streetcar stop. There was the snap of fall in the air, and under the streetlights you could see the rusty brown city leaves about to surrender their grasp on the branches.

"When you dance," I asked Pauline, "are you yourself? Or are you playing a part?"

"It depends. Sometimes you have a role that's acting as much as dancing, like Clara. But when I'm something like a snowflake—that's different."

"I guess it's hard to act like a snowflake."

"I just think of what a snowflake is, how pure they are. Not pure like my mother uses the word, but pure because—well, because a snowflake is entirely what it is, you know?"

"I don't know. I've never actually seen snow."

"Really?" Pauline looked sympathetic. "That's too bad. It's one thing I miss a lot out here."

We walked on a bit in silence. I was about to make a comment about the stylish hat in a shop window we were passing when she spoke again.

"Here's the thing about snowflakes," she said. "They land on your coat, and you can see that they're more than just a little dot. There are actually tiny details, a little design. It's delicate and beautiful. Until it melts, which it always does." She tilted her face to the sky, her expression thoughtful. "So I guess that's what I think of as I dance. That it's something lovely that won't be around for long, but while it's here, it's the most beautiful thing you can imagine. And the world is somehow better because that little snowflake was in it."

TWENTY-FIVE

Max was in a mood. We'd been to the club to discuss the best colors for the carpets, then to a store where I chose the upholstery for the booths and barstools. The war limited our options, but there was a helpful clerk, and we came away with colors not far from my original idea. I did nearly all of the talking, in part because I was growing in confidence and in part because Max seemed miles away. "You all right?" I asked as we got back in the car.

"Fine." But if he could always see through my lies, I could see through his. As he turned to toss his hat on the seat behind him, his face had an expression I don't normally see: like a thundercloud, the novels would say. He accidentally clipped my shoulder as he turned back, and he apologized.

"I don't think you are fine," I ventured.

He started the car and didn't answer. The memory of Cynthia and Fred at the train station shot back into my mind. I looked at his big hands holding the steering wheel.

"Sorry," he said as we paused at a stop sign a few blocks later. "Just something I found out yesterday. I'm not myself."

"Is there anything I can do?"

He turned to look at me, searchingly. For a terrible moment I wondered if he was going to ask me about Cynthia and Fred, if I'd seen something between them in Atherton. If he did ask, I had no idea what I'd say. I could feel myself involuntarily shrinking back against the seat.

There was a honk behind us, and he glanced in the rearview mirror and started driving again. "Yes," he said at last. "You can do something. You can come with me to the beach."

I was relieved, then surprised, for it was nearly dusk. "Now?"

"You've got somewhere else to be?"

I didn't.

We parked by the Beach Chalet and walked out through a break in the low retaining wall dividing the sand from the road. Max leaned against it, and I did, too, wrapping my light coat more tightly around me. He lit a cigarette and in silence we watched the waves.

It was a different scene from the warm crowded beach weeks before, when I'd gone with Trixie and Louise. It was dusk, and only a few people were about, so there was nothing to distract my focus from the ocean, which crashed and thundered before us.

I stared at the horizon. If I got in a ship and sailed off, I would end up in the South Pacific, in names I knew from newspapers. Guadalcanal, the Solomon Islands. The Philippine Sea. Somewhere out there were tankers, airplanes, guns, explosions. The cold stung my eyes.

But there was no evidence of the war here at this beach on the edge of the city, just a straight line beyond which you couldn't see. And the ocean kept on crashing, as it always did and always would, no matter what sort of drama we humans would think to create.

I glanced at Max. He was standing and staring at the waves. The thundercloud had passed; he was not happy, but I could tell he was more like his usual self.

"I'll never get tired of this view," he said. His tone made me realize the subtext of the words.

"When did you first see the ocean?" I asked.

"When I was twenty-four. Not here, back East. I always wanted to see the ocean when I was a kid."

It was something I'd taken for granted, living by the coast. As limited as my orphanage childhood had been, I'd never had to wonder what the ocean smelled like or looked like. I told him so.

"You're lucky," he said. "As a kid I would've given anything for a glimpse of this. When Cynthia and I moved out here it was the first thing I wanted to see." He smiled briefly, almost bitterly, as if saying her name had reminded him of something he didn't want to recall. I waited for him to say more, but he didn't.

"That's how I am with snow," I said. "My whole life I've wanted to see it. Woods in snow." I beat back memories of Johnny, of the conversation in the boat. "Snowy woods."

It was nearly dark now, but I could tell he was looking at me from the angle of his glowing cigarette.

"That's funny," he said after a moment. "I guess snow is the thing I always took for granted."

I shivered and he noticed. "Are you cold?"

"Yes." Before I knew it, he'd whipped off his coat and was putting it around my shoulders. "No, Max, it's fine."

"Take it. It's the least I can do, hauling you out here in the dark."

It was so much heavier than my own coat, substantial and comforting, smelling like him. He turned up the collar around my ears, cigarette held between his lips, his hands brushing my hair. His movements were deft and yet gentle, just as they had been when he'd done up my buttons weeks earlier. When his eyes moved to mine and stayed there, I could feel myself blush.

He stepped away abruptly and I exhaled, which made me realize

I'd been holding my breath. I was warm all over, from my neck down to my feet. "Thank you," I said, feeling almost shy. I ventured a side-ways glance. "But won't you be cold now?"

He shook his head and dropped his cigarette into the sand. "Remember, Irene," he said quietly. "I'm from a place where it snows."

We stood side by side, facing the ocean as the waves broke on the sand. I think we were both aware that the mood had changed.

TWENTY-SIX

Mrs. Anderson, a longtime customer, came by the next morning for the final fitting on her new gray suit. I'd made it out of a suit belonging to her husband, which was pretty common in wartime. It was my third time making one and I had it down to a science, knowing exactly how to turn the pant legs into a neat, trim skirt.

Mrs. Anderson seemed a little apologetic about it all. "Tom will be surprised to come home and find he's missing a suit. But I haven't had new clothes in months."

"He'll probably be so happy to be home he won't care," I said.

I was adjusting something on the lapel when I saw the necklace she was wearing. It was a Miraculous Medal, small and silver, just like the one Sister Margaret had given me. I stared at it a moment too long.

"Is it all right?" She moved her hands to the collar. "Is this going to lie flat?"

"Yes," I said, collecting myself. "When I'm done you won't be able to tell this from any other suit."

"Oh good," she said. Then her face grew wistful. I put a few more pins in the jacket, and after a moment she spoke. "I'm almost glad I have to use his suit," she said with sudden emotion. "It makes him feel closer to me. Until he's back home." Her fingers moved to the medal, holding it, as if she were not even conscious of the gesture.

Our eyes met in the mirror, and I managed to smile. There was nothing I could say so I just turned back to the jacket, silently pinning, trying not to show how much that sight of that medal had affected me.

After Johnny and I finished our tea that night at my apartment, he washed the dishes and I dried. Then he reached into his pocket and pulled out a folded USO furlough guide, the one given to all servicemen on leave in the city. "So we've got till tomorrow morning," he said as we scanned the lists of restaurants, movie theaters, and local attractions. "Where should we go next?"

"What about the Top of the Mark?" I indicated a boxed advertisement. "It's the bar at the top of the Mark Hopkins Hotel."

"Some of the guys were mentioning that. Have you ever been?"

"No, never. I hear the views are amazing."

"Then it's a date," he said with a grin.

I went into the bedroom to renew my lipstick and put on a dress better suited to evening, a long-sleeved green one with a high scoop neck. On an impulse I reached into my jewelry box and took out the Miraculous Medal. Since leaving the orphanage, I no longer wore it every day, but every now and then I found myself drawn back to it. I slipped it underneath the neckline of the dress, where the tiny bit of metal felt cool against my skin.

We found a cab right on Fillmore. I almost never took taxis, and they were a novelty to me, but Johnny slid into the back as if he were right at home. We kissed the whole way there and didn't even notice we had stopped in front of the hotel until the driver said, "Meter's still running, sailor."

We scrambled out. With a sheepish grin, Johnny gave him the fare and a big tip. "Sorry, mister."

"No worries," said the taxi driver, his good humor restored. "Enjoy it while you're young."

The hotel elevator was small and packed. The middle-aged woman in front of us wore a hat with a huge dramatic feather curving down in back, and it kept brushing Johnny's nose and we both had to fight back giggles. She heard us and turned her head, which made the feather catch my nose, and at that he and I both burst out laughing.

"*Well*," she said, eyeing us coldly. From the way she turned and hiked her fur around her shoulders it was clear she thought we were laughing at her.

"Pardon us, ma'am," said Johnny. "We were just laughing because the feather was tickling my nose." I was impressed at how quickly he intuited her thoughts, and how graciously he apologized. She turned back with a visible thawing of her manner and even gave us a brief smile.

On the nineteenth floor, the elevator doors opened to a blast of conversation and laughter. It was an impressive place, with a huge oval bar in the center and small tables set up against the windows on every side. There was a sign saying that servicemen were seated first, but there were so many of them that the line stretched all the way back to the elevator. But being with Johnny, I didn't care how long we had to wait.

After half an hour, we were shown to a small round table with two upholstered chairs. Johnny moved them so they were side by side, and as he did, I took in the walls of windows all around us. Craning to look east, I saw Coit Tower, which seemed oddly tiny; then Alcatraz, a looming bulk in the middle of the black stretch of the bay; and then there were the streets sloping down to the piers; and then the view from our own table overlooking Nob Hill and Huntington Square Park, with a small sliver of the Golden Gate Bridge visible off in the distance. Johnny ordered cocktails and we just sat there, holding hands, my head resting on his shoulder, nothing between us and the city but the smooth wall of glass.

"What a view," said Johnny reverently.

"It's pretty, isn't it?" I felt proud of San Francisco, in a way I never had before. "It's like you could just reach out and pick up those buildings. Up here you forget how big they are."

"That's a good feeling sometimes. Feeling bigger than what's around you."

Next to us an officer and his girl were leaving. They held hands as they threaded their way soberly toward the elevator, and her eyes were glistening with tears. It was a reminder I didn't want to have. Johnny would soon be on a ship in the bay far down below us, sailing out the Golden Gate into a conflict so big it was being fought by the whole world. And yet without that conflict, we'd never have met. It was a wild snow globe, this war. It shook up everything and everyone, Ivy League men from one coast and orphan seamstresses from the other, until we finally settled next to each other in San Francisco on an evening in April.

I leaned my head on his shoulder, loving the way he immediately rested his head gently against mine. "One day," I said, "you can show me New York City. Does it have a place like this where we can admire the view?"

"You bet. There's a band too. We can go there and dance all night." He pressed a kiss to my hair. "And we can remember how we met on a dance floor. Or right next to one, anyhow."

"The place where it all began," I said dreamily.

"Maybe we can go dancing every April seventh. Every single year, for the rest of our lives. People will look at us and say, 'What great dancers they are.'"

It thrilled me, how easily he folded us into the future. "Even when we're old and gray? We'll still be dancing?"

"We'll hobble. People will look at us and say, 'What good hobblers they are.'"

We kissed for a few delicious minutes, until we were interrupted by the waiter offering us more drinks.

In the pause, I gazed out again at the view. Some lights were moving, some still: a city full of lives, full of stories. Our story, Johnny's and mine, was a part of it now.

"You know," he said when my head was back on his shoulder, "I always assumed I'd settle in New York. But I really love San Francisco. Dad wants me to work in his law firm, but I bet he'd come around."

I traced his fingers with mine, feeling suddenly nervous. "Will they like me? Your parents?"

"They'll love you."

"Even though"—I didn't want to say it—"even though I don't have a family?" He turned to look at me. "I don't think I'm part of your world, Johnny. Your family vacations in Europe, and I earn barely enough to pay the bills. Our lives are just—they're so different."

He kept looking at me. Then he turned his whole body, angling his chair toward me.

"Honestly," he said, "that never even occurred to me. Because that's not what matters."

I knew it did matter, to lots of people. But it was a relief to hear him say it out loud.

"Here's what does matter," he said. "That I saw you at the USO and I just knew that there was something about you. That you were going to be something to me that no other girl has been. And that I could fall in love with you." He reached for my hair, looking into my eyes. "And I have. I know it's fast, but I love you, Irene."

"I love you too," I said. I leaned into his hand, eyes closed because of the emotion I was feeling. When I opened them, he was so beautiful, gazing down at me, his brown eyes full of tenderness he didn't have any need to hide. And behind him the dark city glowed with a million lights, like stars.

"Heart and soul," he said softly. "Remember?"

"Heart and soul," I repeated, tracing his lips with my finger.

Nob Hill was quiet when we finally left the Top of the Mark. We walked down toward the bay, finding an all-night diner where we had flap-jacks and eggs at three in the morning, smiling and laughing over the coffee, and even without the coffee I would have been wide awake, because I was with Johnny and we only had a few more hours before he had to go.

We eventually found our way down to the waterfront, walking along the bay as the Italian fishing boats bobbed quietly and sleepily in the water. We sat and looked out over the bay and talked and kissed and planned the future and kissed some more. It was like a dream you don't want to wake out of, and then the fishermen came walking by, a few greeting us with knowing smiles, and one singing something beautiful and sad, his voice trailing off as he clomped along the boards of the wharf. Sea gulls made their high-pitched cries as the boats came to life and I saw the first flush of dawn off to the east, a pink tinge appearing suddenly over the hills and the water.

"I need to meet up with the other guys now," said Johnny. "So we can get back."

He gave me another kiss, a lingering one. I didn't want to let go of him. A fisherman in a nearby boat whistled at us approvingly.

"Let me get you a taxi, Irene," Johnny said. "So you can get safely home."

"I'll be fine, really."

We kissed again. I could feel my cheek already wet with my tears.

"I'll write to you," he said. "And I'm going to tell my parents all about you. Would it be strange if my mom wrote to you? She loves to write letters."

"I'd love it."

"And when this war is over, I'll come back. We'll pick up again, right here. Right where we're leaving off."

On an impulse I stepped back and unhooked the Miraculous Medal from around my neck. "Here," I said, holding it out to him. "I want you to take this. It's a medal the sisters gave me when I was a kid." He angled it to see the tiny figure embossed on the front. "It's supposed to protect everyone who wears it."

His face broke into a smile of recognition. "I've seen this before. My nanny had one. She used to wear it all the time."

"Now you have one too. To keep you safe."

He kissed his thanks for a long moment, then I helped him with the chain. I straightened the medal as it lay on his chest. It belonged there, a piece of my past going with the man who was my future. I was so glad I'd thought to give it to him.

"I almost feel like I shouldn't take it," he said. "I want you to be protected too, Irene. While I'm gone."

"I'll be fine. You need it more than I do."

And then I was crying in earnest, and he gathered me to him and held me. "I'll be back, Irene. And we'll go to New York. We'll go to the snow. We'll walk in the woods and you'll see it falling, just like you always wanted to."

A clock somewhere—the Ferry Building, maybe—began to strike. He bent down for one more kiss. "I love you, Irene."

"I love you, Johnny."

He let go of me at the last possible minute and then turned and walked briskly away. I stood there, watching him through blurry eyes, tears coursing down my cheeks. He turned once and raised his arm, and I blew him a kiss, blinking hard to get one more look at his beautiful smile before he turned away and drew a hand quickly over his eyes. Then he put both hands in his pockets and hurried around the corner into the dawn.

TWENTY-SEVEN

The Monday after my beach visit with Max, Trixie and I went to the USO. I didn't have coffee duty, which meant I was free to play ping-pong, to dance, to sing around the red piano played by an enthusiastic airman. I did all three, but my mind was elsewhere.

The guys there seemed unbelievably young. In reality, they were around my age, but somehow I felt as if I had moved far beyond them. And I realized, as I stood in line for the ladies' room, that it was because of Max.

"You okay?" Trixie broke me out of my reverie.

"Fine. Just off in dreamland."

"Have you talked to Louise lately? I've been so busy with school, I've been a hermit."

"Not for a while." I had an unpleasant feeling of concealment, remembering what Louise had told me last time we'd spoken. "Maybe we can all go out this weekend."

"By the way, Mama called this morning. You're invited for Christmas."

"To Minnesota?"

"I know it's a huge trip and hard to make. But if you can come with me, it would be so much fun."

"Gosh." I was touched. "That's so nice of her." It shouldn't have been a surprise; since leaving the orphanage, I'd spent most holidays with the Dubuques. But it was hard to imagine traveling that far, taking that much time away from my work. "I don't think I can. I'd have to close up shop for a while."

"But I hate to think of you alone on Christmas."

I found myself wondering what the Burkes would be doing. I imagined the Atherton house, decorated with trees and swags of greenery on the banister. It was easy to imagine the McNeils and neighbors sipping eggnog in the library by a roaring fire, much harder to picture Max there with them.

"I won't be alone," I said. "There's the ballet, remember. Their first performance is on Christmas Eve."

"Oh, that's right." She looked happier. "I'm glad you'll have something to do. Well, I'll tell Mama that maybe you can come next year."

Twelve years, Trixie and I had known each other. I was suddenly swept with a wave of gratitude for her friendship. "Hopefully I can join you next year. I'll write to your mother and thank her."

"We'll miss you. And I thought"—she dropped her voice—"well, given everything with Johnny, that you might want a distraction. On Christmas, you know."

We were at the ladies' room now, so there was no time to do anything but say thank you and slip inside.

It hadn't taken long for me to tell my friends about Johnny. The very day after he and I said goodbye at the wharf, Trixie and Louise and I went to J. C. Penney to shop for brassieres, and there, against the incongruous backdrop of girdles and slips, I eagerly told them all about meeting my prince charming.

"He sounds dreamy," said Louise. "A Princeton boy. Pity he's blond, though. I don't like blond men."

"You'd like him," I said, riding a cloud of romantic bliss. "He's the handsomest man I've ever seen."

"Sounds like he said all the right things," said Louise, picking up a satin robe.

The comment stung. "He wasn't just saying them. He meant them."

"Oh, I know," she said.

Trixie gazed at me with wonder. "I can't believe it. You've really fallen in love."

"I have. Isn't it amazing?"

"Well, it's fast. I mean, you hear about wartime romances, but you don't expect it to happen outside the movies."

"I'd never have expected it either. It's just—I don't know, I just knew. We both just knew." I struggled to put it into words, the certainty that Johnny and I had felt. "He talked about the future. He's going to tell his parents about me."

Trixie whistled. "That's serious then."

Louise emerged from behind a rack of clothes holding a long blue satin nightgown, slinky and low-cut. "Buy this. Take a picture of yourself wearing it and send it to him. Give him something to look forward to."

I laughed as she held it up to herself in front of the mirror. "Don't they have people who open and read their mail?"

"Even better. Think of all the sailors you can make happy that way."

"It's all so amazing, Irenc," said Trixie. "I wish I'd been at the USO on Friday, so I could have met him."

"It's fast, I know." Somehow Trixie's approval meant more to me than Louise's.

She shrugged. "Not every relationship is like me and Dennis. You know what my dad says, right? That he wanted to marry Mother the first day they met. I always thought that was so romantic."

It was thrilling to think that I now had a romantic story of my own. One day Johnny and I would tell our children about locking eyes across the USO in wartime. "Sometimes," he would say to them, "you just know."

"As a bridesmaid-to-be," said Trixie, bringing me back to the present, "I'm happy to wear any color but pink. Take note, please."

"It's a deal," I said joyfully.

A saleswoman approached, with an air of imposing efficiency. "May I help you?" she asked. I handed her the brassieres I was holding, and she sailed in the direction of the fitting room. I was just about to follow when I felt something being pressed into my hand. Trixie and Louise, both grinning, were handing me a nightgown of almost-sheer white chiffon.

"You'll need this, too," said Louise with a wink.

As November rolled along, my work for the ballet began in earnest. I loved being part of it. Russell showed me the designs he had painted: a short white tutu with a blue bodice for the Snow Queen, a green empire-waisted ballgown for a party guest, and a muscular gray Mouse King costume with a high crown. Designing for the ballet was unlike designing regular clothes, I realized; it required both whimsy and knowledge of how the dancers would move on stage.

Rationing restrictions meant that the dancers each had to buy their own material, but once they had, the fun began. A few of them could sew or had mothers who did, but the others relied on Inez, the company seamstress, and me. I opened the shop in the evenings and the dancers came by and we worked on the costumes, clouds of tulle and net running through the solid machinery of Anna's Singer.

As we worked, the dancers talked about past productions, current rehearsals, love and war. I learned which girls had brothers or sweethearts overseas and about the struggles to keep the company going with so many of the male members at war. "You know what Mr. C. did?" said Evelyn. "He went to high school football practices and asked the players if they wanted to spend time around girls. And that's how he recruited guys for the production."

"Clever man," I said. "Can they dance?"

"We don't give them the actual dancing parts," said Pauline. "They just have to be able to move without knocking over the scenery."

At times we'd take breaks and have tea, coffee, or Coca-Cola. I'd put on the radio and sometimes the girls would dance to whatever was on: the King Cole Trio, Bing Crosby, the Andrews Sisters. It always astonished me how effortlessly they could move to any sort of music, improvising on the spot. I loved watching them.

I learned that Russell was not just the designer for the ballet but also a character dancer who was playing several roles, including someone called Mother Buffoon. "That dress will be a challenge," he told me when I stopped by the studio with my first finished costumes.

"Who's Mother Buffoon?"

"A mother with a bunch of kids living under her skirt. They come dancing out." He showed me the design; the tentlike dress seemed as much an engineering project as a dressmaking one.

"I grew up in an orphanage," I told him. "The nuns had these big black skirts. When I was very small I used to imagine I could crawl under them and hide." The moment I said it I was surprised at myself; I normally didn't reveal my orphan childhood so casually. Maybe I was feeling more comfortable in my own past. Maybe I was finally becoming *bien dans ma peau*.

My musing was broken by Russell's laugh. "Did you ever try?"

"Never." I grinned. "Just one of life's regrets."

TWENTY-EIGHT

On a relentlessly rainy Thursday, Trixie called just as I was closing up shop. "I got a letter from Dennis," she said breathlessly. "Finally."

"Good news?"

"He sounds the same as ever. Did I just imagine it? I don't know. The war really messes with your mind. Oh, and I have sad news. Sister Rosemary died."

"What? When?"

"Two weeks ago. I think she'd been sick for a while."

"I wish I'd known," I said slowly. I hadn't seen any of the sisters since graduating and moving out of the orphanage. I'd always meant to go back and say hello, but I never had.

"We missed the funeral, too. It was last week."

"Where did you hear all this?"

"From Joan Fallon, down the hall. Her uncle is the pastor at St. Elizabeth's. It's sad, isn't it? Sister was always so kind."

After hanging up I stood in the silent shop, looking out at the street. There were lights on in windows across the way, the cozy witness of people at home on a damp November night, their apartments and houses little bulwarks against the darkness.

I cried for Sister Rosemary, who had been so much a part of my childhood. I remembered her overlapping teeth, her bright eyes, the way she would join in the kids' games on the playground outside the orphanage. She ran in such a funny way, leaning forward at the waist as if leading with her head like a small bull, and the kids would squeal with delight every time. It was Sister Rosemary who had been there when I was dropped off as a newborn and could tell me how much I had been loved. Because of her I'd grown up with a confidence I probably otherwise wouldn't have had.

If only I had asked her more about my past. But I never had, for it seemed there was plenty of time for that. You always think you'll have more time.

I kept staring out at the street, at the lights making haloes on the wet black pavement. Behind me the radio was still going. It was the Hour of Charm, the orchestra coming to me live from a place far away. I was glad for its catchy beat, the deep-toned announcer, and for the applause from whichever audience was hearing it in whichever city, for they were signs of life, and all I could think of in that quiet, dark shop was the opposite.

Three days after Johnny and I said goodbye, I wrote to him. I've never been a great letter writer, maybe because I've never had many people to write to. But sitting at my table where we'd had dinner, looking at the same couch where we'd kissed and talked about the future, the letter seemed to write itself. I told him more about myself, the things we hadn't had time to share. I didn't send a picture of myself in revealing clothing, as Louise had suggested, but I revealed myself in another way by sharing my hopes and dreams and my fondest memories of our time together.

I signed it, *With my heart and soul, Irene.*

Weeks passed, and there was no response. I wasn't alarmed; of course mail going overseas would be slow. I wrote again, sharing all the little nothings I'd have said if he were with me in person. "When I was on Fillmore today, I saw a gray-haired couple holding hands. Do you think they were on their way to the ballroom for some hobbling? That'll be us one day." As before I signed it: *With my heart and soul, Irene.*

"How long does it take you to hear back from Dennis?" I asked Trixie.

"It varies," she said. "I'll hear nothing, and then a few letters come at once. Faye Hilliard's boyfriend is in the Pacific, and she said it took three weeks before she heard anything at all."

I wrote two more letters, four total. No response. The days were longer now, and summer was upon us: a San Francisco summer, meaning banked fog and overcast most days.

Did I worry? No, for I was totally confident in what Johnny and I had. There was a day when Louise asked if I'd received a letter and I said no, not yet, and the look on her face was transparent as glass, pity and cynicism mixed together. *It's not like that*, I mentally argued with her as I returned home from her flat. *Johnny and I love each other. This wasn't just one weekend in wartime.*

I tried to picture his face as my steps took me down Jackson Street, past Victorian houses with bay windows and stunted sidewalk trees. I had no photo of him; we'd been so focused on talking and kissing we'd hadn't thought to step into a booth and take one. It was my one regret from the weekend. As I stood on the corner waiting to cross, I closed my eyes, trying my hardest to conjure him up again: the blond hair, the brown eyes, the slow smile. His face was less clear than I wanted it to be, so I thought of the feel of him, the way he'd held my hands and framed my face and kissed me on the carousel and in the park and in my apartment and at the Top of the Mark and so many places around the city, little holy spots to me, sacred ones. They were all I had of him, these memories.

But he had my medal.

I opened my eyes. Before me, Fillmore Street was its usual bustle of cars and taxis and pedestrians. Johnny had been here; he could picture me in my home and workplace, could visualize exactly what I might be doing at any moment of the day or night. He had the advantage over me, for I could only imagine him in a setting I'd cobbled together from newsreels and movies. Sometimes I pictured him in a hut of some kind under palm trees; sometimes he was lining up for dinner with other men in navy uniforms; sometimes he was on the deck of a huge ship, doing something with rope, the vast blue sea stretching miles around him.

But wherever he was, whatever he was doing, he was wearing my medal. And that made me glad.

It was good I didn't open the mail right away that day in early July. It came while I was with a customer, so I set it aside and forgot about it, only picking it up again after I'd closed up the shop. Among the bills was a letter addressed in an unfamiliar script, with a New York postmark. The reverse side of the envelope was engraved with the name and address of Mrs. Ronald Pendleton.

I looked wildly for the letter opener, my mouth breaking into a grin. "My mother will want to write to you," he'd said, and here it was, the first bit of contact from my future mother-in-law. *I'll have a mother*, I found myself thinking as I finally found the letter opener and clumsily slit open the envelope.

The letter was on monogrammed stationery.

Dear Miss Cleary,

I'm Althea Pendleton, the mother of Johnny. I am writing with the sad news that Johnny was killed in action three weeks ago in the Philippine Sea. We received a telegram and a letter from the war office. He was killed instantly by a bomb blast and buried at sea.

Our grief is beyond words. The knowledge that he gave his life for such a good cause is some small comfort, but the loss is a devastating one. It is a terrible thing to lose a child.

We have received Johnny's things, and I am writing to those who sent him letters. He was a man who made many friends, and I feel it is important to reach out to all who knew him. I am so terribly sorry that you have to receive this letter and to find out in this way. I am so terribly sorry that he is gone. I hope you will pray for us, as we mourn the loss of a son and brother who has been a part of our lives for nearly twenty-one years. May God bless you and may He bless this country and our world.

Sincerely yours,

Althea Pendleton

Shock comes first, before the grief. It feels like everything is cold, like your mind doesn't work right, like something is sitting on your chest. I read the letter a second time, and this time I noticed things, like the fact that Mrs. Pendleton's penmanship grew shaky toward the end of the second paragraph. "It is a terrible thing to lose a child," she had written, and the period was large and blurry, as if the pen had rested there for a while, and I could see a woman sitting at a desk in a library, holding back tears, writing this sentence that she could barely stand to think let alone communicate to others.

I threw myself on the chair and cried in a way I had never cried before.

Trixie was a rock. She came over and made me toast and tea and soup. She called my appointments for the next two days and rescheduled them as I lay on the narrow bed with the busted spring, staring unseeing at the wall.

It had touched me, the war, in a way that was more than blackouts and rationing. It had stretched its tentacles and latched onto my limbs like some awful creature, trapping me, keeping me in bed. I wanted to sleep, for it was my only refuge, but I always had to wake up, and through the open door I could see the corner of the couch where Johnny and I had kissed and taken such delight in each other. The sailor I loved: He was nothing anymore, bits maybe, buried at sea. How much of him had been left after the bomb hit? I remembered reading *The Tempest* in high school, having to memorize Ariel's song. "Full fathom five thy father lies; / Of his bones are coral made; / Those are pearls that were his eyes." Johnny was on the ocean floor, fish swimming past him, his blond hair waving like seaweed. That body I had loved and could have loved even more fully was broken and dissolving, coral for bone, pearls for eyes. The navy uniform would dissolve, too, until there was nothing left.

The medal would stay, though. It would last longer than anything else. The thought of it made me angry, which was an almost blessed reprieve from grief.

The third day I got up, bathed, and washed my hair. Trixie had to go to class but promised to come in with dinner and my favorite cannoli. I sat in the living room in a chair pulled to the window and stared outside. I didn't put the radio on and occasionally sounds from the outside world penetrated my consciousness: a truck backing up, laughter from two children on the sidewalk below, the blare of a horn. People were going about their daily lives, as I would have to myself.

Johnny would become nothing more than a figure from my past. And I had been so sure that he would come back.

Why had I been so sure? Because of fairy tales, and saints' stories, and some naive belief that life favored the good and promises would be kept. Sister Rosemary had been so confident about the little medal around my neck. "It protects those who wear it," she had said, but it hadn't; it had done nothing of the kind. Johnny had been killed, and left behind was a devastated mother in New York and a girl in San Francisco who felt as if her insides had been hollowed out.

It was one o'clock and there was sun in part of the city. Looking toward the west I could see a line, a distinct one, where the fog still lingered. It made no sense to me that I was in the sunny half of the sky.

When Trixie came, she had a small pink box from Lucetti's. "How are you today?" she asked, passing me a cannoli.

"I'm out of bed. I guess that's something." We ate for a moment in silence, her chair pulled next to the window near mine.

"My parents are so sorry. Mama is praying for you and for Johnny's family. She said for you to call if you want to talk to her."

It was nice of her, but I didn't. Not yet. And I wasn't sure what good prayers would do, for mine hadn't done anything to protect Johnny. I couldn't eat any more of the cannoli; it was too sweet for someone steeped in grief.

"I wish I'd slept with him," I said suddenly.

"What?" Trixie looked up from her plate.

"I wish I'd slept with him. I almost did. But then we decided to wait." There was nothing left now of the body that had lain pressed against mine. I had lost my chance to know him completely.

"Don't you think"—I knew Trixie wanted to say the right thing—"don't you think you would have felt worse if you had? I mean, if he'd died, and you—well, you knew what you were missing?" She shook her head in exasperation at herself. "I'm not making sense."

"What's worse, knowing or never knowing?"

"I don't know," she said slowly.

I turned back to the window. The sky was so blue: a brilliant, hard, almost metallic blue.

Around his neck I had put the medal. It had not been miraculous at all. It was just a little piece of stamped tin, worthless, lying at the bottom of the Pacific Ocean.

Life went on, because it had to. The fourth day I opened the shop to customers. It was good to have something to do with my hands, to busy my mind. A few days later I felt well enough to go out with Trixie and Louise. We went to the movies, a comedy, and I even laughed. Two sailors sat in front of us and Trixie, seeing them come in, squeezed my hand in support.

After Trixie had left to catch her streetcar, Louise and I walked along Geary Street. It was a lovely evening; July, as usual, was proving to be both warmer and brighter than June. We passed the Russian church with its beautiful golden domes, making me think of Anna. I thought of how strange it was that within the space of eight months two people close to me had died, for there were very few people who were actually close to me.

Three officers were coming toward us, impressive in their uniforms. They grinned at us, and one touched his hat. "Ladies," he said, eyes on Louise appreciatively.

"Good evening," she said demurely as we passed them.

"Should I turn around to see if they're looking at us?" she whispered to me a moment later.

"If you want to."

She did and turned back with a grin. "The short one was. He was cute." Perhaps out of respect for my loss, she didn't say anything about circling back to approach them, although I knew she would have liked to.

"I'm never going to fall in love again," I said bluntly. "Johnny was enough for me."

Louise gave a shrug. "You can't think of him forever, Irene. I know it hurts," she added, clearly aware of how callous she had sounded. "But life goes on. Someday you'll meet another man."

"I don't think so."

"It sounds heartless, I know. But really, would it have worked out with him anyhow?"

I stopped right in the middle of the sidewalk. "What do you mean?"

"Well . . ." She stood framed by a bakery window, biting her lip. ". . . I wasn't going to say this before, but honestly, Irene, how many of these wartime romances actually last?"

"Ours would have."

"Maybe. But a guy from Princeton, parents with a house near Central Park? My mom's from New York, Irene. You think rich people here are snooty, you have no idea what they're like there. It's like that Edith Wharton novel we had to read in school. They don't like outsiders."

"Outsiders like me, you mean," I said slowly.

"Well, you are, aren't you? You didn't grow up on Fifth Avenue and spend your winters skiing upstate and go to Smith or Vassar. I'm not saying it's right, Irene, but it's how they are. My grandmother is the same way. It's all about who your family is."

"Your mother married an outsider."

"Sure, and my grandparents fought it at first. But Dad's family has a house in the sixteenth arrondissement and a château in Normandy. If he were just some random Frenchman, they'd never have consented."

A random orphan, of course, would never have stood a chance. No house in Paris, no château, no family, no name except the one that the Daughters of Charity had given me. Freckled and working for a living, scraping together just enough money to buy iris flowers for the shop.

I must have been staring at her, for she looked abashed. "I'm sorry, Irene. It's just something that I've been thinking. Shall we?"

We started walking again. I stared unseeing at the busy street ahead of us, my mind stretching to accommodate what she'd said.

"Wartime is strange," said Louise. "Nothing is really normal, is it? But what happens right now is separate from real life. When the war's over we'll go back to how things always were. And maybe it'll help you get over him if you think about it that way."

When I got back home I reread Mrs. Pendleton's letter. I lingered again on a line in the third paragraph: "He was a man who made so many friends." Like an archaeologist with a cipher, I tried to decode her words. Could it be her polite, upper-class way of letting me know I didn't mean as much to him as I had thought? Or that even if I had, she would never have accepted me? Was it her way of keeping me from writing back, as a prospective fiancée would do?

Johnny had said he would tell his family about me. If he had, you'd never know it from his mother's letter. "He was a man who made so many friends." Maybe he had a girl in every port, and I'd been too blind to see it. But no—I closed my eyes and, wrenching as it was, remembered him in Golden Gate Park, in my apartment, at the Top of the Mark—no, I had believed him when he said I was special, and that we had a future together. I still believed him.

But Louise's words were a wedge, a blade prying open the door to the fear that had always been there in my mind. I did not belong in

Johnny's world. If his mother had his letters, then she'd read the things I'd written to him: my dreams for the future, my comments about the elderly couple who would one day be us. I felt sick. She had read my letters, and yet she'd said nothing about them. She had written the same thing to me that she had written to everyone else.

Night was falling. I sat in the gloom and looked around my apartment: at the worn rug on the floor, the mismatched furniture, the small single bed with the sagging spring. I'd done well for myself, as orphans go, but orphans operated on an entirely different plane from people like the Pendletons. My parents had loved me, but they were nameless, faceless, and dead; and I was, in the world of genteel society, an outsider.

And Johnny had never written back to me. Maybe the hesitation I'd shared at the Top of the Mark had echoed in his mind on long days at sea. He'd had time to stare at the horizon and think, time to realize just how ill-suited someone like me was for the life he would return to once the war was over. A weekend was one thing; a lifetime was another.

And then he hadn't returned at all. *Of his bones are coral made.*

I could feel grief starting to threaten me again, the specter of more days spent in bed staring at the wall. I could not let that happen, not when I had just begun to work again, earning money I needed to pay the gas and water bills. I folded his mother's letter and put it in the cabinet under the record player.

Mrs. Pendleton and Louise had made me see the truth. No matter what Johnny and I had felt for one weekend in wartime, our love would never have worked in any other context. Closing the cabinet door with a bang, I was angry at my own naïveté, at the fairy tales of my childhood, and at the belief that a silly medal would guarantee a happy ending. That anger was a flame that I did nothing to extinguish. I let it burn, small but steady, a pilot light that distracted me from pain.

You do that, with grief. You find the thing that hurts less, and you fixate on that instead.

July and August passed as I distracted myself with work, the USO when I could bear it, and outings with Trixie and Louise. I forced myself to go to the beach on a sunny Sunday in August, to look out over the churning ocean. The first time there would be the hardest, I knew, and I made myself do it so I could go back again in relative peace. Whenever Johnny's smile flashed upon my inward eye, I thought about his mother's letter, her polite distance, the harsh but realistic words of Louise. Our love would never have lasted in the real world. Only a fool would believe that it could.

And in September, when that first request came from Cynthia Burke, I was ready for it. If she'd called two months before, in the first raw throes of my loss, I'd never have been able to accept her commission. But when she did call, I was basically myself again, efficient and competent. I was hungry for a challenge, ready to be absorbed by her gown and her glamorous life.

And—this is the part I'd never have expected—by her marriage too.

TWENTY-NINE

Max didn't call me for a week after our visit to the beach, which was just as well; with the holidays approaching, it was a busy time. A society woman all in furs, a referral from Cynthia's mother, had commissioned me to make an entire wardrobe for the doll she was giving her daughter for Christmas, and it was one of the most enjoyable jobs I'd ever had. Mrs. Milton was delighted with the finished product—I'd even made a red skating outfit and a tiny WAVES uniform—and kept saying how clever I was. "This place is lovely," she said, looking approvingly around the shop, making me extra glad I'd whisked the empty mousetrap out of sight. "I'm so happy I've found you."

I happened to be out when Max did call, on a date with a marine I'd met at the drugstore. He was a pleasant fellow, Albert from New Hampshire, and when he invited me to go dancing that evening, I was happy to accept. He was one of those whip-smart fellows who make you wish you'd studied harder in high school, but we had a nice time. When we said goodbye he kissed me lightly on the lips, the first kiss since Johnny. As I opened my door and let myself inside the quiet shop, I was glad, as if it were one more way in which Johnny's ghost could be exorcised. It had been good to have a casual, undemanding date for an evening. As I took off my nylons, I thought wryly that if I were Louise, I'd have invited him upstairs.

Max called me the next day. "I want you to see something," he said. "Something I found at a bar. How about tonight?"

He picked me up at seven and drove below the Panhandle, parking on Clayton Street. "Where are we going?" I asked as we walked down Haight.

"The Persian Aub Zam Zam." He indicated a small facade, nestled in between a hardware store and a butcher shop. It reminded me of pictures I'd seen of Morocco, with its plaster front and narrow window and two thin cylindrical minarets sprouting incongruously out of the roof like mushrooms. "The name means 'Persian oasis.'" He held open the door.

The nightclub was busy and dimly lit, with exotically curved archways and a huge bar. It reminded me of Humphrey Bogart's nightclub from *Casablanca*, on a much smaller scale. We sat down on barstools, and as I looked up I exclaimed in delight at the mural before me: a huge painting showing a woman with long black hair sitting on the bank of a river, in a stylized landscape of forest and rabbits and a dashing man on a white steed. "That's beautiful."

"Nice, isn't it." He lifted his chin at the bartender as he approached. "How are you? A martini for me and one for the lady."

"I'll just have coffee," I told the bartender.

"No," said Max. "You will not have coffee."

"But I have an early appointment tomorrow."

"You're trying a martini. This place is famous for them. If you don't like it, you don't have to finish." The waiter looked to me for confirmation, and I raised my eyebrows in exasperated surrender. He grinned and reached for two glasses.

"I actually called last night to see if you were free," said Max, lighting a cigarette. "But I guess you were out."

"I had a date."

"Someone special?"

"Just a marine I met at the drugstore. We went to the Avalon." He was studying me as if waiting for me to say more. "It was nothing, just a nice time with a guy I'll never see again."

"He treated you well, I hope."

I was surprised. "Of course."

He exhaled a thread of smoke and reached for the ashtray. "I bet you get lots of invitations from servicemen."

"Not so much."

"With all the guys on leave in this town? You're joking."

"There was one, a few months ago. We were—well, serious. But not anymore."

I kept my eyes on the polished bar, bracing myself for the inevitable question: *What happened?* It never came. After a moment I looked up, and he indicated the mural. "So you like this."

"Yes, very much. It reminds me of *The Arabian Nights* stories."

"I was thinking we could put a mural behind the bar. Our bar. It could go the whole length of the front room, show the city's neighborhoods and sights. How does that sound?"

I turned to him in surprise and delight. "Max, that's a brilliant idea. Absolutely brilliant. We can work in so many landmarks that way."

He grinned. "I thought you might like it." He pulled out his pad of paper, and we sat there and brainstormed ideas of what to include: Coit Tower, the Cliff House, Lombard Street, cable cars, the Ferry Building. We could have gone on, but the martinis arrived. I picked up the glass with some trepidation; I'd never had one before.

"Tell me what you think," said Max.

I took a sip. "It's good," I said cautiously.

"You don't like it."

"It's—well, I just didn't know what to expect. I'm still a novice drinker."

"Fair enough." He watched me as I raised the glass to my lips again. I tilted it slowly, looking back at him over the rim. His eyes were lit with curiosity and—I became suddenly, unmistakably aware—with something more besides.

Liquid suddenly coursed down my front, shocking me. "Oh, gosh," I said, putting down the glass.

Max reached into his breast pocket and handed me a handkerchief. "It's clean," he said.

I dabbed at my blouse, glad that the dim light hid my burning cheeks. When I glanced up he was watching me, still with the same expression in his eyes. I had not imagined it. He looked down at his cigarette.

"Very sophisticated," I said when I could control my voice. "I'm not fit to be out in public."

"You're not used to the shape of the glass. It happens. I think the ladies' room is through there."

"I'm fine. And at least it's clear."

He caught the bartender's eye. "A coffee, please."

I indicated my glass. "Do you want the rest?"

"I stop at one, remember."

"Why?"

He stubbed out the cigarette, and I admired the line of his jaw, under the five o'clock shadow. *How on earth*, I wondered, *could Cynthia choose Fred Gibson over him?*

"Because of my mother," he said. "And because there's nothing more dangerous than a bar owner who doesn't know when to stop." He reached for the pad, brushing my arm as he did so. "Sorry," he said, glancing at me. "Are there any parts of the city we've missed?"

With effort I pulled my focus back to the list, studying it in the dim light of the bar. "Probably. There are so many places we could include."

"What about where you grew up?" he asked. "Mount St. Joseph, right?"

"How did you know the name?"

"You told me once. What part of the city is that?"

I hardly remembered having told him. "It's to the south. The bay side of the city, not the ocean side. The orphanage was a big place, brick, with lots of windows. The Daughters of Charity ran it. There were about eighty orphans living there."

"They treated you well?"

"Yes, of course. Some of the sisters were strict, but mostly they were kind and loving. The food wasn't fancy or anything, but we were never hungry." The waiter set down the coffee. "One of the sisters just passed away, actually. I should go back for a visit sometime."

"I'm glad you were happy there," said Max. "I guess that's where you got your confidence."

I didn't always think of myself as confident, but I felt a glow that Max did. I sat up a little straighter on the barstool. "What about you," I said. "Where did your confidence come from?"

He looked surprised at my question, then turned and gazed at the mural behind the bar as if thinking seriously about the answer. I warmed my hands on the cup, watching his profile. At last he turned to me with a smile I couldn't quite read.

"From sheer force of will, Irene," he said.

THIRTY

It's always odd going back to a place you haven't been in years, and as I approached Mount St. Joseph I was heartened to see that it looked the same as ever. The big brick building sat comfortably on its knoll, and there was still the same statue of Mary in the little niche by the front door. Inside was the same echoing foyer with its highly polished tile floor, an entrance that should have been forbidding and yet somehow was not.

I hadn't let anyone know I was coming, and the sisters were surprised and delighted to see me. A few of the children recognized me and smiled shyly or came running up eagerly, depending on their personalities. Danny Gaddini tackled me with a huge hug around my middle, almost knocking me off my feet.

It was strange not seeing Sister Rosemary there. When I said that to Sister Margaret she nodded, a shadow passing over her face. "We feel her absence so strongly. It's been very hard for the children, of course."

"I wish I'd seen her again. I wish I'd come back to visit before . . . the end."

"She knew you loved her, Irene." Sister looked at my coat and hat admiringly. "How stylish you are. Do you have time to visit? Come into my office."

We sat down to tea and bread and butter. "It's providential, you stopping by," she said. "Just yesterday Mrs. Norris donated some bolts of fabric. I was going to call your shop to see if you'd have time to make dresses for the older girls."

"I'd be happy to," I said and meant it. At the orphanage, you generally wore whichever clothes your peers had outgrown; at thirteen, I'd have been thrilled to wear dresses made by someone with an eye for style. "Once I have their sizes, I'll get right to work."

It was peculiar but nice to be in Sister's office as a grown-up visitor. Instead of sitting with the big desk between us, we were in the two small upholstered chairs by the door, angled toward each other for conversation. As a child you knew never to sit in those chairs; I felt almost like visiting royalty.

"We've been blessed with donations recently," said Sister, putting down her teacup. "Not just the fabric. Yesterday we received a check for one thousand dollars."

"My goodness," I said. "What generous trustees."

"This wasn't a trustee, or anyone connected with the orphanage. It was a Mr. Max Burke." Color flooded my face. Sister's expression changed. "Do you know him? I believe he does something with bars and restaurants."

"I do," I said, trying to control my voice. "I made a dress for his wife. And he—I've been helping him with the design of a nightclub he's opening."

"You must have mentioned our name to him at some point."

"I did. He didn't say anything about donating money. I'm surprised."

Sister looked at me with that keen yet gentle way she had. "That solves the mystery," she said at last. "We're so grateful for the money. It means we can repair the radiators in the dormitories. You know how loud they always were."

"I wonder why he didn't tell me," I said, more to myself.

"Many donors like to be anonymous," said Sister. "But tell me more about your business. How is the shop?"

I filled her in, glad to talk about something other than Max.

"I'm not surprised your business is doing well, Irene," said Sister. "I remember you with your paper dolls. Sometimes it's easy to tell in childhood what a person will do as an adult."

It was heartening to be with someone who remembered my early years, who could think back on them fondly. I smiled at her across the teacups, emboldened by the setting to ask her a more personal question than I'd ever have asked before. "What about you, Sister? Did you always want to be a nun, when you were a child?"

She raised an eyebrow at first, as if acknowledging that my question heralded a new tone in our interactions, then smiled. "Actually, no," she said, with the air of sharing something she hadn't expected to share. "When I was a child I wanted to be a writer."

"Really?"

"I wanted to do that for—oh, for quite a while. Until I was twenty or so."

"What happened to change your mind?"

"Life happened," she said simply. "Sometimes we are taken in directions we never knew we would go."

It was the first time I'd ever thought of the sisters as having been my age. They always seemed to have been born as adults, coming into the world already habited in black and white. Sipping the last of my tea, I wondered if this was how it was with girls who had parents. Maybe there came a day where you looked at them in a new light, not as Mother and Father but as people who had once been your own age, who had dreamed and planned and lived all the questions you were living yourself.

"Sister Margaret," I said, putting down my cup, "I wish I'd asked Sister Rosemary more about my parents. I know almost nothing about them."

"That's a natural thing to wonder."

"Is there any way to find out? Maybe she told you something about that morning I was brought here?"

Before she could answer there was a knocking on the open door, and the round face of Sister Bernice appeared. "I'm sorry to interrupt," she said, "but the fire inspector is here."

Sister Margaret thanked her and rose. "It's the yearly inspection. I only need to get him started, and then I'll come back. Are you free to wait, Irene?" I nodded. "Good," she said and disappeared out the door, the cloth of her habit swishing against the wooden doorframe.

Alone, I settled back in the chair, surveying the room I remembered from childhood. Its most dominant feature was the stained glass window behind the desk, tall and rectangular, with bands of color around the edges and the Immaculate Heart of Mary in the center. I knew it was Mary's heart and not Jesus's heart because of the wreath of flowers around it. A sword pierced it at an angle, running in and then back out.

From outside came the muffled shouts of children playing in the yard behind the office. Down the hall I could hear a door closing, then the small high voice of a child and the soothing tones of a sister. My gaze drifted to various things: the glossy houseplant on the bookshelf, the archdiocesan calendar with a picture of the grotto at Lourdes, the empty coat rack, the straight dignity of Sister's wooden desk chair, the wooden file cabinets beyond.

The file cabinets.

What I did next I'd never have dreamed of doing as a child. But I was twenty, an adult visitor; I'd just sat and had tea, talking with Sister almost as equals. She knew I wanted to learn more about my past. Curiosity triumphed over protocol.

The top drawer of the file cabinet was heavy yet glided smoothly. As I'd guessed, it contained records of the orphans, filed by last name. I couldn't find my own, so I tried the second file cabinet. There it was:

a brown folder with *Cleary, Irene Mary* written in beautiful Palmer handwriting.

I took it out, my heart pounding. There were medical records, school reports, and the letter from Mrs. Detweiler announcing my scholarship. There was a record showing my baptism by Fr. Fintan O'Casey, and in the back, there was a yellowed piece of paper. It was handwritten and dated February 25, 1924:

> *Infant girl, one week old, dropped off at 9:20 this morning. Good health. Young blonde woman alone, said having a baby was impossible in her line of work. Asked if father was living and she said he could be one of many different men. Offered to help her find a new job but she said she liked the life she had. Child had no name. Asked if she would later come back for her and she laughed and said no, never. Infant given the name Irene Mary Cleary.*

I read it once, then a second time. My lips felt dry, and nothing seemed to exist but that yellowed piece of paper. It was only when I heard my name that I looked up from the file and saw Sister there, her eyes full of concern.

"Sit down, Irene," she said gently, putting a hand on my arm. "Let's talk."

THIRTY-ONE

"I remember it well," said Sister. "It was my first week here, after coming from Ohio. You were the first child I received at Mount St. Joseph. I wrote down as many details as I could, in case they would be useful later."

"You were there?"

"I was. I answered the doorbell, along with Sister Rosemary. You were asleep in a small crate."

"What did she look like?"

"She had blonde hair." She paused. "I don't believe it was her natural color. Young."

"And she said"—my mouth was parched—"she said my father could have been one of many different men."

"Yes."

"And she liked the kind of work she did."

Sister said nothing, just looked at me with an alert compassion that made me realize, more than words would have done, that I was right in the conclusion I had drawn.

"My mother," I said, "was a . . ." I could not finish.

"If she was," said Sister quietly, "it has no bearing on you. You are not responsible for what your mother did."

"But Sister Rosemary said my parents loved me. That they loved each other."

Sister paused, as if choosing her words with care. "Sister Rosemary was a complex woman," she said quietly. "She had a difficult childhood, Irene. She wanted every child here to feel loved and wanted. It's an admirable motive, but she did, at times, embellish the truth."

"She lied to me."

"She wanted to spare you some of the pain she had known. She wanted to spare you what you are feeling now. They are natural feelings, Irene, even if they are—misguided. Who your parents were makes no difference to who you are."

"But Sister Rosemary didn't believe that. If she did she wouldn't have lied."

"You are your own person, Irene," said Sister, putting equal emphasis on each word. "The same person you were when you walked in this office an hour ago."

I didn't agree. I was different and the entire world was different. "When she—when she handed me to you, did she kiss me goodbye?"

Sister was silent for a moment, which told me the answer before she said it. "She did not, Irene. But I can't say what she did before ringing the doorbell."

"She said she'd never come back to get me. She laughed when you asked. She laughed."

A look came over Sister's face, transparent as water. She was wishing she'd never put that tiny devastating detail into her notes. In all the years I'd known Sister, so calm and unshakeable, I'd never seen her show anything like regret. One more prop that held up my world had been knocked sideways.

Then she reached for my hand and squeezed it gently.

"This does not change you, Irene. Please believe that. Pray for your parents, whoever they were or are; pray in gratitude that your mother brought you to us, where you could be raised by people who love you. I am grateful for your life and always will be."

I knew she meant it. I also knew that I wouldn't pray.

"Will you pray for that?" she asked, looking at me searchingly.

"Yes," I lied. "I will."

But I couldn't look at her as I said it. I stared at the window behind her, at that bright red heart skewered on the sword.

When you've lived all your life in San Francisco, you know about earthquakes. You know that sudden shudder under your chair or bed, coming out of nowhere with a creaking sound and making your heart stop. It doesn't feel like anything else; it's underneath you, it's far bigger than you, and there's nowhere you can go to get away from it. And when you've felt it once, you recognize it instantly.

The revelation about my parents shook me completely. Something on which I had built the house of my very self, my identity, had shifted without any warning, and there was nowhere I could go to escape it. It felt horribly similar to reading that letter from Johnny's mother. You expect that some things will be solid and then they turn to dust before your very eyes.

I'm honestly not sure how I made it home on the streetcar. I was aware of a world around me that looked somehow garish and strange, for I myself was different in it: no longer the beloved child of a happy couple but the unwanted product of a woman who sold her body to so many men she didn't know which one had fathered me. She had laughed and said no, she'd never come back for me. She had laughed, and she had not loved me.

In my abstraction I tripped coming out of the streetcar, and a man who was waiting to board kindly grabbed my elbow. He was middle-aged, with gray hair under a fedora. I thanked him, and as I looked up at his lined face the thought occurred to me: *Maybe this is my father.* Why not? Maybe I would have to wonder that about every man of a certain age now. I imagined myself asking, "Did you pay a blonde woman for sex, around twenty years ago?" I must have been looking at him strangely, for the man's courteous expression gave way to wariness, and he quickly boarded the bus as if glad to get away from me. Irene Mary Cleary, her own kind of leper.

It was dusk when I finally got to my shop. I fumbled with the sticky lock in the front door, almost bursting into tears, and at last it gave, and I stumbled inside. As I did I heard a sound: a rustle, a skitterish squeak, and I saw a small shadow dart behind the curtains. Without thinking I slipped off my right shoe and threw it with great force, missing the sideboard and hitting the wall an inch or two above the ground. Then there were no sounds, only silence, and when I finally pulled aside the curtain to look there was nothing.

Who am I? I thought. *Who is Irene Cleary?* I knew the answer. A girl who was left like a bundle of rags at a junk shop, a girl who is bested by a mouse. A girl who has to fight for almost everything. A girl who keeps on believing beautiful things that never have been true, that never will be true.

I didn't tell Trixie. When she called the next day to remind me about Thanksgiving dinner at her dormitory, I said I had too much work and I'd have to stay home. Maybe I'd tell her someday, I decided as I put down the phone, when it wasn't so raw. She'd be surprised but sympathetic and would probably say what Sister had said, that it didn't change me. On some head level, I knew they were right. But on a soul level—that place, that hidden essential place—I didn't believe it, and I didn't want to pretend that I did.

If I wasn't going to tell Trixie, then I sure as heck wasn't going to tell Louise. I imagined her eyes growing wide, heard her responding in the same thrilled tone she'd had when pointing out the brothel on

Pine Street. And to think I'd been so horrified by that place. For all I knew, I realized grimly as I prepared my Thanksgiving dinner of a can of soup, I had been conceived in a house like that one.

As it happened, Louise called me the next morning. "Irene, doing anything tonight?"

"No. Why?"

"I've got a date for you. I met this soldier—he's so handsome, you've no idea—and he's invited me for drinks. He's got a friend who needs a girl."

"I'm not sure," I said cautiously.

Louise read my tone. "Look," she said, dropping her voice as if the housekeeper might be by, "I know what you're probably thinking. I can go out with a guy and keep it light, Irene. I really can. And this guy's a lot of fun. From Texas. I haven't gone out with anyone from Texas before."

Glancing up, I caught a glimpse of myself in the big mirror on the shop floor. I was wearing a faded pullover sweater and gray skirt, one of the ugliest I had. My hair was lank and uncurled and I hadn't put on makeup in two days. *You're letting yourself go*, said a little voice inside me.

"It's just making two men happy," said Louise. "Like working at the USO. A service for our fighting men."

It was hard to argue with that. And what did it matter anyhow? Why should I care what happened? "All right," I said at last. "I'll go."

THIRTY-TWO

The dress Louise was wearing was new. "That's pretty," I said uncertainly. It was a peacock blue rayon, with a much lower neckline than I usually saw on her.

"You look nice, too," she said, linking her arm through mine. We'd met at the bus stop and were heading to Huntington Park, the pretty square opposite Grace Cathedral. "I always like that color on you."

It was the same red jersey dress I'd worn to dinner at the coast with Max. Even though I was ambivalent about going out, I had to admit it felt nice to put on a pretty dress again.

The two men were standing by the center fountain, heads bent as if sharing secrets, but they whirled around immediately at our approach.

"Helloooo," said Louise gaily. "Hope you weren't waiting too long."

"We'd wait all night for you ladies," said the taller one: Franklin from Texas, Louise's date. He kissed her cheek and shook my hand warmly, then introduced his companion. "This is my buddy, Phil."

Phil had light brown hair and a face that any woman would call handsome, with strong and regular features. His wide-set eyes flickered briefly over my figure before landing on my face.

"I'm Lucille," I said, shaking his hand. "Nice to meet you." I hadn't intended to give a false name and didn't know why I did, but it seemed to come out before I could stop it. Why not be Lucille for a night? I'd never see this man again.

"Lucille," he said in a voice that was deep and relaxed. "Pretty name for a pretty girl."

It was dark, so he probably couldn't see my freckles. Maybe he'd change his tune once he did. I smiled at him like some woman in a movie, cool and appraising, as if I had his number. He smiled back as if he had mine. His teeth were perfect.

"So we're thinking we'll go to the Top of the Mark," said Franklin. "Sound good to you ladies? Phil's never been."

"Lovely," said Louise.

"Why not?" I said.

The first moment she could Louise pulled me aside. "*Lucille?* What on earth?"

"It just came out," I said, glancing at the two men, who had gone ahead in the lobby to buy cigarettes. "I don't know why."

"I kind of like it," she said. "Lucille and Louise. Sounds like a radio show. Isn't Franklin handsome?"

"Older than I expected. They both are."

She shrugged. "Thirty, maybe? I don't ask their age."

The men came back, both smiling at us in the same way. They did look handsome in their belted army uniforms with the wide shoulders, a uniform that somehow makes the navy one look modest in comparison. I tossed my hair back and smiled at Phil, without shyness or hesitation. I was in the Mark Hopkins Hotel, the same place I'd been with Johnny just months before. But it wasn't me this time, it was Lucille. And when Phil slipped an arm around my waist in the elevator it was her waist, not mine.

After a long wait we were seated on the east side, where the lights of the Bay Bridge made a twinkling road across the water. Phil and I were left mostly to ourselves because Louise and Franklin were instantly chummy, heads bent close, ignoring us and everyone else. "Have you known Franklin long?" I asked.

"About a year," he said. He offered me a cigarette, and I took one. He lit it for me and with his face close to mine, something in his features reminded me of a fox. I pulled away and thanked him.

"I've always had a thing for girls with freckles," he said, his voice low, his eyes on me through the smoke.

"Have you?"

"I couldn't believe my good luck when you walked up in the park there."

"Lucky man," I said. A memory of Johnny swept over me, so strong it would pull me under if I didn't do something. What would Lucille do, this creature who had never existed before tonight, who could be whatever I needed her to be?

I looked him in the eye and smiled, leaning back in my chair flirtatiously, like I was Barbara Stanwyck. "You're lucky I was free tonight. My evenings are pretty busy."

"I bet they are." He moved closer so our knees were touching. I drained the last of my drink. "Another cocktail?"

"Why not?" It seemed to be my answer to everything.

Max always stopped at one drink, and I usually did, too, and after the second one I wished I had. There was a slight blur to everything, an awareness that I was having to work harder to focus and keep my wits about me. The Top of the Mark seemed to have grown more raucous, with voices coming at me from all sides. Phil had taken my hand and was tracing my palm slowly and deliberately, which didn't help me feel any more in control. Louise and Franklin had their heads together and I realized after a moment that they were kissing. He pulled back with a smile, and she wiped lipstick away from his mouth as he looked down at her with obvious desire.

"So where do you live, Lucille?" asked Phil.

It took me a moment to realize he was talking to me. "Off Fillmore. The other side of Van Ness."

"How will you get home?"

"I'll take the streetcar."

"You know," he said, now lightly tracing the inside of my wrist, "I've got a nice suite at a hotel not far from here. You could come see it, relax for a bit. Then we'll get you home later."

I'd never had a man touch my wrist like that. He had such huge eyes. It occurred to me that I'd had two drinks, and he'd only had one.

"That's very kind," I said, "but I really should get back now."

Louise and Franklin stood up. "We're going to go for a walk," she said. "Maybe down to the water. Want to come along?"

"Sounds good," said Phil before I could answer. "Shall we, Lucille?" He stood up, picking up my coat. I got up, too, hoping I did not look as unsteady as I felt.

"Just a second," said Louise. "Let me talk to Lucille." She pulled me over toward the bar. "Are you okay?"

"Just a little tired. I think I'll go home."

"Are you sure? Phil will be disappointed. He's so dreamy."

"I'm sure."

She glanced at Franklin, then back at me. "Franklin is so handsome. Such a good kisser, too."

"Louise," I said, "maybe you should go home too."

She opened her eyes wide as if I were being provincial and unreasonable. "Come on, Sister Irene Mary."

"I'm just worried about you."

"I'll be fine. I've already decided I'm inviting him back to my place. He just doesn't know it yet."

The two men were standing together and conferring, glancing at us from time to time. Franklin had his hands in his pockets, looking at Louise with a proprietary smile.

"I think he does know," I said.

Outside the air was cold and clammy with fog. Mason Street had lost its familiar landmarks; even the Burkes' apartment building just a block away had vanished completely in the mist. "Do you want us to help you get a cab?" Louise asked me as she drew on her gloves.

"I'm fine," I said, pulling my inadequate coat more closely around me. "I can catch the streetcar."

"Not the streetcar," said Phil. "Not this time of night. I'll help you get a taxi." He moved a little way down the sidewalk, scanning the street.

"Army men are such gentlemen," said Louise, taking Franklin's arm snugly. "Bye, Lucille. I'll call you soon." They turned and headed east towards the bay, the sound of her heels gradually receding into the night.

I joined Phil, feeling more sober than I had indoors thanks to the cold air. "Any luck?" I asked.

"Not much. Want a smoke?"

"No, thanks." I thrust my hands into my pockets. "Maybe if we head towards Taylor Street we'll find one."

I thought he'd light a cigarette for himself, but he didn't. We walked along, side by side, passing a well-dressed couple walking arm in arm.

"You don't need to stay," I told him. "I'll be fine."

"I wouldn't dream of it." We were passing an apartment building, one of the ornate ones you find on Nob Hill. It had a Christmas wreath in the window, one of the first holiday decorations I'd seen so far, and I was admiring it when suddenly Phil grabbed my arm and pulled me into a small alley on the side of the building.

"What are you doing?" I asked, pulling away, but his grip was too strong.

He didn't answer. The next moment my back was up against the wall and his body was pressing me into it and his mouth was on my neck.

I struggled to push him away but couldn't. "Stop it," I said in a panic. "Stop." This was not Lucille anymore. It was me, Irene Cleary, and I didn't want him anywhere near me.

"Stop?" he said. "No way, honey. You don't come on to me all evening and then tell me to stop." One hand was now on my breast, inside the neckline of my dress. His mouth was on mine, his tongue too, and I finally managed to pull my face away. "This is no way to treat a soldier," he said. I could feel his hand inside my bra, his fingers on my skin, even his nails. I tried to kick but I couldn't; there was nowhere for my legs to go. I opened my mouth to scream but he seemed to sense what I was going to do and his mouth was on mine again, hard, and all I could feel was sheer blinding panic. *It can't happen like this*, I thought as I tried my hardest to break free. *Not like this.*

Then swiftly, without warning, Phil was pulled roughly off of me. He swore and fell back. A man stood behind him, at the entrance to the alley.

"Get the hell away from her," the man said. He stepped toward me, reaching out his hand. "Are you all right, Miss?" Then he recognized me, and his face and voice changed. "Irene?"

"Max." I was breathing so hard I could hardly speak in my relief. "I'm okay." I pulled up the neckline of my dress.

Phil was staring at us, his mouth open. Max turned back to him, barely containing his fury. "You'd better learn something, soldier. When a girl doesn't want it, she doesn't want it. Now get out of here."

"Irene?" Phil was staring at me in confusion, breathing hard. Then his expression turned ugly. "Oh, I get it," he said, looking from me to Max, then back again. "Sure. You're Lucille with me. Irene with another guy. I guess that's how you do it." He glanced at my chest, then at Max. "I guess even the freckled ones can get pimps these days."

I'd seen people get punched in the movies but never in real life. It was much more shocking in reality. Max's fist made contact with a sudden, sickening sound, and Phil staggered, holding his jaw. "What the fuck?" he managed to say.

"If I were you," said Max, "I'd get the hell out of here. Now."

Phil turned back to me, still holding his face. There was a look of pure hatred in his eyes, and instinctively I reached for Max's arm. "You little bitch," he said. Then he turned and ran before Max could react, hurrying across the street and disappearing into the night.

Max took off his coat and put it around me. He scanned my face intently. "Did he hurt you?"

I didn't know how to answer that. Finally I shook my head.

"That fucking bastard." I had never heard Max swear like that before. He smoothed back my hair so it was out of the collar of the coat. "Thank God I was out for a walk. Come on. Let's get you home."

THIRTY-THREE

I barely spoke in the car, just sat huddled in Max's coat. He kept glancing at me sideways. At one point he asked, "So what happened there?" and I told him about the cocktails at the Top of the Mark, about Louise and Franklin leaving me and Phil to get a cab.

"Some friend," said Max. "Leaving you with a guy like that."

It was hard to defend Louise, but I tried. "She didn't know he was like that."

"Then she's a fool," said Max.

We drove for two blocks in silence.

"Why did he think you were named Lucille?" he asked.

"I said that was my name. I don't know why." I pulled the coat more closely around me. "I just wanted to be someone else for a night, I guess. I can't really explain it."

He didn't answer, but there was something in his silence that made me feel understood. And I realized that Maximilian Bukowski, driving his car down California Street, didn't require an explanation.

On my street he parked and walked me to the shop door. "You should fix that lock," he said as I wrestled with the key.

"I should fix a lot of things." I felt like I was going to cry and bit my lip so I wouldn't.

The door finally swung open, and I turned on the light. Max stood on the threshold, hands in his pockets. I was still wearing his coat, and somehow I didn't want to take it off.

"Look," he said. "I know it's late, but I don't like leaving you alone like this."

I didn't want to be alone, either. "Come upstairs then," I said, leading the way.

Once inside the apartment I switched on the light, revealing my home in all its shabby glory. As if he'd been there a million times before he went over to the stove, found a match, lit the burner. "You have tea or coffee?" he asked. "Or milk? Something warm."

"There's tea in the tin on the shelf."

He filled the kettle and put it on the stove, then took a single mug off the hook and added a teabag.

"Aren't you having any?"

"You're almost out," he said. "I don't want to take the last one."

"Take it, Max. I can get more."

He turned to me, then his eyes moved involuntarily down to my chest, and he turned back to the stove. I glanced down. The coat had gaped open, exposing the rip in my neckline. I closed it with my hands.

"Too bad about your dress," he said briefly as he reached for a second mug. "But you can mend it if anyone can."

"I'm not sure I want to wear it again. Ever."

He nodded as if he understood. "Why don't you go change. Put on something new. I'll take care of this."

I took off his coat, leaving it on the chair, then went into the bedroom and closed the door. It occurred to me that there hadn't been a man in my apartment since Johnny. Who had, in fact, been the first man I'd ever invited to my apartment. Maybe it should have felt strange with Max there, moving about my kitchen like a housewife, but it didn't. It was comforting. Natural.

The dress I balled up and put in the hamper. I took off my stockings, too, which had miraculously survived the evening. I found a sweater and a skirt to wear but somehow what I really wanted to do was wash off the evening and the touch of Phil's hands.

I put on my robe and opened the door a crack. "Max? I'm going to take a bath."

"Want me to leave?" he asked.

"No. I won't be long."

The water felt like a blessing. I submerged myself up to my chin, hair pinned on my head, and thought of baptism. I didn't remember my own, of course, but I'd heard there were religions where you were baptized with your whole body, going into a river and emerging ready to start anew. I wanted to wash it all away: the cocktails, the alleyway, Phil's face in my neck, Lucille. There was a scratch on my left breast, the mark of his fingernail making a red furrow across my freckles. I thought about how it would fade each day till it was gone. How ironic that my skin, which I had spent so much time hating, would not fail me. It would heal and make new layers, an automatic act of grace, one that required nothing of me.

From beyond the door, I could hear the scrape of a chair as if Max were sitting down at the table. I felt suddenly aware of my nakedness and got up, drying off and reaching for my underwear, then put on my slip and robe. Pulling the stopper out of the tub felt almost ceremonial, important. I watched the water gurgle away and thought: *This is tonight I am sending down the drain.*

When I came out of the bathroom, Max was standing by the window, looking out at the dark street. I was suddenly aware that anyone looking up from the sidewalk could see in the apartment, and when he saw me in my robe he must have thought the same thing, for he turned back to the windows and pulled down the shades. "Feel better?" he asked.

"Much better. I'll just go get dressed."

"Your tea's ready. You might want to drink it before it gets cold."

I took it and sat down on the sofa, curling my feet under me and making sure my robe covered me decently. Even though there was plenty of room on the couch, Max pulled a chair away from the table so it faced me and sat down with his own mug of tea. He'd rolled up his sleeves and loosened his tie.

"Thank you, Max," I said.

"I hope it's not too strong. I wasn't sure how long to steep it."

"No, I mean for—for being there. For rescuing me."

He looked up, then back down at his tea. "I'm just glad I happened to be walking by."

I warmed my hands on the mug. "Have you done that sort of thing before?"

"Punched a guy?"

"Well, yes. Also, rescued a woman."

"Yes. And yes."

"Have you ever been punched?"

"Yes." He didn't say more, and all of a sudden I remembered what he'd said at the coast, about how his father had broken his nose when he was young. I felt terrible.

"As an adult, I mean?" I asked awkwardly.

He gave me a small smile, as if he had read my mind. "Yes," he said. "I have been punched as an adult. My life's been different from yours, Irene."

Different, and yet the same. I studied him sitting on the chair, leaning slightly forward, holding the mug. He was a man who needed a shave, as he nearly always did, but I could still see in him the young boy without a home, all on his own, making what he could with the only tools he possessed: determination and energy and kindness underneath the rough edges, a kindness that not everyone would see.

I traced the rim of my cup. "Max, you gave money to the orphanage." He glanced up at me in surprise. "I went there a few days ago and Sister mentioned it. She didn't know I know you." He said nothing, so I asked, "Why did you do it?"

He shrugged. "I give money to charity. Lots of people do."

"But why the orphanage?"

"Maybe I just wanted to thank them."

"For what?"

He shook his head slightly as if he shouldn't need to say it. There was a whole box of meaning to unpack there, and somehow I was afraid to start. He nodded toward my mug. "Want me to warm that up?"

"No, it's fine."

"So what were you doing at the orphanage?" he asked, putting his mug on the floor and taking out a cigarette.

"Just visiting. When Sister Rosemary died, it reminded me I hadn't been back in a long time." He got the ashtray from the sideboard then returned to his seat, but in the middle of the floor there was no place to set it. I indicated the other end of the sofa and he sat down, putting the mug and the ashtray on the end table. I turned to face him, modestly tucking my robe around my legs.

"Was it a good visit?" he asked.

"No. I found out something there. For the first time ever I learned how I came to the orphanage. My mother—she was a prostitute." I don't know why I could tell him so easily, when I couldn't tell Trixie or Louise. "She didn't even know who my father was. She didn't want me. I always thought I was wanted, but I was just believing a lie. A story that Sister Rosemary told me just to be kind."

"I'm sorry, Irene," said Max quietly.

"Sister Margaret said it doesn't change anything, but it does. It changes a lot." A tear slipped down my cheek and I dashed it away.

"What does it change?"

It took me a moment to put it into words. "It changes me. The way I fit into the world. Even what that world is." A thought crept into my mind, clearer than it had been before: My history was further proof that I could never have been a part of Johnny's family. The only thing worse than being an orphan was being the child of a whore who had dumped her like a bag of garbage. There could never have been a future with Johnny, beautiful Johnny, who had once sat with me, warm and alive, on this very sofa.

"I loved someone," I said, trying to keep my voice even. "A sailor I met at the USO. We were talking about getting married someday, and then he died in the Philippine Sea. But we could never have had a future together, I know that now. He was rich, he was from a totally different world. It only worked in wartime." I looked up at Max. "See? That's how it is. I keep believing these beautiful things that aren't true. My whole life, believing things that aren't true at all. And I'm tired of it."

He got up and went to his coat and took a handkerchief out of the pocket. I took it gratefully. My head was starting to ache from the crying. He sat back down and stubbed out his cigarette, then turned and faced me, leaning his arm along the back of the sofa.

"You may not believe this, Irene, but who your parents are doesn't matter. What matters is you. That you're here, now. It doesn't matter how you got here."

The words rang a bell, echoing something Johnny had once said. I shook my head, as much to fight off the memory as anything.

"You know about my family," he said. "Sometimes you have to push your parents aside, you have to be who you are in spite of them. Even if they're still alive, sometimes, you have to do that. Family doesn't always make it easier, Irene. Look at Cynthia."

I was surprised. "Cynthia? But her parents are so—so kind."

"Maybe to you," he said briefly. "But it wasn't easy for her, growing up."

This was a revelation, and one that I welcomed as an escape from the grief that was threatening me. "Why not?"

He looked as if he regretted saying it. "Forget it."

"I can't forget it, Max. Not now that you've said it."

He was quiet for a long moment, as if trying to decide what he could share. "I know you don't gossip, Irene," he said at last, "so I'll tell you. For all their wealth and polish, the McNeils are not an easy family to be part of. Not if you're Cynthia. Antonia gets away with everything, but Cynthia has had to be perfect. Her whole life, she's had to be perfect. They won't tolerate mistakes."

I thought of the photograph of young Cynthia on the horse, and how her father had told me, a complete stranger, that his daughter had disappointed him by coming in second. Even at the time, I'd found it an odd thing to say.

"I've seen it myself, Irene," Max went on. "The first time I ever met them, a few months ago, after we'd been married and come home. Her father actually said, in front of all the people gathered at the house, 'Cynthia, you'd better watch it. You're putting on weight.' He actually said that. She looked like she was about to cry. I said, 'With all due respect, sir, that's uncalled for.' One of the first things I ever said to my father-in-law. It didn't go over well."

I pictured the scene: the well-appointed library in the Atherton home; the group of family and friends who had known each other forever; and Max, the outsider, speaking his mind to Mr. McNeil in a way no one ever did. It was a very easy scene for me to imagine.

"Her parents were already angry about our marriage off in Chicago, no big ceremony or reception at the country club. I'd robbed them of that and of their prettiest daughter. It hasn't been a good relationship."

In the midst of these revelations about the past, a more immediate question came to mind. "Max," I asked abruptly, "where is Cynthia? She must be wondering where you are."

It took him a moment to answer. When he did, his voice was quiet and matter-of-fact. "Cynthia is in Atherton. With Fred Gibson. They're having an affair." I couldn't look surprised, of course. He noticed my lack of reaction. "How did you know?"

"When I was in Atherton, Cynthia offered to drive me to the train station. Fred showed up there too. When she thought no one was looking, she pulled him toward her like—well, like they were kissing. I didn't want to tell you. I felt like it wasn't my business." My toes were cold and I tucked them more firmly under the robe. "When did you find out?"

"Two weeks ago. She didn't know I was home and I heard her on the phone, arranging to meet him. The Gibsons have a guesthouse, way back on their property, its own driveway and everything. That's where they meet. But I guess it's been going on longer than I thought."

"I heard they were in love years ago. That everyone always thought they'd get married."

A wry smile crossed his features. "Great-Aunt Mabel?"

"Yes."

"She told me, too. Pointed out the picture of the two of them at the country club, in the dress she wanted you to remake. But I didn't need her to tell me the history between them. Cynthia told me herself."

"She did? When?"

He got up and strode over to the window. The shade was down and there was nothing for him to see, but he stood there anyhow, his hands in his pockets. I stared at the broad expanse of his back, waiting for him to go on.

"I trust you, Irene," he said as he turned to face me. "But you need to promise me that you won't tell anyone. Even if you think it doesn't matter, that they couldn't possibly know Cynthia or Fred or me. Don't let it leave this building."

I nodded.

"Cynthia came to my nightclub the first week she was in Chicago. She was there with an aunt who lives in town. We hit it off right away. It was instant attraction, for both of us. But more than that too." He paused, as if wondering how much to say. "She saw me as a safe place. She confided things about her past, about her life, struggles that most people would never suspect. Things I won't tell even you, Irene. She could do it because I wasn't part of her world, you see. Between that, and the attraction, it was—it was hard to resist. Physically, things moved fast.

"I didn't know then about Fred. She only mentioned she'd loved someone who had married someone else. I had no idea it had happened so recently. If I'd known how recently, how strong those feelings still were . . . well, I might have put the brakes on what happened." He shrugged. "Or maybe not. Anyhow, after a few weeks of this she was pregnant."

I remembered the wedding photo at City Hall. "That's why you got married in Chicago."

"That's why. She was too scared to—well, to get rid of the baby. And she couldn't come home pregnant and unmarried. I thought we'd be happy, that it would all work out in the end. But then two weeks after the wedding she miscarried." He exhaled audibly. "Which was horrible, Irene, in lots of ways. Anyhow, there she was. Married to me, now for no good reason at all. She was stuck with me. I still thought maybe it would work out when we came back here, to a new place. It was only a new place to me, though. To her it was the same old one. With Fred and her family. And I like it here, Irene, but I don't fit into her world."

It was said without self-pity, as if simply stating a known fact, which it was. "Does her family know? I mean, now?"

"About the baby? No. She's terrified about them finding out. No, they think it was a whirlwind romance and marriage, some love at first sight kind of thing. And they all think she regrets it now. Which, of course, she does."

It took a moment for me to process it all, but the story made perfect sense. It was like one of those connect-the-dot puzzles, where you could see a picture slowly emerging. "But her family can't approve of her having an affair with Fred. A married man."

"I'm sure they have no idea. He's the army doctor, the hero, saving lives. Patching soldiers back together. No one knows what he does in his free time."

"I'm sorry," I said. "About all of it. You deserve better, Max."

He smiled briefly. "Do I? Who knows."

I studied him as he stood by the windows, hands in his pockets, eyes fixed on some point on the wall. I'd seen Max in many moods, but never with exactly that expression on his face. I was trying to figure it out when he spoke.

"You know, Irene," he said quietly, "I was actually excited about that baby. It was an accident, sure, but it was a new start. And I think I'd be a pretty good father. I know how not to be one, at least."

Something inside me ached. "Maybe there will be another baby someday."

"Cynthia and I haven't shared a bed since August," he said. "Which is probably more than you wanted to know."

It occurred to me that at the very moment we were speaking, she was sharing a bed with Fred Gibson. Maybe the same thought had occurred to Max, for his face tightened and he picked up the ashtray and moved it back to the sideboard where he had found it.

"How is this all going to end?" I asked him.

"I don't know, Irene," he said. "I don't know." He came back to the sofa and we both just sat there in silence. It was so quiet I could hear myself breathe. "Thanks for listening," he said at last.

"You listened to me too. Thank you for that." I was beginning to feel drowsy, so I put my left arm along the back of the sofa and then rested my head on it.

"You're tired? I should go."

"No," I said. "No, I'm all right." And in spite of my fatigue and the awful start to the evening, I was. Telling Max about my parents had been a relief, a relief I'd denied myself with Trixie or Louise. And knowing that he could confide in me, that he trusted me with the tenderest parts of his life, made me feel secure. I felt strangely rooted somehow, and so much less alone.

"Max," I said as he watched me. "Why did you ask me to work on your nightclub?"

"Because you have an eye for design."

"It wasn't just that."

"No," he said. "No, it wasn't." There must have been a thread on my sleeve for he removed something delicately from the cuff of my robe. I watched him from my strange angle, eyes half-open.

"When you grow up like me," he said, "you recognize other people who have had to work hard. Who've had to make something from nothing. And I saw that in you. Right away, almost, starting with that day you did the pants at the apartment."

"I hated doing those pants."

"I know." He was smiling. I closed my eyes, feeling deliciously sleepy. "I should leave so you can go to bed," he said, and I said, "No, I'm fine like this," and yawned. He moved closer and I moved closer too, putting my head his shoulder, catching a whiff of soap and cigarette. I was more comfortable than I had felt in a long time, with that lovely drowsy feeling you have when you know you should go to bed but the sofa is too comfortable and you drift in and out of awareness, skating on the surface of sleep, secure in where you are and strangely at peace.

THIRTY-FOUR

I came to with a start. I must have been asleep, for I'd been seeing Johnny, his blond hair, his brown eyes, looking at me from the other end of the boat in the park. His smile was going straight to my soul, as it always had. There was a split second when I thought the shoulder that had just been under my head was his, then I remembered: *Of his bones are coral made.* I sat up and then stopped short. "Ow."

"What is it?"

"A crick in my neck." I turned my head, winced. "Was I asleep? How long?"

"Ten minutes, maybe." I felt Max's fingers on my neck. "There?"

"Ow. Yes." I sat forward, back perfectly straight, as he pressed the muscle with a firm touch. I received it gratefully. My sleepiness began to vanish, like fog blowing away over the rooftops.

"What time is it?" I asked after a moment.

"I've no idea. It's late. Or early."

I closed my eyes. For a while the only sound was the hum of the refrigerator off in the kitchen.

As his fingers worked at the knot, I thought of the first day he ever came to my shop, when he'd done up the buttons on my blouse. His hands had brushed my neck, and I'd been frozen in surprise: surprise and, if I was honest, something else too. It was something that I was feeling again, but even more strongly this time. I swallowed, a sound that seemed ten times louder than usual.

"Is this helping?" he asked.

"Yes," I managed to say. "Thank you."

His hands were both expert and gentle. In the part of my mind that was still capable of thought, I remembered Phil, a few hours before. His hands had been on me, too, but it was nothing like this. There was the touch you wanted and the touch you didn't. Max's fingers were giving, not taking.

I opened my eyes.

Before me was my living room, the windows with the shades down, the small low table strewn with magazines, the sideboard in the corner with its record player. I stared at it as his other hand lightly gripped my shoulder, holding me still to get at the right spot. My room, my apartment, my things. My life. My own choices to make.

I had not known you could feel relaxed and wide awake all at once. I had not known lots of things before this evening. The conversation we'd had flitted through my memory, scattered impressions gathering shape and clarity. Max saying he wanted to thank the orphanage. Max and the lost baby. Cynthia and Fred, away, together. A man sitting beside me, carefully kneading away my pain, who had listened as I shared things I was too ashamed to tell anyone else. A man who, like me, had learned how to make his own way and be his own person. Who had become what he wanted to be, the past and others' expectations be damned.

He took his hands away abruptly. "Better now?"

I nodded. Then I turned around, looking at him for the first time since falling asleep.

He sat there on my old sofa, handsome as ever but different too. His eyes had an expression that was at once open and guarded. When his fingers were on my neck I had wondered if it felt good to him, too, not just to me. As I looked at him, I could tell that it had, and that he was trying not to show it. That trying to hide it made all the difference.

"Thank you," I said. It came out as a whisper.

"You're welcome," he said in the same kind of voice.

I did not move my gaze, and neither did he. We regarded each other in silence, with the hum of the refrigerator in the background, and there was also something humming inside me, something insistent and new. I didn't know everything that was in his thoughts, but I knew for sure what was in mine. I was remembering how I'd been good once before, with another man I cared about, on the same sofa. I had been good and then wished I hadn't. It had gotten me absolutely nowhere.

And suddenly, decisively, I was tired of being nowhere.

So I was the one who started it. I put my hand on his face, and his eyes flickered at my touch. His cheek was rough, which was a surprise even though it shouldn't have been. I traced it slowly, looking at his mouth, leaning in, close enough to feel the warmth from his skin. I looked back up into his eyes, unembarrassed by my own desire. And before I could do it myself, Max leaned forward and closed the tiny space between us.

It was not a decorous kiss. I did not want it to be. I didn't want to hold anything back, not this time.

He did, at one point. He pulled back, his hands in my hair on either side of my face. "Irene," he said, his eyes intent. "I don't know. Are you sure you want this?"

Already I was missing the feel of his lips. "Yes," I said, leaning back in. "Totally sure." After a moment of hesitation, it seemed he was sure, too. As if we had one mind between us, we both got up, still holding onto each other, and kissed our way through the doorway into the bedroom.

Twenty minutes later I had my robe back on and was in the kitchen standing at the sink. The light was still on from before, and I reached shakily for a glass. I turned on the faucet and filled the glass almost full, needing something to do, needing a moment alone.

What happened in bed had surprised me. I don't mean the mechanics of it; I'd known all that for ages. I hadn't at any time felt unsafe, nor had I wanted Max to stop. But the actual reality of it, of having another person inside me, had been overwhelming in a way I hadn't expected. There was a moment where the magnitude of it crowded out everything else, and I could no longer lose myself in sensation as I had on the sofa, a moment where I felt abruptly disconnected from the man I'd been so in synch with just minutes before. He obviously felt pleasure at the end, but I had somehow lost the thread, and everything suddenly felt wrong.

The water glass was cold in my hand, and I stood there, holding it, not drinking. I could hear Max come up behind me hastily, with the clink of a belt buckle as if he were pulling on his trousers. "Irene."

I stood there at the sink, my back to him.

"Irene." He put his hands on my shoulders, then quickly took them away as if doubting his right to touch me. "Are you all right?"

I nodded.

There was a pause. "That was your first time, wasn't it?"

I nodded again.

"I'm sorry," he said. "I thought—you mentioned the guy you were going to marry. I just assumed you two had . . ."

"No," I said. "No. We never did."

I could picture his expression as clearly as if he were standing before me. There was a faintly raspy sound, as if he had drawn his hand over his chin. "I'm sorry," he said. "If I'd known it was your first time, I wouldn't have . . . or I would have been more . . ."

He sounded almost anguished. How strange that an evening could switch from pleasure to regret in just a few minutes, for both of us.

"It's fine," I said, trying my hardest to sound casual and offhand. "It doesn't matter, Max. It doesn't matter at all."

We both just stood there at the sink, my back still to him. Max was not usually irresolute or lost for words. A detached part of me was curious at his silence, at exactly the same time that another part of me wanted to cry, because nothing in my life was ever what I dreamed it would be.

Then he put his hands gently on my shoulders and moved closer. I couldn't see him, but I could feel his warm bulk behind me, and I could picture how he would look: his black hair tousled, his eyes dark with feeling.

"Look," he said, quietly and almost humbly, "will you come back? I don't want your first experience to be a bad one. Let me make it right. Let me give you that at least."

In the long pause that followed I could somehow see us, both of us, as clearly as if I were outside myself looking on. I could see us standing in my tiny shabby kitchen under its weak light bulb, a dark sleeping city outside the window. I saw myself in my red terry robe, and Max with pants not yet fastened, shirtless, his feet bare. Max, standing behind me, offering me himself, waiting for me to choose.

I saw something else too. I saw that this moment, even more than the one on the sofa, was the turning point. I knew I could say no and cut it off there, leaving it at one disappointing but isolated experience. I could say no, and I almost did. But his tenderness for me, mixed with the desire that was once again lighting little flares along my veins, was too potent to resist.

There's choosing to do a thing once, and there's choosing to keep on doing it. When I finally put down the glass and turned to face him, when I reached up to put my hands behind his neck and looked into his eyes, I was choosing the latter.

He smiled at me. It was a grateful smile, as if I were giving him something instead of the other way around. For a while we just stood like that, the moment growing large around us.

Then he kissed me, and I kissed him, for a long while. When he could tell I was ready he gently picked me up off my feet, and, still kissing me, took me slowly back to start again.

THIRTY-FIVE

Red velvet was everywhere, yards of it covering the sofa in the ballet studio waiting room, draped over chairs and boxes alike. Three dancers were bending over it with shears, carving it into smaller pieces. "What's all this?" I asked, taking off my coat.

"This is providence." Russell was visibly excited. "The Cort Theatre closed down and they gave the curtains to Goodwill. Ten dollars later they were mine."

"Ten dollars? For all this?" I reached out to finger the material, which gave me the instant thrill that velvet always did. "You're kidding."

"Amazing, isn't it? We have enough for the Act One coats, and more besides."

"Maybe you can redesign my snowflake costume," said Pauline, who was one of the cutters. "One red snowflake would look good, wouldn't it?"

"Sorry, Pauline," said Russell with a grin. "You're still going to have to stand in line for that tulle."

I opened my bag and took out my own pair of shears. "I'm ready and willing. Just tell me where to go."

Working on a table set up in a free corner, I laid out a piece of velvet and pinned the pattern pieces down, deftly and efficiently. It was four weeks until the performance and everyone was feeling the crunch, Russell in particular. Costumes were still being made all around town—dancers, their mothers, volunteers like me doing their part—but with Thanksgiving behind us, there was a renewed sense of urgency.

I've always loved working with velvet. As I pinned I remembered the first time I'd ever felt it, when one of the trustees' wives had worn a green velvet coat to a Christmas party. I'd been tiny, four or five at the most, and she'd kindly let me hold the coat until she had to leave. I remember the velvet even more fondly than the baby doll I received that year as a gift.

Even back then, it seems, I had been sensitive to touch. The memory of Max's lips on my spine washed over me, and I could feel my cheeks burn as I pinned.

That second time in bed had been a revelation. There were worlds of feeling out there that I'd never suspected, feeling that left me breathless and unable to speak, and he had held me afterwards and I had felt my heart slow down, gradually, as his cheek rested in my hair. I remember noticing light around the edges of the bedroom shade, gray light. It was morning and a whole night had passed. From the Top of the Mark to my own bedroom I'd been on a journey from the terrible to the sublime, in the space of less than twelve hours, and I felt my life would never be the same.

I had to pause and look around the studio to break my reverie. I must have been flushed, for one of the ballerinas smiled sympathetically. "Wish we could open a window. It's stuffy in here."

Russell approached, his arms full of folded velvet. "Here's more. When you're done with the pieces, I'll pass them on to Dorothy and she'll take them to her mother to stitch up."

"A real assembly line."

"You bet." He beamed, still savoring his triumph. "We got so lucky with these curtains."

"What do you still need for material?"

"Some of the girls need to pick up their tulle for the snowflakes and the flowers. Only a few . . . we're in pretty good shape there. I'm stuck on the Chinese costumes, though. We've got the stuff for the pants, but I'm coming up short for the coats."

I thought of the sketch he'd shown me of a high-collared Mandarin coat with toggles. "What were you thinking?"

"I'd love something embroidered, something authentic and colorful. But there's nothing left in the budget." He stared off in the distance as if imagining the ideal coat. "I have this vision of something blue. With a big print, that the audience can see."

"Something like flowers, maybe?"

"Exactly. Wish I could snap my fingers and make the cloth appear."

For a moment I was back in the guest bedroom in Atherton, and Mrs. McNeil was handing me the folded cape. "Make it into something new," she had said. My face broke into a smile at the thought.

"I have just what you need," I said. Russell's eyes widened in surprise. "It's a long story, but I have some Chinese silk. I'll bring it on Thursday."

"Brilliant. That would be brilliant." Before he could say more, he was called away by a question across the room. He made a small bow of thanks before leaving.

I turned back to the velvet, feeling buoyant and alive. Picking up the shears, I heard Anna's voice: *Measure twice, cut once.* With more energy than usual I sliced my way recklessly through the red.

For two days after my night with Max, I moved about in a sort of fog, both distracted and keenly alive. Memories kept coming back at random times: memories of things he'd done, even things I'd done, and they were so vivid that I was sure others could see into my brain as if my head were made of glass. I learned to switch back and forth between the memories and whatever I was doing: working with a client, boarding a bus, paying for a loaf of bread . . . it was a strange integration of the past and present, the ecstatic and the mundane.

My view of the world was different too. On Fillmore Street I found myself looking at strangers and wondering about their private lives, dividing them into two camps, those who had slept with another person and those who hadn't. That white-haired matron with the sensible shoes and the wedding ring, toting a shopping bag—she must have known what I'd known, impossible as that seemed. That young girl wistfully watching the couple standing before the jewelry store: No, she couldn't possibly know, not yet.

Louise knew, of course. Part of me wanted to tell her about Max so I could process the whole experience. But I didn't, for I was far too cautious. And if I hadn't instinctively known to be discreet, Max had said as much as he put his shirt back on, standing before my bedroom mirror while I sat in my robe and watched him.

"I probably don't even need to say this, Irene," he began, and I finished for him.

"I know. I won't tell anyone."

"I'm not just thinking of myself here," he said, turning to look at me. "I'm thinking of you." His expression was sober. "Actually, I'm thinking mostly of you."

A cold draft went up my back, the recognition that I'd done something that most of the world would condemn, something that I myself would have condemned in the abstract. *But this is different*, I told myself. *Cynthia doesn't even want him. She's with another man. And it's wartime and everything has changed.* But I didn't like feeling that draft.

"Will I see you again?" I asked.

"Of course."

"I mean"—I felt suddenly very vulnerable—"like this?"

He stood in his shirt and pants and bare feet, tying his tie, looking at me. Outside you could hear the milk truck driving along the street, making its rounds. There was light in the room, and I suddenly wanted nothing more than to scroll back a few hours, to have him standing behind me in the kitchen so I could have none of it over and all of it before me.

If the moment at the sink had been my decision point, this was his. I could see it in his expression and his hesitation. I realized that my every thought, my every feeling, was nakedly transparent on my face. But I'd never been much good at hiding my feelings with Max.

"Do you want to?" he asked.

"I do," I said, almost awkwardly. "Do you?"

In his eyes I saw the caution give way to something like tenderness. He looked at me sitting on the edge of the bed, and then the tenderness itself shifted into something else and he crossed the room in two large strides, took my face in his hands, and kissed me. His kiss was still new enough that I was flooded with wonder along with everything else. It was another hour before he left.

The next time we met, it was at the club. The floor in the front room had been restained and carpet was being installed in the other two. The walls had been painted and the upholstery shop was turning the orange-red silk into curtains dividing the foyer from the main bar. "It's actually happening," I said, looking about me in delight.

Max lit a cigarette. "It is." He waved out the match, dropped it in an ashtray on the bar. "This is the exciting phase, when things really happen. Tangible things, being put into place."

"How many bars have you opened?" I asked, watching him. He was so handsome, head tilted back, looking at the ceiling.

"Four. All in Chicago."

"Who's running them now?"

"People I know and trust. I'll be heading back there soon, just to check in."

The thought of him leaving town made me feel suddenly bereft. "When?"

"In a few weeks, before Christmas." He looked at me and our gazes held, and he smiled. It was the kind of smile that made me instantly recall the night and morning we'd spent together. The sound of one of the workmen approaching made me look hastily away.

"Mr. Burke? We've got a question when you're free."

"I'll be right there." He took my elbow, turned me about to face the bar. I found myself inching closer to him. "So that space, all along there. That's where the mural will be."

"Have you found an artist yet?"

"There's one up in Marin County, Victorine Kaufmann. I'm calling her tomorrow." He put down the cigarette. "Let me see what those guys need over there, then we can go." He hesitated, then added, "Cynthia's still in Atherton. We can grab some dinner together, if you want."

When we came back to the apartment after dinner, I went over to pull down the shades. He stood, hands in his pockets, looking about him. I saw his eyes rest on the place above the sideboard where Anna's icon of Christ used to hang. I'd taken it down the evening after we'd been together; his solemn gaze seemed like a reproach, and I did not want any reproaches.

For a moment Max and I just looked at each other across the apartment. I don't know why it felt so awkward all of a sudden, but it did.

"I'm glad you're here," I said finally. It was the truest statement I could think of. I needed to say something to break the silence.

"I feel like this is a very selfish thing," he said. "On my part."

I hadn't expected him to say that. It altered the mood, taking it in a direction I didn't want. "I'm getting as much out of this as you are," I said. "Maybe the selfish one is me. I mean I." I gave a little laugh. "I never know which one is right."

"Neither do I." The flicker of a smile touched his face, then it passed, and he was sober again. "I don't know how all this is going to end, Irene," he said.

End was a word I didn't want to hear, didn't want to think about. I'd had enough things end on me in the last year.

So I didn't say anything. The opposite of an end is a beginning, so I went over to him, slipped my arms around his waist, and rested my head on his chest. A moment later I felt his hands in my hair. He tipped back my head and put his lips on mine, and it all began again.

It's wrong to say that I felt no guilt. There were plenty of moments, in the days that followed, where certain things—a bride and groom in a magazine advertisement, or the sound of bells from St. Dominic's Church a few blocks away—made me feel a stab of remorse. I always fought it back with cold logic. *Cynthia is the one who ended it first. She's the one who left him. I'm not taking anything she wants.*

Sometimes I would tell myself, *Nothing matters anymore. Everything has changed. Look at Louise. Look at the war, at the headlines full of battles, casualties, deaths.* A few days after my second night with Max, I took a dress to a client on Broadway, and afterwards, feeling restless, I walked down the Lyon Street Steps, the long staircase running along the flank of the Presidio. Ghostlike eucalyptus trees loomed to my left, their fallen pods releasing the astringent scent that could not be mistaken for anything else. Letterman Army Hospital was not far away, where Fred Gibson worked. I remembered what he'd said at the

McNeils' party and thought of the wounds he must have encountered. I recalled how once in Union Square I'd seen a young man in crutches, his leg entirely gone below the knee. Perhaps it had been the result of a bomb blast, blowing it clean away. But it was more likely that a doctor like Fred had taken a saw and had to carve away the ragged ends. I winced.

From the steps you had a good view of the bay, off beyond the antique-looking temples of the Palace of Fine Arts. There were battleships, as there always were now. I paused to gaze at the water, and into my memory flashed the face of Rear Admiral Callaghan, killed at Guadalcanal in '42. The photos in the paper showed a handsome man with white hair that was a striking mismatch for his young-looking face. He was a native of San Francisco, so his death had been much mourned in town; I was living at the boardinghouse, and that was all anyone could talk about. "They say he was hit by an exploding shell," said one of the girls in the dining room, in a hushed voice. "Can you imagine? You probably can't even tell it's a person anymore. It's just body parts all over." I remember wishing I hadn't heard that, that I'd left the room a few seconds earlier so I didn't have that image in my head, where it had haunted me for weeks. A memorial Mass was said for him in town, but there was no funeral, for he'd been buried at sea.

He'd been blown into pieces, and he had been buried at sea.

I pulled my coat more firmly about me, then turned and went back up the steps so I would not have to see the water or the ships. As I climbed, I let myself think of Max. I ran through memories of him, letting myself get lost in the thoughts of where his lips and hands had been. It worked until I paused to catch my breath and glanced up at the house to my left. A gold star was in the bow window, looking back at me like an all-knowing eye.

THIRTY-SIX

I'd forgotten all about my promise to make dresses for the orphan girls, so I was surprised a few days later by the delivery of two bolts of fabric and a large envelope addressed in Sister's beautiful handwriting. Inside was a list of the girls' sizes, along with a note for me. "I have been thinking of you ever since you were here the other day, Irene. My prayers are with you. You are a blessing and a joy in my life, and to so many others. God bless you, Sister Margaret."

I lifted one of the bolts to my nose. It was kelly green cotton printed with tiny flowers of burgundy and navy blue, and it smelled clean, dry, and intoxicating, as new fabric always does to me. I decided to make the dresses totally unique, each one with its own look, so the girls wouldn't have to suffer the embarrassment of being dressed alike. As I sketched a few ideas my excitement rose, and I turned to my precious store of buttons and lace and trim for even more inspiration. If I finished the dresses quickly, the girls could even wear them on Christmas.

Laying out pattern pieces for the first dress, I was glad to have a new project to absorb my thoughts. Max had said he would stop by later that night, and thoughts of him jarred oddly with the sight of Sister's letter on the counter. I felt the unfamiliar sensation of having a secret life, one that I could not hold up to the light.

To distract myself I turned on the radio. Judy Garland was singing the new song "Have Yourself a Merry Little Christmas," and though it was beautiful, its wistfulness was too much for me. A turn of the dial brought me to Bing Crosby singing "White Christmas," but that reminded me of Johnny. Finally I found a radio show, a silly soap opera about a nurse and an army doctor. I worked steadily, time seeming to fly as it always does when I'm working on something I like.

Max arrived at seven, bearing a paper bag. "Dinner," he said. "I know cooking isn't your thing." The blinds in the shop were down, so I greeted him with a kiss, which became long and lingering.

Dinner was a pair of calzones, which we ate upstairs, supplemented by a can of applesauce I'd found in my cupboard. "By the way," he said as we finished, "I'm sending a locksmith tomorrow to fix that lock on your front door."

"You are?"

"Yes. I know it's been a problem for you."

"Thank you," I said. For some idiotic reason this little act of kindness, so typical of him, made tears start to fill my eyes. I had to look down and blink several times to hold them back.

"What is it?" he asked.

I couldn't answer. How could I say that for all my bravado, I'd just seen into my soul and realized that there was more feeling there than I had admitted? I didn't want to say it, and I couldn't say it without driving him away, without dismantling the fragile structure of casualness I'd built for myself after our first night together.

So I looked up and smiled. "Nothing," I said brightly. "Nothing at all. Thank you for arranging it, Max." I took our plates to the sink, rinsed them off, and took out the dish soap.

I felt him come up behind me and slip his arms around my waist. I leaned back against his chest, losing myself in the feel of him. We stood that way for a while as the water ran, filling the sink, and finally he reached up and turned it off.

"What are you doing a week from Sunday?" he asked.

"Sunday? I have the USO. No, wait, that's Saturday. Nothing, I guess."

He turned me around. "Come up north for the day, to Point Reyes Station. I'm going to meet that artist about the mural."

"I'd like that."

He rested his forehead against mine, eyes closed. We were silent, standing that way, the only noise the radiator in the other room. For a moment I thought of asking him to leave, saying I had too much work to do. Given how much I'd ached all day to be with him it was crazy that I would even think that, but for some reason I did. But then he lifted my chin and set his mouth gently on mine, and that was the end of my brief moment of clarity.

After he left two hours later I took a bath, feeling relaxed and drowsy, then decided to return to the sewing. I put on my pajamas and the red terry robe, made myself some tea, and went back downstairs to the quiet shop.

Sister's letter was nearby, still folded on the side counter near my cutting table. As I pinned I thought of my visit to the orphanage. It was strange to realize that although the discovery about my parents had shaken me to my core, I'd hardly even considered it since. Max had driven all thoughts of it out of my mind.

But as I fit the pattern pieces onto the cloth as economically as I could, my mind went back to what I had learned in Sister's office. My cherished image of the shabby man with the basket was gone, and I would never get it back. It had been supplanted by the discovery that I'd been created in a moment of transactional sex, between two people who might not even have known each other's names. That was the reality. That was the truth.

And as I stood there in my red bathrobe, bending over the fabric, I could see faces where before I had only been able to see a harsh and bare outline. I could picture a young woman with blonde hair and hazel eyes that tapered at the corners, smoking a cigarette, staring out the window at a happy couple walking by and feeling a pang at the sight of them as she waited for her next client. I could see her burying old childhood dreams under the necessity of paying for food and rent, but those dreams did not entirely go away. They lingered below the surface, threatening her ability to survive, so she worked hard to keep her veneer of flippancy and carelessness. If you pretend it doesn't matter, then maybe one day it won't.

I could see a young man with freckles, maybe recently moved to town, wanting comfort, wanting to connect with someone in this gray city by the water. I could see him climbing the stairs to her room, on the one hand hating himself for what he was about to do, on the other hand aware of the gaping need inside him for the touch of another human being. He would know it wouldn't last, but for a few brief minutes he could forget, could believe in the fantasy that he was loved, that someone in this foggy, windy town cared whether he lived or died.

He knocks, tentatively. She stubs out the cigarette and opens the door. They look at each other. She puts on her working face, and he puts on an expression of nonchalance, as if he has done this kind of thing many times before. And the door closes behind them.

I looked up, staring at the light bulb above the table. It was so vivid to me, that scene. Maybe it was just another fiction, a ridiculous made-up story, like the crying man with the Moses basket. But something inside my bones, something that had not even existed there the week before, knew that it was the truth.

THIRTY-SEVEN

Trixie and I met at Union Square the next evening to look at the department store Christmas windows. It was something we'd done every December since starting high school. Now, of course, everything had a wartime feel; the window at I. Magnin was set up to look like a living room, with a fake fireplace with stockings and a table where two young women in matching red velveteen dresses were selling war bonds. Customers lined up in the store to wait their turn, and when they went up into the window, the girls sat them down with a warm smile. Once they'd bought their bonds, the girls gave them a peppermint stick and, if the customer happened to be male, a kiss on the cheek, which always made the crowds outside cheer and clap. "That's one way to spread the Christmas spirit," said Trixie. "I'd sure be embarrassed to be on display, though."

We drifted among the festive crowds to the windows at Gump's, where beautiful housewares gleamed on green damask tablecloths. NEXT YEAR, HE'LL BE HOME FOR CHRISTMAS, said a large sign showing a soldier embracing a woman at the front door of a trim yellow house.

"Do you think that's true?" asked Trixie thoughtfully. "Next year, they'll all be back?"

I knew she was thinking of Dennis. "I hope so."

We ended up at Bunny's Waffle Shop, in a small booth with a paper bell hanging on the wall beside us. "How is your designing going these days?" asked Trixie. "For Max Burke? I've been so busy I've barely asked you."

"Fine," I said, looking down quickly. But I could not stop the rush of color that flooded my face. And Trixie knew me too well.

"What's going on?" she asked me. "Is everything okay?"

I didn't mean to tell her, I swear. But it took me so long to decide how to respond that she, always the good observer, sensed what I was going to say. I could see the sudden awareness of it in her eyes.

"What happened?" she asked in a low voice, with an audible tinge of alarm.

Quietly, against the incongruous backdrop of Dinah Shore singing "Jingle Bells," I told her about the night at the Top of the Mark, the way Max had rescued me, the night at my apartment, the other two times he had stopped by. I didn't tell her about Cynthia's affair with Fred, or about the pregnancy that had led to the Burkes' marriage; those weren't my secrets to tell. She listened to me, her face intent and sober. I could tell she was worried, which made me want to reassure her.

"It sounds awful, I know," I said. "But it's just something that happened. And I know it won't go on forever. I just"—I looked down at my empty pie plate—"I just figure, why not?"

"But he's married."

"His wife doesn't want him. I wish I could tell you more, Trixie, but I can't. I promised I wouldn't. But please believe me when I say I'm not hurting Cynthia, at all. I'm not."

"I don't know," she said helplessly. "I don't know. I'm just surprised."

I knew exactly how she felt, for I'd felt the same when Louise had confided in me. "I'm the same me," I said, realizing that I was echoing Louise's words. "This doesn't change me."

"Of course it changes you. Everything we do changes us. That's just life."

"I guess what I mean is"—I paused as the waitress refilled our coffee cups—"because of the war, the things that used to matter don't matter anymore. Don't you ever feel that way, Trixie? Like the world we knew in high school no longer exists?" I gestured to the street. "Look at the shop windows. They never used to have anything to do with war, only Santa and bells and carolers. Everything's different now. The old rules don't apply."

She kept looking at me, steadily, and in her brown eyes I did not see disgust—or judgment, thank God. I saw gradual, dawning understanding.

"What are you thinking?" I asked.

"I'm thinking," she said quietly, "that you still haven't gotten over Johnny."

I was not expecting that. There seemed to be a small explosion somewhere in my chest, as if something I'd carefully built inside myself had just been destroyed. But I smiled, even laughed. "Come on, Trixie. It was one weekend in wartime. It would never have lasted afterwards."

"You keep saying that," she said thoughtfully.

To hide my emotion, I took out my compact and powdered my nose. I did that for a while, avoiding looking into my own eyes.

"Look," I said, snapping it shut and putting it away. "I'm sorry to shock you, I really am. And I'd probably think the same if the shoe were on the other foot. But I'm not taking anything Cynthia Burke hasn't already given up, truly I'm not. I'm not hurting anyone."

She finally smiled, though she still looked worried.

"I believe you when you say she doesn't want him," she said. "I honestly do. And I think—well, I can see how this could happen, I really can." She blushed lightly. "Look, if Dennis were actually here in town, I'm not sure I'd care too much about waiting until we got married. But I don't want you to get hurt, Irene."

"I won't," I said resolutely. "It's just temporary with Max. I'm under no illusions." I opened my pocketbook and took out my coin purse to pay the bill. "Illusions are for the old me, not this me."

Trixie pulled out her own pocketbook. "I'll pay for this, Irene."

"Why? Because I'm such a deserving and upright character?"

She glanced up, saw I was smiling, and smiled too. "Yes," she said earnestly, taking out some coins, "and because you're my best friend and always will be. Ever since we were eight years old."

"When we were young and life was simple," I said breezily, but I had to blink back tears as I said it.

The USO was full of holiday spirit. There was hot apple cider and gingerbread men, and the place had been decorated with paper cutouts of reindeer and snowmen along with menorahs and dreidels, two things which I was embarrassed not to know and which an earnest soldier from Long Island kindly explained to me. The guys seemed more nostalgic than usual, as if the holiday atmosphere just emphasized the difference between home and war.

"What are you missing most?" I asked a friendly soldier as we sipped our cider.

"Everything," he said. "The baking my mom does, and the caroling. Buying gifts for my brothers and sisters and then hiding them. And snow. This is a great city, but there's no snow. It doesn't really feel like Christmas."

I nodded. The song had just ended so I put down my cider. "Want to dance?" I asked.

It felt odd, having another man's arms around me. For some reason it felt like a betrayal of Max. When I realized what I was thinking, I was shocked and did an extra spin to hide my confusion. "Gee, you're really good," said the soldier. He couldn't have been more than eighteen.

At nine o'clock Mrs. Latham clapped her hands for attention. "We have a special guest tonight," she announced.

"Lana Turner?" asked one of the men hopefully, prompting laughter from the crowd.

Mrs. Latham gave an indulgent smile. "We'll try to get her next time." She gestured to a stout middle-aged woman, who came forward from the group of senior hostesses. "No, this is Madame Rosalie, who will tell your fortune if you'd like."

The USO often varied the program by bringing in performers, magicians, and sketch artists, but this was the first time I'd been there when they had a fortune teller. Madame Rosalie had a dramatic red shawl, long strings of beads, and a plain but kind face. She sat at a small table in the ping-pong room, greeting each serviceman with a maternal smile.

I moved about the room, watching the ping-pong players, chatting with various guys. I felt odd doing it. So much had happened since the last time I'd volunteered: learning about my parents, Phil, Max. At one point I realized I was staring off into space and not listening to the sailor next to me. I came to with a start. "Sorry. I'm scattered these days."

"No problem." He nodded toward the corner where Madame Rosalie was studying the palm of a gawky soldier. "Should I have my fortune told?"

"I'm not sure I would."

"No?"

"I wouldn't want to know how my life will turn out. It might make me live it differently."

"Like *Macbeth*. 'All hail, Thane of Cawdor.'"

I laughed. "Exactly." He kept looking at the fortune teller, holding his cider cup to his lips but not drinking. I thought of where he would be going next: the Pacific Theater, where so many men had died.

A sailor came up to us through the crowds, nodding at me, and slapped my companion on the back. "Hey, Stew. Gonna learn your future?"

"Nah," said Stew, "I don't think so. Not sure I want to know what's coming."

"I wouldn't worry about that," said his friend good-naturedly. "I've been standing by her table the whole time and listening. She's telling every single guy that he's going to come home all right."

We all looked over at Madame Rosalie's table. The gawky soldier was standing up, relief written clearly all over his face.

Stew drank the last of the cider. "Well," he said, "if you're just going to make something up, it might as well be that."

THIRTY-EIGHT

Max called the next morning as I was opening the shop. "Can I stop by sometime today?" he asked. "Just briefly. Just to talk something over."

He showed up at two minutes after noon as I was finishing the seams of a wool coat. He smiled to see me behind the sewing machine. "Look at you. Working that machine like a professional."

"I *am* a professional," I teased him.

He glanced about as if to make sure no one walking on the sidewalk could see us, then leaned over and kissed me quickly. "Can we talk upstairs?"

I offered him lunch, afterwards realizing that the only thing I had was a can of onion soup. "Soup's fine," he said, sitting back at the table and lighting a cigarette. It felt strange for him to be there during the day, and I said so. "I've got an appointment tonight, at a jazz club on Market. Trying to find the best musical talent. Want to come?"

"I can't, sorry. I've got Pauline coming over to work on her costume."

"Right, the ballet. How's that going?"

"It's been wonderful. Getting to know the dancers, seeing the production from the inside."

"You'll see it from the outside, too, I'm guessing."

"Pauline promised me a seat for the first performance, on Christmas Eve Day."

He took the soup bowl I offered him, and I sat down. For a moment we ate in silence.

I looked up to find his eyes on me. They were intent and thoughtful. "What is it?" I asked.

He put down his spoon. "Cynthia was back at the apartment last night. She told me about her and Fred. She didn't know I already knew."

"Oh," I said. I put down my spoon too, wiping my lips with the napkin. Then I frowned. "Why did she tell you?"

"Because she wants a divorce."

"A divorce? So she can marry him?"

"Yes."

"But he's married."

"Apparently she thinks he's going to divorce his wife."

"No," I said. "No. That can't be." I tried to imagine it. "He wouldn't do that to Betty." I thought of the McNeils in the conservatory the morning I arrived, of Mr. McNeil saying that members of his family only married once. "How could Cynthia possibly think her family would approve?"

"I asked the same thing. She thinks it would blow over in time. That he's so much a part of their world, of their family almost, they'd be forgiving. They couldn't get married right away, for appearances' sake, but they could eventually."

I thought of Betty Gibson, so young and hopeful, a newlywed in love. This would devastate her. The saltiness of the broth was overpowering, and I got up for a glass of milk. I offered Max one, and he lifted a hand in refusal.

"What did you tell her?" I asked as I sat down again.

"I told her to be sure she really wants a divorce. And I said I'd think it over."

Do you want to divorce her? I almost asked. But I didn't ask, because I didn't want to know the answer. It would be terrible to hear no, and it would be somehow frightening to hear yes.

"Did you—did you tell her about me?" I asked.

"Of course not."

"Do you think she suspects anything? About us?"

"I doubt it. Why would she? She's in Atherton most of the time. If not at his place, then with her parents."

"But they won't be able to keep meeting there," I said. "When Fred's wife comes back to town."

"One would think."

"Did she—did she seem sorry at all? I mean, telling you about Fred?"

He pushed his empty soup bowl away and leaned back in the chair. "Yes," he said quietly. "She feels bad about hurting me."

It might have been wishful thinking on his part. But as I studied Max, saw the look in his brown eyes as he stared at the window, I knew he was right.

One time at the boardinghouse, shortly after I moved in, I remember opening my bureau drawer to get out a necklace. All three of the ones I owned—the Miraculous Medal, the locket Trixie had given me as a birthday gift, the fake pearl pendant that I'd bought to wear with my senior prom dress—had somehow gotten tangled together, their chains in a snarl. I had no choice but to sit there under the strongest light I could find, using a safety pin to tease the little knots apart so I could gradually separate the necklaces. It had taken a full half hour, but even in my frustration I couldn't help being impressed at how thoroughly and neatly three different things could get tied together.

After Max left and I was washing the lunch dishes, I thought of the Burkes and the Gibsons. They were like those necklaces now, tangled together in a way that would be very difficult to put right. And though no one knew it but Max, I was right there, too, caught up in the middle of it all.

My afternoon appointments passed in a haze, my mind spinning on what Max had told me. I looked forward to Pauline coming over that evening; her playful humor was always a good distraction. But when she came in, a package of white tulle under her arm, I could tell immediately that something was wrong. "What happened?"

"It's my cousin Edith. Her husband was killed in action."

"Oh, Pauline. No."

Tears shone on Pauline's cheeks. "She left today to go back to Utah. It's just so unfair. They were so in love."

I'd only met Edith the one time, but I remembered her bandana and lunchbox, her cheerful optimism, her anticipation at seeing her husband again one day. "I'm so sorry," I said, blinking back tears of my own. "Is there anything I can do?"

"Just pray for her, I guess. And his parents and sister. And let me come here and blubber if I need to."

"Anytime," I said.

She dashed her tears away with the sleeve of her coat, then handed me the tulle. "Here. I finally bought the silly fabric."

I was glad to have something solid to hold, even tulle, to distract me from the news. "I'm pretty quick with these now. I can have it done by Monday. Want a drink, something to eat?"

She shook her head, moving toward one of the already-completed tutus lining the back wall. As if nothing mattered, she rifled the white layers of the nearest skirt, then watched them settle back. "What the heck am I doing, Irene?" she asked suddenly. "Dancing around like a snowflake when people are dying. It just seems so pointless somehow."

The next morning I woke up earlier than usual, and on an impulse I bundled up in my wool coat and went outside. It was bright and crisp, one of those chilly mornings where you instinctively cross to the sunny side of the street to get as much warmth as possible. I saw the milkman making his rounds and a deliveryman unloading a van at Gino's Grocery. At the streetcar stop I saw a young Black woman in a heavy coat and coveralls, her hair tied up, holding a metal lunchbox. Another Edith, going off to build ships, probably holding in her mind the image of a man—a sweetheart, a brother, a cousin—who was somewhere across the seas. Everyone knew someone. Everyone had lost someone.

I walked up Fillmore with no particular destination in mind, but at the intersection with Jackson I paused. There was the violin player, in the clothes he always wore, with the addition of a shapeless coat and a muffler. He was opening his case, flexing his fingers, ready to make music.

I wondered why he did it. It wasn't for money, for he never put out a cup for coins. He could play at home where it was warm, instead of standing in the cold archway of a church on a December day. "Dancing around like a snowflake when people are dying," Pauline had said. "It just seems so pointless somehow."

Finding a little patch of sunlight on the pavement, I stepped into it. I don't think he saw me, even though I was only a few feet away; he never seems to see anyone. He raised his bow, closed his eyes, and began. The piece was from *Swan Lake*, a song that always made Anna close her eyes as if doing so would let the notes sink ever more deeply into her soul.

I closed my eyes, too, and pictured her again: her figure not fat, not slim, but somewhere in between; her dark gray hair, always pinned up in back; the glasses she wore when doing any sort of detailed work;

the quiet smile she'd give me when I'd done something really well. She was an intensely private person, which suited us both; she'd never have worked well with a more gregarious girl. Still, I wish now that I'd asked her more about herself. After her death I'd found some photographs, along with various documents and personal letters written in Russian. I had saved them because it felt wrong to discard them.

The song floated in the morning air. A man waiting at the streetcar stop lowered his paper to listen. The workman unloading a crate by the curb paused, putting his hands in his armpits for warmth. And I, standing in the patch of sunlight, remembered a day when Anna and I had heard the song on the radio. It was a break between customers, and we'd been drinking tea with strawberry jam in it—she always made it that way—and eating Russian cookies, and out of nowhere she said one of the most personal things I'd ever heard from her. "A beautiful thing, the ballet," she'd said. "Some people ask why I spend so much money on a ticket, because what do you keep, when the evening is over? But you keep the memories."

I turned and walked home even though the song wasn't over. I did not want to hear it end.

THIRTY-NINE

I was surprised the following morning to get a call from Betty Gibson. "I'm just back in town from Florida," she said, "and I have a dress that needs altering. May I come by sometime today?"

I offered to come to her apartment, but she said she'd like to come to the shop. She arrived at two o'clock in a pretty green tartan coat and matching hat, but her face was puffy and there was a redness about her eyes, which I noticed with feelings of both sympathy and guilt.

The dress was an evening gown of blue, which she was hoping to wear for the holidays. "I'm wondering if you can let it out," she said. "It's tighter than it used to be."

It was a very good quality dress, with generous seams. "I believe so. Let me measure you to be sure."

She forced a smile. The perky warmth of a few months earlier was gone; she seemed like a much older woman. I offered her tea or coffee, and she shook her head quickly. "No, thank you."

As she undressed I asked if she'd had a nice trip.

"Very nice. My sister just had a baby. A girl." She stood in front of the mirror in her slip, and I took up my tape measure and notebook.

"Actually," she said abruptly, "I'm having a baby too."

She hadn't needed to tell me; I've been a seamstress long enough that I could tell the signs in her figure. "Congratulations," I said. "That's wonderful news." My mind, of course, was racing.

"It is," she said. "I hope." Then she put her hands to her eyes and began to sob.

I immediately fetched her a handkerchief and gently ushered her to the chair. She sat down in her slip, sniffling as I stood awkwardly by, twisting the tape measure around my finger.

"Thank you," she said at last. "I'm not crying about the baby. I'm crying about—something else." And she began to sob again.

I got her a glass of water and stood helplessly by. Her naked misery was a terrible thing to see. But all I could do was try to comfort her and pretend I knew absolutely nothing about why she was crying.

In bed that night I opened a book Trixie had lent me, but it was too hard to focus, so finally I put it aside and stared at the ceiling. I wished Max were there, not only for the obvious reasons but to have someone there to distract me from my thoughts. I kept thinking of the day I'd first met Betty at her apartment on Nob Hill. I remembered the buttercup yellow silk she'd been so excited about, and the huge wedding picture in the living room, Cynthia there among the party.

I recalled Dolores Kittredge, smoking a cigarette and gossiping about the Burkes and their marriage. "I suspect," she'd said about Max, "he knows how to behave in the bedroom." My face turned red, even though I was all alone.

Glancing to the other side of the bed, I thought of the times in the last few weeks that I'd had Max lying next to me. I felt worlds different from the girl who had made notes in her book and pretended not to be listening to the gossip about him. I'd travelled so far since then, so far into a world of pleasures and delight, that I had no idea how to get back to the old world. It was hard to imagine ever wanting to.

As if my thoughts had summoned her, the very next day Dolores Kittredge herself entered the shop. She was with a beautifully dressed woman, thirty-five or so, with an aquiline nose and an elegant fur coat. I got quickly up from the sewing machine, hiding my surprise, and went over to greet them.

"Just wondered if you could mend this for me," asked Dolores, opening an alligator skin bag and taking out a folded garment. It was a long satin nightgown, like something a starlet would wear in a movie. There was a rip along one sleeve.

"Of course, Mrs. Kittredge." I glanced at the clock. "I can even do it now, if you can wait. It shouldn't take more than a few minutes."

"Perfect," said Dolores. She was wearing a dramatic copper-colored hat and a matching suit with a draped front that flattered her angular figure. "This is Mrs. Marion Ramsey, by the way. She lives on Pacific Avenue, not far from here. Miss Cleary did that yellow suit for Betty Gibson," she said, turning to her friend. "Now you know she's here if you need any work done."

I nodded politely to Mrs. Ramsey, offered them both tea, which they refused, and sat down to pin the sleeve.

"Such an elegant nightgown," said Mrs. Ramsey. "How on earth did it get ripped?"

"It caught on a latch. The stupidest thing."

"That's too bad." Mrs. Ramsey dropped her voice, adopting a just-us-girls tone. "I thought maybe Gordon did it."

"What, in bed?" Dolores laughed. "Hardly. That's not his style. Though when you've been married as long as I have, you'd welcome a little variety." She lit a cigarette and her tone changed. "Speaking of variety—"

"Yes?"

Dolores lowered her voice, but I could still hear clearly. "Cynthia has been spending a *lot* of time in Atherton. Did you know?"

"I know she wasn't in town for the Red Cross last week, or the week before. Or for Ellen's baby shower."

"Fred Gibson's been down there a lot, too." Dolores paused, apparently for effect. "Gordon keeps inviting him to things but he's never in town."

"No," said Mrs. Ramsey as if the word were delicious to say. "No. They wouldn't." She paused. "Would they?"

"Cynthia's carried a torch for Fred for years. Everyone knows that."

"But he'd never do that to Betty."

"She's a doll, of course. But Cynthia was there first." Glancing up from my pinning, I could see them standing by the vase of iris, Mrs. Ramsey leaning forward avidly. "And Betty's been in Florida for nearly two months, just got back. I have no proof, Marion, so don't spread anything around. Just saying it's possible."

I had to turn on the sewing machine, whose rat-a-tat-tat drowned out whatever was said next. It was actually a relief, for I did not want to hear more.

FORTY

On Sunday morning Max picked me up at ten for our outing to Point Reyes. "I'm glad you're coming today," he said as we drove off under gray skies. "I've never interviewed a muralist before."

"I've done it loads of times," I said glibly. "Just leave it all to me." I glanced up at the heavy, dark clouds. "Hopefully the rain will hold off."

It was exciting to be going somewhere new and positively thrilling to go over the Golden Gate Bridge. As we drove under the huge orange towers, my head kept swiveling from side to side. I hardly knew where to look: toward the bay to my right, toward the ocean to my left, or at the sweeping hills up ahead. The bridge and the views were so magnificent I got a lump in my throat. "This is beautiful," I managed to say.

"Have you been on the bridge before?" Max asked.

"No, never. I went to Marin County when I was a kid, but by ferry. They were building the bridge at the time."

"What were you doing up there?"

"An orphanage picnic. One of the trustees knew someone with a dairy farm and they thought we might like to get out of the city for a day. It was so exciting, seeing the bridge being built." I'd never seen anything like it, those huge unfinished towers rising out of the gray waters of the bay. All of us kids and even the sisters had leaned against the ferry rail, speechless with wonder.

"You know," said Max, "I was talking to a sailor the other day. The Golden Gate is the last bit of home they see when they head out. He said the whole ship of guys goes quiet when it goes under the bridge, totally quiet. It's almost spooky, he said."

I looked out of the mouth of the bay to the ocean beyond. Johnny had been one of those men. He'd sailed out to sea, my little medal around his neck, my voice still fresh in his ears.

"Sorry," said Max. "That was a little depressing."

"It was," I said, hiding my emotion under gaiety. "Just for that you'll have to kiss me."

"Later. When we have time to do it right."

I put my hand on the back of his neck and left it there. He leaned back into it as if he liked it.

It was nice to be away from the bustle of the crowded city. We drove through the eucalyptus-covered hills of Sausalito and through the lovely small towns of Ross, San Anselmo, and Fairfax. We passed under the canopies of redwoods and out into the country, where gently rolling hills were gold-brown and damp with the recent rain. There were large barns, white farmhouses with gables and porches, cows in herds grazing unconcernedly under the gray skies. Mrs. Bliss had taken precise directions from the artist, which was helpful, for there was none of the geometric regularity of the streets of San Francisco.

Outside the tiny town of Point Reyes Station, we found the yellow cottage home of Victorine Kaufmann, a fiftyish woman with graying black hair tied in a kerchief. She wore denim slacks and a man's sweater and was candid about the proposed commission. "I don't go to nightclubs," she said, "never have. But a mural of San Francisco is too enticing to turn down." A barn served as her studio, and she showed us the paintings stacked about, landscapes and men and women that were at once realistic and stylized. As she talked to Max, I wandered about to study her work.

One painting in particular moved me. It was a young girl with dark hair holding an abalone shell. The shell mirrored the shape of the girl's face, and its iridescent interior was echoed in the tints of the girl's complexion.

I wondered what had inspired Victorine to paint it. I could see her standing before an empty canvas, brush poised, exhilarated by a new idea. To create something out of nothing, especially when it's something that only you can make: perhaps that's as close to heaven as you can get on Earth. And it suddenly occurred to me that as solitary as I've been for much of my life, when I'm creating something I'm excited about I never feel lonely. It was astonishing that I had never realized that fact before.

Half an hour later, our business was concluded with a handshake and a pot of tea brought out by Victorine's teenage daughter. I commented on the beauty of the hills around us, and the artist smiled. "It's magical," she said. "I'm from New York City and the first time I ever saw this place it went right to my bones. As if I'd been here before, in another life." She nodded out the studio door. "If you aren't in a hurry to get back, there's a gate just down the road, with a footpath through the trees. Worth a ramble."

I was glad I'd opted to wear stylish slacks and low-heeled shoes rather than a skirt and pumps. We found the gate easily, and a short walk through a tawny field led us into a forest of redwoods, oaks, and the occasional bay tree. Lichen grew on the trunks of the oaks and ferns flourished on the banks of a small clear brook, which sparkled in the rare moments of sunlight that occasionally broke through the clouds. It smelled achingly beautiful, a combination of wet soil and leaves and the slightest hint of the ocean. Max took my hand and we walked along slowly through the trees. “It’s a fairy-tale forest,” I said. “It’s like we’re Hansel and Gretel or something. Should we leave a trail of breadcrumbs to find our way out again?”

“That didn’t work out so well for them, did it,” said Max.

Birds flitted above, and I heard a rustling at one point that could have been a rabbit. Shafts of light occasionally pierced the leafy canopy over our heads, beaming down like pictures from a holy card.

“You can really believe in heaven in a place like this,” I said.

“You don’t believe in it, in the city?”

“I don’t know. It’s harder, somehow.”

His hand still held mine, a point of warmth in the cool forest air. I paused and pointed to a place just off the path where a fallen tree was overhung with branches and vines, making a space underneath. “It looks like a little nest, doesn’t it. Like a forest room.” I squeezed his hand. “Maybe we could live out here, Max. We could make a home out here and never go back.”

I meant it jokingly, but he stopped and turned to face me, his expression serious. “You’re an astonishing woman, Irene Cleary.”

“Astonishing.” I laughed. “Just for pointing out a fallen tree?”

In an answer he drew me to him and pressed his lips to mine. It was the first time we had ever kissed outside my apartment. There was no one to see but the trees and the brook and a doe I saw when we finally pulled apart. She gazed at us calmly, no judgment in her gentle eyes.

The forest was enchanting but we soon grew hungry, so after half an hour we turned and retraced our steps. As the brook tumbled along in its red-brown banks, I told Max about my epiphany at Victorine’s studio. “I realized I’m never lonely when I create. When I’m working on a project I really believe in.”

"But you're lonely the rest of the time?"

"Well, I do live alone. And even at the orphanage I was sort of on my own. We all were, really."

He laced his fingers with mine. "Tell me how you got interested in dressmaking."

I told him all about the paper dolls, about the extra clothes I sketched so happily as a child. "It worked out so well, being placed with Anna. She was the perfect teacher for me."

The air felt cooler as we emerged from the forest and back into the open space. A huge bay tree rose up to our left, and to our right was open space beyond a low fence, a cow standing in the middle of the field.

"What about you?" I asked as we drew closer to the gate leading to the road. "When did you want to be a nightclub owner?"

"When I was eighteen or so."

"And what did you want to be when you were really young? When you were seven, eight?"

My question hung in the air, for Max didn't answer until we had reached the gate. He paused by it and looked off in the distance, at the rolling hills, at the sky with its gray clouds. I was not expecting the answer he gave.

"I wanted to be a hero," he said, more to the landscape than to me. Then he unlatched the gate and held it open, giving me a kiss as I passed through.

FORTY-ONE

There weren't many places to eat so far out in the country. "Something's bound to turn up," I said as we drove along the two-lane highway.

"Do you need to be back at a particular time?" Max asked.

"No. Do you?"

"No. Cynthia's in Atherton again." The car moved along in silence. I wished I hadn't heard her name; it brought to mind the conversation with Dolores and Mrs. Ramsey. I fiddled with a button on my coat, wondering if I should say anything.

"What is it?" he asked. I had to admire his ability to sense when I was troubled by something.

"Just that—well, I think she should be careful." I gave him an account of the conversation between Dolores Kittredge and Marion Ramsey. When I glanced at him, his face was like stone.

"Dolores Kittredge is poison," he said. "Sheer poison." A few raindrops fell on the windshield, big ones. He turned on the windshield wipers. "Maybe I should tell Cynthia to be careful."

I thought about what a strange world I was in, one where a man's wife has a lover and he warns her not to be reckless so she won't get caught. We passed a farmhouse where a woman was running outside to gather laundry off the line. I pulled the coat about me and buttoned it, and he turned up the heater.

"As long as Dolores doesn't know anything about you," he said suddenly.

"About me? Oh, you mean about you and me." I held my cold hands to the vent. "Why would she?"

He shook his head. "I can't think of a reason. But it would be terrible for you if she did."

A few miles later we came upon a brown-shingled building with a sign which read STAN'S RESTAURANT. We parked in the small lot and ran to the door, dodging the raindrops. Inside was a large dimly lit room with a big stone fireplace and about eight tables laid for dinner. On the wall behind the front desk, the eyes of a mounted deer head stared at some point a few feet above us, giving the room the look of a hunting lodge.

At our arrival a man with a well-trimmed gray moustache stood up smartly, folding the paper he was reading. "Good day," he said. "Dinner for two? It is early but we have just opened." He had an accent, one that reminded me somewhat of Anna's.

I waited for Max to answer, but he was suddenly tense and wary, as if something had put him on the defensive. "Yes," I finally said. "By the fire, if we may?"

We followed the man past a wall partition hung with colored pictures of what looked like cities in Eastern Europe. He set down the menus and disappeared behind the partition where we heard him speaking to someone in the kitchen in a language I didn't recognize.

The menu, printed on cardboard, had the usual fare: soup, pork chops, roast beef, omelet, hamburger. But there were other things too, listed under a heading called Specials of the House. Stuffed cabbage leaves. Kielbasa (homemade). Pierogi (dumplings filled with mushroom and cheese).

I looked up in sudden awareness and Max met my eyes. "He's Polish," he said briefly.

"You knew right away, didn't you?"

He nodded and lit a cigarette, offering me one, which I refused. He stared at the pictures on the walls, the closest one an image of a dark-skinned Madonna in an ornate dress and crown, holding the infant Jesus. "Our Lady of Czestochowa. My mother had the same picture," he said without smiling. "So did everyone in our neighborhood."

The man returned with a plate. "Caraway bread, made this morning. Are you ready to order?" Max said nothing, just kept smoking and looking past him into the fire. "Our specials are quite good," said the man hopefully, but Max did not respond.

"I'm sure they are," I said, smiling to break the awkwardness. "But I think I'll just have a hamburger." The man nodded, trying to conceal his evident disappointment. He turned toward Max, opening his mouth to ask for his order, but before he could say anything Max leaned forward, with brisk, sudden decision.

"No, Irene," he said. He put his cigarette resolutely in the ashtray. "I can't let you order that." He looked directly at the man, smiled briefly, and said something in Polish.

The change in the man was instantaneous. His eyes widened and his face lit up with excitement. His answer was in Polish, and so was Max's response, and I looked from one to the other in astonishment, like a spectator at a tennis match. After a while the man held up an eager hand as if to say, "Wait, wait," and he hurried behind the partition, reappearing with a gray-haired woman wiping her hands on an apron and a boy about sixteen. Max got to his feet and introductions were made—I heard "Irena," and Max pointed to me—and though I couldn't follow, I was beaming too.

The man indicated me and seemed to be asking if I spoke any Polish. Max shook his head, and the man made a gesture of apology. "Excuse us, please. But how joyful, to speak our language with a customer. We cannot often do so in California."

The bell at the front door announced the arrival of a middle-aged couple with an umbrella. The waiter, still smiling, excused himself and went to welcome them.

Max sat down again. The wariness was gone; there was an ease about him I hadn't seen since we'd walked in the front door. "I thought you didn't speak Polish anymore," I said.

"It's like riding a bicycle. You never forget." He nodded behind the partition, where the wife and son had returned to the kitchen. "Stan and Alicja and their son Janusz, from Krakow. Came here in the thirties. They have another son, off in the war." He gazed at the fire, as if seeing images that made him thoughtful. "They're good people."

Under the table I reached for his hand. He turned to me, surprised out of his reverie, then took my hand and put it on his knee. "So," I said. "What did you order for me?"

"Something far better than a hamburger." He nodded toward the door, where Janusz was coming out with two steaming bowls. "Here's the first course."

It was soup, cloudy and thick with bits of carrot and celery. It was also surprisingly, deliciously sour. "It's like a pickle," I said.

"Dill cucumber soup. My mother used to make it," said Max. "When I was a kid I'd eat three bowls at a time." He took a spoonful, smiling reminiscently. "It's been years since I tasted this."

We ate by the glow of the fire as the restaurant began to fill. There were five other tables of diners, but no one I recognized. I knew Dolores or Mrs. Ramsey would never end up in such a place, and I felt so safe at my cozy table with Max. Rain drummed on the roof and the soup warmed my insides. I tried to picture him as a young boy, sitting before a steaming bowl at a Chicago kitchen table.

"Max," I asked, "what was your mother's name?"

He put down his spoon and wiped his mouth with his napkin. "Her name was Beata."

"That's pretty. Does it mean something?"

"Blessed." He smiled, ironically. "Not very prophetic, as names go."

I was moving slowly on my soup now, not wanting to be done. "What was she like, Max? I mean, when she wasn't—"

"Wasn't drunk?" He didn't say it with bitterness. "She was . . ." He stared once more into the flames. "She was very bright. Loved to laugh. I remember how when something amused her, surprised her, she'd drum her feet on the floor really quickly, like she had to react with her whole body." He smiled at the memory. "And generous. One time in first grade I needed a costume for a school play. We didn't have any money to get fabric, so she cut up her favorite tablecloth to make it. When I realized what she'd done, I went out and shoveled snow for the neighbors, swept their front steps, saving pennies so I could buy her a new one. On her birthday six months later, I finally had enough."

Stan appeared again. "You enjoyed the soup?" he asked me.

"Delicious," I said. "The best I've ever had." We paused while he picked up the bowls and removed a speck of dirt seen only by him.

When he was gone Max took my hand. "You know," he said, "for a long time, I blamed my mother for her drinking, for not knowing how to stop. But I've realized that it didn't come out of nowhere. It must have been a response to something else. Some unhappiness or pain."

"What kind of pain, do you think?"

"I have no idea." He traced my thumb thoughtfully. "But there must have been something that happened in her life, some point where it all went wrong." He paused and the fire crackled. "If only I knew what that point was. If I could go back, find it. Though I guess it doesn't matter anymore, now."

"Maybe we all have a point in our lives where everything changes," I mused. "But we can't see it until it's too late. Until the damage is already done."

He raised his eyes to mine. The look in them startled me. He looked as if he were thinking something about me, something that caused him almost physical pain. *I wasn't talking about myself*, I wanted to say, *I wasn't talking about us*, but then Stan and his son appeared with the next course on trays, and I never actually said it.

That dinner has a dreamlike quality, now: the dim and cozy restaurant, the rain pouring outside, the fire leaping in the stone fireplace. The food, so much of it, heaps of pierogi filled with mushrooms and cheese, cabbage leaves like a limp pale skin rolled tightly around spiced minced meat, steamed cabbage that was inky-purple in color, creamy rice pudding for dessert. Every course prompted Max to share something about his childhood, little things, good things, and whenever Stan stopped by the table Max would shift back into Polish and I would listen in wonder to the sound of it, absorbing a side of Max that I'd never seen before, a side at home with his past or at least starting to become so. And there was amber liquid served in small goblets, honey liqueur, which was unlike any drink I'd ever had and which I can still taste.

Then the rain stopped, and we drove home through the damp-smelling hills, through the quiet towns of Marin County, over the bridge and back into the city, twinkling like a Christmas tree beyond the black sheet of the bay at night. Max came upstairs, and it was somehow different than it had been the other times; I don't know why exactly, but I know that I cried afterwards, with something that wasn't exactly sadness. In his arms I let the tears fall and they wet the hollow of his shoulder, and he put his lips in my hair, tightening his arms as if he understood. And we said nothing, just lay in my quiet apartment in the big sleeping city, on the edge of emotions that neither one of us wanted to formalize with words.

It was, in so many ways, the last bit of calm. For the next day, we learned that just as we were sitting knee to knee in Stan's restaurant, Fred Gibson took a gun and shot himself in his parents' guesthouse in Atherton.

FORTY-TWO

Max called me with the news. I had just finished with my last customer of the day, and his words shocked me so much I had to sit down. "What happened?" I asked when I could speak.

"It was around seven yesterday evening. A worker on their estate heard the sound of a gunshot, and they found him."

I thought of his mother, so gracious and kind, sitting next to me in the McNeils' home. I could not imagine her grief. Or Betty's, for that matter, so young and vulnerable.

"His wife is pregnant," I said. "Did you know?"

"I didn't." He exhaled. "That poor woman. She's just a kid, really."

"Cynthia wasn't with him?"

"No, she was out with some friends. She called me with the news this morning." His voice was even more grim than before. "She's—I've never heard her like that. Her parents are looking after her. I'm going down in an hour."

"Do they know why he did it?"

"There was no note or anything. Apparently he'd not been himself for a while. The work at the hospital—he's seen some awful things."

I remembered his face, when Antonia had asked him about the worst injuries he'd seen. How abruptly he'd turned and walked out, only coming back after Cynthia had gone out to soothe him.

"No one suspects about him and Cynthia, do they?" I asked.

"I don't think so."

But in a way it didn't matter, because of course Fred himself knew. And I could imagine how a man already grappling with demons would react, realizing his sweet young wife was pregnant, that there was no way out of his situation but to devastate one of the two women he loved and who loved him back. I wished I knew nothing, nothing about any of it. And somehow, I wanted Max with me more than ever.

"I'll check back with you in a day or two," he said. "I'm supposed to go to Chicago on Saturday. I'll see how Cynthia is before I go."

"Of course." I twisted the phone cord around my finger, staring at the darkened street outside the shop.

There was a pause. "You're all right?" he asked gently.

"I'll be all right. It's all so sad, though."

And when he had said goodbye and hung up, the tears came. I was crying for Fred, for his family, for Betty, even for Cynthia, I suppose. I was crying for the tragedy that crept everywhere like an implacable fog, stretching its cold white fingers from a library in a home in New York into a quiet guesthouse under the oaks in California.

I hadn't seen Louise since the night at the Top of the Mark. She'd been planning to go Christmas shopping with Trixie and me at Union Square, but she'd had to cancel due to a cold. She and I met at the Oyster Loaf for dinner, a restaurant decorated with fake seagulls and other marine decor. Her manner was subdued as we settled into a small table.

"I'm going to New York, Irene," she said without preamble after we ordered. "On Thursday."

"For Christmas?"

"For the rest of the war, basically." She lowered her voice so as not to be heard by the party at the nearby table. "My mother found out about . . . me."

"Oh."

"Hetty told her. She heard me come back with Franklin that night. I guess we were—well, louder than I realized." A slight blush crept over her face. "Anyhow, she called Mother, who is appalled, so I'm being taken back to New York in disgrace."

"I'm sorry."

"No, it's fine. At least Dad doesn't know. He's pretty old-fashioned, so Mother wants to keep it that way." She pleated her napkin. "So my career as the female Casanova is over. It was fun while it lasted."

"I guess it's good that it ended before something bad happened."

"Getting knocked up, you mean?"

"Well, yes."

"True. I've been spared that at least."

The waitress arrived with our drinks. Louise stared at her glass with a pensive expression, something I wasn't accustomed to seeing from her. "You know," she said when the waitress had left, "I think I'm always going to wonder about those guys. All of them. If they make it back all right or if they died out there. Franklin especially."

I didn't know what to say. Finally, I said, "I think it's good that you think about that."

She looked at me, her eyes suspiciously bright. She blinked a few times, then shrugged and gave a casual laugh. "Well, c'est la vie. Off to New York I go. Mother is already talking about making me volunteer for the Red Cross."

"Maybe you'll like it."

"Maybe." The waitress put down our soup bowls and I took a spoonful, blowing on it first to cool it. Looking up, I saw Louise's gaze had drifted over my shoulder, and she was smiling. I turned and saw a marine at a table fifteen feet away, grinning at her in frank admiration. When I turned back, she opened her eyes wide in innocence. "I'm just looking, Irene. It's all right to look."

She took a spoonful of chowder. "Oh, I never asked. How did it go that night?"

"Which night?"

"You know, after the Top of the Mark. With Phil."

I took my time crumbling a cracker into my soup. When I looked up her gaze had drifted over my shoulder again, a smile touching the corners of her lips. *Louise*, I thought with a mix of affection and sadness, *will always be Louise*. I answered accordingly.

"It was fine," I said. "Fine."

Christmas was a season I usually loved. At the orphanage the sisters had always tried hard to make it festive with a tree and candy canes, and one year we even made gingerbread houses, a whole neighborhood of ramshackle lean-tos studded with gumdrops along the rooflines. After leaving the orphanage, I'd spent Christmas at the Dubuques' home, where there was mistletoe in the dining room archway and stockings along the mantel, including one for me. I've always loved carols, twinkling lights, and the general feeling of excitement that comes with the holiday.

But as I walked along Fillmore, hearing the ring of Salvation Army bells, it just wasn't the same. Christmas felt different, and I realized it was because I was different. The Irene who had sipped eggnog at the Dubuques' home last year hadn't yet met and designed a dress for Cynthia Burke. She had not given her heart and soul to a sailor with a beautiful smile. She had not yet given her body to a man who surprised her at every turn with his own capacity to give. It took the sameness of the holidays, maybe, to show me how much I'd changed in one short year, how much wider and more complicated the world had become.

I worked furiously all the next day, wanting to keep myself busy, but I kept thinking of Fred Gibson. There was a funeral at noon at a church in Atherton. His obituary in the paper had said nothing about the manner of his death. I wondered how one managed to keep that a secret.

It was too terrible, thinking of the gunshot, the blood, the scene found by his parents. I could hardly imagine Cynthia's pain. She knew that something more than war wounds had made him take up that gun. I sewed a button on a blouse and felt sympathy for her, an intense sympathy that surprised me. Some part of her might even have felt responsible. There was no one in whom she could confide.

No one but Max.

I pricked myself with the needle, something I almost never do. It hurt so much I had to put the blouse down and close my eyes.

When Max called at nine the next morning, I was relieved to hear his voice, even though we couldn't talk for long. "Can you meet me at the club?" he asked. "Five o'clock? There's something I want you to see."

I closed early and put on the blue jersey dress and the red hat and crossed town, arriving fifteen minutes late due to traffic. Max opened the door for me, but we weren't at home so I could hardly greet him with a kiss, much as I wanted to. The main room of the club smelled of fresh paint, and the orange-red drapes were hanging in vivid splendor. The refurbished bar gleamed in the light, below the empty spot where Victorine's mural would go. "What did you want me to see?"

"This." Max took me into the second room. The carpet was laid, the walls were painted, and the booths had been upholstered. It was exactly the effect I'd wanted: a symphony of moss green, forest green, and light green, highlighted with mauve and white. But what drew my eye most of all were the photos, large black-and-white ones in gilt-edged frames that made them seem to leap off of the walls. The windmill. The bison in his pen. A path leading into a grove of cypress. And three carousel animals, two horses and a lion.

"They put them up today. What do you think?"

"It's perfect," I said. It really was. "Who took the pictures?"

"Fellow by the name of Frank Delgado. He did a great job."

One of the carousel horses was white. I moved closer and studied it. It looked just like the one I'd ridden with Johnny. "He sure did," I said.

Max squeezed my elbow. "I thought you'd like to see it. Something to cheer us both up." He paused, and his tone shifted. "Irene, there's something—"

We heard footsteps and he dropped my arm. We both turned.

Two men were standing there, one with a large camera and one with a pad and pencil. "Mr. Burke?" said the one with the pad. "Jim French, *San Francisco Chronicle*. I know we're early, but we happened to be in the neighborhood. Is this a good time?"

"Of course," said Max, striding toward him and shaking his hand. "Of course, Jim. How are you." He shook hands with the man with the camera, who introduced himself as Al Brinker. "This is Irene Cleary. She helped with the designs." We exchanged the usual pleasantries, Jim making a notation in his pad. "They're going to do a write-up about the club," said Max to me. "Advance publicity."

I checked my watch and nodded an apology to the two men. "I should really be going anyhow. It was nice to meet you."

"Look around for a bit," said Max to the two men. "I'll be right with you." He walked with me back into the main room, pausing by the curtains. "Sorry, I thought they were coming by later," he said, lowering his voice. "I need to stay here a bit. Can I stop by later?"

"Sure. I'll be at home."

He smiled briefly, encouragingly, before turning back to Jim. "So," I heard him say as they walked off toward the bar, "we're still waiting on the mural. It'll go up along the wall there."

I lingered a moment by the curtains, looking in my purse for the streetcar fare before going back out into the cold. I had just glanced up when I heard the sound of a camera and saw the flash of a bulb. Max and Jim were deep in conversation off by the bar, but Al was a few feet away from me, lowering his camera, nodding toward the front door. "Nice framing," he said. "With the curtains."

I had no idea what he was talking about, but I wasn't terribly interested either. I smiled, said goodbye, and left.

FORTY-THREE

When Max came by at seven, I offered him dinner. "Have you already eaten?" he asked, shrugging off his coat.

"Not yet. I've got two pork chops. I can fry them up."

He sat down at the table, and I put on an apron and lit the stove. I set out two napkins, silverware, glasses. *This is what being married would be like*, I thought.

"Sorry we got interrupted there at the club," he said. "I wanted to tell you something. Something I found out just yesterday."

"What?" I asked as I put the chops in the pan.

"It's Cynthia," he said. "I was down in Atherton yesterday. We went out for a drive, the two of us. She told me that she's pregnant."

I stared at him. "Pregnant?"

"She found out about a week ago." He answered the question in my eyes. "And yes, she told Fred. Two days before he shot himself."

"Is that why he did it?"

"She thinks so."

I sat down at the table. "And of course she can't tell anyone," said Max. "Except me." He was silent for a moment, his eyes focused on a space on the wall, clearly replaying a conversation. "She blames herself. It was a relief for her to tell me."

"And no one else knows about them?"

He shook his head. "She thinks Betty might have suspected

something, but according to Fred, he never told her. So you know, and I know. And that's all."

I traced the pattern on the oilcloth tablecloth with my finger. "Except the people who suspect. Like Dolores Kittredge, or Marion Ramsey."

"But they suspect with no proof. Which is how it needs to stay. For the sake of everyone, really."

There was a loud sizzle behind me, and I turned down the gas burner. It gave me time to think, to recognize the magnitude of the scandal that would break open if those suspicions were confirmed, if people knew that Fred had fathered not one but two children who would never know him. I had the sudden, shocking awareness that I held Cynthia Burke's happiness in my hands. It was a power I would never use, but it was somehow terrifying simply to know that I had it.

I sat down again, and Max reached for my hand. He traced it, searching my face. "Somehow, Irene, you've landed in the middle of this crazy drama. I'm sorry."

It was the first time he'd touched me since coming into the apartment, and I didn't want him to stop. I stared at the black hair at the base of his wrist. "She probably doesn't want a divorce anymore, then."

"It didn't come up," he said quietly. "I'm leaving for Chicago tomorrow, that trip I had planned. I offered to cancel it, but she said she'd be okay. I hope she's right."

"She has her family," I said weakly.

"True," he said. "For all their faults, they're good at a time like this. She won't be alone."

But I will be, I found myself thinking, and the thought shocked me. I jumped up, busying myself with taking down plates.

He came up behind me and put his arms around me, and I leaned back into him as I'd done before, his solid arms circling my waist and his mouth somewhere above my temple. We were that way for a full minute, at least; then, just as precisely as if we had choreographed it, he let go of me at exactly the moment I stepped away, and I turned back to the stove.

We didn't sleep together that night. The mood wasn't there, for either of us. We ate dinner, listened to the radio, talked. I took out the cherry brandy and we drank the last of it as Artie Shaw played on the radio and we sat on the couch, my hand on his knee and his hand on mine, each thinking our own thoughts.

At quarter to eleven we said goodbye. He held my head, looking into my eyes.

"Can I bring you anything from Chicago?" he asked. "A Christmas gift?"

"I don't need anything."

"You sure?"

"You've given me so much already, Max."

His left thumb traced my cheekbone. For some reason a phrase popped abruptly into my mind, like an absurd jack-in-the-box: *He giveth and he taketh away.* I blinked and then closed my eyes and after a few seconds I felt his lips on mine. I opened my eyes and he was looking at me, his gaze troubled and tender. He kissed me again, took up his coat, and was gone.

I stood in the window to watch him go. It was late, only a few pedestrians on Sacramento Street, probably coming from the movie theater on Fillmore. Two young women strolled by, arm in arm with two sailors, and a well-dressed couple paused under a streetlamp as the man lit a cigarette. I heard the sound of my shop door closing, then I saw Max directly below me, walking out to the car parked along the curb.

If I'd moved back a second earlier, I wouldn't have seen it. But I was still by the window, leaning out, and as his car lights went on I saw that the woman under the streetlamp was Mrs. Ramsey. She was staring at his car as it backed up, then she nudged her husband, and I could almost hear what she was saying: *Isn't that Max Burke in that car?*

Then she looked up. She looked right into the lighted window of my apartment, and I instantly backed away, fumbling for the cord on the window shade, quickly pulling it down.

Five minutes later, standing in my quiet kitchen, I felt my heartbeat return to normal. *No*, I told myself. *She couldn't possibly have seen me. Of course not*. I ran water to wash the stacked dishes, then paused, picking up the glass Max had used. I traced the rim lightly with my finger.

FORTY-FOUR

The next morning I woke up to fog, thick and clammy. Everything outside my window was blurred by the mist. There was no point in trying to do anything with my hair because dampness always made the curl fall right out, so I pinned it up, went downstairs, and got to work.

Mrs. O'Leary came by in her old brown coat, this time with a pin the shape of a Christmas angel on the lapel. My attention was so focused on the suit I was piecing together, and on avoiding thoughts of Max, that it was an effort to smile and be welcoming. "Terrible day, isn't it?" she said, setting down her ubiquitous shopping bags. I offered her a seat and she was there for twenty minutes, chatting about various things. "I like your hair up like that," she said at one point, studying me. "You look so much older than you used to."

It wasn't the hairstyle that made me look older. I didn't even want to think about what was making me look older. I gave a brisk smile. "I'm very sorry," I said, "but I really need to get back to work."

"Of course. You have such important customers now," she said humbly. "I don't want to keep you. I just stopped by to give you this and wish you a Merry Christmas." "This" was a small lumpy bundle, wrapped in a napkin and tied with a limp red ribbon. "I always made plum cake for Anna," she said a little sadly. "It wouldn't feel like Christmas without bringing it by."

I felt terribly ashamed. "Thank you, Mrs. O'Leary. Yes, I remember. Anna used to share with me. It's delicious."

"Well, it's not as good as usual. Wartime, you know, it's hard to get all the ingredients. But we just work with what we have, don't we?"

She took up her shopping bags and turned to the door. I went over to hold it open for her.

"You know," she said, looking at me, "you've done so well here, Irene. Anna would be so proud of you."

That evening and all the next day, I thought of Max. I imagined him on the train in a small compartment like in the movies, with a porter carrying his luggage. I imagined him sitting in a window in a dining car, cigarette in hand, staring at the landscape as the wheels moved inexorably through frozen fields to Chicago.

Unlike a train, my own thoughts wouldn't stay on a single track. I finished the edging on the final Chinese coat, the last costume I was making for the ballet. The silk made me think of the McNeils, and then it was hard not to dwell on Cynthia, her guilt and her secret, a secret that I was privy to even though she had no idea that I was. Again I was aware that I could destroy her with what I knew. To have such power was utterly alien to me, and I kept returning to the thought with a sort of scared fascination. Her parents, her neighbors, Great-Aunt Mabel, the likes of Dolores and Mrs. Ramsey: a frail wall, held up by Max and me, was all that kept her from their contempt and scorn.

It was strange to think that I had once seen her as an example of all that I lacked. Her life had seemed so polished and perfect, but I'd seen the underside now, the raw edges and knots. Some of her story, of course, was still hidden from me; she'd confided things in Max that he had not told me, rightly so, and I could only wonder at what they might be. I felt a tremendous compassion for her.

But at other moments my thoughts ran into the past, into Max. Like a movie reel, moments played through my head: his arms around me as we stood at the sink, his keen and eager gaze as he looked around my shop, the cozy dinner we'd shared at Stan's Restaurant. Emotion made my eyes water. I had to put down the coat because I could not see.

Whatever he was thinking on the train pulling into the Chicago station, whatever he felt for me, I knew that Cynthia would not divorce him now. She would stay with him and have a baby which would, to all the world, be Max's child.

As long as he agreed to stay with her, of course.

I pulled my arms around my waist, holding myself tight. I let myself imagine another ending: the shop door opening, and Max entering and taking me in his arms. *I love you, Irene. I want to be with you. It doesn't matter what she wants. I'm choosing you.* I let myself imagine it, the feel of his lips on mine and the smell of him, and his arms around me, in that coat I knew so well. It felt like a movie: beautiful, intoxicating, and utterly a fantasy.

I don't know how this ends, he had said before our second night together. But there was only one way my relationship with him could end, and I'd always known it. I think we both had.

FORTY-FIVE

The next evening I set off for the ballet studio on Van Ness. I'd promised to drop off the finished costumes, and then Trixie and I were going to meet for dinner before I went to the USO. The fog was gone, thankfully; I always found it disconcerting when the usual streets looked like places I'd never seen before.

When I took out the jackets, there was a chorus of admiration from the dancers. "Where did you get that fabric?" asked Gina. "It's gorgeous!"

Katherine, one of the Chinese dancers, slipped a jacket on over her practice tunic. "This is by far the nicest costume I've ever worn," she said, smiling at her reflection in the mirror. "Too bad that dance is so short. This deserves more time on stage."

Russell was beaming. "These are perfect. Exactly what I hoped for but never thought I'd find." He turned to me gratefully. "I can't thank you enough, Irene, truly. You didn't have to give this up for us."

He was right. I could have turned that precious material into a dress or a wrap, something I'd keep for years. Maybe it was a waste to use it for a two-minute dance, done for two performances only and then tucked in a storeroom.

But for those two performances, the silk would blaze in orange and blue and yellow across the stage. It would make the dancers feel the part and would help an audience of San Franciscans, weary after years of war, be transported for an evening to a world of magic and delight.

"There's nothing I'd rather do with it," I said.

Over dinner at the coffee shop I passed along my gifts for the Dubuques and one for Trixie herself, a peasant blouse I'd made and embroidered along the neckline. She gave me a wrapped present, too, and we both pledged not to open the gifts until Christmas Day. Her train was leaving the next morning for Minnesota. "I wish you were coming along," she said, tucking the presents into her shopping bag.

"Maybe next year." I played with the saltshaker and tried to imagine Christmas 1945. A world without war, hopefully? But a year from now yawned like a huge wasteland.

"How is everything?" asked Trixie delicately. "With—you know?"

I shook my head. "He's in Chicago now. But something happened." Her face was curious and compassionate. "It's not something I can tell you about, Trixie. But I think—I know—it's over. Between us, I mean." It was the first time I had said the words aloud. It was hard to say them, hard to hear them even from my own mouth.

"Does he think it's over too?"

"I haven't talked to him about it yet. He's still gone a few more days."

"I guess you knew it wouldn't last," Trixie said tentatively.

"I know." The waitress came with our sandwiches, and we ate for a moment in silence.

"At least it was only a few weeks," she said. "Right? It would have been harder to end if it had gone on for months and months."

"Probably," I said. But time had nothing to do with depth of feeling; my weekend with Johnny had shown me that. With great effort I smiled. "I'll be fine."

"I know you will. You're a strong person, Irene."

"I'm good at faking it," I said, half-joking.

"No, you really are strong," she said staunchly. "And at least it's ending before anyone knows about it. Besides me, I mean. It could have been so much worse, really."

I nodded, putting down my sandwich, pushing aside the thought of Mrs. Ramsey under the streetlamp.

We said goodbye in front of the restaurant, and she went home to finish packing while I threaded my way through holiday crowds to O'Farrell Street. I was sorry she wasn't going to the USO with me.

The moment I entered, in fact, I wished I hadn't come. My mood was so far from the innocent, lighthearted one of the club. Mrs. Latham seemed to be in a mood as well; she greeted me briskly, but without her usual warmth. "I guess the holidays have everyone in a dither," I said to Vicky Bergman as we freshened up in the ladies' room. "Mrs. Latham seems different tonight."

"I don't think it's the holidays," she said. "I think she's just sort of surprised about you."

"What do you mean?"

"Because of the newspaper."

I stared at her blankly.

"You haven't seen it? Come here." She led me through the knots of servicemen and girls, threading our way into the reading room. Searching among the newspapers and magazines on the table, she found the *Chronicle* and turned to the page she wanted.

It was an article about the Golden Gate Club, "the brainchild of Max Burke." There was a photo of him leaning against the bar, looking dashingly handsome. There was a photo of the Golden Gate Park room, with its beautiful framed images. And there was a picture of me, standing by the curtains, with a caption:

Caught in the evening light is Miss Irene Cleary, whom Max Burke introduced as a designer for the club. She left as quickly as Cinderella at the ball, but we're intrigued by this young lady, who somehow managed to get involved in one of the most talked-about projects this fall.

The photo showed me just looking up from my handbag without smiling. It was the unguarded expression of someone who doesn't know her picture is being taken, the kind of expression that looks at once naked and guilty.

Fear pounded along my veins. "Oh gosh," I said feebly. "Gosh."

"Mrs. Latham and Mrs. Cohen were talking about it before you got here," said Vicky. "They were pretty surprised." She regarded me expectantly.

No wonder they were surprised. If only the expression on my face were less furtive. If only I had talked to the reporters like a real designer instead of leaving like someone with something to hide.

I stared at my own face in the grainy newsprint. If only I had said something to Cynthia about helping with the club, that night in Atherton. My silence now could be read as deliberate. I folded the paper and put it down.

Vicky was looking at me curiously, waiting for me to explain. I had no idea what to say.

To my relief, two marines came up, grinning boyishly. "Pretty girls who aren't dancing," said one. "I think we need to fix that. Right?"

From the dance floor I could see Mrs. Latham at the coffee table. She was watching me, her expression thoughtful and grave, as if I were a girl she'd never met before.

FORTY-SIX

It's strange how having your photo in the newspaper makes you feel utterly exposed. As I boarded the streetcar a few hours later, it seemed everyone was staring at me. The man with the gray mustache, the girl reading the Chinese newspaper, the middle-aged woman with a hotel maid's uniform under her coat—their eyes all seemed to linger on me as I got on and found my seat. Or maybe I was just imagining it, seeing the world through the lens of guilt. I turned my head away and stared out at the hotel and apartment windows passing by, lit from within like rectangles of life in a dead city.

It occurred to me that this must be how Cynthia felt, all the time. Her whole life, I realized, she'd been in the public eye. No wonder Chicago had represented a certain freedom for her. And now, carrying Fred's baby, she was surely in a panic of discovery.

The streetcar approached my stop, and I turned from the window, gathering up my pocketbook. The pretty woman with the Chinese newspaper was still staring at me. *She's probably wondering how a girl like me ends up being the "designer" for Max Burke*, I thought uncomfortably. If I'd been wearing a scarlet letter I couldn't have felt more conspicuous.

Then she leaned forward. "Excuse me," she said. "There's a smudge of dirt on your cheek." She indicated the corresponding area on her own face.

I thanked her and pulled out my compact. She was right. I wiped it away, feeling both ridiculous and relieved.

Things always look better in the morning. Sister Margaret used to say that, and as I toasted the bread for my breakfast the next day, I realized she was right. I'd clearly been overreacting about the newspaper. Really, how many people had seen it? And if they had, what did it matter? Everyone knew that a single picture didn't tell the whole story.

The day was dedicated to finishing the dresses for the orphan girls. They'd turned out even better than I'd expected, each one pretty and unique. I decided I'd take them to the orphanage the next day; the girls would be excited to wear them for Christmas.

It was good to have a set plan, for as the day dragged on and the fog came in my mood shifted into thoughts of Max, and there was no Trixie or Louise in town to distract me. At five o'clock I took a long walk west, down Jackson Street and past the fine homes backing up to the Presidio, huge mansions with their own little yards and some with lighted Christmas trees visible in the windows. The walk tired me enough that, thankfully, I fell asleep without much trouble.

The next morning at nine I put the sign in the shop window—BACK AT NOON. I was just putting on my coat and wrapping up the dresses to take them to Mount St. Joseph when the telephone rang.

"Miss Cleary?" said the instantly recognizable voice. "It's Cynthia Burke."

I nearly dropped the receiver. "Good morning, Mrs. Burke," I managed to say, my heart pounding so fast that I was sure it was audible on the line. "How are you?"

"I'm just fine, thank you," she said. "I was wondering if you were free to come by today? Around eleven? I've got a garment I'd like to ask you about."

Her voice was the same as ever: clear, warm, no hint of anger or suspicion. It made it easier for me to respond in a normal voice.

"Is it possible for me to come by later? Perhaps about three?"

"I'm afraid not. Before lunch is my only open window today."

"I see," I said, rapidly recalculating. I could take the dresses to the orphanage after meeting with her. "Yes, I believe I can make it work."

"Oh, good," she said. "Thank you for being so flexible. I'll see you at eleven o'clock then. Goodbye."

As I put down the receiver I was flooded with relief. There was no way she would sound that way if she had any suspicions. I would go, and it would be fine. Max would not be there, and everything would be absolutely businesslike and cordial, and I would banish all thoughts of Cynthia's own secrets from my mind.

And if she mentioned the article in the paper? "Yes, Mrs. Burke," I would say, with an apologetic smile. "I have been helping Mr. Burke on the nightclub designs. I was about to tell you in Atherton but then we went in to dinner and I forgot to mention it." As I put on my lipstick I actually said it to the mirror, practicing a few times and adding a self-deprecating laugh, until it sounded natural.

I imagined her smiling in response, putting down her teacup with graceful ease. "I was surprised to read it, Miss Cleary," she would say candidly. "But I know how talented you are, and in that way it's not surprising at all."

For all my brave thoughts, as I approached their apartment it was hard not to feel a flutter of apprehension. Riding up in the elevator, I knew that the first moment of greeting would be the hardest. If I could smile at her without nervousness or guilt, I'd be fine. If she smiled at me the way she always had, I'd know it would be all right.

To my great relief, Cynthia greeted me at the door with her usual warmth. "Thank you so much for coming on such short notice." There were slight shadows under her eyes, a puffiness to her face that hadn't been there when I'd last seen her in Atherton, but otherwise she looked as pretty as ever. "Please, come in."

I followed her through the elegant foyer and into the living room. What I saw there stopped me in my tracks. Dolores Kittredge and Marion Ramsey were sitting on the divan, side by side, watching me keenly. An instinct, an almost animal one, filled me with sudden fear.

"You know Mrs. Kittredge and Mrs. Ramsey, I think," said Cynthia, and her tone was different than it had just been at the door, cold and portentous.

"Yes," I said, managing to nod politely even though my heart was hammering in my chest. "How do you do?"

"Miss Cleary and I are almost neighbors," said Mrs. Ramsey, her tone significant, as if she was also remembering the night she'd looked up to my apartment window. I sat down in the chair indicated by Cynthia, every nerve taut. Dolores Kittredge was holding a cigarette, watching me over the smoke. There were china cups and a silver pot of tea on the low coffee table in front of them, but this time Cynthia did not offer me any.

Silence fell. I could hear the clink of dishes far off in another room, as if a maid were setting a table for lunch. All three women were regarding me, and I felt exposed, naked, as if I were in a spotlight at a burlesque show. I summoned my courage and spoke, making my voice as steady as possible. "There was a garment you wanted to ask me about, Mrs. Burke?"

"Oh, yes," she said. "When we were in Atherton my mother showed you a cape, antique silk. From China. She loaned it to you, and I would like it back."

My lips went cold. "You need it back?"

"Yes. I've contacted a dressmaker and I'm going to have it made into a coat." Her glance flickered to the women on the sofa, then turned back to me. "I'd like you to return it, please."

"I'm sorry," I said, my heart pounding. "I understood that it was a gift."

"It was a loan," said Cynthia evenly. "You wanted to sketch the pattern on the fabric, as I recall. And now I need it back."

It was so utterly a lie I could only stare at her, dumbfounded. It took me a moment to respond.

"I'm very sorry," I said, striving to make my voice even. "I understood it was a gift. For helping with the wedding."

"Perhaps you heard what you wanted to hear," said Cynthia. "Mother would never have given it away."

I glanced at the women on the sofa. With their fancy hats and the china in front of them they looked like women at a tea party, but their avid attention made them more like spectators at a tennis match. I remembered the relish with which they'd discussed Cynthia and Fred, that day weeks before in my shop.

And even in the midst of my fear, I sensed what was going on. Cynthia was trying to stamp out one bit of gossip by deliberately creating more. I was the target she'd chosen.

"Apparently you don't have it anymore." Cynthia's voice broke the silence. "You've already made it into something for yourself."

"I donated it to the ballet," I said, my voice growing stronger. "For costumes for their new production." I turned to include the other women in my explanation. "If you go to *The Nutcracker* on Christmas Eve, you'll see it. In the Chinese dance."

For a moment Cynthia looked surprised, as if I had veered away from the script she'd imagined. Then the cold look returned. "That's a shame," she said, "that silk was extremely valuable. Too valuable to use for costumes. My mother will be terribly disappointed."

Even in the horror of my present circumstance, even with my fear and my racing pulse, I was stubbornly determined not to capitulate. "I am sorry for the misunderstanding," I said, emphasizing the last word. "I was told by your mother that it was a gift."

Cynthia lifted her chin slightly. "Well," she said carefully and distinctly, as if it were a line she had rehearsed before I came, "I suppose I shouldn't be surprised." She fixed me squarely in her gaze, her eyebrow lift giving significance to what she said next. "You seem to make a habit of taking things that don't belong to you."

There was no mistaking her meaning. If she had called me a whore to my face, I could not have been more stunned. Involuntarily I looked at the other women. Dolores was holding her cigarette perfectly still, eyes wide as if not wanting to miss a thing, and Mrs. Ramsey was watching me with immense satisfaction, as if the part she had played in this drama were everything she had hoped it would be.

There was nothing I could say. Denial was useless, for my rising color had already spoken for me. And it was totally clear to me what Cynthia was doing, and why. Having a husband who had strayed was a scandal she could bear, one she herself could survive. It was like lighting a new fire to distract from an old one. That was her intention, and there was nothing I could do to save myself.

Except one thing.

Fight fire with fire. The proverb sprang into my mind, from somewhere deep in my memory. And as I sat on the edge of the chair, caught in the triangle of the three women watching me, an awareness of my own power suddenly surged inside me. I could rewrite the scene Cynthia had orchestrated. I could give it a totally new ending with a few well-chosen words. *I saw you and Fred Gibson in Atherton. Max knows all about your affair. You're going to have Fred's baby and pass it off as Max's.* I could turn to the ladies on the sofa, who would sit there open-mouthed. *Your suspicions about Cynthia and Fred, that day in my shop? They are true, all of them.*

It was a loaded gun lying just within reach. All I had to do was pick it up, aim, and pull the trigger—and even I, with no experience using such a weapon, could not fail to hit the mark.

But I didn't do it. Something stopped me, or maybe lots of things. Betty Gibson's tears at my shop and Mrs. Gibson's kindness to me, the outsider at the Atherton dinner party. My own innate kindness, which had never been tested like this before. My promise to Max. And also, most of all, the thought of that child not yet born, a child whose life would be changed forever by what I said.

I couldn't say it. I didn't want to say it.

Instead, I picked up my handbook and stood, raising myself to my full height. I nodded to the women on the divan, then turned back to Cynthia. She was staring at me with a different look on her face: not the proud and cold one, but something less calculated, something that was suddenly almost vulnerable.

"I am sorry for the misunderstanding about the silk." My voice sounded rusty even to my own ears, as if it had been years since I'd last spoken. "I hope you have a good Christmas, Mrs. Burke. Goodbye."

As if I were someone, I walked out of the room. When I reached the foyer I glanced back, where all that was visible was the fireplace and the chair where Cynthia still sat. She was looking after me, her face turned away from Dolores and Marion, and on it I saw embarrassment, an involuntary slipping of the mask. *I had to do it*, her eyes seemed to say. *Forgive me.*

I did not answer them. I turned, opened the door, and left.

FORTY-SEVEN

Once in high school, before the war made us have to worry about enemy ships coming across the sea, a group of us girls went to Ocean Beach for a June picnic and bonfire. Molly LaMotte built the fire, and the cold and foggy evening was magically transformed by the orange flames. We'd roasted hot dogs and marshmallows on sticks and because the school year had just ended, someone had the idea of writing memories on notebook paper and feeding them to the fire. It had been fascinating to watch the paper catch and twist in the flame, our school year gradually consumed. Sitting there with blankets around our shoulders, we were all mesmerized by the bonfire. After looking at it against the black sky and ocean, it was hard to see anything else.

I didn't go to the orphanage that day to deliver the dresses. I went back home in a daze, for the scene at the Burkes' apartment had burned itself into me and I could not see anything else. The CLOSED sign went in the window, and I went directly upstairs.

There was no one I could talk to about what had happened. Trixie was in Minnesota. Louise was—well, even if she weren't in New York, I wouldn't have confided in her anyhow. Max was in Chicago, but even he—how on earth could I tell him what his wife had said and done?

I drew a bath and sank into it. There was a wet spot on the ceiling I'd somehow never noticed before. I wondered, rather numbly, how it got there and how I would clean it. But then I didn't see it anymore, for the flames burned again in my memory.

There would be no more Nob Hill commissions. My budding career as a society designer was gone, consumed like those notebook pages. My professional hopes had been sacrificed on the altar of Cynthia's self-preservation.

And there was no one to defend the reputation of Irene Cleary, seamstress and orphan. No parents, no friends in town, no husband. No Johnny.

"No one can know about this," Max had said, knotting his tie that first morning. "I'm thinking mostly of you." I'd known that by continuing our affair I was playing with fire, but it hadn't mattered at the time. Love, idealism, caution: all that had died with Johnny, and I was older and wiser, more adult, less likely to be hurt. Or so I had wanted to think.

If you had only lived, Johnny, I thought. The water was cold now, and my many tears did nothing to warm it.

The next day, December twenty-first, I kept my head down and worked. Pauline stopped by to deliver homemade cookies from one of the ballet mothers. "And here's your ticket," she said, handing me a small envelope. "December twenty-fourth, two o'clock. You can see your beautiful handiwork on stage." She looked at me curiously. "Is everything okay?"

"I look that bad, do I?" I joked.

"No, just like something is on your mind. Something more than, you know"—she gestured as if to indicate the war—"everything."

"It's hard to explain."

"A man?" I nodded. Her face changed. "Sorry. I've been there."

I doubted she had been there—who else had been involved in

exactly this kind of tangle?—but I was touched by the sympathy. “Thanks, Pauline. It’s nothing I can talk about, for a few reasons, but I just feel like everything’s a mess.”

The jingle of the shop bell heralded the arrival of Mrs. Mendoza, her toddler in tow, coming to pick up her new skirt. I helped her over the screams of her child, who was pulling on her arm trying to break free and play with the sewing machine. “I’m sorry,” she said, lifting her voice to be heard over the wails. “He’s in a terrible mood today.”

“Can I offer him a c-o-o-k-i-e?” I knew from the orphanage that spelling was safer where tiny kids were involved.

“Oh, yes,” she said gratefully. It did the trick: the little boy gnawed his animal cracker happily and peace reigned. Mrs. Mendoza thanked me effusively, tipping me a quarter and wishing me a very merry Christmas as she left.

“How is Edith?” I asked Pauline as I put the money in the cash register.

“All right. We talked just yesterday. It helps for her to be home,” said Pauline, lifting an iris flower from the vase and twirling it between her fingers like a pinwheel. “But she’s coming back here after New Year’s. To keep on working at the shipyard.”

“Is she really?”

“Says she needs to keep doing something to help the other soldiers. And other wives.”

I took the ticket Pauline had given me and put that carefully in the register too. “I admire that,” I said. “Doing something with the pain. Making it into something.”

“So do I,” said Pauline. “A few days ago I felt so stupid, just dancing my way through the war.” She stopped twirling the iris and looked at it thoughtfully. “But at rehearsal yesterday—well, there’s something about ballet, about doing something so precise and beautiful. I realized that maybe I’m putting order back into a world that’s falling apart.”

She returned the iris to the vase, moving it carefully to the right place. "And maybe that means something after all."

FORTY-EIGHT

The first dress rehearsal of *The Nutcracker* was on December twenty-second. Russell had invited me to come backstage and help as needed, but I couldn't go; the drama with Cynthia Burke had set me back and there was still a blouse to finish and a child's green taffeta party dress to shorten. In the middle of the day I paused and ate some of Mrs. O'Leary's plum cake, which in turn reminded me of past holidays when Anna would share hers. I pictured Mrs. O'Leary standing in a kitchen, an apron tied around her middle, having to substitute ingredients in a recipe she knew by heart. The war had crept into every part of life, even sugarplum cake.

Finally, it was five o'clock. As I pulled down the shades, I thought of the dresses for the orphans. I felt guilty for not calling Sister to explain why I hadn't delivered them when I'd said I would. Just as I was going to the phone to pick up the receiver, there was a knock on the door. It was Max.

He stood on the threshold in his coat, an echo of the time he'd arrived right after closing as I froze guiltily in his wife's dress. It seemed like something that had happened a century before. I stepped back to let him in.

"Irene. Hello."

"When did you get back?" I asked, closing the door behind him.

"Earlier today."

He didn't move to embrace me, and I didn't move to embrace him. We just stood a few feet apart.

"How was Chicago?" I finally asked, striving for a casual tone, pulling out a chair for myself and sitting down.

"It was good." He found a chair and sat down, too, leaning forward slightly in that way he had.

"Cold, I bet. Was there snow?" It was a casual question, but then I remembered the conversation at the beach and how he'd wrapped his coat around me and his hands had brushed my hair. I blushed.

"There was," he said in a restrained tone that made it clear he was remembering too. He looked down at his clasped hands, then back up at me.

Neither one of us spoke. The silence was so complete I could even hear two women walking by outside, the thin staccato of their heels on the sidewalk, the lilt of their voices as they talked and laughed. "Did she *really*?" I heard one of them say as they rounded the corner, then the sounds trailed off to nothing.

"It's all right, Max," I said finally. "I know it's over."

His expression changed. I saw relief that I'd brought it up, and I focused hard on that relief, because I didn't want to think about the pain that was also visible in his eyes.

"There was no other way it could end," I continued, keeping my voice even. It was hard to maintain my resolve, with him sitting a few feet away, looking at me that way. "I knew it and you knew it too. You knew it all along."

"Yes," he said slowly. "I did. Though for a time I thought, maybe—" He broke off, paused, then shook his head. "Never mind," he said quietly.

I hadn't expected that. A swift, treacherous hope surged in me like a wave, but I knew that if I asked him to explain I would only regret it. It felt like I was hanging onto a cliff face, and only sheer force of will was keeping me from letting go. I dug in my fingers.

"Have you seen Cynthia yet?" I asked.

"Briefly. I stopped at home before coming here."

"Did she know you were coming here?"

"No. She doesn't know about us, Irene."

It was rare for me to feel older than Max, to feel wiser, and it was a strange sensation. If he didn't know about Cynthia's carefully planned ambush, then I was not going to tell him. A dangerous feeling of tenderness washed over me, watching him sitting in that chair with his hands clasped, leaning forward.

"It was good, being in Chicago," he said. "I spoke Polish again. I had some dill cucumber soup." He grinned. "Almost as delicious as Stan's. But it was also good being there, where Cynthia and I first met. Remembering the conversations we had." He gazed down at the floor, a foot or two in front of me, as if seeing the past. "Like going back to the beginning, to what was once there and maybe still is."

"Was she happy to see you today?" I asked after a pause.

He looked up at me, then down. "Yes," he said quietly. "She was."

He had wanted to be a hero, that little boy. He still did. It was in his blood and bones, that instinct to protect the vulnerable. I had seen it more than once, had been saved by it myself. I had been grateful for it, just as Cynthia was now.

"Will you be able to do it?" I asked after a moment. "Raise a child that you know is—that you know isn't yours?"

He seemed surprised that I would ask. "A child isn't his parents," he said. "And in the end, I don't think it matters. I'll just be glad that he—or she—is here."

He meant it, every word. I nodded at the floor because I couldn't look at him. Too much inside me was hurting. "You'll be a good father," I managed to say.

"Thank you," he said quietly. The floor suddenly went blurry, and I blinked hard.

"Honestly, Irene," he said, and I could hear it again, that note of anguish I'd heard in his voice once before. "I don't know how to say it, how to say everything that I feel here. Only that I wish, somehow—" He stopped, and a long time passed before he spoke again. "Only that I won't forget you."

I looked up and our eyes met.

The radiator started, with its clanking sound. I hadn't even noticed how cold it was in the room. It was impossible not to think that at one time he would have pulled me into his arms to warm me. I wrapped my sweater more closely around me and stood up. He did the same.

"Max, I hope"—my voice was hard to control—"I hope you'll be very happy. You deserve it."

He stood a few feet away, a line between his brows.

"Will you be okay, Irene?" he asked. It was not a casual question. He really wanted to know.

And I knew that if I said no, he would not be able to say goodbye. Somehow, he would have to protect me. What that protection would look like I didn't know, and he probably didn't either, but he would stay in my life and I would see him again, and for a brief moment I almost released my hold on that cliff. But below me was the deep blue sea, and I had to stay on land.

"I'll be fine, Max," I said. "I'll be fine." I was so firm I almost believed it myself.

We stood there, looking at each other as the radiator hissed. It seemed suddenly unbearable to me that the last kiss had already happened, that I hadn't known at the time that I needed to memorize it. For a fleeting moment I thought of slipping my hand behind his neck and lifting my face to his, one final time.

But I didn't. We both stepped away from each other, almost at exactly the same moment. And he reached out his hand and grasped mine, squeezed it once, then let go.

"If you ever need anything, Irene."

"Thank you." I managed a smile. "Goodbye, Max."

He gave me one last look, then turned quickly away and opened the door. And I listened to his footsteps down the sidewalk until I couldn't hear them anymore.

Tears came, and I let them fall. I had learned it twice in the past six months. You don't always know when a kiss is the last kiss. You don't always get to decide.

FORTY-NINE

Months ago, even before I met Johnny, I was at the USO one evening. I was drinking a Coke and laughing with a few servicemen when I noticed a soldier staring at me from across the room. He was tall and gangly like Jimmy Stewart, and he kept looking at me in a way that was not attraction or desire but something that I knew instinctively was bigger and more interesting. I couldn't help glancing back, and after about twenty minutes of this he came over.

"Excuse me, Miss," he said apologetically. "I know I've been staring. It's just that you remind me of my girl, back in Nebraska."

He showed me a picture, taken carefully out of his wallet. She was standing arm in arm with him in front of what looked like a farmhouse of some kind with a vine crawling up the porch post. We had similar hairstyles and the same build and yes, visible even in the photo, were freckles.

"She has a sweater that color too," he said, indicating my blue pullover.

"What's her name?" I asked.

"MaryLou. MaryLou Halverson." He put the photo carefully away. "It's strange to say, but when I look at you, it's like I can pretend it's her. For just a little while I can pretend she's here." He looked embarrassed. "You must think I'm a real sad sack."

I didn't. I was touched. I asked him to dance, but he declined, instead thanking me formally and going back to stand again on the other side of the room. I knew why he'd said no. At a distance he could pretend that I was MaryLou, while actually dancing with me would break the spell. And in the middle of a strange city, right before shipping off to the world of war, he wanted to live just a little longer in a beautiful fantasy.

Maybe Max had been my substitute for Johnny. Maybe he'd been my way to pretend that Johnny was still here, to live in a spell of my own where we could do the thing we hadn't done and never would. If some analyst looked at the events of 1944, he'd probably see it that way. Why else would sensible Irene Cleary, just five months after losing the man she had loved, turn to a married man in the small hours of the night and lead him to her bed?

I lay in the gray dawn the next morning after a tearstained night. "I think," Trixie had said when she learned about Max, "that you still aren't over Johnny." She was perceptive, Trixie, and always had been. She had always known me well.

But even if it had started that way, it hadn't finished that way. I lay in the bed Max gave me and there was no question what I was feeling. As much as I'd tried to be cavalier about our relationship, I loved him. Two very different men, as opposite as night and day: I had loved them both, and I had lost them both.

And it hurt. It hurt in my skin and bones, in my heart and in my soul.

I couldn't listen to Christmas carols the next morning. Every one made me cry. It seemed to be all that was on the radio, but finally I found a station playing songs from *Oklahoma*, the musical.

I thought about Oklahoma as I basted the hem of an evening gown. It was a place far away from the mess I'd made at home. Looking up, I saw myself in the mirror. My hair was pinned up; I hadn't had the energy to curl it. I wasn't wearing any lipstick. I wore an old tweed skirt and purple sweater and every time I moved my arms, I caught the sharp smell of my own sweat, faint but unmistakable. The last time I'd worn the sweater I'd told myself it was time to have it laundered, and then I'd totally forgotten about it.

The woman on the radio was singing about love. A man sang back. Tears blurred my vision, and I had to put the dress down and fold my arms on the table and rest my head on them, which only made me smell it again: my own sweat, my own failure.

At the ring of the shop bell, I lifted my head quickly. Filling the doorway like a white sail was the headdress of a nun. It was Sister Margaret.

"Good morning, Irene," she said, closing the door behind her.

"Sister." I scrambled to my feet, dashing at my eyes. She'd never come to the shop before.

"I'm sorry not to call first. I had a dentist appointment on Fillmore, and I thought I'd stop by."

"Oh, the dresses." Guilt suffused me. "I'm so sorry I didn't bring them by, Sister. I—something came up." I found the dresses in the back room, and when I returned she'd taken a seat at the end of the cutting table. I turned off the radio and took a chair facing her.

She looked at each dress, not unfolding them, but admiring the trim and collars and buttons. "Oh, these are lovely. The girls will be so excited. And you've made each one look totally different. You know, don't you, what a girl likes to wear."

"I'm sorry I didn't come the other day. I was going to, but . . ."—I pulled the sleeves of my sweater down, covering my hands—"then I couldn't."

I've been around sisters all my life, but in the unfamiliar setting of my shop I realized how the habit of a nun covered things that you normally see. I couldn't see Sister's hair and I wasn't distracted by her clothes, so I couldn't really get away from her eyes, which were somewhere between brown and green. They were fixed on me, in a way that was not intrusive and not unkind. I looked away anyhow.

"I've been thinking of you, Irene," she said, carefully setting the dresses to the side. "And praying for you. Ever since that day we spoke in my office. I know the news was a shock to you."

It had been, at the time. "It's fine," I said. "I don't think about it anymore." That was true.

"Then it must be something else you're thinking about," she said quietly.

I nodded. I wasn't going to say more, but her eyes were so grave and encouraging. From where I sat, my back was to the windows and the shop door and I saw only her and the back wall, and it felt like a tiny private place, like a confessional or something, one where I could unburden myself and be safe with a woman who had known me since there was anything about me to know.

"I want to tell you something, Sister," I said. "If you have the time."

There was something about Sister Margaret: She had always been able to give the effect of an understanding smile without actually smiling. "I'm in no hurry at all, Irene."

It took a while to tell it all. Johnny, our weekend together, how I gave him the Miraculous Medal. The letters I'd written, and the terrible letter from his mother. Phil, and the Top of the Mark. Cynthia's affair—yes, I told her that, though I kept the name of her partner hidden—and Max. It was hardest to tell her about Max. But her face showed no judgment, only the same quiet gravity. And I told her about what had happened at Cynthia's apartment, and Max's last visit the night before.

"I thought I was in control of how I felt about Max. That it was just"—I could feel myself blushing—"just having a good time. I thought I'd been cured of wanting love, after Johnny died. But I guess I wasn't strong enough."

"Because you love Max."

I nodded and fumbled in my pocket for a handkerchief. "I'm more hurt now than I was before. And I did it to myself."

"Love isn't convenient," said Sister. "We can't always control when or how it comes. As much as we might wish to." She paused while I wiped my eyes. "And I would suggest, Irene—well, I think it's a good thing that you love him."

"Why?"

"Because it means that you are still open. It means that a part of you, the tenderest part of any woman—or any man—did not die when Johnny did. Even when you tried to stamp it out, it couldn't be killed."

"I'm not sure I want to be tender."

"I know. But tenderness is tied in with all that is good in life. Things like hope, and faith. The ability to feel what another person feels. To care about things, and people."

I seemed to hear Louise's voice: *I'm always going to wonder what happened to those guys*, she said. *If they lived or died out there.* But the mention of hope and faith made me think of the little medal I'd put around Johnny's neck, now fathoms deep in the waters of the Pacific. It was a tender memory, one that still hurt with the sting of betrayal.

"I gave him my medal," I said. "I believed it would protect him, and it didn't. He died anyhow." There was defiance in my voice. "It wasn't true, any of it. Just a story for children."

"I remember the day I gave you that medal," said Sister. "Do you remember what I told you?"

"You said that it would give me the graces I need. That it would protect those who wear it."

"You're half right," said Sister, as if we were in a classroom. "I told you it would give the graces you need. I didn't say that it would protect you."

I looked up to argue, then remembered. "It was Sister Rosemary who told me that."

Sister nodded. "It's never been my way to make promises of that kind. Not even in matters of faith. But I have always believed that wherever we find ourselves, we are given the graces we need."

"But Johnny didn't get those graces. He was killed."

"But how do you know, Irene, what that little medal did give him? Perhaps it gave him comfort. Perhaps it gave him beautiful moments at sea, thinking of you. It was a reminder of love, of the people we meet who change us for the better, even if we don't have them for very long. Those are graces, all of them. They give us the courage to face whatever life brings us."

I had to wipe my eyes again. "When I gave it to him, he said it reminded him of his old nanny. She had one like it."

"Then he had double the reminders of love. You gave it to him not even knowing how much it would mean to him. But your instinct was to share it."

I thought of Johnny, that last morning by the bay. The rose of the sky behind him, the delight in his eyes at my gift. He was the first man who had loved me, the only one who had said it in so many words. For a moment I wished there had been no Max, that there had only been Johnny, golden in my memory. *But no*, I thought confusedly, *I cannot wish Max away*.

"I don't know who I am anymore," I said helplessly. "I've lost myself. I don't know who I am."

Sister was thoughtful for a moment. "I think you do," she said at last. "What you feel now, after all these new experiences . . . well, it's only natural to feel lost. But there's an essential you that doesn't change, Irene. Something in your soul. The Irene that dreamed about your parents, about being born because of love: I think that Irene is still there." She saw my face and nodded in acknowledgment. "Yes, maybe it wasn't their love that brought you here, but there's a bigger love that did. A love behind everything in the world that's good, including you. It's the love that made you dedicate hours to making these girls' dresses unique and special. It's the love behind every creative impulse, every effort to bring something good out of nothing. Even in wartime, where so much is being destroyed, that love is there. It can't be stopped."

Instinctively I reached out to the folded dresses, tracing the collar of the top one. My Point Reyes epiphany rang in my mind like a bell. I still had the desire to create; that drive hadn't died, even with all that had happened since.

"I thought I was starting something new," I said half to myself. "Making dresses for the ladies of Nob Hill. Making a name for myself." I'd made a name, but not the one I'd intended.

"If I know you, Irene," said Sister, "you'll weather this storm. You will even make something good from it. And this is a big city, one that's constantly changing. New worlds will open for you."

Her certainty made me feel better. I straightened in my chair. "I've been doing some sewing for the ballet. For their new production."

"They are very fortunate to have you."

I looked up at her grave face. She'd known me my whole life, the closest thing to a mother that I'd ever had, besides Mrs. Dubuque. I wondered how old she was. It struck me as astonishing that we had talked as we had so frankly, that I had opened up to her about things that were hard to say even to myself.

Behind her, on the wall, was the picture of Notre Dame cathedral.

Johnny had stood before it, hands in pockets, studying it and smiling. I wondered when I would be able to look at it without instinctively thinking of him.

"It would never have worked out with Johnny anyhow," I said, as if Sister had just argued the opposite. "It was just one weekend in wartime. He was from a totally different world."

"We do this, don't we," said Sister thoughtfully. "We close ourselves off into little worlds. And then we're astonished when we find that the other worlds aren't actually so different from our own."

The clock struck the noon hour. "Am I keeping you, Sister?"

"I should think of starting back soon. Tomorrow is the Christmas party, and the children are livelier than usual."

"I remember." I hugged my arms around me, smiling at the memory of Christmases gone by. Life used to be so simple: good was good, bad was bad, one was rewarded accordingly. Now it was murkier.

"I'm proud of you, Irene," said Sister. I looked up, surprised. *How can you be*, I almost asked, *after what I've done?* But in the face of her clear nonsmiling smile, I felt my question die away. A feeling of warmth flooded through me, a glow of something hopeful that I hadn't felt since that day at Cynthia's apartment. And something else, too, a little question that had been there ever since she had listened, so calmly and without shock, to my story.

"How do you know so much about all this, Sister?" I asked. "About—about everything?"

This time she actually did smile. It was a kind of smile I'd never seen from her: quick, almost mischievous, as if letting me in on a shared secret.

"Because, Irene," she said simply. "I was twenty years old once myself."

After Sister left, I closed up for the lunch hour and took up my coat and walked out to Fillmore and down toward Geary. The business district had the bustle of people two days before Christmas, everyone doing last-minute errands. I had nothing to buy. I just wanted to think.

As I walked I couldn't help reflecting on how much the neighborhood had changed in three years' time. There used to be fancy decorative iron arches stretching across the street, but they'd been taken down, the metal too precious not to be used in the war. On my walk I counted two gold stars in apartment windows above the storefronts. I'd gotten so used to seeing signs selling war bonds that I had to remind myself they hadn't always been there. Before December of '41 I never saw men in army or navy uniforms, or women in the uniform of the WAVES.

I passed the shop that had once been the Yamagamis'. It was something different now, a shoe repair. I lingered there for a moment, thinking of them somewhere else, in some dusty camp in the southwest. What graces would keep them going and hoping? In the upheaval of their lives, would their son still play baseball, would Helen still read Steinbeck? Would they find solace in the memory of rows of chrysanthemums, still blooming somewhere, all the colors of sunset?

I closed my eyes. It had been a while since I had prayed, and it wasn't anything like the ones I used to say. *We are astonished to find our worlds aren't actually so different after all*, Sister had said. I prayed that it might be so, for all of us.

FIFTY

The next morning I woke up early, even before my alarm, and lay in bed staring into the gray room. When I realized what day it was, I felt a little flicker of the old Christmas Eve excitement. This time, it didn't come from the thought of presents, but from the knowledge that I was going to see *The Nutcracker*. It would be my very first time at the ballet. I could almost see Anna smiling.

As I was finishing my toast a half-hour later, the phone rang. "It's Pauline. I have a favor to ask you. A huge one."

"Go ahead."

"So our dress rehearsal yesterday . . . well, let's just say it's good we're only doing two performances. Some of the costumes are already ripping. It's the material," she added hastily, "not the sewing."

I wasn't offended; with the exception of the red velvet and Chinese silk, the fabrics were definitely below par. "How can I help?"

"I hate to ask, but I'm going to anyhow. Would it be all right if you stayed backstage during the performance today, on-call for repairs? I'll get you a ticket for the performance next Wednesday instead, I promise."

I wasn't upset at all. It felt wonderful to be able to help. "I'll be there, with my trusty thimble."

I thought I'd have a leisurely few hours until Pauline came by to meet me, but a young woman showed up needing emergency alterations on a dress—"I'm singing in a Christmas service tomorrow, I have nothing else to wear!"—and before I knew it the morning was gone. After my customer left I hurried upstairs for a hasty lunch and was just putting on my lipstick when Pauline rang the bell.

"Sorry," I said as I opened the shop door. "I had a customer with an emergency. I'm almost ready."

"Everyone needs you today," said Pauline. "Irene the Indispensable."

I grabbed my sewing bag after first making sure I had it all: scissors, pincushion, thread of a few colors to match the costumes. I was just turning off the light when Pauline stooped down and picked up a pile of envelopes, handing them to me. "Your mail."

I thrust the envelopes into my sewing bag, closed and locked the door. Thanks to the locksmith Max had hired, it worked more smoothly than ever, which still surprised me each time. The thought of him made me feel a sudden pang, and I was glad when Pauline took my arm chummily and distracted me with tales of rehearsal as we hurried to the bus.

We entered the Opera House through the small and unassuming stage door. Pauline led me into a maze of corridors and to the dressing rooms, past hallways where costumes were hanging on racks. "Guess who's here to save the day?" she announced to the dancers, some of whom cheered.

It took a while to assess the needed alterations. Most were simple and easy to do, with the exception of a "Waltz of the Flowers" tutu. "I tried to mend it," said the dancer sheepishly, "but I think I just made it worse. I'm afraid it'll rip on stage, and whoosh! There goes the illusion."

"I'll do my best to prevent disaster," I promised her. "And I'll be on call for anything you need during the performance."

I was happier than I'd been in days. Happier even than I'd have been sitting in the audience. It was exciting to be on the inside, swept up in the excitement and energy of the dancers as they did their hair and makeup.

The minute I'd finished the tutu, Pauline pulled me out of the dressing room. "If we go quickly I can give you a tour." We moved up to the wings and peeked onto the stage, which displayed the painted backdrop for the Sugar Plum Fairy's palace. It was a fantasy of lollipops, ice cream cones, cupcakes, and gingerbread men, bright with vivid colors like a child's Christmas dream. I exclaimed over it and a stagehand, a burly man with a cigarette hanging from his lips, nodded. "Pretty, ain't it?" he asked.

It was such a contrast, the whimsy of the scenery and the utilitarian world of backstage, where ropes were hanging like jungle vines and lighting fixtures were clustered like huge eyes. Before I knew she was doing it, Pauline had pulled me out of the wings and onto the stage. "I shouldn't be here," I said.

"Sure you should. You can see what we see. Only the house is dark for us, of course."

The view from stage was breathtaking, red plush seats and gold opulence rising in tiers above me. I tried to imagine every seat filled with people eager for the ballet to start. Below in the orchestra pit a few men were seated, leafing through music or sitting with closed eyes as if resting. One looked up at us and nodded in greeting. "It's a whole world of its own, isn't it," I said as Pauline led me back to the dressing rooms.

You could feel the energy change as the performance drew near. Willam seemed to be everywhere, answering last-minute questions; he'd be the Cavalier to the Sugar Plum Fairy, danced by his sister-in-law Gisella. "His brother Lew is off in the army," said Pauline as she took a last glance in the mirror. "I wonder what his Christmas is like."

Russell had said I could watch the ballet from the wings, but I felt awkward about doing so and stayed in the ladies' dressing room. It was oddly cozy, being there alone and listening to the sprightly melody of the overture. As the first act began I wandered about, checking on the racks of clothes: the gray mouse suits, the soldier uniforms, the pastel tutus for the "Waltz of the Flowers." Russell's Mother Buffoon costume was hanging from a separate hook, its voluminous folds pleated on the ground like curtains. The snowflakes would dance holding large wands with stars on the end; they shimmered even under the harsh backstage lightbulbs.

I lingered for a moment at the Chinese coats. Taking one hanger off the rack, I studied the blossoms and butterflies. That fabric had traveled across the world, from China to San Francisco to Atherton and now to the Palace of the Sugar Plum Fairy. I'd expected to feel a pang at the sight of it, at the memory of the last time I'd seen Cynthia, but I didn't. *You are exactly where you should be*, I silently told the silk.

The party scene costumes held up well, minus the waist of one dress. Russell, who had been one of the guests in a black Empire coat and ruffled shirt, narrated what was happening onstage: Clara sleeping, then the Nutcracker coming to life, and the battle with the mice. "You should go up to the wings and watch," he said.

I decided to wait until after the snowflakes were dressed for their dance, which was a good call as the simple act of putting on the costumes prompted one hasty repair. Jocelyn looked down apprehensively at her short Snow Queen tutu. "I've already mended this bodice once. I'm afraid it'll give way when I'm on stage."

I'd seen the dance being choreographed, so I knew that she and the Prince danced on and off a few times. "Tell you what," I said. "I'll stay in the wings with my sewing bag. I can do a quick repair offstage if you need it. You won't even need to take it off."

"Better you than Onna," said Pauline. "Last week she tried to sew her costume while she was still wearing it, and we had to cut her out of the sewing machine." Onna, tying the ribbon on her toe shoe, made a good-natured face at her across the room.

And then it was time, and with a flurry the dancers grabbed their starry wands and hurried off. I picked up my sewing bag and followed them.

In the wings you could see a slice of the stage, where the Nutcracker, now a prince, was dancing with Lois as Clara. There was a stool off to the side under a single lightbulb on the wall, and I settled there with my sewing bag in my lap. The snowflakes lined up in a whisper of tulle, their wands glistening in the half-light. One of the dancers checked a seam and flashed me a hopeful smile.

I reached into my bag to make sure I had the pincushion at the ready, and as I did so I found the letters I'd dropped in my bag on my way out the door. I glanced at them under the lightbulb. One was an electric bill; one looked like a Christmas card from the Dubuques; one appeared to be a payment from a client.

And a thick one was from Mrs. Ronald Pendleton, New York City.

I didn't see the dancers dance onstage or hear the music shifting into the waltz. With my heart pounding I slit the envelope open.

December 20, 1944

Dear Miss Cleary,

I hope this letter finds you well and in good health. As you know, Johnny's things were returned to us upon his death in June. Just last week, we were surprised to receive some letters he had written but had not mailed. They had been taken to be read by the censors, and for that reason were not with the others. There was one for us and this one, for you.

Having a surprise letter from him has brought us so much joy and peace in this difficult Christmas season. It has also helped us see what you meant to him. I hope your letter brings you the same comfort and happiness.

With our warmest wishes for Christmas and always,

Althea Pendleton

There was another letter in the envelope, still sealed. I took it and opened it. My hands were shaking, and I could barely hold it steady.

June, 1944. At sea.

Dear Irene,

I'm writing this at night, under a sky full of stars. I'm on watch, which is dull, but a good time to write.

Your letters have made me so happy. They came all at once, after a long delay; it's how things happen here, I guess. I got a bunch from my family too. There was a drawing from Hildy, of me on a sailboat, going to an island with a palm tree. It's really cute.

I wrote back to my family first. Some guys here slip carbon paper under their letters so they can make copies, but you deserve a letter all your own, so it's taken me a while to write you. But you're always in my thoughts.

Does it feel like a dream, that weekend we had together? Sometimes it does to me. My life now is a big ship, lots of guys, water all around. Most of the time it's peaceful, sometimes it's not. I am allowed to say we've seen a little action and I'm all right. But it sobers you right up. It's funny that as a kid my friends and I would play war, as if it were a game. It's actually a time when people die, guys my own age, sometimes with no warning. They are here one moment and then they're not. I've seen some pretty terrible sights. There are some I keep seeing at night and wish I could forget.

I didn't write that to my family. I hate to worry them, especially my mom. So it means everything that I can say this to you, Irene.

Remember at the Top of the Mark, when you said you wondered if my family would like you? I've been thinking of that a lot lately. You stare out at the water here, and on a good day there's nothing out there to see, so you can't help thinking. I told you my family would love you, and I meant it and still do. But maybe I didn't understand how much it worried you. I hope you're not still worrying about it.

Just before writing this letter, I wrote one to my parents and told them about you. They'll know I've found the girl who is different from any other. I know they'll be so happy to meet you one day. (There's a record player on the ship, and one of the records is "Heart and Soul"! I listen to it so often it's driving the other guys a little crazy.)

It's a calm night, Irene. I wish you could see the stars here, so many more than you see in New York or San Francisco. I like to imagine you here, my arm around you, looking at them together.

I said it feels like a beautiful dream sometimes, our weekend together. Sometimes, when things are really hard here, I wonder if I just imagined it all. But you know what? It wasn't a dream, it was real. I know because of that little medal you gave me. I wear it all the time and I can always feel it against my skin. It's proof of our time together and of your love for me. You don't know how much this medal has helped me, being out here, seeing what I've seen.

I'd better wrap this up for now. It's funny: I look up at these stars, and they make me think of snow. I imagine them as snowflakes falling on me. I imagine you and me, seeing those winter woods like you always wanted to. I can't wait to share that with you.

I love you, Irene. Heart and soul.

Johnny

Through the blur of my tears I looked up from the letter. In the dark space beyond the light bulb, I seemed to see Johnny standing before me. He was in his uniform, white hat on his blond hair, the tiny glint of my medal on his chest, smiling at me exactly as he had there at the wharf in the dawn. I had never before been able to remember his face so clearly. I smiled back.

And then he was gone, and I was looking at a dark wall of ropes and light switches, but I couldn't forget what I had seen. I held the letter to my heart. It was full, as if something had cracked it right open, but in a way that did not hurt at all.

For a moment I just sat there, crying, hugging the letter to my chest. Then I became aware of the music. It had been playing the whole time I'd been reading, and it still was.

And when I turned toward it, I was looking into a winter forest. The beauty of it made me catch my breath. There were stars and there were snowflakes, a sky full of them, delicate and light. In the footlights they danced, whirling for a brief moment in time, filling the world and me with grace and more grace.

EPILOGUE

The war ended nine months later. Here in the city, it ended with rejoicing in the streets, which turned into drunken brawls that Trixie and I missed entirely, as we'd gone home long before nightfall. "It's such a shame," said Mrs. O'Leary the next day, watching me pin the pieces of a skirt, "that people can't just celebrate without causing all that ruckus." Then she brightened. "But isn't it a wonderful feeling, waking up to peace?"

"Yes," I said, looking up and beaming. "Absolutely wonderful."

It's June of 1946 now. The city has changed, as we all have. The USO has closed, and the City Hall barracks are gone. You can actually buy things like nylons again. There's a feeling of possibility, of a fresh start, of having been through something terrible and come out the other side. But you also still see the scars of war: gold stars still in windows, and families without brothers or husbands.

The Yamagamis returned, although many of their neighbors have not; the war workers who moved into their neighborhood seem to have decided to stay, even though there are no more ships to build. When I saw Mr. Yamagami for the first time, he greeted me with real warmth underneath his usual courtliness. The shop was clean and organized but looked somehow bare, as if little things that used to be there had been lost. I asked after Helen, and her father said she was living with her aunt and uncle in Monterey County now. He promised to give her my best wishes.

When I left the shop, I glanced back and saw him gazing out the window at the street. *I am back in the same place*, his face seemed to say, *but it's no longer the same, and neither am I.*

The next time I brought some work to him, I also brought a small bouquet of magenta chrysanthemums. It was a little thing, but I could tell that he was moved. He put them carefully in a vase, and as he did so I saw that behind the counter he had once again hung the photograph of his son in a baseball uniform. I was surprised how happy it made me to see it again.

Max's nightclub opened a month after *The Nutcracker*. He sent me a note inviting me to the grand opening, the first contact we'd had since saying goodbye in my shop. *This club wouldn't be what it is without you*, he wrote in his dark scrawl. *But if it's too awkward for you, I understand.* It was too awkward for me. I didn't go.

Finally, last month, I did. I invited Trixie, Dennis, and Charlie, a man I met while waiting for the streetcar. He's a structural engineer from Portland who talks about bridges the way I talk about clothes, and we're always able to make each other laugh. I wore a dress I'd just designed, savoring the freedom of not having to ration fabric. It was a gorgeous rust color, with a scoop neck and a fuller skirt than usual. With my hair pinned up I felt like I'd finally grown into the woman I always wanted to be.

As we entered the club Trixie kept glancing at me anxiously, and I smiled at her to let her know I was fine. How amazing that I could look at all the things that held such memories—the orange-red curtains, the framed carousel prints, the upholstery I'd chosen for the booths—with pride rather than pain.

"You helped design this?" asked Charlie as we took our seats. "That must be quite a story."

"It is," I said simply. Maybe I'll tell him more someday. He seems like the kind of man you could tell anything.

My eyes drifted to the mural Victorine had painted. I'd never seen it before, only a small photo in the newspaper. There was the city that Johnny had loved, that we'd explored together: Union Square, Golden Gate Park, the wharf. There were the places I'd been with Max, like Chinatown and Ocean Beach. I found the Opera House, where I still help with the ballet. And there were places I'd seen from afar but never yet up close, like Coit Tower and the Cliff House.

"You never get to the end of this city, do you," I said. I didn't realize I'd said it out loud until Trixie looked up and smiled at me across the table.

It's been more than two years since I met Johnny. I still think of him often. When I do, it's with a sense of peace. That weekend in wartime, with all its joy and love and wonder, shines in my memory like a jewel.

I wrote to his mother a week after getting her letter, and Johnny's. She wrote back right away, with a heartfelt and humble invitation to share whatever I wished to share about his last weekend in the States. The request moved me. I realized that she could tell me things about him that I never got to know, and I could do the same for her. We've had a regular correspondence since then. When Trixie and I go to New York next month to visit Louise—my first trip out of California—I'll spend a day with the Pendletons. *You feel almost like family to me now, Irene*, his mother wrote in her last letter.

"Everything that happens to us changes us," Trixie once said. He was only in my life for a short time, but Johnny showed me what it meant to love and be loved. He was the first to do that. He will always be the first.

Yesterday I closed up shop at two so I could deliver a dress to a customer. It's rare for me to take time off lately, for I've never had more business. Last week it occurred to me that I could train a girl from the orphanage as an apprentice, and I'm seriously considering it. I like the idea of being Anna for someone else.

The dress was going to a wealthy elderly woman who lived in Nob Hill, a woman whose arthritis makes it hard to cross the city herself. I get a few society commissions every now and then, but I don't seek them out; I realized the other day that I have nothing to prove, to myself or anyone else. It was an astonishing and liberating thought, and I pondered it as the streetcar carried me east.

The day was sunny and mild, so after delivering the dress I took an impromptu stroll past the cathedral. And just across the street, I saw Cynthia and Max standing on the sidewalk in front of the park.

I paused and watched them. Cynthia was wearing a beautiful green suit and hat and her arm was threaded through her husband's. Max was pushing a black baby carriage. After a moment he hailed a taxi, and when it pulled to the curb Cynthia raised herself on her toes and kissed his cheek. She got inside and he closed the door for her, then smiled and lifted his hand in a wave. And as the cab pulled away I made my decision.

Max was folding back the hood of the carriage and didn't see me until I was a few feet away. "Irene," he said, straightening, surprise and genuine pleasure on his face. "Hello."

"Hello," I said. "I saw you across the street."

In the stroller, a little girl about a year old was sitting up in a nest of blankets. She had blonde hair and wore a pink coat and matching bonnet. She stared at me, with that wide-eyed, fascinated expression babies sometimes have.

"I heard you had a little girl," I said. "She's adorable, Max."

"Sharp as a tack too," he said. "Just about to start walking. And she's already talking."

"What was her first word?"

"Dada." There was no missing the love and pride in his voice.

It was so different to see him with a baby carriage, but otherwise he was exactly the same, with that ever-present five o-clock shadow. His mouth still turned up at the corners and there was still the same tenderness in his eyes as he looked at me.

"You're doing well?" he asked abruptly. "Business is good?"

"Never been better." I held out my index finger and the little girl grabbed it, still staring at me. "I finally went to the nightclub last month," I said. "It's beautiful, Max. Really special."

"It is, isn't it? We did a good job. You did a good job, I should say."

"I'm glad I got to be a part of it." It was the truth. "I learned a lot."

"I'm going to open one like it in Chicago. We're moving back there in a few months."

"Are you?"

"We both decided it's the right place to be. It'll be good to be back."

The little girl had released my finger, so I was able to turn and face Max again. For a moment neither one of us spoke. We stood there by the baby carriage, two people with a shared past that neither one of us would mention but that neither one of us had forgotten. I could see the memory of it in his eyes as he looked at me, just as he could surely see it in mine. But I felt no anguish, no awkwardness, only gratitude.

"I'm glad I got to see you again, then," I said. "Before you leave."

"I'm glad too. Maybe we'll meet again here someday. I want Beata to know the city where she was born."

"Beata?"

"Beatrice. We call her Beata." He said it with a slight lift of one eyebrow, a gentle acknowledgment of what I knew.

I turned back to the little girl. She stared at me, then grinned, showing two bottom teeth. If you were looking for Fred Gibson you could find him in her features, but she suddenly grabbed for her stuffed rabbit with a determination that reminded me of Max.

"That's beautiful," I said. "And so is she." I smiled up at him. It took no effort to do so for I was happy, and I could tell that he was too.

"Goodbye, Max," I said. "And good luck."

"Goodbye, Irene." His eyes were fond. "Take care of yourself."

When I got to the corner, I paused and turned back. Max was leaning over the carriage and tucking the blanket carefully around his daughter. I could just imagine what he would be saying to her, something silly and affectionate and sweet.

The sun warmed my face as I continued on my way. Beata. *Blessed.* There was no better name for that little girl, growing up with a father who loved her, who had already proved how far he would go to protect her.

As I neared the Mark Hopkins, a taxi pulled up to the curb and a young couple got out, laughing in that way you do when you've just fallen in love. Johnny and I had scrambled out of a taxi together in exactly that spot, in exactly that mood, on that April night. We'd sat by the huge wall of windows and looked down on the astonishing city and felt the wondrous, exhilarating sense of what was possible.

Continuing along the street, I thought of how much had happened since that night. There had been grief and pain and mistakes, both my own and other people's. But there had also been beauty and friendship and an opening of what was possible, in this city and in myself. Maybe it's simplest to say that there had been grace, all the way through.

And it occurred to me, as I looked down at the sparkling bay, that I was blessed too.

When I got back to my neighborhood it was late afternoon. The sun was slanting from the west, and I walked down Jackson Street from the bus stop, passing the big school and the grocery.

At the corner I paused. On the other side of Fillmore, the violinist was on the church steps, setting his case down at his feet. I hadn't seen him there in months.

I crossed the street and stood on the sidewalk right before the church. He was still in his brown suit, gold vest, and green tie, and his gray hair still touched his collar. He seemed to move a little more stiffly than before as he took out the violin and tucked it under his chin. I stood on the sidewalk in the sunlight, not in any hurry, waiting for him to begin.

He looked up. He looked right at me. I think he smiled.

Then he raised his bow and began to play.

THE END

AUTHOR'S NOTE

In December 2019, my family and I went to see the San Francisco Ballet's *Nutcracker*. It happened to be the seventy-fifth anniversary of the ballet's first performance in San Francisco, and as I read the program, I was struck by the fact that the production on Christmas Eve in 1944 was the first time the entire ballet had been performed anywhere in the United States.

That was surprising, because *The Nutcracker* is such an established part of the holiday season. It's certainly been part of my life as long as I can remember. As a child I was a rather clumsy mouse in a local production, and once my sister and friends and I staged an entire performance in my friend Jenn's living room, complete with shredded Kleenex "snow" thrown from offstage by Jenn's mother. Even for the less ballet-obsessed, there's no avoiding *The Nutcracker*; its music creeps into holiday car commercials and the characters dance across coffee cups. It is so ubiquitous that, as I sat in the War Memorial Opera House in 2019, waiting for the curtain to rise, it was difficult to imagine a time when the ballet was essentially unknown to the American public.

Hours later, in the car on the ride home, I couldn't stop thinking about that first San Francisco performance. I was struck by fact that this whimsical, fantastical ballet had its first American performance during the fourth year of a world war. The juxtaposition of the two intrigued me. My writer mind began to spin.

The World at Home is the result.

In writing about that 1944 *Nutcracker*, I have done my best to stick closely to the facts. That was easy to do because the facts are, quite frankly, fascinating. When director Willam Christensen decided to stage *The Nutcracker*, he was choosing a ballet that he had never even seen in its entirety. To fill in the gaps, he sought out members of San Francisco's Russian expatriate community who remembered the ballet from the Maryinsky Theatre, also interviewing dancers George Balanchine and Alexandra Danilova when they came through town on tour (a decade later, Balanchine himself would famously bring *The Nutcracker* to New York City Ballet).

The costumes for the first performance were in fact designed by nineteen-year-old Russell Hartley, a character dancer with the company. My descriptions of them are based on his drawings and on photographs of the first production (with the exception of the Chinese tunics, for which I allowed myself some dramatic license). Hartley successfully met the challenge of producing 143 costumes in a time of fabric rationing, helped out by those famous red curtains from the Cort Theatre (which, he would later explain, supplied the ballet company with velvet for the next ten years). Although Irene is a fictional character, she represents the pitch-in-and-help spirit of the volunteers who brought Hartley's designs to life under the direction of seamstress Inez Dodson. During the writing of this novel, I had the privilege of accessing the Russell Hartley archives at the Museum of Performance and Design in San Francisco, a museum which was founded by Hartley himself. I was also helped by the books *San Francisco Ballet: The First Fifty Years* by Cobbett Steinberg and *The Christensen Brothers: An American Dance Epic* by Debra Hickenlooper Sowell.

Although *The Nutcracker* was the catalyst for *The World at Home*, it quickly became clear to me that at its core, this story was not about ballet, but about a city in wartime. In his book *Cool Gray City of Love: 49 Views of San Francisco*, Gary Kamiya writes, "You could put a plaque to memorialize World War II on hundreds of places in San Francisco, because the war touched everyone and everything." One of the most obvious places was Fort Mason, from which 1,647,174 troops shipped out to war. As Kamiya observes, for the thousands of them who did not survive, San Francisco was the last bit of home soil they ever touched. The latent awareness of this fact, and the sheer volume of young people coming in and out of San Francisco, created a charged and sometimes hedonistic atmosphere.

It was a city with many temptations (including, for those with means, Sally Stanford's infamous brothel on Pine Street), which led concerned civic leaders to offer wholesome counterprogramming. The USO on O'Farrell Street was one of thousands across the country, established with the goal of offering clean entertainment for young men on leave. Irene's experiences as a junior hostess are based on the accounts of the women who volunteered, as shared in the fascinating book *Good Girls, Good Food, Good Fun: The Story of USO Hostesses During World War II* by Meghan K. Winchell. Another helpful and poignant resource for me was an actual USO San Francisco Furlough Guide from January 1945, a folded magazine listing entertainment and dining options, local attractions, houses of worship, and other resources for those on leave in the City by the Bay.

The treatment of Japanese Americans during the second World War, in San Francisco and across the country, is a particularly shameful episode in our national history. I placed Mr. Yamagami's fictional shop on Fillmore Street, in the heart of what was a thriving

Japantown prior to 1942. Although Mr. Yamagami comes back after the war, not everyone did; only about half of the displaced residents of San Francisco's Japantown returned to their former homes. As further evidence of how deep the prejudice was during the war, the Japanese Tea Garden in Golden Gate Park was in fact renamed the Oriental Tea Garden; its original name was restored in 1952.

To learn more about San Francisco in the early forties, I recommend *The Bad City in the Good War: San Francisco, Los Angeles, Oakland, and San Diego*, by Roger W. Lotchin. *San Francisco in World War II* by John Garvey and the California Center for Military History offers a rich visual overview of civilian and military life in the city. The 1944 novel *Shore Leave* by Frederic Wakeman supplied a fictional male character's take on the social dynamics of wartime San Francisco. I want to give a special mention to Herb Caen, legendary *San Francisco Chronicle* columnist, for the vivid vignettes of the city in his 1949 book *Baghdad-by-the-Bay*. *Letters from the Pacific: A World War II Romance as Told Through the Letters of Jane and Chuck Flynn*, compiled by Kathy Flynn de Gaxiola with Luz Gaxiola Flynn and Mica Gaxiola Flynn provided a window into the correspondence that crossed oceans during the war. Lastly, *Our Mothers' War: American Women at Home and at the Front During World War II* by Emily Yellin is an excellent resource for anyone curious about the female experience of this unique time in history.

One final note: Max was correct when he observed that the war would make people discover and fall in love with San Francisco. The city left a strong impression on the servicemen who passed through, and many chose to come back to start their postwar lives. The Bay Area population exploded in the years following the war, with some of its suburban towns quadrupling in size. The world had found San Francisco, and there was no going back.

ACKNOWLEDGMENTS

This book is, above all, a love letter to San Francisco. I'm grateful to all who preserve its history. It's a city like no other, and a darn good place to leave your heart.

I've had the privilege of personally knowing two World War II veterans, my great-uncles Walter Wolf, Jr. (Army) and Robert Wolf (Navy). I wish I'd started this book thirty years ago so I could have asked them directly about their experiences. Thank you, my beloved great-aunt Carol Ann Marshall, for sharing war reminiscences from your early years. You are such a blessing in my life.

Thank you to all my friends for your love and encouragement. A special shoutout goes to Tarn Wilson, Angela Dellaporta, and Diane Ichikawa for reading this manuscript at three different points and offering candid and insightful feedback. As ever, I want to honor Mary Donovan-Kansora, who I suspect would have loved Irene and fully identified with her creative spirit.

Thank you once again to the fabulous team at She Writes Press, especially Brooke Warner, Lauren Wise, and Shannon Green. Many thanks to Anne Durette and Laura Matthews for the editorial help and to designer Julie Metz for getting Irene out there by the Golden Gate. It's a delight to work with Caitlin Hamilton Summie and Rick Summie, excellent partners in publicity. I'm also very grateful to Supriya Wronkiewicz, San Francisco Ballet Archivist, who made it possible for me to spend a fascinating afternoon with the Russell Hartley archives at the Museum of Performance and Design.

My grandparents Alice and Alfred Kubitz used to take me to the San Francisco Ballet *Nutcracker* as a child, which is where the very first seed of this story was planted. Grandma, thanks for letting me borrow your Polish heritage for Max. I'm grateful to my mom, Linda, for being such an enthusiastic reader of my novels and for sharing them with everyone she knows (I'll do my best to keep writing them, Mom, so you have more to read). Thanks to my dad, Alan, for passing on his reverence for history and beautiful music. Dad, you'll notice that both found their way into this book. Amy, you were my partner in ballet crime for many years, and that *Nutcracker* at the Groenevelds' house was an extraordinary creative feat for a gaggle of nine- to eleven-year-olds. Thanks for the memories.

Matthew and Luke, you have both grown so much since I started this journey. What hasn't changed is how grateful I am to be your mom. (Spoiler alert: that's never going to change.)

Scott, I'll always bless the snow globe that landed us in the same San Francisco park at the same moment in history. It's ironic that it took a New Yorker to show this California girl some of the most fascinating places in the city. Lucky me.

ABOUT THE AUTHOR

Photo credit: High Tea Photography

GINNY KUBITZ MOYER is the author of the novels *A Golden Life*, named one of Kirkus Reviews' Best Indie Books of 2024, and *The Seeing Garden*, which won Silver in the 2023 Foreword INDIES Book of the Year Award for Historical Fiction. She lives in the San Francisco Bay Area with her husband, two sons, and one rescue dog.

Learn more at www.ginnymoyer.org.

Looking for your next great read?

We can help!

Visit www.shewritespress.com/next-read or scan the QR code below for a list of our recommended titles.

She Writes Press is an award-winning independent publishing company founded to serve women writers everywhere.